Nate shifted so that his shoulder brushed against hers, and he lowered his mouth closer to her ear.

"Since that kiss we shared under t̶h̶e̶ ̶m̶i̶s̶t̶l̶e̶toe, I haven't been able to go much ̶ ̶ ̶ ̶ ̶ ̶ ̶ ̶ ̶thout thinking about you ̶ ̶ ̶ ̶ ̶ ̶ ̶ ̶ ̶ ̶ ̶kiss, I remember how ̶ ̶ ̶ ̶ ̶ ̶ ̶ ̶ ̶ ̶ ̶and how surprised—a ̶ ̶ ̶ ̶ ̶ ̶ ̶ ̶ ̶ ̶ ̶he passion of your res̶ ̶ ̶ ̶

"You're right," Allis̶ ̶ ̶ ̶ ̶ ̶ ̶ ̶ ̶es are different. But considering that ̶ ̶ ̶ ̶ ̶ ̶ing to be working closely together, I think it would be best if we both just forgot about that kiss."

"I already know that I can't."

"Maybe you just need to try a little harder."

"Are you saying that you have forgotten?"

"I'm saying that I'm not going to let anything interfere with our working relationship."

"I know how to separate business from pleasure," he assured her.

"Let's keep the focus on business," she suggested.

"That doesn't sound like nearly as much fun."

"I like my job and I want to keep my job. Which means I'm definitely not going to sleep with my boss."

His lips curved. "I'm not your boss yet."

Those Engaging Garretts!
The Carolina Cousins

...key turned, so that his shoulder pressed against hers, and he lowered his mouth closer to hers...

...the mistakes...

...for much longer than that will one minute as... was. And when I think about that kiss I... When my... good body felt against mine, and how wild... and incredibly turned on—I was by that... so quick a response."

...Alison said, "Our memories of that time... I still we're going to... would be best if we forget about it...

...a good use to use all of...

...

THE DADDY WISH

BY
BRENDA HARLEN

MILLS & BOON

Published in Great Britain 2015
by Mills & Boon, an imprint of Harlequin (UK) Limited,
Eton House, 18-24 Paradise Road, Richmond, Surrey, TW9 1SR

© 2015 Brenda Harlen

ISBN: 978-0-263-25110-4

23-0215

Harlequin (UK) Limited's policy is to use papers that are natural, renewable and recyclable products and made from wood grown in sustainable forests. The logging and manufacturing processes conform to the legal environmental regulations of the country of origin.

Printed and bound in Spain
by CPI, Barcelona

Brenda Harlen is a former attorney who once had the privilege of appearing before the Supreme Court of Canada. The practice of law taught her a lot about the world and reinforced her determination to become a writer—because in fiction, she could promise a happy ending! Now she is an award-winning, national bestselling author of more than thirty titles for Mills & Boon. You can keep up to date with Brenda on Facebook and Twitter or through her website, brendaharlen.com.

Writing is often a solitary venture…but not this time! During the writing of much of this book, I was blessed with the company of an incredible group of women, and I would like to dedicate this story to the CBs who were an integral part of the process: CMS, JenB, RSS, GP and Theresa, with an extra special thank you to JenB and "Mr JenB" for their generosity and hospitality. (xo "35")

This story is also dedicated to Becky with thanks for the tour, the stories, and answers to my endless questions. All the good stuff is hers—any mistakes made or liberties taken are my own.

Prologue

The Garrett Furniture Christmas party was held at the Courtland Hotel in downtown Charisma, as it had been for each of the past six years that Allison Caldwell had worked for the company. The main ballroom was decorated for the occasion with miles of pine garland, dozens of potted evergreens twinkling with lights and white poinsettias at the center of every table. The meal was a traditional roast turkey dinner served family style, with stuffing, mashed potatoes, gravy, buttered corn, baby carrots, green beans and cranberry sauce.

The Garretts always treated their staff well—from holiday parties to summer picnics, from comprehensive benefit packages to generous vacation allowances—and Allison would always be grateful that a three-week temp position had paved the way to her becoming the executive assistant to the CFO. Tonight, she was seated at a table with three co-workers from the finance department and their respective spouses, and throughout the meal, conversation flowed as freely as the wine. No one seemed to notice or care that she was on her own. No one except Allison.

She'd been married once—for all of two minutes. Actually, it had been two and a half years, but that two-and-a-half-year marriage had ended six years earlier. Since the divorce, she'd become accustomed to attending social events on her own, and she usually preferred it that way.

But on this night, only twelve days before Christmas, as

she watched various couples snuggle up to each other in the corners or move together on the dance floor, she was suddenly and painfully aware of her solitary status. Aware that she would be going home to a dark and empty apartment because Dylan was spending the weekend with his dad's new family. Her eight-year-old son was the light of her life, the reason for everything she did, and she missed him unbearably when he was gone.

A surreptitious glance at her watch confirmed that it was almost eleven o'clock— still early for the die-hard partyers but an acceptable time for her to head out. She wished her boss and his wife a merry Christmas, then made her way to the cloakroom to get her coat.

She paused in the wide arched entranceway when she heard voices emanating from within. It took only a few seconds for her to realize there was only one voice—and that it was a familiar one. Nathan Garrett, the CFO's nephew and heir apparent, who would be her boss one day, was talking to someone on the cell phone that was pressed up against his ear. Glancing up, he flashed her the quick, easy smile that never failed to make all of her womanly parts tingle.

All of the Garretts—men, women and children—were beautiful people, and Nathan was no exception. He stood about six-two, with a lean but powerful build that was showcased nicely in formal business attire. His hair was dark, his eyes were an amazing gray that—depending on his mood— looked like smoke or steel, and dimples flashed when he smiled. It was those dimples that got to her, every time.

Not that she'd ever let him know it. Because the man was a major player, and Allison had learned her lesson about players a long time ago.

He disconnected his call and dropped the phone into his jacket pocket.

"I didn't mean to intrude," she said.

"A beautiful woman is never an intrusion," he assured her.

She stepped into the room and began looking for her coat, silently berating herself for the warm flush that colored her cheeks. She didn't respond, because what could she say in response to flirtatious words that came as naturally to him as breathing? And how pathetic was it that she could recognize the fact and still not be able to control the tingle?

"You're not planning to leave already?"

She'd assumed he'd gone and was startled to hear the question, and his voice, so close to her ear.

"It's a great party," she said. "But—"

"So stay and enjoy it," he interrupted.

"I can't. I've got a busy weekend." She told herself that wasn't really a lie, because she did have to get Dylan's Christmas presents wrapped, and that was a task easier done when her son wasn't around.

Finally spotting her coat, she tugged it off its hanger.

"Well, you can't go just yet," he insisted.

"Why not?"

He stepped closer, so close that their bodies were almost touching. She wanted to step back, to give herself space to breathe, but the rack of coats at her back prevented her from doing so.

Nate lifted a hand and gestured to the arched entranceway. "Because you stepped under the mistletoe."

She frowned at the sprig of green leaves and white berries and tried to ignore the wild pounding of her heart inside her chest. "Why would someone put mistletoe in a cloakroom?"

"I have no idea." He crooked a finger beneath her chin to tip her head up. "But tradition demands that a woman passing under mistletoe must be kissed—and I'm a traditional kind of guy."

She couldn't think, she didn't know how to respond to that, and before her brain could scramble to find any words at all, his lips were on hers.

And…oh…wow.

The man definitely knew how to kiss.

Of course, she would have been disappointed to learn otherwise. After all, he had a reputation for seducing women with a word, bringing them to orgasm with a smile and breaking their hearts with a wave goodbye. She'd always assumed those rumors were at least slightly exaggerated, but as his mouth moved over hers, promising all kinds of wicked, sensual pleasures, she was forced to acknowledge that she might have been wrong.

A slow, lazy sweep of his tongue over her lower lip nearly made her whimper. The sensual caress did make her lips part, not just granting him entry but welcoming him inside.

His free hand slid around her back, gently urging her closer. She didn't—couldn't—resist. The coat slipped from her fingers and dropped to her feet, forgotten. There was so much heat coursing through her system, she might never need a coat again. Her hands slid up his chest to his shoulders and she held on, as if he were her anchor in the storm of sensations that battered at her system, pounding self-preservation and common sense into submission.

His tongue danced with hers, a slow and seductive rhythm that teased and enticed. Somewhere in the back of her mind, she knew she should be disappointed to realize that she was no different from any other woman who had succumbed to his charms. But in the moment, in his arms, she really didn't care.

While her body might urge her to let one kiss lead to a mutually satisfying conclusion, she still had enough working brain cells to acknowledge that tangling the sheets with a man who would one day be her boss could be a very big mistake. She eased away from him.

"That's some powerful mistletoe," she said, trying to make light of the intensity of her response.

"I don't think we can blame that on the mistletoe." He bent down to retrieve her coat, then helped her into it. "I'm leaving in the morning to go skiing with some friends, but I'll see you when I get back."

He smiled again, but she ignored the tingles, reminding herself that her job was too important for her to jeopardize for the pleasure of a few hours in his bed. So she only responded with, "My ride should be here by now."

He walked out with her, and she stopped beside the cab that was idling at the curb. "Merry Christmas, Mr. Garrett."

He reached past her for the door handle, but didn't immediately open it. "Don't you think, after that kiss, you could drop the formality and call me Nate?"

No, she couldn't. Because calling him by his given name implied a familiarity she wasn't ready for. "Have a safe trip, Mr. Garrett."

He shook his head, but he was smiling as he opened the door. "I'll talk to you soon, Allison."

She slid into the backseat and gave the driver her address.

He stood on the curb, watching as the cab drove away, but she didn't let herself look back.

Chapter One

Allison wasn't usually the type to spend too much time fussing over her appearance. She never left her apartment looking less than professional—that was a matter of pride—but she didn't usually bother with more than a cursory brush with the mascara wand to darken her fair lashes and a quick swipe of gloss to moisturize her lips.

On the first morning after the holidays, when she found herself digging into her makeup bag for rarely used eye shadow and lipstick, she told herself that she simply wanted a new image for the new year. That the extra care she was taking with her appearance was in no way linked to the possibility that she might cross paths with Nathan Garrett at the office today.

Finally satisfied with the results of her efforts, she poked her head into her son's bedroom. "Come on, Dylan. You don't want to be late on your first day back."

"Yeah, I do," he told her. "School sucks."

She held back a sigh. It worried her that he had such a negative attitude toward school when he was only in third grade, but she'd long ago given up trying to change his opinion and focused her efforts on getting him to class on time. "Okay, but *I* don't want to be late on my first day back."

He eyed her suspiciously. "How come you're all dressed up?"

"What do you mean? I wear this suit to work all the time."

"But you don't wear all that gunk on your face."

She had no ready response to that. If the "slight" improvement she'd been aiming for was obvious enough that her eight-year-old son noticed, she'd definitely gone overboard.

"And your hair's different," he said.

"Go eat your cereal, then brush your teeth," she told him.

It had taken her almost twenty minutes to do her makeup and hair, and less than five to wipe the color off her face and tuck her hair into its usual loose knot at the back of her head.

Dylan didn't comment on the changes, which she interpreted to mean that she now looked as she usually did. She certainly wasn't going to turn any heads when she walked into the office, and maybe that was for the best. Far too many women tripped over themselves trying to catch Nathan Garrett's eye, and she'd always taken pride in the fact that she wasn't one of them.

After dropping her son off at school, she drove across town to the offices of Garrett Furniture, trying not to think about what had happened at the company Christmas party.

Of course, her efforts were futile. It didn't matter that she hadn't seen or heard from Nathan in the twenty-three days that had passed since they'd connected under the mistletoe—she hadn't stopped thinking about him or THE KISS.

Which was ridiculous, because he really wasn't her type. Not that she had a type—she couldn't even remember the last time she'd had a date. But if she *did* have a type, it would *not* be a too rich, too sexy, too good-looking and far too self-assured man who had a reputation for enjoying women of *all* types.

She decided it was a good thing that she'd wiped off her makeup and tied back her hair. The last thing she needed was for Nathan Garrett—or anyone else in the office—to think that she was interested in him.

Maybe her response wasn't about the particular man so much as the fact that she hadn't been kissed (even in lowercase letters) in a very long time. Maybe that was the real reason he'd stirred up desires so long dormant, she hadn't been certain she was capable of feeling them anymore. Maybe she didn't want her boss's nephew so much as she wanted to connect with someone. *Anyone.*

As a single mother, she didn't have time to be lonely—except for every other weekend when Dylan was with his dad, and Dylan had been with his dad the night of the Christmas party. She never would have stayed out so late, or let herself drink so much, if her son had been waiting for her at home. Not that she'd had so much to drink—probably not more than three glasses of wine. But she'd decided that being under the influence of alcohol was a convenient explanation for her uncharacteristic behavior.

And now she was acting like a schoolgirl with a crush on the most popular boy in class—trying to pretty herself up to get his attention. It was pathetic, especially when she wasn't even sure that she liked the guy all that much.

Not that she *dis*liked him.

Allison blew out a frustrated breath. This was ridiculous. *She* was being ridiculous—spending far too much time obsessing over THE KISS and in danger of starting to think about Nathan Garrett as THE MAN. He was simply *a* man— no more and no less. Even if he was a man who could kiss far better than any other man in her experience.

She pulled into her usual parking spot and turned off the ignition. After the holiday, she was eager to get back into the familiar routines of work again, but she stopped by the break room first to grab a cup of coffee. While there, she wished a happy New Year to Melanie Hedley, who was doing the same.

"How was your holiday?" Melanie asked.

"Quiet," Allison said. "Yours?"

"Amazing." The other woman fairly gushed the word. "I went to Vail before Christmas and stayed at this *fabulous*

condo resort that had fireplaces in *every* bedroom and hot tubs on *all* the decks. And Nate and I discovered the most *incredible* little café tucked away in the foothills."

Allison sloshed coffee over the back of her hand and sucked in a sharp breath as the hot liquid scalded her skin. "That does sound…amazing," she said, grabbing a paper napkin to wipe the spilled coffee off her hand.

"Lanie—" Enrico Sanchez poked his head into the room "—we need you on that conference call."

"Oh, right." Melanie smiled at her. "We'll catch up more later."

Allison added a splash of cream to her cup, stirring mechanically while all the excited anticipation that had fueled her buoyant mood only a few minutes earlier fizzled out like air from a balloon.

She wasn't unaware of Nate's reputation, but it still hurt to realize that, only a few days after he'd kissed her, he'd been dining with Melanie in Colorado. It shouldn't. She had no right to be upset or disappointed or anything. He'd certainly never made her any promises, and she wouldn't have believed him if he had.

So why had she let her own imagination paint unrealistic dreams? Why had she ever let herself believe that THE KISS had been anything more than a kiss?

She hated being taken for a fool. Worse, she hated *being* a fool. She sat down at her desk and turned on her computer, determined to put all thoughts of the man from her mind once and for all.

John Garrett walked in while she was still reviewing email messages that had come through over the holidays. He was a good boss and a genuinely wonderful man, and she greeted him with a sincere smile.

The smile froze on her lips when he said, "I'm glad you're here—I need to talk to you about Nathan."

* * *

Allison took her iPad into John Garrett's office.

Though he'd said he wanted to talk to her about Nathan, she didn't think there was any way he could know what had happened at the Christmas party. But HR frowned upon personal relationships in the workplace, and her heart was hammering against her ribs as she perched on the edge of the chair facing his desk.

The CFO looked uncharacteristically burdened and weary. She could practically feel the knots forming in her belly—twisting and tightening—as it occurred to her that she might very well be on the verge of losing her job because she'd had too much to drink and had foolishly and impulsively let herself get caught under the mistletoe by her boss's heir apparent.

"You're no doubt aware that Nathan has been chosen to take over as CFO when I retire," John continued.

She exhaled slowly, reassured by his opening that whatever this was about, it wasn't about the kiss. (The brief exchange with Melanie in the staff room had succeeded in relegating the event to lowercase status.) Her relief was so profound, it took several seconds longer than it should have for the rest of his statement to sink in.

Retirement? Why was he mentioning it now?

"But that's not until June," she noted. And only then if he didn't decide to postpone it again, as he'd done twice already.

"Actually, I'm going to be finished here as of the end of January."

"What? Why?"

"I had a little bit of a health scare over the holidays," he admitted.

She was instantly and sincerely concerned. John Garrett might be her boss, but over the six years that they'd worked together, he'd also become a friend and something of a father figure to her. "What happened? Why didn't anyone call me?"

"It was just a minor blip with my heart—nothing too serious."

The fact that he was sitting behind his desk and not in a hospital bed confirmed that it wasn't too serious, but she knew him well enough to suspect that he was downplaying the "minor" part.

But what did this mean for her? Would she be let go? Was John telling her now as a way of giving her notice that she would be out of a job at the end of the month?

"Nathan's worked hard for the company for a lot of years," he continued. "He's not getting this promotion just because his name is Garrett but because he's earned it."

She nodded, her heart sinking as she considered the repercussions of his announcement. She was confident that she could find another job; she knew John would give her a glowing recommendation. But she wasn't nearly as confident that she would find another job with the comprehensive health-care benefits she needed for the ongoing treatment of her son's asthma.

"That being said, I wanted to be certain that you don't have any concerns about working with him."

"Working with him?" she echoed.

"Is that going to be a problem?"

"No, of course not," she hastily assured him, because she wouldn't let it be a problem. Because he was offering her the chance to keep her job—and her benefits—and she would make it work.

As for the mind-numbing, bone-melting kiss she'd shared with her soon-to-be boss...what kiss?

"I just assumed he'd want to choose his own executive assistant," she said, still not entirely sure Nathan wouldn't do exactly that.

"We've already discussed it," John said. "He wants you."

She knew he only meant that his nephew wanted her to

work for him, but that knowledge didn't prevent her cheeks from flushing in response to his words.

"Now that that's settled, I need you to book a flight to St. Louis for next Thursday," he told her. "There are some minor discrepancies in their numbers that need to be looked at."

Which could probably be done via email, but John had always preferred a hands-on approach.

"Considering the 'minor blip' with your heart, I'm surprised your doctors have given you the okay to fly."

"They haven't," he admitted. "So you'll be going with Nathan."

Allison had to bite her tongue to hold back her instinctive protest as she rose from her chair. It wasn't unusual for John to request that she accompany him on his business trips, but going anywhere with the man who'd kissed her more thoroughly than anyone else in recent memory—maybe ever—filled her with apprehension.

Thankfully, St. Louis was only a two-hour flight from Raleigh, which meant that the trip would be completed in one day. It would be a long day—with a departure at 8:35 a.m. and a return fourteen hours later—but only one day. The trips that the CFO made to review the books of the Gallery stores—more upscale showrooms that carried exclusive, higher-end inventory—located in Austin, Denver, San Francisco, Saint Paul, New York, Philadelphia and Miami, required more time and attention, sometimes necessitating a two or three-night stay.

As Allison returned to her desk, she could only hope that Nathan would decide he didn't need his executive assistant to accompany him on those, because she didn't trust herself to spend that much time in close proximity to the man. Sex had never been casual to her. Even when she was in college, she'd never hooked up with a guy just for a good time. And she'd tried to steer clear of the guys who were reputed to sleep with different girls every weekend. No doubt, Nathan Garrett had been one of those guys.

She'd heard rumors of his extracurricular activities, and while the whispered details might vary, the overall consensus was that the current VP of Finance definitely knew how to pleasure a woman.

Which was definitely *not* something she should be thinking about right now—especially when the man himself was standing in front of her desk.

He was the only man she'd ever met who managed to make her feel all weak-kneed and tongue-tied in his presence. She hadn't worked at Garrett Furniture long before she'd recognized that the family had won some kind of genetic sweepstakes. The three brothers who ran the company were of her parents' generation but still undeniably handsome, and all of their children—most of whom were employed at the company in one capacity or another—were unbelievably attractive.

It had been an impartial observation—nothing more. She'd been too busy trying to settle into her new job, put her life back together and be a good mother to her toddler son to be attracted to anyone. And then, in her second year of employment in John Garrett's office, his nephew Nathan moved back to Charisma.

By then, Allison's wounded heart had healed and her long-dormant hormones were ready to be awakened again. And they had jolted to full awareness when Nathan walked into the office and found her struggling to fix a paper jam in the photocopier.

He'd come over to help, and just his proximity was enough to make her skin prickle. When he'd reached around her, his chest had bumped her shoulder, and the incidental contact had made her nipples tingle and tighten. He'd dislodged the paper, she'd stammered out a breathless "thank you" and then he'd gone in to see his uncle.

Four years later, she still wasn't immune to him. She'd learned to hold her own in conversations with him, but she hadn't learned to control her body's involuntary response to his nearness. Even now, even with him standing on the other side of her desk, her blood was pulsing in her veins.

She forced a smile and desperately hoped that her cheeks weren't as red as they felt. "Good morning, Mr. Garrett."

His answering smile didn't seem forced. It was effortless and easy and so potent; she was grateful that she was sitting down because it practically melted her bones. "Good morning, Allison."

She forced herself to glance away, down at the calendar on her desk. "Your uncle is free, if you want to go in."

"I will," he said, but eased a hip onto the edge of her desk. "But first I wanted to apologize for not calling you when I got back from my ski trip."

"Oh, well." She kept her gaze focused on the papers on her desk, because his proximity was wreaking enough havoc on her hormones without looking at him and remembering how his mouth—somehow both soft and strong, and utterly delicious—had mastered hers, or how those wickedly talented hands had moved so smoothly and confidently over her body. "I know the holidays are a busy time for everyone."

"And then Uncle John had his heart attack the day after Christmas." She glanced up and could tell, by the seriousness of his tone and the bleakness in his eyes, that he was still worried about his uncle.

"So it was more than a minor blip," she remarked.

"Is that what he told you?"

She nodded.

"The doctors did say it was minor, but it was definitely a heart attack."

"That must have come as a shock to all of you," she said.

He nodded. "Aside from smoking the occasional cigar,

he didn't have any of the usual risk factors, but the doctors strongly urged him to make some lifestyle changes."

"He's already asked me to look into that cruise he's been promising your aunt for the past few years."

"Retirement is going to be a big adjustment for him, so it will be good for him to have something to look forward to."

"It's going to be a big adjustment for the whole office," Allison agreed.

"And not exactly the adjustment I was hoping to make in our relationship," Nate said.

Our relationship.

She wasn't exactly sure what that was supposed to mean, but her heart gave a funny little jump anyway—before she ruthlessly strapped it down. "Mr. Garrett—"

"Really?" His brows rose and his lips curved in a slow, sexy smile that made her want to melt into a puddle at his feet. "Are you really going to 'Mr. Garrett' me after the—"

"There you are, Nate."

She exhaled gratefully when John poked his head out of his office and interrupted his nephew. Because whatever he'd been about to say, she didn't want to hear it.

Nathan held her gaze for another moment before he turned his attention to his uncle. "I didn't mean to keep you waiting."

"Normally I wouldn't mind," John told him. "But we've got a lot of ground to cover in the next twenty-five days."

Nate nodded. "I'll look forward to catching up with you later," he said to Allison, already moving toward the CFO's office.

She didn't bother to respond, because as far as she was concerned, there wasn't anything to catch up on.

Whatever might have started between her and her soon-to-be boss under the mistletoe was over when he flew off to Vail with Melanie Hedley the next day. And that was for the best. Not only because she didn't want to make a fool of herself—again—where Nathan Garrett was concerned, but because any fantasy she might have had about getting naked with the VP of Finance was inappropriate enough, but the same fantasy with the company CFO could be fatal to her employment.

And that was a risk she wasn't willing to take.

"How was your first day back?" Allison asked when she picked her son up from his after-school program.

Dylan made a face as he buckled up in the backseat.

"Do you have any homework?"

"Yeah. I've gotta write a stupid journal entry about my holiday."

"Why do you think it's stupid?"

"Because it's the same thing Miss Cabrera made us do last year. And because I didn't do anything really exciting. Not like Marcus, who went to Disney World. Or Cassie, who got a puppy."

His tone was matter-of-fact, but she was as disappointed for him as he obviously was. Unfortunately, peak-season trips weren't anywhere in her budget, and pets—especially dogs—weren't allowed by the condominium corporation. "But we had a nice holiday, anyway, didn't we?" she prompted.

"I guess."

"What was your favorite part?" she asked, hoping to help him focus on the highlights.

"Not being at school."

She held back a sigh. Her son's extreme shyness made it difficult for him to make friends, but she didn't understand how he could prefer to be alone playing video games rather than interacting with other kids his own age. At the first parent-teacher meeting of the year, Miss Aberdeen had suggested that he was bored because the work was too easy for him, but when she offered to give him more advanced assignments, Dylan had been appalled by the prospect of being singled out. So he continued to do the same work as his classmates and continued to be bored at school. "What was your favorite part aside from not being at school?" she prompted.

"I had fun at the cartooning class at the art gallery," he finally said.

"So why don't you draw a comic strip about your holiday?"

His brow furrowed as he considered this suggestion. "Do you think that would be okay?"

"I think Miss Aberdeen would love it."

So once they got home, Dylan sat at the table, carefully drawing the boxes for his comic strip while she made spaghetti with meat sauce for dinner. As she stirred the sauce, she kept an eye on her son, pleased by the intense concentration on his face as he worked.

If she'd told him he had to write a paragraph, he would have scribbled the first thing that came to mind and been done with it. But he was obviously having fun with the cartooning, and she was pleased that he didn't just want to draw a comic strip but wanted to draw a good one.

When the outlining was done, he opened his package of colored pencils, and she felt a wave of nostalgia as she remembered when he used to sit at that same table with a box of fat crayons and scribble all over the pictures in a book. He'd been a fan of single-color pictures and would cover the page with blue or green or red or brown, but rarely would he use a variety of colors.

She'd always loved him with her whole heart, but she couldn't deny that there were times when she missed her little boy. The one who would crawl into her lap for a story at bedtime, who looked to her as the authority of all things and whose boo-boos could be made better with a hug and a kiss. He was so independent now—in his thoughts and his actions. Her little boy was growing up, and he didn't need her in all the ways that he used to.

She was proud of the person he was becoming, and more than a little uncertain about her own future. Being a mother had been such a huge part of her identity for so long, she'd almost forgotten that there were other parts. Being with Nathan Garrett made her remember those parts. He made her think and feel and want like a woman, and she wasn't sure that was a good thing.

Chapter Two

Allison was avoiding him.

It was a fact that baffled Nate more than anything, but he couldn't deny it was true.

Over the next few days, their paths continued to cross in the office. But every time he walked past her desk on the way to see his uncle, she seemed to be on the phone. And every time he walked out again, she scurried away from her desk to retrieve something from the printer or the photocopier or to water the plants on the window ledge.

At first he was amused by her obvious efforts to avoid any continuation of the conversation that had been aborted on their first day back after the holiday, but his amusement soon gave way to exasperation. As a Garrett and VP of Finance in the company, he was accustomed to being treated with respect, even deference.

He was not accustomed to being ignored. Especially not by a woman who had been sighing with pleasure in his arms only a few weeks earlier.

She was acting as if the kiss they'd shared had never happened, and maybe she wished it hadn't. But he could still remember the taste of her lips, somehow tangy and sweet and incredibly responsive; he could still remember the heady joy of her slender curves pressed against him; and he could still remember wishing that he didn't have to be on a plane at six fifteen the next morning, because he could think of all kinds of wicked and wonderful things they might do if they spent the night—and maybe several more—together.

For just a minute, maybe two, he'd considered forgetting about the trip with his buddies. Because the warm softness of Allison's body was a hell of a lot more tempting than the promise of fresh powder on the black diamond trails.

But then she'd pulled away. When she looked at him, he saw in her melted chocolate–colored eyes a reflection of the same desire that was churning through his veins, but there was something else there, too. Surprise, which he could definitely relate to, not having expected a minor spark of chemistry to ignite such a blaze of passion, and maybe even a hint of confusion, as if she wasn't quite sure how to respond to what was suddenly between them—yet another emotion he could relate to.

Even after more than three weeks, he couldn't forget about that kiss and he couldn't stop wanting her. And he wasn't prepared to pretend that nothing had happened. Had he taken advantage of the situation? Undoubtedly. But he hadn't taken advantage of *her*. In fact, she'd met him more than halfway.

And when he got out of his Friday afternoon meeting with his uncle, Nate was going to hang around her desk until Allison had no choice but to acknowledge him. Except that it was after six o'clock when he finally left the CFO's office, and she was already gone.

He caught up with his older brother instead.

"Don't you have a wife and a daughter waiting for you at home?" Nate asked, surprised to find him fiddling with design plans on a tablet.

Andrew shook his head. "They've decided that the first Friday of every month is girls' night out. Tonight the plan was for pedicures, dinner and a movie. And they dragged Mom along, too."

"I doubt much dragging was required," Nate commented,

well aware of how much Jane Garrett doted on all of her family—and especially her grandchildren.

"Probably not," his brother allowed. "But since no one's at home, I decided to take the time to polish up the details on the new occasional tables that should hit the market before next Christmas."

"You do realize it's the ninth of January?"

"Product development takes time and attention to detail," Andrew reminded him.

Nate shrugged. "Right now, I'm more interested in dinner. Did you want to grab a burger and a beer at the Bar Down?"

Andrew saved his progress and shut down the tablet.

"So you know why I was working late on a Friday night," Andrew said, when they were settled into a booth and waiting for their food. "But why were you hanging around the office?"

"I had a meeting with Uncle John that went late."

"I imagine you'll have a lot of those meetings over the next few weeks."

Nate nodded. "He's been in charge for a long time— I know it's not going to be easy for him to let go."

Their uncle had been talking, mostly in vague terms, about retirement for a couple of years now. Now Nate would be sitting behind the big desk in the CFO's office by the end of the month. And from behind that desk, he would have a prime view of the CFO's undeniably sexy executive assistant.

"So why don't you seem thrilled that your promotion is coming through sooner than you'd anticipated?"

"I'm happy about the promotion," Nate said. "I just wish it wasn't happening for the reasons it is." Although he'd frequently lamented the fact that his uncle kept pushing back his retirement, he never wanted it to be forced upon him.

"Now he can finally take Aunt Ellen on that cruise he's been promising since their fortieth anniversary."

"How long ago was that?"

"Almost four years." Andrew sipped his beer. "But somehow I don't think you're thinking about their vacation plans."

"I was just wondering why Uncle John was so insistent that Allison Caldwell stay on as my executive assistant."

"Probably because she's been doing the job for more than six years and knows the ins and outs of the office better than anyone else," his brother pointed out. "Do you have a problem with Allison?"

"No," he said quickly.

Maybe too quickly.

His brother's eyes narrowed. "Tell me you haven't slept with her."

"I haven't slept with her." Nate thanked the waitress who set his plate in front of him and immediately picked up his burger, grateful for the interruption as much as the food.

"Keep it that way," Andrew advised when the server was gone. "She's a valuable employee of the company."

"I'm aware of the code of conduct in the employee handbook," Nate reminded his brother. "I helped write it."

"Along with Sabrina Barton from Human Resources."

Nate bit into his burger.

"Tell me," Andrew said, dipping his spoon into his Guinness stew. "Did you sleep with her before or after the handbook went to the printer?"

"It was a brief fling more than three years ago, *after* she gave notice that she was leaving the company," he pointed out. "And *she* threw herself at *me*."

"The curse of being a Garrett," his brother acknowledged sarcastically. "But you could exercise some discretion and not catch every woman who throws herself at you."

"It's basic supply and demand—and with the number of single Garrett men rapidly dwindling, the unmarried ones are in greater demand." And he very much enjoyed being in demand.

Andrew shook his head as he scooped up more stew. Nate focused on his own plate, and conversation shifted to the hockey game playing out on the wide TV screen over the bar.

The waitress had cleared their empty plates and offered refills of their drinks. They both opted for coffee.

Andrew's cup was halfway to his lips when his cell phone chimed. He read the message on the display, then looked up.

"Problem?" Nate asked.

His brother glanced past him and smiled. "Not at all."

Over his shoulder, Nate saw that Andrew wasn't looking at something but some*one*. Rachel Ellis—now Rachel Garrett—his wife of four months.

She slid onto the bench seat beside her husband and brushed her lips over his. "Hi," she said, her tone soft and intimate.

"Hi, yourself," he said. "How was girls' night?"

"Fabulous." She snuggled close. "We got our toenails painted, then had dinner at Valentino's—with triple-chocolate truffle cake for dessert. But there weren't any good movies playing, so Maura went to your parents' house for a sleepover."

Andrew gestured for the waitress to bring the bill.

Nate sighed. "Whatever happened to bros before—" he caught Rachel's narrowed gaze and chose his words carefully "—sisters-in-law?"

"I'd say sorry, bro, but I'm not," Andrew told him.

"I know you're not."

And Nate *was* happy for his brother. Before he met Rachel, Andrew had spent a lot of years grieving the loss of his first wife and trying to raise his daughter on his own. With Rachel, Andrew and Maura were a family again.

"Why are you hanging out with your brother tonight instead of seducing a beautiful woman?" Rachel asked him.

"I've given up any hope of finding a woman as beautiful as you," Nate replied smoothly.

"Which is the same thing you'd say if Kenna was here instead of me," Rachel guessed.

"Because both of my brothers have impeccable taste."

Andrew signed the credit card receipt and tucked his card back into his wallet.

"What happened to the girl you were with at the Christmas party?"

The mischievous glint in his sister-in-law's eyes made him suspect that she wasn't just fishing for information but had actually seen something that night. "I wasn't with anyone."

"I know you didn't take a date," Rachel acknowledged. "But I definitely saw you come out of the cloakroom with someone."

Nate sipped his coffee and pretended not to know who she was talking about.

Huffing out a breath, she turned to Andrew. "You must have seen her. Pretty blonde in a green dress."

"Sorry," he said. "I didn't notice anyone but you."

"That's so sappy," she said, but she was smiling.

"And true," her husband assured her.

Nate rolled his eyes. "Don't you guys have an empty house waiting for you?"

"As a matter of fact," Andrew said.

"He's changing the subject," Rachel pointed out. "Because he doesn't want you to figure out who she was."

"I didn't leave with anyone that night," Nate said. "I had a six a.m. flight the next morning."

"I didn't say you left with her," she said. "Just that you were in the cloakroom with her."

"Maybe we both went to get our coats at the same time?" he suggested.

Rachel shook her head, unconvinced, but she let her husband nudge her out of the booth. "If your memory clears, you should bring her to dinner Sunday night."

Nate knew that wasn't going to happen. Stealing a kiss from a coworker at the company Christmas party was one thing—inviting his executive assistant to his parents' house to meet the family was something else entirely.

Friday nights always loomed long and empty ahead of Allison after she gave Dylan a hug and a kiss goodbye and sent him off to his dad's house for the weekend.

She tried not to resent the fact that Jefferson and his new wife had a three-bedroom raised ranch on a cute little court in Charisma's Westdale neighborhood. She'd always wanted her son to have a backyard in which he could run and play, and now he did. She just wished it was something she'd been able to give to him every day and not every other weekend when he was with his father.

But she was grateful that they had a nice two-bedroom apartment on the fifth floor of a well-maintained building with a park across the street. The rent wasn't cheap, but after she paid the bills each month, she was able to put aside a small amount of money into a vacation fund. Last summer, they'd gone to Washington, DC. This year, she intended to take him camping—to give her city boy a taste of the outdoors. She had some concerns as to whether or not he'd be able to survive a whole week without television or video games, but she wanted to try.

However, it was only January now, which meant she didn't have to determine their summer plans just yet. In the interim, she should cherish this time on her own: forty-eight hours in which to do whatever she wanted. She could lounge around in her pj's and eat popcorn for dinner while she watched TV if she wanted. She didn't have to prepare meals for anyone else or pick up dirty socks that missed the hamper in the bathroom or pull up the covers on a bed that had been left unmade.

But the sad reality was that she had no life outside of

work and her son. She could go to the bookstore and lose herself in a good story for a few hours, but lately even her favorite romance novels had left her feeling more depressed than inspired.

She wanted to believe in love and happy-ever-after, but real life hadn't given her much hope in that direction. And if she let herself give in to her desire for Nathan Garrett, she was more likely to end up unemployed than marrying the boss, and she had no intention of jeopardizing her job for a hot fling with a man who probably wouldn't remember her name the next day.

Instead, she called her friend Chelsea, thinking that they might be able to catch a movie. As it turned out, her friend was working, but she convinced Allison to come in to the Bar Down for a bite to eat. The sports bar was usually hopping on weekends, so she didn't think they'd have much time to talk, but her growling stomach and the promise of spinach dip were a stronger lure even than her friend's company.

To her surprise, there were only a handful of tables in use, and more of the seats at the bar were vacant than occupied.

"I don't think I've ever seen it so quiet in here on a Friday night," Allison remarked.

Chelsea set a glass of pinot noir on a paper coaster in front of her friend. "It might pick up a little bit later, but the first weekend after the holidays is always slow. Most people are dragging after their first week back at work—or too worried about paying their credit card bills—to want to go out."

"I can understand that," Allison acknowledged.

"And I'm guessing the only reason you're here is that it's Dylan's weekend with his dad."

"Yeah," she admitted. "I've got a thousand things to do at home—with a thousand loads of laundry being at the top of the list—but it just felt too quiet tonight."

"Did you come in here to see me or in search of some male companionship?"

Allison's eye roll was the only response she was going to give to that question.

Her friend sighed. "When was the last time you went out on a date—the night Dylan was conceived?"

"I date," she said.

Chelsea's brows lifted.

"I do. I even let you set me up on that blind date with your cousin Ivan not too long ago."

"Evan," her friend corrected. "And that was more than three years ago."

"It was not."

"It was," Chelsea insisted. "Because he didn't meet Wendy until a few months after that, and they just celebrated their second wedding anniversary."

"Oh." She picked up her glass, sipped. "It really didn't seem like it was that long ago."

"You're a fabulous mother, but you're also a young and sexy woman hiding behind your responsibilities to your son. There should be more to your life."

"I don't have time for anything more."

"You have to make time," her friend insisted. "To get out and meet new people."

"Why can't I just hang out with the people I already know?"

Chelsea sighed. "How long has it been since you've had sex? No—" She shook her head. "Forget that. How long has it been since you've even kissed a guy?"

Sex was, admittedly, a distant and foggy memory. But every detail of that kiss under the mistletoe was still seared into her brain despite all of her efforts to forget about it, tempting her with the unspoken promise of so much more.

"Oh. My. God."

She blinked. "What?"

"You've been holding out on me."

"What are you talking about?"

"I mentioned the word *kiss* and your eyes got this totally dreamy look and your cheeks actually flushed."

Allison's cheeks burned hotter. "It really wasn't that big of a deal."

"I'll be the judge of that," her friend decided. "When? Where? And who?"

Because she knew Chelsea wouldn't be dissuaded, she answered her questions in order. "Before Christmas, at a party. It was just one kiss, and no way am I telling you who."

"*Before* Christmas? And I'm only hearing about this *now*?"

"It wasn't a big deal." Which was a big fat lie, but she mentally crossed her fingers in the hope that her friend might believe it.

"Just one kiss?"

She nodded.

"Honey, if you're still blushing over one kiss more than three weeks later, it isn't just a big deal, it must have been one helluva kiss."

"I haven't been kissed like that in…" Allison tried to think back to a time when another man had touched her the way Nathan had touched her, kissed her as if he wanted nothing more than to go on kissing her, and her mind came up blank "…ever."

"Ty—" Chelsea called out to the man working the other end of the bar. "Can you cover for me for a few minutes?"

He winked at her. "Your wish is my command."

Chelsea rolled her eyes as she came around to the other side of the bar and slid onto the empty stool beside her friend, so they could talk without their conversation being overheard.

"Tell me about your holidays," Allison suggested, hoping to redirect her friend's focus.

Chelsea shook her head. "Uh-uh. This is about *you*, not me."

"But your life is so much interesting."

"Not this time."

Allison traced the base of her wineglass with a fingertip. "It really was just one kiss, and it's not going any further than that."

"Why not?" her friend demanded.

"Because it was the office Christmas party."

"It was someone you work with?"

She nodded.

"How closely?"

"Does it matter?"

"Of course it matters."

"Too closely."

Chelsea sighed. "Can't you give me at least a hint?"

She wished she could. In fact, she wished she could tell her friend everything. But Chelsea was a die-hard romantic, and the last thing Allison wanted or needed was any encouragement. Because even knowing all of the reasons that getting involved with Nathan Garrett would be a mistake, even knowing he'd been with Melanie Hedley in Colorado, she couldn't help wishing he would kiss her again.

"No, because you'll encourage me to do something crazy, and anything more than that one kiss would be totally crazy."

"He really has you flustered," Chelsea mused.

"It looks like Ty could use a hand behind the bar."

"He's fine." Then her attention shifted, and her lips curved. "Although maybe I should vacate this stool for a customer—because there's one headed in this direction who should be able to make you forget the mystery kisser and probably your own name."

Allison turned her head to follow her friend's gaze and sucked in a breath when her eyes locked with Nathan Garrett's cool gray ones.

She immediately turned back to Chelsea. "Are you crazy? He's practically my boss."

She didn't know if it was the words or the heat that she could feel infusing her cheeks, but somehow her response magically tied all of the loose threads together for her friend.

"It was *him*," Chelsea stated. "You kissed Nathan Garrett."

"*He* kissed *me*," she clarified. "And it was only because of the mistletoe."

"If he'd kissed me, I wouldn't have let it end there."

"You mean he hasn't kissed you?"

Her friend's brows lifted. "I know he has a reputation, but it isn't all bad. In fact—" she grinned "—most of it is *very* good. And if he's half as good a kisser as his brother Daniel, I can understand why your pulse is still racing."

"My pulse isn't still racing," she denied.

Chelsea just smiled, rising from her stool as the soon-to-be CFO slid onto the vacant seat on Allison's opposite side.

"What can I get for you, Nate?" Chelsea asked, returning to her position behind the bar.

"I'll have a Pepsi."

"Straight up or on the rocks?"

He smiled. "On the rocks."

The bartender stepped away to pour his soda, and Nate turned to Allison. "You skipped out early today."

She shook her head. "I only take a half-hour lunch each day so I can finish at four on Fridays."

"I wasn't aware of that."

"Is that going to be a problem, Mr. Garrett?"

"I don't see why it would."

Allison picked up her wine, set it down again. Dammit— Chelsea was right. Her pulse was racing and her knees were weak, and there was no way she could sit here beside him, sharing a drink and conversation and not think about the fact that her tongue had tangled with his.

"I think I'm going to call it a night."

"You haven't finished your wine," he pointed out.

"I'm not much of a drinker."

"Stay," he said.

She lifted her brows. "I don't take orders from you outside of the office, Mr. Garrett."

"Sorry—your insistence on calling me 'Mr. Garrett' made me forget that we weren't at the office," he told her. "Please, will you keep me company for a little while?"

"I'm sure there are any number of other women here who will happily keep you company when I'm gone."

"I don't want anyone else's company," he told her.

"Mr. Garrett—"

"Nate."

She sighed. "Why?"

"Because it's my name."

"I meant, why do you want my company?"

"Because I like you," he said simply.

"You don't even know me."

His gaze skimmed down to her mouth, lingered, and she knew he was thinking about the kiss they'd shared. The kiss she hadn't been able to stop thinking about.

"So give me a chance to get to know you," he suggested.

"You'll have that chance when you're in the CFO's office."

She frowned at the plate of pita bread and spinach dip that Chelsea slid onto the bar in front of her. "I didn't order this."

"But you want it," her friend said, and the wink that followed suggested she was referring to more than the appetizer.

"Actually, I want my bill. It's getting late and…" But her friend had already turned away.

She was tempted to walk out and leave Chelsea to pick up the tab, but the small salad she'd made for her own dinner after Dylan had gone was a distant memory and she had no willpower when it came to the Bar Down's three-cheese spinach dip.

Allison blew out a breath and picked up a grilled pita triangle. "The service here sucks."

"I've always found that the company of a beautiful woman makes up for many deficiencies."

It was, she was sure, just one of a thousand similar lines that tripped easily off of his tongue. And while she wanted to believe that she was immune to such an obvious flirtatious ploy, the heat pulsing through her veins proved otherwise.

Then he smiled—that slow, sexy smile that never failed to make her skin tingle. It had been a long time since she'd been an active participant in the games men and women played—so long, in fact, that she wasn't sure she even knew the rules anymore.

What she did know was that Nathan Garrett was way out of her league.

Chapter Three

Nate didn't usually have any trouble reading a woman's signals, but while Allison's words were denying any interest, the visible racing of her pulse beneath her ear said something completely different.

She didn't want to want him, but she did. That wasn't arrogance but fact, and one that was supported by the memory of the kiss they'd shared. A kiss that, for some inexplicable reason, she was pretending had never happened. He was tempted to ask her why, but he decided it wasn't the time or the place. Because he knew if he pushed, she'd just walk away—and he didn't want her to walk away.

So he picked up his glass and gestured to the plate in front of her. "Are you going to share that?"

She took her time chewing, as if thinking about his request. Then she shrugged and nudged the plate so that it was between them.

He'd eaten dinner with his brother, but she didn't know that, so he selected a piece of bread and dunked it. He was usually a meat-and-potatoes kind of guy, but the grilled bread in the warm cheesy spinach dip was surprisingly tasty. "This is good," he said.

"And addictive," Allison agreed, popping another piece into her mouth. "Which is why I rarely come here."

"Not because of the poor service?"

Her lips curved, just a little. "That, too."

Her smile, reluctant though it was, stirred something low in his belly.

She was pretty in a girl-next-door kind of way, her sexiness tempered by sweet. Definitely attractive, just not his type. Or so he'd always thought. He'd had countless conversations with her, sat in numerous meetings beside her, and never felt anything more than mild interest.

Until the Christmas party.

When Allison walked into the ballroom that night, it was as if a switch had flicked inside him, causing awareness to course through his blood like a high-voltage electrical current. And he didn't even know why. Sure, she looked different—but not drastically different.

Her hair, always tied in a knot at the back of her head at the office, was similarly styled, but the effect was softer somehow, with a few strands escaping to frame her face, emphasizing her delicate bone structure and creamy skin. Her eyes seemed bigger and darker, and her lips were glossy and pink, and deliciously tempting.

He wasn't sure if he'd ever seen her in a dress before. Certainly he'd never seen her in a dark green off-the-shoulder style that hugged her slender torso and flared out into a flirty little skirt that skimmed a few inches above her knees. Or in three-inch heels that emphasized shapely legs and actually made his mouth water.

She sat with a group of coworkers from the finance department for the meal, and he found himself sneaking glances in her direction—trying to figure out why he was so suddenly and inexplicably captivated by a woman he'd known for four years. He saw her dancing a couple of times early in the evening. She seemed to be pretty tight with Skylar Lockwood, his cousin's office administrator, and they looked to be enjoying themselves. The music was mostly fast and upbeat, with the occasional slow song thrown in to give the dancers a chance to catch their collective breath.

During one of those times, he watched his dad lead his mom to the dance floor. Even after more than forty years of marriage, they had eyes only for each other, and the obvious closeness and affection between them warmed something inside him. He'd never wanted what they had—and what each of his brothers had found with their respective spouses. And yet, he'd recently found himself considering that he *might* be ready for something more than the admittedly shallow relationships that had been the norm in his life for so long. Not that he was looking to put a ring on any woman's finger, but maybe a toothbrush in her bathroom wouldn't be so bad.

The vibration of his phone against his hip had him moving out of the ballroom to respond to the call. The name on the display gave him pause. Mallory was definitely not a woman with whom he would ever have something more, although there had been a time when he'd believed otherwise. Then he'd found out that his flight attendant girlfriend had also been dating a pilot she worked with, an Australian entrepreneur and a French banker during the time they were together.

More than a year after their final breakup, he had to wonder why she was reaching out to him now. And because he was curious, he answered the call. The connection wasn't great, so he moved into the cloakroom—where it was a little bit quieter and more private—to talk to her. While her claims of missing him had soothed his bruised ego, he wasn't at all tempted by her explicit offer to reconnect when she passed through town again.

He'd just tucked the phone back into his pocket when Allison had come in to get her coat. And in that moment, he completely forgot about Mallory and every other woman he'd ever dated. In that moment, he wanted only Allison.

And when he noticed that someone had pinned a sprig of

mistletoe in the center of the arched entranceway, he couldn't resist using it to his advantage.

"Refill?"

The question jarred him back to the present. He glanced up at Chelsea, who was pointing to his empty glass.

"Sure."

The bartender nodded, then shifted her attention to Allison. "One more?"

She shook her head. "No, I'm going to head home."

"Alone?"

"Yes, alone," she said firmly, definitively.

"But it's late," Chelsea protested, looking pointedly in Nate's direction.

"I live down the street," Allison reminded her.

"Down a dark street."

She shook her head. "Could I have my bill, please?"

Her friend looked at Nate again before she moved to the cash register to calculate the tab.

He knew how to take a hint—and he appreciated the opportunity the bartender had given to him. "I can give you a lift home," he told Allison.

"I really do live just down the street—it's not even far enough to drive."

"Then I'll walk with you," he said.

"I appreciate the offer," she said. "But it's not necessary."

"Chelsea thinks it is."

"I don't think that's what Chelsea's thinking," she admitted to him.

His brows lifted at that; Allison just shook her head.

When Chelsea returned with the bill, Nate passed her his credit card. "Add my drink and put it on that."

"I can pay my own bill," Allison protested, but her friend had already walked away again.

"You shared your spinach dip with me," Nate reminded her.

"I wouldn't have eaten the whole thing by myself—or

shouldn't have, anyway." But when he signed his name to the credit card receipt Chelsea put in front of him, she accepted that it was an argument that she wasn't going to win. "Thank you, Mr. Garrett."

"Nate," he reminded her.

She slid off of her stool and picked up her coat. He rose to his feet, intending to walk her to her door.

"I'm just going to the ladies' room," she told him.

"Oh." He sat down again, and watched out of the corner of his eye as she headed toward the alcove with the restrooms.

Chelsea finished serving another patron at the bar, then came back to him, shaking her head. "You're too accustomed to women falling at your feet, aren't you?"

He frowned. "What are you talking about?"

"I'm talking about the fact that you just let Allison slip out the door."

"She just went to the ladies' room."

"With her coat?"

He swore under his breath as he reached for his own.

Chelsea put her hand on his arm, shaking her head. "If you chase after her now, you're not only going to look pathetic, you're going to scare her away."

He scowled at that.

"I thought you'd appreciate the opportunity to walk her home," she continued. "But maybe you're not as interested as I thought."

"Just because you once dated my brother for a few weeks doesn't give you the right to pry into my personal life."

"No," she agreed. "But the fact that I'm Allison's best friend gives me the right to pry into hers."

"Then why aren't you talking to her?"

"I tried," she admitted. "But she doesn't kiss and tell."

However, the twinkle in her eye in conjunction with her word choice suggested that she knew more than she was letting on.

"Neither do I," he said.

"So don't talk," she said. "Just listen."

He picked up his soda and sipped.

"She doesn't date—or hardly ever, and she definitely doesn't sleep around. So if you're not looking for anything more than a good time, you should look elsewhere."

"I don't know what I'm looking for," he admitted.

"Then you better figure it out. And if you decide you want Allison, be prepared for the obstacles she'll put in your path every step of the way."

"Is that supposed to be a challenge or a warning?"

"That depends entirely on you," Chelsea said.

Nate considered what she'd said as he walked out of the bar. She was right—he could take her words as a warning and decide to forget about the sexy executive assistant, and that was probably the smart thing to do. On the other hand, he was more intrigued by Allison Caldwell than he'd been by any other woman in a very long time—and he never turned away from a challenge.

"Come on, Dylan. Your breakfast is on the table."

It was the third time she'd called to him, and finally he wandered out of his bedroom, still in his pajamas, his hair sticking up in various directions. She looked at her sleepy-eyed son and felt the familiar rush of affection.

She hadn't thought too much about getting married or having a baby before she found herself pregnant at twenty-one, but she'd never believed her son was anything but a gift. He wasn't always an easy child—there were times when he challenged and frustrated and infuriated her, but she loved him with every ounce of her being.

As he passed her on the way to the table, she gave him a quick hug and dropped a kiss on the top of his head. "Good morning."

"Mornin'," was his sleepy reply. He settled into his usual

chair at the table and scowled at the box of cereal on the table. "Can't I have waffles?"

"Not this morning," she told him.

His scowl deepened as he poured the Fruity O's into his bowl, then added milk. "Can I have pizza in my lunch?"

"We don't have any pizza." She cut the sandwich she'd made in half diagonally and put it in a snap-lock container.

He responded with something that sounded like, "Idon'wannasan'ich," but the words were garbled through a mouthful of cereal.

"It's ham and cheese," she told him. "Your favorite."

"M'favrit'spza."

"Don't talk with your mouth full."

He swallowed. "My favorite's pizza."

"We don't have any pizza," she said again, adding grapes and cookies to his lunch box.

"Can we have pizza for dinner?"

"You're going to be at your dad's for dinner," she reminded him.

He shoveled another spoonful of cereal into his mouth. "I'sThursdy."

"Yes, it is."

"Joslynsgot—"

"Chew and swallow, please."

He did so. "Jocelyn's got piano and Jillian's got dance."

"Lucky for them."

"Not for me," he grumbled. "'Cause I get dragged everywhere with them."

She wasn't without sympathy. She could only imagine how painful it was for an almost-nine-year-old boy to sit around while his younger sisters were involved in their own activities.

"Take your 3DS," she suggested, expecting him to jump at the offer.

"We're not s'posed to have 'lectronics at school," he told her.

She held back a sigh as she zipped up his lunch box and slid it into the front pocket of his backpack, double-checking to ensure that his rescue inhaler was where it was supposed to be. "Keep it in your locker."

He shoved more Fruity O's into his mouth, but he chewed and swallowed before speaking again. "Where's St. Louis, anyway?"

She opened the atlas she kept on hand to assist with his geography homework and pointed out Missouri. "Right there."

He studied the map. "It's a lot farther than Washington."

She knew he meant Washington, DC, which they'd visited the previous summer. "Yes, it is," she confirmed.

"Why do you hafta go there?"

"It's a business trip," she said, trying not to sound impatient as she glanced—again—at the clock.

"When are you gonna be home?"

"Tonight," she said. "And I'll pick you up straight from the airport."

"Promise?"

"I promise."

He pushed back his chair and started to carry his empty bowl and juice cup to the dishwasher. She was trying to teach him to pick up after himself—an uphill battle, to be sure—but she decided that today wasn't a day for lessons. Not if she wanted to get Dylan to school and herself to the airport on time.

"I'll do that." She took the dishes from him. "You go brush your teeth and get dressed."

Thankfully, he didn't drag his heels too much while doing so, and they were only three minutes behind schedule when they walked out the door. If the traffic lights cooperated, she might be able to make up that time on the way. But before Dylan climbed into the backseat of her car, she took the time to give him a hug and a kiss, because she knew he wouldn't accept any outward displays of affection when she dropped him off in front of the school.

He didn't say too much on the drive, and she knew that his mind was already shifting its focus to the day ahead. She was pleased that he did well in school, and frustrated by the realization that his success hadn't led to enjoyment. She thought he might like it more—or at least hate it less—if he made some friends, but he didn't choose to interact with many of the other students, except if the teacher forced them to work in groups, and even then, he didn't say much as he quietly did the work that was assigned.

She pulled up in front of the school as the bell rang and watched as he walked up the front steps to the main doors. It seemed like only yesterday that he'd refused to let go of her hand on his first day in kindergarten. The years had gone so fast, and so much had changed since then. Now he was in third grade, and she was lucky if he bothered to wave goodbye when she dropped him off.

He did today, lifting his hand as he glanced over his shoulder before he pulled open the door and disappeared inside, and the casual gesture tugged at her heart.

Then she pulled away from the school and turned toward the airport.

The acting CFO was already at the gate when Allison arrived.

Nate offered her a smile and a large coffee. "Cream only."

She didn't ask how he knew, she just accepted it gratefully. "Thanks."

As she sipped her coffee, she tried to focus on what she'd told her son—that this was a business trip, not unlike so many other business trips she'd made with John Garrett in the past. Except that this time she was traveling with her boss's nephew, and the memory of that one stolen kiss was still far too vivid in her mind.

When they boarded the plane, she was grateful that flying business class meant they wouldn't be sitting as close together as they would if they were in coach. Although Nathan didn't have the same girth across his belly as his uncle, he was a couple inches taller, his shoulders were broader and his legs were longer.

He paused at the aisle to let her precede him.

"You don't want the window seat?"

"No, I like the aisle."

"Oh. Okay." She slipped past him and into her seat.

He settled beside her and buckled his belt.

His choice of aisle over window wasn't a big deal, except that she couldn't help feeling as if she was trapped between the wall and Nate's body. Nate's long, lean and delicious-smelling body.

She tried to ignore his proximity, but every time she drew in a breath, she inhaled his scent and felt a little quiver low in her belly.

Seriously, the man was dangerous to her peace of mind.

While everyone else was boarding, she kept her attention focused on her tablet, checking her calendar for the dates and times of meetings in the next couple of weeks. Nate, she noted, was reading a newspaper, but he tucked it away when the flight attendant began to review the safety procedures of the aircraft.

Most of the passengers in business class were frequent fliers who probably knew the spiel as well as the staff, and she didn't doubt that he was one of them, but he gave the flight attendant his attention anyway. Or maybe it had nothing to do with the safety procedures and everything to do with her big…smile.

When the presentation was finished, he turned to Allison. "Are we being picked up at the airport?"

She shook her head. "John always preferred to have a rental car rather than be at the mercy of someone else's schedule. I didn't think to ask what arrangements you wanted made."

"I would have told you to make the usual arrangements," he said, and smiled.

And damn if that smile didn't make her toes want to curl.

In an effort to refocus her thoughts, she said, "Did you want to review any of your uncle's notes before the meeting?"

"I did that last night."

"Do you have any questions?"

He shifted in his seat, so that he was facing her more fully. "As a matter of fact, I do."

"Okay."

"Why are you pretending that nothing happened at the Christmas party?"

She felt color climb up her neck and into her cheeks. So much for her determination to stay focused on business. "I meant—do you have any questions about the meeting?"

"No," he said. "But I want to know why you're pretending the kiss we shared never happened."

Since he obviously wasn't going to let her ignore his question, she decided to answer it succinctly and dismissively. "Not making a big deal out of it isn't the same as pretending it never happened."

"So you do remember it?"

She scrolled through the notes on her tablet. "I remember that it was late, there was mistletoe, we both had a little too much to drink and got caught up in the spirit of the holiday."

"Do you want to know how I remember it?"

"I'm actually a little surprised that you do."

"What is that supposed to mean?"

"I would have thought your sojourn with Melanie would

have eradicated one meaningless little kiss from your mind," she said.

"Let's put aside the inaccuracy of your description until after you explain who the hell Melanie is."

"Melanie Hedley," she said.

"The name sounds vaguely familiar," he admitted.

"Perky blonde, works in marketing."

His confusion finally cleared. "You mean Lanie?"

"Yeah, I guess I have heard some people call her Lanie."

"And the sojourn?" he prompted.

"Your ski trip."

He shook his head definitively. "I didn't go with Lanie."

"And yet she couldn't stop talking about the wonderful lunch you had at a fabulous little café by your hotel."

"We did have lunch together one day," he admitted. "I ran into her in the lobby of the hotel when I was heading out to grab a bite and invited her to join me. It wasn't anything more than that."

"You don't have to explain anything to me," she told him.

"Apparently I do," he said. Because he could tell by the tone of her voice that she'd arrived at her own—and obviously erroneous—conclusions. "Do you really think I was sleeping with another woman the night after I kissed you?"

"I really didn't give it much thought at all," she said, shifting her gaze to the clouds outside the window.

If he hadn't already suspected that she was lying, her refusal to even look at him would have triggered his suspicion. "Yes, I went away with some friends. And yes, I received a couple of offers to hook up while I was there.

"But I didn't consider any of them for more than two seconds—" he shifted so that his shoulder brushed against hers, and lowered his mouth closer to her ear "—because since that kiss we shared under the mistletoe, I haven't been able to go much longer than that without thinking about you.

"And when I think about that kiss, I remember how good

your body felt against mine, and how surprised—and incredibly turned on—I was by the passion of your response."

"You're right," she said shortly. "Our memories are different. But considering that we're going to be working closely together, I think it would be best if we both just forgot about that kiss."

"I already know that I can't," he told her.

"Maybe you just need to try a little harder."

"Are you saying that you have forgotten?"

"I'm saying that I'm not going to let anything interfere with our working relationship."

"I know how to separate business from pleasure," he assured her.

"Let's keep the focus on business," she suggested.

"That doesn't sound like nearly as much fun."

"I like my job and I want to keep my job," she told him. "Which means I'm definitely not going to sleep with my boss."

His lips curved. "I'm not your boss yet."

She lifted a brow. "Your point?"

"We could use the next few weeks to get this…attraction…out of our systems, so that it won't be an impediment to our working together."

"Thank you for that uniquely intriguing offer," she said primly, "but no."

Despite his blatant flirtation on the plane, when they got to the St. Louis store and started to review the books, Nathan proved that he did know how to separate business from pleasure.

Allison was impressed by his knowledge of the company's history and employees and the diligence of his work. She hadn't assumed he was moving into the CFO's office because his name was Garrett, but she had suspected the familial connection had paved the way. Watching him work, she realized that had been her error. Nate was going to be the new CFO because he was the most qualified person for the job.

Still, it took several hours before the discrepancy was found. Working together to match invoices to payment receipts, it became apparent to both Nate and Allison that some numbers had been transposed when the deposit was made. Instead of $53,642 being deposited, the amount was noted as $35,264—a deficit of $18,378. But what seemed like a simple accounting error was further complicated by the facts that the payment had been made in cash (apparently office furniture for an upstart law firm that didn't yet have a checking account) and no one seemed to know where the $18,378 had gone—or they weren't admitting it if they did.

To a company that did hundreds of millions of dollars in business annually, the amount was hardly significant. But the misplacement of any funds, whether careless or deliberate, was unacceptable from an accounting perspective. The head of the store's finance department agreed and promised to locate the missing money before the end of the week.

"I'm surprised you're going to leave it for Bob to deal with," Allison said when they'd left the man's office.

"They're his people," Nate said. "And I have no doubt he already knows who is responsible for making that eighteen thousand dollars disappear."

"So you don't think it was a mistake?"

"I would have believed the transposing of the digits was a mistake if the correct amount had actually been deposited—the fact that it wasn't proves otherwise."

"You don't want to know who did it?"

"I will know," he said confidently. "But I don't need to know today."

"In that case—" she glanced at her watch as they made their way toward the exit "—we should be able to get to the airport in time to catch an earlier flight back to Raleigh."

"That would be good." He stopped to pull his phone out of his pocket and frowned at the message he read. "But I don't think it's going to happen."

"Why not?"

"Apparently a storm has moved into this area. I just got a notification from the airline that our flight has been delayed."

She pulled out her phone and found that she'd received the same message. "There has to be a mistake—the forecast was clear."

"Then the forecast was wrong."

She halted beside him at the glass doors and blinked, as if she didn't quite believe what she was seeing. Or rather *not* seeing, since the blowing snow made it impossible to see anything past it.

Nate was focused on his phone, checking for updates from the airline. "All flights are canceled for the next twelve hours."

"So what are we supposed to do?" She couldn't help but think of the promise she'd made to Dylan that morning.

"Find a hotel," he said easily. "Hopefully one that isn't too far away from where we are right now."

"A hotel?" she echoed.

"Unless you want to bunk down here?"

"Of course not." What she wanted was to be back in Charisma, in her own apartment with her son—not stranded in St. Louis, and especially not with a man who made her feel nothing but heat despite the obviously frigid temperatures outside.

"There's a Courtland not too far from here," he said. "Let me just give them a call and see if we can get a room."

"Two rooms."

But the room situation wasn't really her biggest concern—nor was the fact that she hadn't packed an overnight bag. She was more worried about the fact that she hadn't packed anything for Dylan. Of course, her ex-husband knew that Mrs. Hanson, the widow who lived across the hall from Allison and Dylan, had a spare key and could let him in to get whatever he needed. She just wasn't sure that Jeff would know what their son needed.

Did he know that Dylan had specific pajamas that he liked to wear when he stayed at his dad's house? Would he remember to pack Bear, the little boy's ancient and much-loved teddy bear? Would he make sure that Dylan did his homework? Would he remember to pack his lunch for the next day? She worried about all of those details while Nathan made a phone call to secure their hotel rooms.

Less than five minutes later, they battled the blowing snow and howling wind toward their rental car in the parking lot. Despite the wild weather, Nate went around to the passenger side to open the door for her, an unexpectedly chivalrous gesture that reminded her there was more to the man than his reputation implied.

She slid into her seat and buckled up, aware that the roads were going to be icy and slick—and still not nearly as dangerous as spending the night in a hotel with Nathan Garrett.

Chapter Four

It took nearly twenty-five minutes to travel the six miles between the store and the hotel.

And for every single one of those minutes, Allison was grateful that Nate was behind the wheel. She considered herself a good driver, but she had little experience driving on snow-covered roads and absolutely no experience navigating unfamiliar streets in whiteout conditions.

As Nathan eased to a stop at a red light, he glanced over at her. "Are you okay?"

"Fine. Why?"

"You're clutching your bag so tight your knuckles are white and you haven't said a word since we pulled out of the parking lot."

"I wanted you to be able to focus on the roads."

"I've driven in worse," he assured her.

"Really?"

"I went to New York University," he said.

"You have to be crazy to drive in New York City on a good day."

"A little bit," he agreed, easing into the intersection when the light turned green.

"There's the hotel," Allison said, recognizing the distinctly scripted *C* that was the Courtland trademark.

He pulled into the underground parking garage and found a vacant spot. "At least we won't have to brush snow off in the morning."

"I'm hoping it will all be melted by the morning."

"That's definitely wishful thinking," he told her. "But as long as the storm has passed, we'll get home tomorrow."

She nodded and followed him to the elevator.

"Ever checked into a hotel without a suitcase before?" he asked her.

"No," she said, just a little primly.

He waggled his eyebrows. "Does it make you feel like you're on your way to an illicit rendezvous?"

"No," she said again, because that was something she definitely did *not* want to be thinking about. "I don't do things like that."

"Never?"

"Never."

He flashed that tingle-inducing smile. "Too bad."

When the elevator opened up on the main level of the hotel, he went directly to the check-in desk and spoke to the woman behind the counter. The name on her tag was Sheila, and she smiled warmly at Nate.

Part of the customer service or proof of the effect that he had on all females? And why should she care? He could flirt with the desk clerk and every other female in a ten-block radius, if he wanted—and he probably did. She just wanted to get to her room to make a phone call.

"We're almost at capacity because of a veterinarian medicine conference," she told him. "So we weren't able to find two rooms…"

Allison's breath caught—

"…on the same floor."

—and released.

"We're just happy you were able to accommodate us at all," Nate assured her.

"The storm caught a lot of people unaware," Sheila said. "The phones have been ringing almost nonstop for the past hour as stranded travelers scramble to find beds."

Allison felt a slight twinge of guilt that they were taking two rooms—no doubt each with two beds—until she reminded herself that this wasn't the only hotel in town.

"If I could just get a credit card for each room?" Sheila prompted.

Allison reached for her wallet but Nate was already passing his corporate credit card across the desk. "Put both rooms on this."

"I can pay for my own room," she protested.

"And if this was a vacation, I'd let you," he said. "But this was a business trip, so the hotel is a business expense."

"I don't imagine accounting will be happy to reimburse for two rooms for what was supposed to have been a quick day trip."

His brows lifted. "Are you offering to share a room?"

"No."

He grinned at her immediate and vehement response, then lowered his head and his voice. "I promise—I don't snore."

"I don't care," she assured him.

He lifted one shoulder in a half shrug. "Your loss."

She didn't doubt that it probably was, but she'd learned a long time ago that impulsive actions could have extensive repercussions. She didn't do impulsive anymore.

Sheila came back to the counter. "You're in room 542, Ms. Caldwell, and you're in 913, Mr. Garrett." She passed their respective key cards across the desk. "Neither of you has any luggage?"

"No," Nathan answered for both of them. "Our trip wasn't supposed to be longer than a few hours."

Sheila reached into a drawer and pulled out a couple of clear plastic bags with various sundries, including toothbrush, toothpaste, comb, cotton swabs, disposable razor and sample size deodorant. "If you need anything else, there's a clothing boutique, general store and pharmacy on the lower level. There's also Prime—our steak and seafood restaurant, the Martini Bar and the Gateway Lounge, so you should be able to find something to suit your palate."

"Thank you," Allison said, gratefully taking the key and kit.

Nathan followed her to the elevator. "Are you hungry?"

"Starved," she admitted.

He pressed the buttons for five and nine. "Do you want to try the restaurant?"

Her stomach growled at the thought of a thick, juicy steak, but her mind warned of the dangers of enjoying a cozy dinner with her sexy boss. "I'll probably just grab a sandwich from the lounge and eat in my room."

His brow furrowed. "A sandwich? Really?"

She felt her cheeks flush. "I've got some phone calls to make."

"I do, too." He glanced at his watch. "Let's meet back downstairs at six."

She'd never said she would have dinner with him; he'd just steamrolled over her protests. Of course, he was accustomed to being the man in charge at the office—and probably in his relationships. And although she instinctively balked at the take-charge attitude that was far too reminiscent of her ex-husband's demeanor, she realized that he was paying for her room and most likely her dinner, too, which made it a business dinner. It wasn't as if he was asking—or demanding—that she go on a date with him.

"Six-thirty," she finally relented when the bell chimed to announce their arrival on the fifth floor. "I'll meet you downstairs then."

The first call she made was to her ex-husband, to tell Jeff that she was stuck in St. Louis. Since it was past the time that he should have picked up Dylan from school, she frowned when the call went immediately to voice mail. She left a message, asking him to call her back when he had a chance. After that, she spent some time responding to emails that had come in throughout the day, periodically glancing at her silent phone as if she could will it to ring.

Dylan had mentioned that Jillian had dance and Jocelyn had piano—or was it vice versa? She never seemed to be able to keep the girls' activities straight, which wasn't relevant anyway. What was relevant was that she'd never known Jeff not to have his phone literally attached to his hip. And with each minute that passed, her anxiousness increased. In the absence of any response from her ex-husband, how could she even be certain that he'd picked their son up from school?

Logically, she knew that the school would have called if Dylan had been left there. But the boy had been in an obviously disgruntled mood that morning—disgruntled enough to leave the school yard on his own? She didn't think so, but it was hard to remain rational when she was so far away and helpless to do anything but wait for Jeff to respond to her message.

Well, not entirely helpless. She picked up her phone again and called her apartment, neither surprised nor reassured when the answering machine clicked on. She considered trying Mrs. Hanson to ask if she'd seen Dylan, but she didn't want to worry her elderly neighbor unnecessarily. Because although Allison was worried, she acknowledged that she might be overreacting to the situation.

Instead of calling Mrs. Hanson, she tried Jeff's number again—and got his voice mail again. Then she called a number she very rarely dialed: her ex-husband's new home.

Jodie answered, sounding breathless and annoyed, on the fifth ring. "'Lo?"

"Hi, Jodie. It's Allison."

The other woman huffed out a breath. "This really isn't a good time—I'm trying to get little Jefferson down for a nap and he'd just started to drift off when the phone rang."

In the background, she could hear distant crying. "I'm sorry," she apologized automatically, "but I haven't been able to reach Jeff and I wanted to make sure he remembered to pick up Dylan from school."

"Of course he remembered."

"Usually he sends me a text to confirm."

"Well, usually we don't have three kids needing to be in three different places and then, on top of all of that, you dumped Dylan on him without even asking if it was convenient, so perhaps he was just a little busy."

Allison bit her tongue so hard she thought she might draw blood. When she could finally speak without letting loose on her ex-husband's new wife, she only said, "In case he doesn't get the voice mail message I left for him—" she didn't admit that she'd left three "—can you ask him to give me a call when he gets in?"

"Sure. But aren't you supposed to be here to pick Dylan up in a couple of hours?"

"That was the original plan," she agreed. "But a snowstorm stranded me in St. Louis."

"Oh." Somehow there was a wealth of disapproval—and accusation—in that single syllable. "I guess that means he'll be staying here tonight."

"Since Family Services generally frowns upon eight-year-olds being left alone when a parent is out of town, I guess it does," she confirmed.

"I'll make sure Jefferson gives you a call."

"Thank you." Allison disconnected and blew out a breath.

She was generally an easygoing person who liked almost everyone, but no matter how hard she'd tried—and she really had tried—she'd never managed to like Jodie Daley-Caldwell.

From day one, her ex-husband's new wife had treated Allison as though she was "the other woman." Yes, Jeff and Jodie had dated all through high school, but they'd gone to different colleges after graduation and decided to end their relationship shortly after that. It was more than two years later before Allison even met Jeff, so she could hardly be accused of coming between them.

And while she might have had nothing to do with their breakup, her marriage to Jeff had certainly been an impediment to their reconciliation, albeit one that he'd quickly rectified when he realized he was still in love with his high school sweetheart. Allison knew that Jodie wished she could pretend her husband's first marriage had never happened—but Dylan's existence and regular visitation with his father made that impossible. And Allison couldn't help but resent her son's stepmother treating him like he was an inconvenience.

She was still trying to shake off the weight of the conversation when a knock sounded at the door. Frowning, she squinted through the peephole to find Nathan standing outside her room.

Drawing in another deep breath, she opened the door. "I thought we were meeting downstairs."

"I wanted to make sure you didn't change your mind."

"Was changing my mind an option?"

"No," he admitted. "Which is why I'm at your door."

She still hadn't talked to either Jeff or Dylan, but they both had her cell phone number so she didn't have to wait in the room for a return call. And although she knew she wouldn't completely relax until she'd heard from her son, she tucked her key card in the pocket of her blazer, slung her purse over her shoulder and stepped out into the hall.

Reassured that Dylan was safely in his father's care, the knots of anxiety in her belly hadn't dissipated but they did loosen enough to make her realize how very hungry she was.

Then Nate put his hand on her back to guide her toward the elevator, and the awareness that her stomach was empty was supplanted by an entirely different awareness.

Over the six years that Allison had been John Garrett's executive assistant, she'd gotten to know her boss very well and she'd never felt the least bit uncomfortable with him. Of course, she'd never been kissed by him the way Nathan had kissed her at the Christmas party.

Which had been more than four weeks ago. Not exactly ancient history in her world, but certainly enough time had passed that the memory of it shouldn't still make her pulse race. Except that it did. And standing beside Nate in the elevator, just the two of them in the confined space, her pulse was definitely racing.

When they arrived on the main floor, he gestured for her to precede him, then he splayed his hand on her back again. She was wearing a silk shell and a tailored jacket, but she was as aware of his touch as if there was no fabric barrier between his wide palm and her bare skin.

The restaurant hostess led them to their table, and she noticed that the larger booths had rectangular tables and straight bench-style seating on three sides; the smaller booths had round tables with semi-circular bench seating designed to allow couples to snuggle close together if they chose.

Allison sat as far away from Nate as possible. But even then, the curved design of the booth and the flickering candle on the table provided a romantic ambience that she didn't want to feel. The hostess handed them menus, recited the daily specials and promised that Stefano would be right over to take their drink orders.

She opened her menu and skimmed the offerings, wondering why it felt so much like a date when it clearly wasn't. She was here with Nate only because they were stranded. As soon as the storm blew over—please God, let it be gone by the morning—they would be on their way back to North Carolina and their separate lives. But while they were stuck in St. Louis, they were having dinner together only because they both had to eat. It absolutely was *not* a date.

"Red or white?"

The question seemed to come from out of nowhere, and she looked up at Nate. "Sorry?"

"Wine," he clarified.

"Oh. Um." She figured adding wine to the situation could only equal trouble, so she looked at the waiter with an apologetic smile. "I'll just have a glass of water."

"And a bottle of the Woodbridge cabernet sauvignon," Nate said.

"Good choice, sir," Stefano said, then retreated to get their beverages.

"Do you know what you want?" Nate asked.

She forced her gaze to stay focused on the menu. "The peppercorn sirloin sounds good."

"It does," he agreed. "I was looking at the same thing."

The waiter returned with two glasses of ice water and the bottle of wine. Stefano deftly popped the cork and poured a sample for Nate to approve. He sipped, savored, nodded.

Stefano, apparently having forgotten as quickly as Nate that she'd said she didn't want any wine, tipped the bottle over her glass. She decided it was ridiculous to worry that a single glass of wine was going to override all of her inhibitions and entice her to drag her soon-to-be boss into her hotel room to have her way with him.

But she picked up the glass of water first.

"Are you ready to order?"

Allison went with the peppercorn sirloin—medium well, with a side of wild rice and a green salad. Nate opted for the ten-ounce sirloin—medium, with a baked potato, fully loaded and cauliflower au gratin.

When the waiter had gone, Nate offered her the bread basket, but she shook her head.

"I know we worked through lunch," he said, as he tore open a warm multigrain roll. "So how are you not starving?"

"I am," she admitted. "But I'm waiting for my steak."

"I'm just glad to see that you aren't one of those women who thinks that lettuce is a meal."

"Why would my eating habits be of any concern to you?"

He broke off a piece of bread and popped it in his mouth. "Because now I know that, when I finally convince you to go out with me, I can take you to a real restaurant and not just a salad bar."

"You definitely don't need to worry about that, because I wouldn't go out with you."

He didn't argue, he just smiled.

That smug, sexy smile that made her realize he could probably convince her of anything if he made the slightest effort.

She tried to remember all of the reasons that getting involved with him on a personal level was a very bad idea—most notably that the man was going to be her boss and an affair would do nothing to enhance her credibility in the office. Focusing her attention on the forthcoming changes at Garrett Furniture, she said, "How do you think your uncle is going to adjust to retirement?"

"Reluctantly," Nate admitted. "My aunt Ellen has been pressuring him to retire for the better part of four years, and he kept saying he would, and then he kept putting it off."

"He can't put it off any longer."

"It certainly doesn't look that way. But there are still two more weeks before the end of the month, so I'm not rearranging the furniture in his office just yet."

Beneath the words, she heard just a hint of the frustration that had been building over those four years since he'd been brought back to Charisma in preparation of taking over the position. "For what it's worth, he has no doubts about your abilities to do the job."

"Then why did he keep postponing his retirement?"

"Because he's sure that he'll go crazy inside of two

weeks." She smiled in response to the lift of his brows. "His words."

"Aunt Ellen will probably drive him crazy," Nate acknowledged. "She'll make him eat a heart-healthy diet to stay alive, but she'll drive him crazy."

Despite the disparaging words, she heard the affection in his voice.

Over the years that she'd worked for John Garrett, she'd learned that the company history was also family history. Garrett Furniture was founded almost sixty years earlier by Henry Garrett, who worked in the tobacco fields during the day and puttered with wood in his workshop at night. His first project was a dining room table and chairs for his family; then he designed and built a cabinet for his wife to display the heirloom china that had come down to her from her grandmother.

Visitors, friends and family alike, were usually surprised to learn that he'd made the furniture that filled the home, and he was soon being asked to make pieces for others. A few years later, he quit his job in the tobacco fields to focus on building furniture full time. A few more years after that, the first Garrett Furniture store opened.

When he finally retired—forced to do so because of hands that were so twisted with arthritis, he could no longer hold the tools that had built his business—he turned the reins over to three of his sons: David, John and Thomas. (A fourth son, Edward, had gone to medical school up north and, after graduation, settled down to practice in Pinehurst, New York.)

David was the CEO, John was the CFO and Thomas was the COO. Allison thought it was interesting that each of the men had three children, and while some of those offspring had chosen to do other things—David's son, Daniel, had been a network security specialist before he decided to invest in a stock car racing team; John's son, Justin, was an ER

doctor; and Thomas's daughter, Jordyn, was the manager of
O'Reilly's Pub—most worked for Garrett Furniture in one
capacity or another. And despite their large number and
disparate career choices, they were a close family. They all
came together for the company Christmas party, the annual
summer picnic and countless birthdays and anniversaries
and weddings. (The three cousins in Pinehurst—Matthew, a
surgeon; Jackson, an attorney; and Lukas, a veterinarian—
had all married within the past couple of years.)

Stefano delivered their plates, and they each dug into their
meals with enthusiasm. Between bites, Allison sipped the
wine in her glass. She was halfway through her steak when
Nate asked, "What are you worrying about now?"

"Why do you think I'm worried?"

"Because you've got that little line—" he touched a finger to illustrate the spot between his own brows "—you get
when you're worried about something."

She was surprised by both his observation and insight,
and she couldn't deny that she was worried. "I wasn't able
to get in touch with Jeff to let him know that I wasn't going
to be back tonight."

"Who's Jeff?" he asked.

"My ex-husband."

Above those warm, smoky eyes, his brows lifted. "Why
would your ex-husband care that you're stuck out of town?"

"It probably won't bother him as much as it will bother
Jodie," she admitted. "Because they weren't planning on
keeping Dylan overnight."

He speared a floret with his fork. "And Dylan is?"

"My son."

Chapter Five

Nate paused with the fork halfway to his mouth and tried to absorb what she'd just told him.

My son.

The words echoed through his mind like a clanging bell—an unmistakable warning.

He'd always appreciated all kinds of women. It didn't matter to him if they were blonde, brunette or redhead, skinny or curvy, tall or short. He didn't have any specific type—except that women who were tied down by familial obligations were definitely *not* his type.

And Allison Caldwell had a kid.

He popped the cauliflower into his mouth and tried to wrap his mind around the fact that the sexy woman seated across from him had carried and borne a child.

How had he not known that she was a mother? It seemed unlikely to him that the existence of her son hadn't come up in conversation at some time over the past four years. Or maybe it had, and he just hadn't paid much attention.

When he'd first moved back to Charisma, he couldn't help but notice that his uncle had a new executive assistant—or that she was young and very attractive. He also knew that his transfer to the head office of Garrett Furniture was a huge step up the corporate ladder and, determined to focus on his career, he'd made every effort to steer clear of the temptation that was Allison Caldwell.

The fact that she had a kid was just one more—and possibly the biggest—reason that he should walk away from her. A better man would claim that revelation didn't change anything. Nate had never claimed to be a better man. And even though both of his brothers had wives and children, he wasn't eager to go down that same path.

He had no interest, not right now or in the foreseeable future, in doing the whole family thing. If he had a choice—and he did—he would avoid getting tangled up with a woman who was already tangled up by domestic responsibilities.

He cut off a piece of steak, chewed. He knew that being a mother was more than a title; it was an intrinsic part of a woman's identity. But when Allison had been in his arms, responding to his kiss with a passion that matched his own, he knew without a doubt she sure as heck hadn't been thinking or feeling like a mother.

The fact that she had a child did nothing to dampen his desire for her, but it did make him realize that pursuing a relationship with her would be more complicated than he'd imagined. Maybe more complicated than he wanted.

With the exceptions of only his niece and his nephew, kids were way outside of his comfort zone. Although he hadn't completely disregarded the possibility that he might want one or more of his own someday, that someday was somewhere in the distant future. And even then, he wasn't sure he wanted to take on the responsibility of someone else's kid—no matter how much he wanted the kid's mother.

"How old is he?" he asked.

"Eight. Almost nine."

Which was older than he'd expected, but still young enough that the kid would be the focus of most of her time and attention. "You must have been young when you had him."

"Not yet twenty-two," she confirmed.

"Were you married then?"

She nodded. "We got married in September. Dylan was born in March. Our divorce was final two years after that."

"It must have been hard for your son, being so young when you split."

"Actually, I've always thought it was good that because Dylan was so young, our separation wasn't a big traumatic event in his life. In fact, he has no memories of his dad and me together." She picked up her glass of wine and sipped. "Of course, our marriage was so brief—and so chaotic as we struggled to get used to being married and dealing with a brand-new baby—that *I* barely have any memories of his dad and me together."

"Do you still love him?" He wasn't sure why he asked the question, why her response mattered to him, but it did.

"I never really did," she admitted. "We were just a couple of college kids who weren't always vigilant about birth control yet somehow naive enough to be shocked when I ended up pregnant.

"Jeff asked me to marry him because he felt it was the right thing to do, and I accepted his proposal because marrying a guy I didn't know all that well was a slightly less terrifying prospect than having and raising a child on my own.

"He's a good dad," she said. "At least, he tries to be. He picks Dylan up from school every Wednesday and has him overnight every other weekend, but he doesn't often make extracurricular activities or school events because he's got another family now."

"He's remarried?"

"Exchanged vows with his high school sweetheart only a few days after our divorce was final."

Her tone was neutral, almost too neutral, making him suspect that she'd been more hurt by the event than her matter-of-fact statement revealed.

"That was—" so many words came to mind: cold, cruel and heartless were only a few, but he settled on "—quick."

She smiled at that. "Yes," she agreed. "But not really surprising. Because even when he asked me to marry him, he was still in love with her. Of course, I didn't know that until after we split up." She frowned into her glass of wine, as if it was somehow responsible for her rambling. "I'm sorry—I don't know why I'm telling you this."

"I asked," he reminded her.

"And now I'll bet you're sorry you did."

"Not at all. I'm just surprised that I've known you for more than four years and never knew that you had a child."

"I guess you're not the only one who knows how to separate business and pleasure." She glanced away as her cell phone vibrated on the table. Whatever she saw on the screen made her lips curve in a smile that was as quick as it was genuine.

"Your son?" he guessed.

She nodded. "Excuse me," she said, and rose from the table to answer the call.

Allison was as relieved as she was pleased to hear Dylan's voice. Not just to know for sure that he was okay, but because the call gave her an excuse to step away from the table and the seductive gaze of Nathan Garrett.

"Hi, honey. How was school today?"

Dylan ignored her question to ask his own. "Where are you?"

"I'm still in St. Louis."

"You said you were going to pick me up," he reminded her, his tone querulous.

"I didn't know that they were going to close the airport because of a snowstorm."

"It's not snowing here."

"Remember when we looked at the map this morning?" she asked him. "Missouri is a long way from North Carolina."

"I don't wanna stay here tonight. Why can't I have a sleepover at Aunt Chelsea's?"

It wasn't so long ago that he used to love going to his dad's, staying at his dad's, but that was before he had to share his dad's attention with three other kids. "Because she has a class on Thursdays and, even if she didn't, it's too late to make other arrangements."

On the other end of the line, her son was silent.

"Did your dad take you home to get your overnight bag?"

"Yeah. And he made me pack extra stuff 'cause he said I'm gonna stay for the whole weekend, but I was here last weekend."

"I know," she acknowledged. "But your dad and Jodie are going to be out of town next week so they asked if they could change the dates."

"You could've said no," he told her.

Yes, she could have, but she tried to be accommodating, to ensure that her son got as much time as possible with his father. But there were times she couldn't help but feel that her ex-husband took advantage of her flexibility without regard to their son's schedule or his feelings.

"We'll do something special next weekend when we're together," she promised.

"Like what?"

"I don't know what. Why don't you think on it and we'll discuss some ideas when you get home?"

"You mean when you get home."

"Sure," she agreed. Provided it stopped snowing overnight, she should be home the next day, and then she would have two nights alone before he got back on Sunday. But she didn't want to think about that when she was already missing him so much.

"Where are you now?" he asked. "Are you on the airplane?"

"No, I'm at a hotel near the airport."

"You don't have Bear," he said. "'Cause he was still in my bed when Dad took me home to get my stuff."

As a baby, Dylan wouldn't go to sleep unless his favorite teddy bear was in his crib. As he got older, he grew less dependent but still usually packed the toy when he would be gone overnight. And a couple of years earlier, he'd started packing Bear in his mom's suitcase whenever she had to go away, so she wouldn't be lonely.

"I didn't bring Bear because I didn't think I would have to stay overnight," she reminded him.

"I wish you had him with you, so you don't have to sleep alone."

It was the innocent suggestion of a child, but his words brought to mind all kinds of not-so-innocent possibilities.

Maybe she should consider Nathan's offer to get the attraction out of their systems—except she was no longer certain the offer was on the table. She could tell that he'd been taken aback to learn she had a child, and she suspected the revelation had diminished the attraction—at least on his part.

"I'll be okay by myself," she promised him.

"I love you, Mom."

"I love you, too, Dilly Bug."

As she disconnected the call and tucked her phone into the pocket of her jacket, she heard the echo of Chelsea's voice in the back of her mind.

How long has it been since you've had sex?

She honestly wasn't sure. She'd had only two lovers in the six years that had passed since she'd divorced, and neither had been anything more than a temporary diversion. She hadn't wanted anything more. And she didn't want anything more now, but she couldn't deny that being with Nathan Garrett made her want.

Bad idea, she reminded herself sternly as she made her way back to the table.

When she got there, Stefano was clearing away their plates.

He asked if they wanted dessert and coffee; she declined the former but accepted the latter. Nate ordered the New York–style cheesecake with chocolate-cookie crust and strawberry-Grand Marnier topping.

When it came, the square plate was drizzled with chocolate sauce and sprinkled with powdered sugar, with the thick slice of cake at its center. There were also two forks.

"Try it," Nate instructed.

She couldn't deny that she was tempted—and annoyed with Nate for putting the temptation so squarely in front of her. "Do you ever take no for an answer?"

He smiled at the frustration in her tone. "It's just cheesecake."

And he was right, but she was afraid if she didn't say no and mean it now, she wouldn't be able to say no to anything else that he asked of her.

He picked up one of the forks, broke off a piece of the cake and held it toward her.

"I said I didn't want any dessert."

"Your lips are saying no but your eyes are saying yes."

She rolled her eyes at the cliché, but she couldn't deny that it was true. She loved cheesecake, and her mouth was practically watering in anticipation of the rich, creamy flavor, but she kept her lips firmly closed.

"Are you always this stubborn?" he asked.

"How is refusing dessert stubborn?"

He moved the fork away from her lips and slid it between his own. "You're denying yourself something that you want for no reason other than to be difficult."

"You ordered the cake—I would think you'd be happy not to share it."

"Food is a necessity, but dessert is a pleasure. And pleasure—" he scooped up another bite "—should be shared."

"Are we still talking about cheesecake?"

His eyes held hers as he guided the fork closer to her mouth. "You tell me."

He was temptation personified, and she could no longer resist.

Her lips parted, and he slid the fork between them. Her eyes closed and a hum of satisfaction echoed in her throat.

"It's good, isn't it?"

She held up a hand. "I'm having a moment."

He chuckled softly and nudged the plate closer to her.

She picked up the second fork and took another bite of the cake, savoring the creaminess of the cake and the sweetness of the strawberries on her tongue.

"This is—" she couldn't find words that would adequately describe the taste "—even better than sex."

Which was not something she ever intended to say out loud—especially not in front of Nate Garrett.

His only response was a lift of his eyebrows as he took another bite of the dessert. "It's very good," he confirmed. "But if you think it's better than sex, you need a different partner."

"Or at least a partner."

He picked up his coffee. "That would be a good start."

She shook her head. "And that is why I usually don't have more than one glass of wine—because I lose the filter between my brain and my mouth."

"I like you like this," he said. "Saying what you're thinking instead of censoring your thoughts and weighing your words."

"Lillian—my former mother-in-law—used to admonish me all the time for speaking without thinking."

"Because your thoughts weren't in line with hers?"

"Because *Mrs.* Jefferson Caldwell the Third didn't have any thoughts that didn't echo those of *Mr.* Jefferson Caldwell the Third. And, if I was ever going to be a good Southern wife, I needed to take my cues from my husband."

"Jefferson Caldwell the Fourth?" he guessed.

She nodded.

"I'll bet you didn't score any points by choosing a name for your son that wasn't Jefferson Caldwell the Fifth."

"You'd be right," she agreed. "But what else could they expect from a Yankee?"

"You're not a North Carolina native?"

"I was born there, but my parents weren't. They moved from New Jersey shortly after they were married."

"Do your parents still live in the area?"

She shook her head. "I was an only child born long after they'd given up hope of ever having a baby. My dad was a heavy smoker for almost forty years and died of lung cancer when I was in high school, and my mom suffered a fatal heart attack a few years after that, before Dylan was born. Which means that my former in-laws are the only grandparents he has. Unfortunately, they weren't ever able to forgive me for getting pregnant—or Dylan for being the product of that unplanned pregnancy."

He frowned at that. "You're kidding."

She shook her head. "Jeff dated Jodie all through high school. They lived in the same neighborhood growing up. Their mothers were best friends. Everyone expected they would be together forever. Jeff went to UNC Wilmington for occupational therapy; Jodie went to Asheville to study music. Halfway through their first year, they broke up.

"I met Jeff when I was in my third year of economics at the Cameron School of Business, and a few months later, I got pregnant. But now, much to Lillian's delight, Jefferson and Jodie are together again—happily married and the doting parents of Jocelyn, Jillian and Jefferson the Fifth."

"For real?"

"As if I'd make something like that up."

"How does your son feel about his dad's other family?"

"It is what it is," she said. "When Jeff first got remarried, he was great about spending as much time as he could with Dylan. When Jeff and Jodie bought their house, Dylan got to help decorate his room and he loved going there for sleepovers. Then Jodie had a baby and all of their attention shifted. But Dylan doted on his little sister and—fifteen months later—his second little sister, too.

"Then Jefferson the Fifth was born. Instead of making the girls share a room, they put the crib in Dylan's room, since—as Jeff explained—he's not there all the time anyway. Which wouldn't have been a big deal except that his race car posters were taken down and a mural of a big orange giraffe with a balloon bouquet was painted on the wall."

"Race car posters?"

"Dylan's a huge racing fan," she told him. "Even when he was in kindergarten, the age when most kids wake up early Saturday morning to watch cartoons, he was watching race highlights on the sports channel."

He smiled at that. "Has he ever been to a race?"

"His dad's taken him to a couple of amateur races at the dirt track outside of Charisma."

"Stock car racing isn't your thing?"

"I don't mind watching it on occasion, but I don't understand all the lingo, and Dylan usually ends up rolling his eyes when he tries to talk to me about bump drafting or restrictive plates."

"Restrictor plates," Nate corrected.

She shook her head. "I still have no idea what they are."

"Metal plates with holes in them, installed at the intake of an engine to limit its power."

"But why would you want to limit its power?"

"To slow it down."

"Which doesn't make any sense to me," she confided.

"Isn't the whole point of a race to go fast? Isn't that how you win?"

"Sure," he agreed. "But on super speedways, the use of restrictor plates is designed to reduce the number of high-speed crashes."

"I guess I'll have to take your word for it."

"So if stock car racing isn't your thing—what is?"

"I don't know that I really have a thing," she hedged.

"Everyone has something," he insisted. "Like skydiving or stamp collecting, foreign films or French cuisine."

Her brows lifted. "Are those your hobbies?"

He laughed. "I like football and baseball. I prefer movies with action and explosions and thick steaks cooked on the grill. I also like camping under the stars, classic rock played loud and big, slobbery dogs."

"That's an impressive list."

"Now it's your turn," he told her.

She considered for a minute. "I can't stand football but I don't mind baseball, I like walking barefoot in the sand, the scent of freshly cut grass, movies that make me laugh, books that make me cry, dinner by candlelight, dark chocolate, red wine, spring flowers, small dogs, big hugs and the sound of a baby's laugh."

He nodded approvingly. "That recital of facts told me something else about you."

"What's that?"

"You're competitive."

"How do you figure?"

"You had to make sure your list was longer than mine."

"It's not the size of the list that matters—it's the self-awareness." Though her tone was solemn, the sparkle in her eye told him that she was teasing.

And while he wasn't sure about the "self" part, he was definitely aware of her.

He understood why she didn't want to get involved with

him. He'd thought her reservations centered on an unwilling-
ness to complicate their working relationship, but he knew
now that her reasons went deeper than that. And while he
couldn't deny the validity of those reasons, he still wasn't
ready to back off.

Yeah, the kid was a complication. But the kid was in
North Carolina, while he and Allison were stranded together
in St. Louis. And it had been a long time since he'd been so
completely and thoroughly captivated by a woman.

He'd often found himself attracted to a pretty face and
womanly curves, and although Allison had both, she also
had a sharp mind, a sense of humor and an honest sincerity
that was, in his experience, far too rare.

"So if a man wanted to impress you, he should bring you a
bouquet of tulips and take you out for a candlelight dinner?"

"That would be a good start," she agreed. "Except that
I don't date."

He signed the check that Stefano delivered. "Ever?"

"Rarely. And I'm definitely not going to date my boss."

"I'm not your boss yet," he pointed out to her.

"But you're the VP of Finance of the company that signs
my paychecks."

"Chelsea warned me that would be an issue for you." He
pushed his chair away from the table and stood.

"Chelsea needs to mind her own business."

"She likes me," he said mildly, offering his hand to her.
"In fact, most people do."

After a moment's hesitation, she put her hand in his and
rose to her feet. "Yeah, I've heard that."

"Have you ever considered the possibility that my reputation might be the tiniest bit exaggerated?"

"No," she admitted. "Because your reputation isn't really
any of my concern."

He guided her into the elevator. "It is if it's a factor in
your refusal to go out with me."

"Only one of many."

He rubbed his thumb over the back of her hand, tracing the ridges and valleys of her knuckles in a slow, sensual caress. "Such as the fact that you're not attracted to me?"

She tugged her hand away. "Attraction is nothing more than a trick played by our hormones."

"You can't really believe that."

"Actually, I do," she told him. "And if a relationship is built on nothing but physical attraction, there's nothing left when that attraction fizzles."

"You're letting your experience with your ex-husband color your judgment."

"Perhaps," she acknowledged.

"There's something between us, Allison. Maybe it's attraction, maybe it's more, but I think we need to figure it out."

She watched the lights above the doors indicate their ascension toward the fifth floor. "The only thing we need to do is to work together."

"And we will." He stepped closer to her. "But right now, I want to kiss you."

Her fingers tightened around the key card in her hand, so much that the edges of the plastic dug into her palm. She wanted to shove him away, to distance herself from the temptation that was Nate. But even more than she wanted him gone, she wanted him to kiss her. She knew that she shouldn't, that even one kiss could be dangerous. But she was lonely and he was so damn sexy and just being in close proximity to him made her blood hum.

"There's no mistletoe this time," he told her. "No reason or explanation aside from the fact that I haven't been able to think about anything else since I kissed you at the party."

His tone was as seductive as the words, weaving a spell around her, drawing her in.

"But if you don't want me to, just say the words and I'll walk away."

She wanted to say them—she *needed* to say them. But when she opened her mouth, the words refused to come. Because the truth was, she *did* want him to kiss her. She wanted to feel the way she'd felt the night of the Christmas party, when he'd taken her in his arms and held her as if he'd never let her go. When he'd kissed her as if he could go on kissing her forever.

She laid her palms on his chest, where she could feel the beating of his heart—strong and steady—and moistened her lips with her tongue. "I don't want you to walk away," she admitted. "I want you to kiss me, but I'm afraid it won't end there."

"I'm not going to push for more than you're ready to give."

The steady gaze and sincere tone convinced her that he meant what he'd said, but his promise did nothing to reassure her. Because she knew that it wouldn't take much persuasion for her to give him anything, everything.

And then he tipped her chin up and lowered his head. His lips brushed against hers softly, gently. It was a tantalizing caress more than a kiss, an invitation rather than a demand. She responded. Her hands slid over his shoulders to link behind his neck as his lips continued to move over hers, tempting, teasing.

The need started low in her belly, then spread through her veins. His hands moved over her, hotly, hungrily, and everywhere he touched, she burned. She could feel the press of his arousal against her, and thrilled in the knowledge that he wanted her as much as she wanted him. And she did want him—she couldn't deny that simple truth any longer.

He lifted his mouth from hers when the elevator dinged to announce its arrival on the fifth floor. "I'm sorry," he said.

She touched a hand to lips that were still trembling.

"Not for kissing you," he quickly clarified. "For pushing when I said I wouldn't."

"You didn't push," she assured him. "But I did promise myself that I wouldn't invite you into my room."

"Then I should let you get to bed," he said, holding the elevator doors open.

"Wait." She laid a hand on his arm, felt the tension practically vibrating in his muscle. She hadn't realized how much effort it took for him to hold his desire in check, and how much she wanted to unleash it.

She drew in a deep breath and looked up at him. The heat in his gaze burned straight to her core, but she held it without flinching and stepped forward, breaching the distance he'd deliberately put between them.

"Allison," he said, and her name on his lips was as much a warning as a plea.

Her hand slid down his forearm, her fingers skimming over the sleeve of his jacket to link with his.

"I promised that I wouldn't invite you into my room," she said again. "But I didn't promise that I wouldn't go back to yours."

Chapter Six

The elevator seemed to take forever to reach the ninth floor.

Realistically, Nate knew it couldn't have been more than a minute or two, but it felt like forever. He held his breath as the seconds ticked away, certain that each second that passed would be the second that Allison announced she'd changed her mind. He really didn't want her to change her mind.

She squeezed his hand, whether seeking or offering reassurance, he didn't know. But when he glanced into the warmth of those chocolate-colored eyes, he couldn't deny that he wanted her as he hadn't wanted any woman in a very long time.

"You're not having second thoughts, are you?"

"No," she assured him. "But I do think we should establish some ground rules."

She was wearing a silky purple top beneath a belted black blazer and slim-fitting black pants. The material was dark but sheer enough that he could see the lace edging of a camisole. He couldn't wait to strip away her clothes to admire what she wore beneath. He was hoping for a thong to go with the lacy camisole. For all he knew, she might wear white cotton granny panties, but it was his fantasy, so he was going with the thong.

"Nate?" she prompted, as they exited onto his floor.

"Ground rules," he echoed.

She nodded. "If we're going to do this, we should be clear on a few things first."

"What kind of things?"

"That this can be nothing more than a moment stolen from our normal lives. Not only will it not happen again, we won't even mention it when we go back to Charisma."

He slid his key card into the slot; the light blinked green. "You want a one-night stand?"

"It's the only way this will work."

"Why do you say that?" he asked, more curious than offended.

"Because my life in Charisma is complicated enough without adding a relationship—however casual or temporary—to the mix. And aside from that, at the end of the month, you're going to be promoted and there is no way I'm going to be the clichéd secretary screwing around with her boss."

"You can be the sexy executive assistant screwing around with her boss," Nate said, unfastening her jacket and slipping it off of her shoulders.

"No." She tugged at the knot of his tie. "Not going to happen."

His hands found their way under the silky top, his palms gliding up her sides. "So you want to ensure that I don't have any expectations?"

"I just want to be sure that we're in agreement." Her fingers worked the buttons of his shirt.

"I do have one question."

"What's that?"

"If we're only going to have one night, can you stop talking so that we can get to it?"

She laughed softly. "Okay, Mr. Garrett, show me what you've got."

Then she reached between them and stroked the hard length of him. The touch of her hand, even through the fabric, made him suck in a breath.

He lowered his head to capture her mouth. "Nate," he

admonished, nibbling on her bottom lip. "I want to hear you say it."

"Nate." She stroked him again. "I want you, Nate."

"Well, that's convenient—because I want you, too." He unhooked her pants and pushed them over her hips to pool at her feet. Allison stepped out of them and kicked them away.

She wasn't wearing a thong, after all, but a skimpy lace bikini. He wasn't disappointed—and that was even before he saw the thigh-high stockings. He whisked the purple top over her head, dropped it on top of the pile of discarded clothing on the floor, then took a step back. She was still wearing the camisole and panties, stockings and heels, and just looking at her made his mouth water.

"You are...so...beautiful."

She shook her head. "I have stretch marks and small—"

He touched a finger to her lips, silencing her words. "Beautiful," he said again. "Perfect."

Her cheeks colored, as if she was unaccustomed to hearing such words. He wondered what was wrong with the men she'd dated that they obviously hadn't appreciated who she was—and what was wrong with him, that he'd overlooked her for so long.

He was determined to make up for that oversight now.

He lowered his head and touched his lips to the racing pulse point beneath her ear. Then his lips skimmed down her throat, across her collarbone, over the gentle curve of her breast. The tips of her nipples pushed against the lacy fabric, as if begging for his attention. He was more than happy to give it. He traced circles around one rigid peak with his thumb, the other with his tongue, and felt her shudder.

He had a feeling it wasn't going to take much to push either of them to the brink, but he didn't want it to be over fast. He wanted their lovemaking to last all night, and he wanted to savor every minute. If they could have only this one night, he was determined to make sure it was a night she'd never forget.

So while he wanted nothing more than to lay her back down on the bed and bury himself in the wet heat between her thighs—

He sat up abruptly and swore.

Allison propped herself onto her elbows. "What's wrong?"

"I'm not in the habit of carrying condoms in my wallet anymore," he admitted. "And I didn't anticipate that this would happen."

She let out a long, unsteady breath. "I didn't plan for this to happen, either."

"There's a pharmacy downstairs," he remembered. "Just give me five minutes—"

"Wait." She slid out of bed, taking the sheet with her, and rummaged in her purse. "I didn't plan for this," she said again, "but I decided a long time ago that one unplanned pregnancy was enough."

He took the condom she handed to him. "Just one?"

"I have a couple more, but I didn't think you'd need more than one at a time."

"No," he confirmed. "I just wanted to know if I'd have to make a trip to the pharmacy."

Her brows lifted. "Maybe tales of your stamina haven't been exaggerated."

He pulled her into his arms and tossed the sheet aside. "You can let me know later."

She had a moment to wonder: What was she doing? Why was she letting herself believe that sleeping with her soon-to-be boss could be anything but an unmitigated disaster?

Then he kissed her, and all the doubts and recriminations faded away. She couldn't think about anything but how much she wanted this—how much she wanted *him*.

Especially when he eased his lips from hers to ask, "Okay?"

The fact that he did ask, that he was giving her the opportunity to make a different choice even at this late stage of the game, reassured her that this was the right choice. The only choice. Even if they couldn't have more than this one night.

"Okay," she confirmed.

His lips curved, and her insides twisted into knots that were equal parts anticipation and apprehension. It had been a really long time since she'd been naked with a man, and her almost-thirty-year-old body wasn't as sleek and firm as it had been ten years ago. Then he kissed her, and she stopped wondering why he would want her and let herself enjoy the fact that he did.

He lifted his mouth from hers to strip her camisole over her head, push her panties over her hips and roll her stockings down her legs. Then he got rid of his own clothes, kicking off his shoes and socks, tossing his shirt and pants on the floor with hers. But he kept his briefs on, though they barely contained the impressive bulge of his erection.

She reached a hand out, wanting to touch, but he caught her wrist, circling it with his fingers.

"You convinced me that pleasure should be shared," she reminded him.

"And it will be," he promised, easing her back onto the bed. "Soon."

But first he kissed her again, long and slow and deep. And while his mouth patiently and thoroughly explored hers, his hands did the same to her body, following the curves and contours with gentle, leisurely strokes that made her quiver and sigh.

Then his mouth moved over her jaw, down her throat, across her collarbone. He found her nipple with his tongue, flicked it playfully, then blew gently on the moist peak. She gasped and arched beneath him, silently begging for more.

His hands took over, continuing to tease and caress the aching peaks as his mouth moved lower, his tongue trailing a path down her belly as he nudged her thighs farther apart with his knees.

Her breath caught and her fingers fisted in the sheet as his fingers found the soft curls at her center. Everything inside her was tense, quivering. She wanted him to touch her, but she was already so close to the edge, she knew that if he did, she would fly apart.

"Nate—please. I want you inside me."

"Soon," he said again, then groaned as he slid a finger between the slick folds of skin and into her.

She bit down on her lip to keep from crying out as he withdrew, then sank in again, deeper. When his thumb brushed over her tight, throbbing nub, she could hold back no more. She cried out in shock and pleasure as her body erupted. And still he continued to stroke her, causing wave after wave of sensation to wash over her, the first crashing into the next, relentless and unending.

"Now, Nate. Please."

But instead of giving her what she thought she wanted, he gave her more. His head dipped between her thighs and his mouth settled over her. He nibbled and sucked the tender flesh, his tongue sweeping in and out, quick licks alternating with leisurely strokes that drove her up—high and ever higher.

She wanted to protest, to tell him that he'd already given her so much—too much. But she couldn't find the words. She couldn't even catch her breath. She simply had nothing left, and she knew there was no way—

Oooh.

Her head fell back against the pillows as a kaleidoscope of light and color erupted behind her closed eyelids. Apparently there was a way, and he had found it, and he groaned in appreciation as he tasted her pleasure.

And…*oooh…yesss.*

He gripped her hips in his hands, holding her immobile as he continued his sensual onslaught, as wave after wave of pleasure washed over her and…finally…ebbed.

Then, and only then, did he ease away from her, kissing his way up her body, and finally reach for the condom he'd put on the bedside table. He discarded his briefs, tore open the wrapper and quickly sheathed himself.

Though her heart was still pounding and her skin still tingling, she was aware of the harshness of his breathing, of his eagerness to join his body with hers. She wrapped her arms around him, taking him into her embrace, welcoming him into her body, hoping to give him even a fraction of the pleasure he'd already given her. When he drove into her, the size and strength of him stretched her, filled her, fulfilled her. And—though she would have sworn it was impossible—she came again.

He caught her hands in his, linked them above her head, as he moved inside her. Long, deep strokes that seemed to touch her very center.

"You feel…so…good."

She heard his voice as if from a distance. She blinked, tried to focus, but the world was spinning. She lifted her legs, hooked her ankles together, anchoring herself to him, against the storm of sensations that battered at her from every direction.

His hands slid up her torso, cupped her breasts, his thumbs stroking the peaks of her nipples as he drove into her. She arched up, meeting him thrust for thrust, taking him deeper inside.

She felt connected to him in a way she hadn't experienced in a very long time—if ever before. Their bodies moved and merged together, their breaths—quick and shallow—

mingled and their hearts pounded in synchronized rhythm as they raced not against but beside each other, and finally reached...ecstasy.

When Nate returned to the bed after disposing of the condom, Allison was snuggled beneath the sheets, a soft, satisfied smile on her lips. She truly was beautiful, and already, he wanted her again. He wanted to explore every inch of her soft, silky skin with his hands and his lips. He wanted to touch and taste, and drive her as crazy as she drove him with her soft sighs and breathless gasps.

He'd thought of no one but her since that stolen kiss before Christmas, wanted no one but her. He'd been certain that *having* would do away with the *wanting* and was surprised again to find it wasn't so. If anything, the first taste had only whetted his appetite.

He pulled back the sheet and lowered himself onto the mattress beside her. Her eyelids flickered, opened, and she offered him a shy smile. "I should probably head back to my own room."

"Why?"

"So that you can sleep."

"I don't want to sleep." He stroked a hand down her side, following the feminine dips and curves, and she sighed contentedly. "I don't think I'll ever be able to look at you seated behind your desk and not remember the way you look right now."

The pleasure in her eyes dimmed, just a little. "This is nothing more than a stolen moment," she reminded him. "Not to be spoken of again after tonight."

"One night," he confirmed, and kissed her softly, gently. "But the night isn't over yet."

Much to Allison's relief, the storm had cleared up by morning and the airport was reopened, planes landing and taking off again as scheduled. Allison wanted to call Dylan, to let him know that she would be home today, but there didn't seem to be any point when she wouldn't see him until the end of the weekend anyway. But she did call the airline, because it had always been part of her job to take care of the travel arrangements and because doing so now was a timely reminder that Nate was the acting CFO of Garrett Furniture and she was his executive assistant. Their brief time as lovers was finished, even if she knew it would never be forgotten.

As she took her seat on the plane, she didn't—couldn't—regret those stolen hours of bliss, which had been so much more than she'd imagined. She hadn't intended to stay through the night, but she'd fallen asleep in his arms and awakened the same way. Though she'd been reluctant to slip from the comfort of his embrace, she'd known it was necessary. But he'd caught her at the edge of the mattress, pulled her back to the center of the bed and shown her the heights and depths of pleasure again.

It had been a long time since she'd been with a man—but she wasn't inexperienced. She'd had several lovers before she'd hooked up with Jeff, but she'd never had a lover like Nathan Garrett.

She didn't think there was anything he didn't do well, and now she could add lovemaking to the list. Of course, she shouldn't be surprised—if even half the rumors that circulated through the break room were to be believed, he'd certainly had enough practice. And somehow he'd turned a physical act into a lovely and breathtaking art.

And now, after only one night, she was turning into a romantic fool. Thankfully, they'd both agreed to the one-night deal. It wouldn't do for her to be caught daydreaming about the boss when she was behind her desk at Garrett Furniture. She needed to get back home, to get her feet back on solid ground, to remember all the reasons that they weren't right for each other—even for the short term.

The plane touched down smoothly, but she felt the jolt of the landing inside her. It was over now. They were back in North Carolina, back to reality. She slung her messenger bag over her shoulder, he picked up his briefcase and they walked out of the airport together.

The air was cold enough that she could see her breath in the air, but the sky was clear, the ground barely dusted with snow. Further proof that they were miles away from St. Louis and the intimacy they'd shared.

But Nate stood close enough that she could feel the heat from his body, and her own stirred with memory, with longing. She took a deliberate step away from him as she dug into her purse for her keys.

"I'm going to send John a text, to let him know that I'm stopping at home for a quick shower and change of clothes before I head into the office."

"I'm going to do the same," he told her.

"Don't forget you have a three o'clock meeting with your uncle and the incoming VP of Finance."

"I won't forget—you programmed the reminders for all of my meetings for the next two weeks into my phone."

"I did." She remembered now, and felt foolish that she'd forgotten. But so much had happened in the past twenty-four hours, so much had changed—not just between them but within her—that she was having trouble finding her footing and clearing her head.

"So…I'll see you at three," he said.

"I'll see you at three," she confirmed.

His smoky eyes held hers for a long minute and he looked as if he wanted to say something more, but in the end, he only nodded and turned away.

It was both unrealistic and naive to think that having sex with a woman wouldn't change things between them.

Nate was neither unrealistic nor naive, and while he knew

that Allison's concerns about their working relationship were valid, he was confident that they could both move forward with their professional relationship.

Some women tended to romanticize sex—wanting to turn the physical act into a meaningful relationship. Thankfully, he didn't have to worry about that with Allison, because she was the one who'd insisted that their one night together wouldn't ever be anything more.

The problem was that when he went to the CFO's office for his meeting and saw her sitting behind her desk, he realized that the one night they'd spent together had done nothing to conquer his desire for her. If anything, he only wanted her more.

As John went over the most recent numbers from their Gallery stores, Nate found his attention continually shifting to the woman outside. She was wearing a different pantsuit now—this one was charcoal gray with a subtle pinstripe. Beneath the jacket she wore something lacy and pink that immediately brought to mind the camisole he'd stripped from her body the night before.

"Any questions?"

Nate forced his attention back to his uncle. "Um, no. I think that covers everything."

"Keep an eye on New York," John suggested. "It might be that we'll want to expand there in the very near future."

He nodded and made a note on the page.

"Of course, Allison will undoubtedly send you a reminder to check in with Seth Overton—the manager there—after the fourth-quarter numbers are in."

He nodded again as his uncle's phone buzzed.

John picked up the receiver. "I know," he said without preamble. "I'm on my way now."

He chuckled as he listened to the response on the other end before hanging up.

"I've got a doctor's appointment," he told Nate. "Allison wanted to make sure I wouldn't be late."

"She keeps track of your personal appointments, too?"

"She keeps track of my life," John said, pushing his chair back from his desk. "Last year, when we were in the midst of that audit in San Francisco, I almost forgot my anniversary. Allison made the arrangements to fly Ellen out to California, had flowers waiting in our hotel room when she arrived, a spa appointment booked and dinner reservations made so that all I had to do was show up at the restaurant."

He took his coat off a hook behind his door. "I honestly don't know what I would have done without her for the past six years. She's not just an asset to this office but an incredible person."

He slid his arms into the sleeves. "Although I'm sure you figured that out for yourself last night."

"What?"

"Last night—when you were stuck in St. Louis," John prompted. "I hope you spent some time getting to know her."

Probably more intimately than his uncle could imagine— definitely more than he would approve.

"We had dinner at the hotel," he said, because that was both a true and safe response. "I found out that she has a kid."

His uncle nodded. "Dylan—a great kid. Although incredibly shy."

"You know him?"

"Sure. Allison usually brings him to the summer picnic. And she would sometimes pick him up from school and bring him back to the office if she was working late on something."

The summer picnic was very much a family thing, which was why Nate had preferred to avoid it if at all possible. And it was usually possible.

The phone on John's desk buzzed again.

He opened the office door. "You nag worse than my wife," he told his executive assistant.

"She was nagging on behalf of your wife," Ellen said to her husband, who looked duly chagrined.

"You didn't have to come over here to go with me," he protested. "It's just a checkup."

"It's the only way I can be sure you don't edit the doctor's instructions when you pass them on to me," his wife said.

John's heavy sigh was confirmation that he did just that. "Have a good weekend, Allison. And you, too, Nate."

Allison smiled as she watched them make their way to the elevator, bickering affectionately all the way.

"They're good together," she noted. "Even after forty-four years, you can tell they still love each other."

"The true test is going to come when Uncle John is at home full-time."

"You're probably right."

"Why are you still here?" he asked. "I thought you usually finished early on Fridays."

"Usually," she agreed. "But Jeff has Dylan for the weekend, so there was no reason for me to rush off."

"You're on your own tonight?" He couldn't help but feel hopeful that her solitary status might allow a repeat of the previous night's activities, despite her explicit statement to the contrary.

"Just me and all the chores that get overlooked day to day."

"That sounds…" He wasn't sure how to finish the thought. Chores definitely didn't sound as interesting as what he'd been thinking, but he couldn't share those thoughts with her now.

She smiled. "Incredibly mundane and boring?"

"Actually, yes," he admitted. While he wasn't a stranger to washing dishes or doing laundry, neither was on his list of plans for a Friday night.

"My life, for the most part, is incredibly mundane and boring."

"Including last night?"

She dropped her gaze as color filled her cheeks. "Last night was definitely…out of the ordinary."

"Extraordinary," he agreed, and the color in her cheeks deepened.

"Did your uncle mention a possible expansion of the Gallery in New York?" she asked, in a deliberate attempt to shift the topic of conversation back to more neutral ground.

He'd obviously flustered her, and he was gratified to know that she wasn't as unaffected by the intimacy they'd shared the night before as she wanted him to believe. Satisfied with that, at least for now, he responded to her question. "He said we should look at it after the final numbers are in for the fourth quarter."

She nodded. "I'll make a note to do that."

But as she shut down her computer, he suspected that she had already done so. She was, as his uncle had said, an asset to the office. He had yet to figure out what other role she might play in his life, but he knew that they weren't finished yet.

Not even close.

Chapter Seven

Most of the time, her life was incredibly mundane and boring, and Allison was okay with that. She liked predictability and routines and quiet nights at home. Okay—she liked steamy-hot sex with a certain corporate executive, too, but the night she'd spent with Nate had been pure fantasy, and it was time for her to focus on reality again. And her reality right now, after having finished the first load of laundry and vacuuming through the apartment, was figuring out a dinner plan.

She'd intended to meet Chelsea at Marg & Rita's, the local Mexican restaurant, but her friend had texted earlier to say she had to work because Ty was off with the flu. Allison considered walking over to the bar to grab a bite and share some conversation with her friend, but she wasn't in the mood for the crowd.

Unfortunately, since grocery shopping was still on the part of her to-do list that was not yet done, she didn't have a lot of options for dinner. There was a pizza in the freezer, and though it didn't look very appealing and she didn't know how long it had actually been in there, she set the oven to preheat.

She was scrolling through the Netflix menu when a knock sounded at the door. Since no one could get into the building without being buzzed through the secure door in the lobby, she assumed it was probably Mrs. Hanson from across the hall.

The old woman liked to bake, but she always seemed to

be in need of a stick of butter or a cup of sugar or a package of semisweet chocolate chips. Allison had learned that keeping those staple ingredients on hand meant she and Dylan would reap the benefits of whatever Mrs. Hanson baked.

Anticipating her elderly neighbor, she was surprised to find Nate standing on the other side of her door.

"Nate. Um, hi." She was suddenly conscious of the fact that she was wearing a pair of yoga pants and an old UNCW T-shirt with her hair pulled back in a haphazard ponytail and her feet bare.

He smiled and offered her the bouquet of flowers in his hand. "Hi."

"Oh." She was touched by the unexpected gesture, and just a little wary. "Thanks."

"My sister-in-law, Rachel, is a florist—Buds and Blooms."

"Not that I have any objection to getting flowers," she said. "But why?"

"Because I wanted an excuse to drop by," he admitted.

"How did you get into the building?"

"An older woman who said she lives across the hall from you," he told her.

"Mrs. Hanson?"

He nodded. "That was her name. As I was looking at the tenant directory, she came through the lobby and asked who the flowers were for. When I mentioned your name, she said that spring flowers always made her think of sunny days and that it was about time you had a devastatingly handsome man bring you flowers and put some sunshine into your life."

She lifted a brow. "Devastatingly handsome?"

He grinned. "I might have embellished a little."

"Well, I guess I should invite you to come in while I find a vase for these."

He followed her into the kitchen. She opened the cupboard above the fridge and pulled out a Waterford crystal

vase—a memento of her long ago and ill-fated wedding—
then filled it with water.

"I heard what you said—about last night being only one
night. I didn't come here expecting to take you to bed but
hoping that I could take you out to dinner."

"Why?"

"Maybe I was hoping dinner with me would be a step up
from mundane and boring," he suggested.

"And it would be," she agreed. "Several steps up, in fact.
But it wouldn't be a good idea."

"Valentino's is always a good idea."

"Until someone we know sees us together, then it's a date
and the hot topic of office gossip."

"I'm sure people have better things to talk about than
my personal life."

"Where do you think I heard about your ski trip with
Lanie?"

"I already told you—it wasn't a ski trip with Lanie, we
just happened to be at the same resort."

"And I believe you," she told him. "But rumor is always
more interesting than truth."

"If you won't go to Valentino's with me—will you let me
bring Valentino's to you?"

Sharing a meal with him in the privacy of her apartment
might protect her reputation, but it could also jeopardize her
heart. Because the more time she spent with him, the more
she saw different facets of his personality, and the more she
realized that she actually liked him. And that was dangerous
because he didn't do relationships and—what happened in
St. Louis notwithstanding—she didn't do flings.

But he looked so earnest and she really wasn't in the
mood for frozen pizza. So instead of sending him away, she
replied, "Only if it's lasagna."

* * *

Half an hour later, he was back with lasagna and garlic bread and a bottle of pinot noir.

They chatted easily while they ate. More easily than she would have expected, considering that only twenty-four hours earlier, they'd been naked and horizontal together. But they kept the conversation fairly neutral.

She was surprised to learn that he'd turned down a baseball scholarship to Stanford because he wanted to go to NYU. It was only when she prompted him for more details about his decision that he admitted his grandmother had been ill at the time and he also didn't want to be too far away from his family. Apparently he'd played second base at Hillfield Academy with fifty-two home runs and a .384 batting average over four years—which were also details she had to pry out of him. Though she didn't know much about baseball, she knew the statistics were impressive. But even more impressive to Allison was that he'd wanted to be part of his family's company more than he'd wanted to pursue the possibility of playing professional ball.

Although they didn't touch on anything too personal, she couldn't deny there was a hum of something in the air. Or maybe it was just that her head was buzzing from the wine, because Nate had limited himself to a single glass so he could keep a clear head to drive home. She half wondered if he made the statement in the hope that she would tell him he could stay, if he expected that the pleasure he'd given to her the night before would entice her to want to repeat it. But though she was undeniably tempted, she said nothing.

She was, after all, the one who had established the ground rules. If she changed her mind now, if she pushed aside the barriers that she'd erected, she couldn't expect him to respect them in the future. On the other hand, he was Nate

Garrett, and the idea that his interest would extend so far in time to anything that might be considered "future" was improbable if not impossible.

In fact, his interest had probably already waned because, aside from showing up at her apartment with flowers and inviting her to dinner, he seemed perfectly content to play by her rules. He hadn't touched her or kissed her or given any indication that he was aching for her the way she was aching for him. And she was, admittedly, more than a little disappointed.

But as they cleared away the dishes in the kitchen, she felt something in the air between them. And when she looked at him, she saw the want in his gaze.

"I guess I should be going."

"That's probably a good idea," she agreed.

He picked up his jacket and made his way to the door. "Thanks for dinner."

"Thanks for not making me eat alone on a Friday night."

"I have no doubt that you would have found someone else to have dinner with if I'd sent you away."

"I didn't want to have dinner with anyone else." He lifted a hand and cupped her cheek. "I don't want anyone else."

She swallowed. "We had an agreement," she said, to remind herself as much as him.

"I wasn't of sound mind when I accepted your terms."

"You weren't of sound mind?"

His thumb traced the curve of her bottom lip. "I was crazy with wanting you."

And he was making her crazy now. He'd barely touched her, but her blood was pulsing, her body quivering.

"I'm not going to have an affair with my boss," she said, though without much conviction.

"I'm not your boss yet," he reminded her.

"You tried that argument once before," she reminded him.

"It's still a valid point."

"What happened last night…I don't do things like that. I'm not spontaneous and impulsive and irresponsible—not anymore. I can't be."

He tipped her chin up, forcing her to meet his gaze. "How about beautiful and sexy and passionate? Because you're definitely all of those, no matter how much you try to deny it."

"And you know just what to say to make me forget all of the reasons I decided that what happened last night couldn't happen again."

"So maybe they weren't very good reasons," he suggested.

"Maybe they weren't," she acknowledged, linking her hand with his. "Are you going to stay?"

"I thought you'd never ask."

It wasn't just a fact but a matter of pride that Nate didn't chase after women. He'd never had to. Since he'd hit puberty, women had chased him and, when the attraction was reciprocated, he happily let himself get caught. But never for the long term.

His mother frequently lamented his penchant for frequent and casual relationships, and although Nate didn't like disappointing her, he had no intention of settling just to make her happy. He enjoyed the company of women, both in and out of bed, but he didn't play fast and loose with their emotions. He was always careful to select women who wanted the same thing he did—a good time.

Allison Caldwell was not his usual type. She was beautiful and sexy and smart—which were all qualities he admired in a woman—but she had a kid, and the whole family thing had never been his scene. Sure, he enjoyed hanging out with *his* family—his parents and brothers and aunts and uncles and cousins—even the little ones. But he had no desire to be part of a core family unit.

He'd let himself forget that when he was with Allison. He

couldn't claim that he didn't know about her son, but when they'd been stranded together in St. Louis, her kid had been more than eight hundred miles away. Of course, she'd given him absolutely no reason to believe that she expected—or even wanted—anything more than what they'd shared that night. He was the one who had stopped by her apartment, unannounced and uninvited. He was the one who'd spent the night with her in a bed less than eight feet across the hall from her son's bedroom. Not that he'd been there—but that wasn't the point.

Actually, he wasn't even sure that there was a point, except that showing up at her apartment—with flowers no less—made him worry that he was chasing her. When they were stranded together, it was easy to blame the circumstances of the storm, the temptation of proximity. But as soon as they got back to North Carolina, that should have been the end of it. She'd told him that would be the end of it.

But he'd been unable to let her go. He'd spent both Friday and Saturday nights with her, in her bed; he'd shared the narrow shower in her en suite bathroom; he'd eaten breakfast at the little bistro table in her kitchen; and even when it was time to head to his parents' house for Sunday night dinner, he hadn't wanted to leave her.

He'd actually, for just a minute, considered inviting her to go with him. And that, he suspected, would have been a disaster of monumental proportions. Not just because everyone knew her as his uncle's executive assistant, but because he hadn't invited a woman to his parents' home in probably ten years.

Thankfully, sanity had reigned and he'd kissed her goodbye and went to Sunday night dinner alone. But that moment of consideration had shaken him. After only a few days and nights, he couldn't seem to get her out of his mind. Which was why, when he found himself with nothing to do the following Saturday night, he called his cousin Ryan and arranged to meet him at O'Reilly's Pub.

But even that choice had been colored by his determination to push all thoughts of Allison out of his mind. Ryan had suggested the Bar Down, but Nate knew that if they went there, chances were good that Chelsea would be working, and seeing Chelsea would make him think about Allison and he was determined not to think about Allison tonight—except that he was only halfway through his first beer and doing a lousy job of controlling his thoughts already.

"This must be my lucky day," Jordyn said, sidling up to the other side of the bar. "Two of my favorite cousins in one place."

"She wants something," Ryan said to Nate.

He nodded. "The question is—what?"

"*I* don't want anything," Jordyn assured them. "But I know Lauryn would really appreciate some help putting up the shelves she bought for the baby's room."

"Shouldn't her husband be able to do that?" Ryan asked.

"You'd think so. Unfortunately, Rob doesn't seem to know the difference between a hammer and a drill." Jordyn's disgusted tone left them in no doubt about her feelings toward her sister's husband.

"Which doesn't mean that she'd be willing to accept our help," Nate pointed out.

Because Lauryn hated that everyone knew Rob had taken the money her parents gave them for a down payment on a house and used it instead to prop up his failing business. Especially when, three years later, the business was still on shaky ground.

Nate always thought it was both a blessing and a curse to be part of a large, close-knit family. The blessing was that there was always someone ready to lend a hand when it was needed; the curse was that there was no way to hide the fact that it was needed. Lauryn and Rob had gone through some rough patches in their marriage recently, and when Lauryn had called everyone together at the end of the previous summer, there was speculation within the family that they might call it quits. Instead, she'd announced that she was pregnant.

With a baby on the way, Lauryn had been determined to move out of their apartment and into a house—and she refused to take any more money from her family. They used their limited funds to purchase a fixer-upper that Rob promised to fix up for their new family, but it was still in rough shape and mortgaged to the hilt.

"She keeps insisting that Rob will get around to doing the things she wants done," Jordyn told them, "but I know that if he doesn't do them soon, she will. And I don't think, at seven and a half months pregnant, she should be climbing a ladder."

Ryan frowned. "She wouldn't."

Nate didn't like to think so, but he had to disagree with his cousin. "She would."

Jordyn nodded.

He sighed. "When?"

"Tomorrow would be great."

"I'm not doing anything," Nate confirmed.

"I'm going to be out of town," Ryan said.

"Convenient," Jordyn said.

"No, really, there's a thing I have to go to in Winston-Salem."

"I'll snag Andrew to help," Nate decided. "He's the carpenter."

"Thank you." Jordyn poured another draft, set it in front of him. "Sincerely."

He just nodded.

"What about me?" Ryan lifted his half-empty glass.

She put another under the tap, filled it. "His is on the house—you're paying for yours," she said. "And don't forget to tip your server."

Nate waited until Jordyn had moved down the bar to serve another customer before he turned to his cousin. "A thing in Winston-Salem? What kind of thing?"

"The baptism," Ryan admitted. "My friends Darren and Melissa's little guy."

"That's right," Nate suddenly remembered. "You're going to be the godfather."

His cousin nodded.

"Does it freak you out?"

"Why would it?"

Nate shrugged. "I don't know—the whole idea of being responsible for someone else's kid seems pretty scary to me."

"It's not like I really have to do anything other than sign my name to a piece of paper," Ryan said.

"And smile for pictures."

"Yeah, that might be a challenge."

"Why do you say that?"

"Because Harper Ross is going to be Oliver's godmother."

"The maid of honor?"

Ryan nodded again.

"I thought you liked her."

"No, I said she was hot."

"My mistake." Nate picked up his beer again and settled back to watch the game.

On the thirtieth of January, there was a big party in the office for John Garrett. Allison had taken care of all the details: streamers and balloons, the banner proclaiming Congratulations on Your Retirement, the enormous sheet cake and bowls of punch and urns of coffee.

It was the end of an era for Garrett Furniture, and she was feeling a little nostalgic as she wandered around the now-empty office. She really was going to miss seeing John on a daily basis. On a more positive note, she felt pretty good about working with his nephew. Over the past couple of weeks, she'd sat in on numerous meetings with Nate and had countless conversations with him, and had managed— mostly—to stay focused. It was almost as if those few nights they'd spent together had never happened.

But when she was alone in her bed, she couldn't help but remember those nights that she hadn't been alone. It wasn't just that her body ached for his touch; she found that she actually missed his company. Maybe it was a sign that she was ready to start dating again. Now that Dylan was older and more independent, maybe it was time to find someone to share her life. Except that when she thought about dating, she couldn't help thinking about the awkward getting-to-know-someone moments, and she didn't miss those at all.

As she made her way around the office, looking for empty cups and forgotten plates, she tried not to think about the fact that this would be her last time tidying up John's office, because it was now Nate's office. And she tried not to wonder where her new boss had gone. He'd been there for the party, of course, but he'd slipped out to take a phone call. Less than a minute later, Melanie had followed.

She believed that nothing had happened between them in Vail. Certainly he had no reason to lie to her about the fact. It was equally evident that the other woman was hoping to rectify that situation. Allison didn't blame her—Nate Garrett was, by all accounts, quite a catch. The only problem, as she saw it, was that he had no intention of ever being caught.

She didn't regret the time they'd spent together, but it was hard not to wish there had been more of it. Her choice, she knew, and the right decision. She didn't ever want to be like Melanie, chasing after a guy who clearly didn't want the same things she did.

She was almost finished tidying up in the CFO's office when Nate returned.

"We do have a cleaning service, you know," he said to her.

"I know," she confirmed. "I'm just giving them a hand."

"I'm starting to realize that you do a lot more around here than I ever suspected."

She shrugged. "My job description is pretty vague."

"Does it including putting up nameplates?" He gestured to the engraved brass on the door.

"I put it up," she acknowledged. "But it was your uncle's idea."

"It's a nice touch," he said. He moved a little closer. He didn't touch her, but he was near enough that she could feel the warmth of his breath on her cheek, and her own caught in her throat.

"I've missed you."

"You've seen me almost every day."

"You know what I mean," he chided.

She nodded, because she did. "But we both knew it was going to be like this."

"It's funny," he said. "I've been waiting for my uncle to retire for more than two years. Now that it's finally happened, I can't help wishing he'd stayed on another six months so that we could have had that time to figure out what's between us and where to go from here."

"Six months wouldn't make any difference," she told him. "We'd still end up exactly where we are now."

"How do you know?"

"Because you don't do serious and I don't do casual."

"But we both have to eat," he pointed out.

"Most people do," she agreed.

"I know you would have left two hours ago if your son wasn't with his dad this weekend, so why don't you come back to my place for dinner tonight?"

She shook her head regretfully. "I appreciate the offer, but I can't."

"Okay, we'll skip dinner and go straight to sex."

She managed a laugh. "Tempting, but no."

"C'mon, Alli. Meet me halfway."

"Halfway to what?"

Before he could respond, Melanie peeked around the door. "There you are," she said to Nate. "I've been looking all over for you."

The teasing glint in his eyes faded; his expression grew wary. "Is there a problem?" he asked.

"Of course not—I just wanted you to know that a bunch of us are heading over to Tonic to continue the party."

Nate lifted his brows at the mention of the trendy dance club that was popular with the twenty-something crowd. "My uncle's going to Tonic?"

Melanie giggled. "No—this party is for the new CFO."

"Oh. Well. That's very kind but—"

"Don't say you can't come to your own party," Melanie admonished.

He looked helplessly toward Allison. "Will you come, too?"

"I can't," she said. "But I'm sure you'll have a great time."

Nate looked disappointed by her response, but she refused to feel guilty that she'd abandoned him to the company of an obviously willing woman. Instead, she turned and exited the CFO's office, not wanting to hear the rest of their conversation.

If Nate truly had missed Allison, she had no doubt that Melanie would ensure he didn't continue to miss her for long. And maybe that was for the best.

Chapter Eight

From the moment Nate took over the corner office, he was a consummate professional and perfectly circumspect in his behavior toward Allison. She was the one who couldn't seem to stop thinking about the fact that she'd been naked with him. But she was confident that the memories—and the longing—would fade in time.

He made a three-day trip to Austin in early February. He asked her if she wanted to go with him, but didn't push when she said that she couldn't. She wasn't sure if she was relieved or disappointed, but she knew it was for the best. Her job was much more important than her tumultuous feelings for her boss—a fact of which she was clearly reminded when she got called to the school because Dylan was having an asthma attack.

It turned out not to be serious. In fact, by the time she arrived, he'd treated himself with the rescue inhaler he carried in his backpack, but the episode terrified her—as such episodes always did. Thankfully, her son's attacks were now fewer and further between than they'd been a few years back, but they always made her take stock of what was most important in life—and the answer was always Dylan.

Of course, Chelsea was fond of pointing out that Dylan wouldn't always be a little boy, that someday he would go off to school and a life of his own, leaving Allison alone. She was prepared for that—but she wasn't prepared to ever let her son feel as if he wasn't the most important person in her life, especially since he knew his place in the hierarchy of his father's family and it wasn't at the top.

Sure, there were times that she wondered if she might ever be anything more than a mother—when she thought about how she'd felt in Nate's arms and wished she could reconcile her responsibilities and her desires. But for all she knew, Nate had already lost interest in her. Sometimes when she was working, she'd glance into his office and find him looking back at her, but she was never able to interpret what those looks meant. Or maybe she just unwilling to let herself hope.

Nate might not have realized it was Valentine's Day if not for the enormous bouquet of flowers on Alli's desk. But he couldn't even glance into the outer office without seeing the colorful blooms that spilled out of the tall frosted-glass vase beside her computer monitor. They'd been delivered early that morning—a beautiful and elaborate arrangement of orange and pink gerberas mixed with red carnations and purple alstroemeria (and he admittedly only knew what that was because he'd asked Rachel when he saw it in her wedding bouquet). There was a card peeking out of the top of the arrangement, but he wasn't able to get close enough to see it without making it obvious that he was looking.

He didn't care—he *shouldn't* care. It wasn't any of his business who was sending her flowers. Allison was no longer his uncle's executive assistant, but his own, and she'd made it clear that she wasn't going to get involved with her boss. But he didn't like to think that she was involved with anyone else, either. She hadn't mentioned that she was seeing anyone, but she wouldn't. She didn't talk about her personal life. Ordinarily, he would appreciate that kind of discretion, but now, wanting to know the identity of the man who had sent her Valentine's Day flowers was driving him to distraction.

And what if he did see the name on the card? What if the card was signed "All my love, Gunther"? He didn't know any Gunthers, but it was a pretty fair bet that he wouldn't be able to track the guy down on the basis of his name. And even if he could, what was he going to do about it? Show up at his door and beat him up because he had the right to send a bouquet to Allison and Nate didn't? Besides, he didn't want to send her flowers. Flowers—especially Valentine's Day flowers—implied a relationship they didn't have.

He'd given her flowers once—a simple bouquet of spring flowers because she'd told him that was what she liked. Either the sender of this arrangement didn't really know her taste or was determined to make a statement about their relationship.

Just because they'd spent one weekend together four weeks earlier didn't give him any proprietary claim, and just because he wasn't seeing anyone else didn't mean that she couldn't be. But the possibility did not sit well with him.

He went to her desk to pick up the latest sales reports from San Diego.

"I was going to bring those in to you before your conference call," she told him.

"I didn't realize you were even there," he lied. "I couldn't see you past the flower shop on your desk."

Her cheeks colored as she glanced at the bouquet. "A little over the top, isn't it?"

"It definitely tips the scales on the opposite side of subtle," he acknowledged. Then, in a deliberately casual move, he shifted so that he could read the message buried in the flowers.

Thinking about you—today and always! Love, C.

"Who's C?"

She glanced up. "Sorry?"

He gestured to the card. "Who's C?" he asked again.

"Oh." The color in her cheeks deepened as she shook her head. "A friend."

"Those flowers make a pretty strong statement from a... friend."

"No doubt that was the intention. Everyone who saw the delivery arrive has been whispering and wondering," she told him. "So far speculation has ranged from Cody in service to Chad in HR to Carter in marketing."

"Apparently no one is aware of your refusal to date someone you work with," he mused.

"It could be argued that I don't really work with Cody, since our paths have never crossed during the workday."

"Are you saying that they are from Cody?"

She shook her head. "I was only making the point that I don't work with Cody. In fact, I don't even know him."

"So who are they from?" he pressed.

"Chelsea," she finally admitted.

"Chelsea Lawrence?"

She nodded. "It started several years ago, when she broke up with her boyfriend only a few days before Valentine's Day. She was more upset than the breakup warranted and finally confessed that she just wanted to have one Valentine's Day that she didn't spend alone.

"It can be a difficult day for single women—so I sent flowers to cheer her up. The next year, I did the same, and so did she. Since then, it's become a tradition."

"Even when she was in a relationship, a couple of years ago, she told her boyfriend that she couldn't go out with him on Valentine's Day, because she had plans to hang out with me."

"Is that what you're doing tonight—hanging out with Chelsea?"

"Yep. With pizza and wings from Valentino's and a pitcher of Chelsea's trademark sangria." Her fingers continued to move efficiently over the keyboard as she spoke. "What are your plans?"

He shook his head. "I have none."

She seemed surprised by that. "You don't have a date on Valentine's Day?"

"Not unless you invite me to share your pizza and wings."

"Sorry," she said, not sounding sorry at all. "Girls only."

"What about your son?"

"Dylan's with his dad this weekend," she said, then glanced down as a reminder chimed from her computer. "You've got that conference call in fifteen minutes."

He nodded, grateful for the reminder and the redirection. She'd told him, and more than once, that their interlude together was over. If he thought it had been far too brief, apparently he was the only one. By all appearances, she was content in her role as his executive assistant and didn't want anything more.

He couldn't deny that he still wanted her—but he'd be damned before he'd beg. He took the file back to his office to prep for his conference call.

Since Valentino's was between Chelsea's town house and Allison's apartment, Chelsea picked up the pizza and wings on the way. Allison put the food in the oven to keep it warm while Chelsea made the sangria.

Her friend seemed preoccupied with her thoughts while she worked, making Allison wonder if she was unhappy to be spending yet another Valentine's Day with her best friend rather than a romantic liaison. She put out a tray of veggies and dip that she'd prepared earlier and nibbled on a carrot stick.

"Something unusual happened when I went to pick up your order at Valentino's," Chelsea said, as she poured the wine into two glasses.

"Marco flirted with you," Allison guessed.

"Marco flirts with every female who crosses his path—that's not unusual."

"True," she acknowledged. "So what was the something unusual?"

"The pizza and wings had already been paid for."

Allison paused with a cucumber slice in the dip. "What?"

"That was my reaction, too," her friend admitted. "But Gemma said that someone had come in and specifically asked if there was an order for Allison Caldwell. She was worried that she'd misunderstood what time it was supposed to be ready and told him that the pizza was still in the oven—he said he wasn't there to pick it up, just to pay for it."

"That is strange." She popped the cucumber into her mouth.

"So who knew that you were having pizza and wings from Valentino's tonight?" Chelsea asked.

"I mentioned it at the office," she admitted.

"To anyone in particular?"

"It was just a passing comment—I didn't think he was even paying attention."

"Nate Garrett," her friend guessed.

She nodded and picked up her sangria.

"And the plot thickens."

"There is no plot—nothing to thicken."

"You kissed him at Christmas and he bought you dinner on Valentine's Day," Chelsea noted. "It makes me wonder what might have happened in between that you haven't told me."

She sipped her drink. "Mmm—this is fabulous sangria."

"Come on, Alli. I know when you're holding out on me."

"And I only hold out on you when I know you're going to make a big deal out of something that isn't."

"*What* isn't a big deal?" Chelsea demanded.

"Sex in a St. Louis hotel room."

Her friend choked on a cherry tomato.

Allison thumped her on the back.

Chelsea held up a hand to ward her off as she lifted her glass and swallowed a mouthful of sangria. "For real?"

She nodded, then gestured to the DVDs she'd selected from her collection. "What's it going to be tonight—*The War of the Roses*, *The Break-Up* or *Thelma & Louise*?"

"Forget the movie," Chelsea said. "I want details about St. Louis."

"It wasn't a big deal," she said pointedly. "It was attraction fueled by proximity and a very nice cabernet."

Her friend frowned. "That's it? That's all the detail you're going to give me?"

"And cheesecake." Allison took the pizza and wings out of the oven. "There was this incredible cheesecake with strawberry-Grand Marnier topping."

"A true friend shares details about getting naked with a hot, sexy guy like Nathan Garrett when she knows that her BFF isn't getting any," Chelsea admonished.

"I'm not getting any anymore, either," Allison said.

"It was just that one night?"

She took her time transferring a slice of pizza to her plate, then added five wings. "One weekend," she admitted.

"He slept with you and then he dumped you?"

"There was no dumping to be done—we both agreed at the outset that we weren't going to get involved."

"Why not?"

"Because he's the CFO and I'm his assistant and we both have to focus on doing our jobs. Because Nate Garrett isn't the daddy type and I have an almost-nine-year-old son who is the center of my world."

"He'd love Dylan if he ever had the chance to meet him."

"Not going to happen."

Chelsea sighed, obviously disappointed. "I felt the sizzle between you when you were both at Bar Down. I was sure he was the one for you."

"Even if I were looking for a relationship—which I am *not*—I would not look in Nate Garrett's direction."

"He does have a reputation for being difficult to pin down," her friend agreed. "And yet…"

Allison refused to take the bait, biting into her pizza instead.

"And yet," Chelsea continued, "he went out of his way to buy you dinner on Valentine's Day."

"You can't know that he went out of his way," she argued. "More likely he stopped at Valentino's to pick up something for himself, remembered that I'd mentioned our plans for tonight, and decided that paying for our pizza would be a nice gesture from a boss to his employee."

Chelsea considered that possibility as she nibbled on a chicken wing. "What did he think about the flowers?"

"He said that he hoped Chad and I would be very happy together."

Her friend frowned. "Who's Chad?"

"He works in HR and was widely speculated to be the 'C' who signed the card."

"And Nathan won't go out with you but he's okay with you fraternizing with some guy in HR?"

Allison picked up the pitcher of sangria to refill their glasses. "Actually, I told him that the flowers were from you."

"Why?"

"Because he asked."

"Aha!"

"There's no 'aha.'"

"But there could be," Chelsea insisted.

She shook her head. "I'm not going to jeopardize my employment—and my employee benefits—for a temporary relationship with a guy who isn't capable of anything more."

"How do you know he isn't capable of anything more?"

"The guy is a serial dater."

"I'm not so sure," her friend said. "A true serial dater lives for the chase, and as soon as he gets a woman into his bed, he's ready to move on."

"Exactly," Allison agreed.

"Except that it doesn't sound to me as if he's moved on. In fact, the last time he was in the bar with his brother and Josh Slater, I saw a woman slip him a cocktail napkin with her name and phone number on it—and he crumpled it up and dumped it in the trash."

"Obviously he's a changed man."

Chelsea scowled at the sarcasm. "So what's the office gossip these days?"

"I haven't heard much of anything," she admitted. "But people might be more careful about what they say around me now because they know that he's my boss."

"Or maybe there isn't anything to say." Her friend nibbled on a wing. "You should call him."

"Why?"

"To thank him for dinner."

Allison knew she was right. And if it had been anyone but Nate, she wouldn't have needed her friend to remind her. But initiating contact with her boss, on a weekend, to discuss something that had nothing to do with work, seemed to cross that line she didn't want to cross. "Maybe," she finally said. "But not tonight."

"Why not?"

"Because this is supposed to be our anti-Valentine's Day celebration and men are not invited or discussed, so drink up your sangria and pick a movie."

Chelsea lifted her glass. "Okay, but I have one more thing to say first."

"What's that?" she asked warily.

"I think he could be good for you—and Dylan—if you gave him a chance."

Allison randomly picked a DVD. "*The War of the Roses* then."

Chelsea made a face. "That movie is so depressing. Let's go with *Thelma & Louise*."

"Yeah, because that one has a happy ending," she said drily.

"Maybe it's not happy," her friend acknowledged. "But at least they're together in the end."

"We're going to need another pitcher of sangria, Thelma."

"I'll take care of that, Louise, while you set up the movie."

Nate was scrambling eggs the next morning when his cell phone beeped to announce a text message.

Thanks for dinner.

And reading those three words, his mood lifted.

Usually when a woman says those words to me in the morning, it isn't via text message.

No doubt—apologies if I've interrupted your "morning."

No interruption. I was just making breakfast. As if on cue, the bread popped up out of the toaster.

Breakfast? It's almost lunchtime—she's probably starving by now.

He responded to her message: Okay—we'll call it brunch. But there's no one else here...unless you want to join me?

I don't think so.

He chuckled at the predictable response, could almost

hear the prim tone of her voice as he read the words on the screen. I thought maybe you mentioned dinner as a prelude to another meal.

No, I just mentioned it to say thanks.

He scraped the eggs out of the pan and onto his plate. Before he could reply, she sent another message.

Actually, I wasn't sure if I should text you.

Why not?

Because I only have access to this number because we work together.

So? He poured hot sauce onto his eggs and lifted a forkful to his mouth.

So I wasn't sure if it was inappropriate conduct.

I don't feel as if I'm being stalked...but I haven't completely given up hope.

LOL

He shoveled in another forkful of eggs, because his mother had never reprimanded him about texting with food in his mouth. Do you want my address?

NO!

He chuckled again. Since you're not having brunch with me, how about dinner?

No thanks.

Movie? He bit into a piece of bacon.

No thanks.

A polite brush-off is still a brush-off.

Agreed.

He finished off the eggs, typing awkwardly with one thumb. That sound you can't hear is my ego deflating.

I don't think I can be held responsible for any shrinkage.

Hey!

She didn't respond to that, and he could picture her staring at her phone, her teeth sinking into her bottom lip as she wondered if she'd crossed a line with her response. And though he was admittedly just a bit worried about pushing her beyond her comfort zone, he couldn't resist teasing her a little: Are you…sexting me?

Her response this time was immediate and definite: NO!

Because it sounded like sexual innuendo to me.

It wasn't. Or not intentional, anyway.

Accidental sexual innuendo?

I'm going to do my grocery shopping now.

Is cheesecake on your list? ;)

GOODBYE, Nate.

He let her have the last word, confident that she was at least thinking about him. As he was thinking about her as he finished up his breakfast and put his dishes in the dishwasher.

She was beautiful and sexy and smart and funny. He appreciated that she had her own thoughts and ideas and wasn't afraid to share them. A lot of the women he'd dated seemed to think they needed to echo his opinions or share his interests—which frequently made for boring conversations. He was never bored with Allison.

He hadn't yet figured out how he felt about dating a woman with a child—of course, Allison would be the first to say that they weren't dating. But he wasn't ready to give up on the possibility that they might get there.

When Jeff brought Dylan home the following Wednesday night, Allison decided it was a good opportunity to discuss their son's upcoming birthday.

Jeff, always impatient, glanced at his watch. "I'm well aware that Dylan's birthday is in less than three weeks."

She ignored his defensive tone. "Do you know what you're planning to get for him?"

"What does he want?"

"A Ren D'Alesio jacket and a video game—in that order. I thought I'd give you first choice."

"D'Alesio?" he scowled. "I thought he was a Rayburn fan."

"No—you're the Rayburn fan," she reminded him. "Dylan has always liked D'Alesio, and he's been bugging me about the jacket since he found it online before Christmas."

"Fine—I'll get the jacket."

"You'll have to order it. It's not something you'll be able to pick up the day of his birthday."

"I said I'll get the jacket," he repeated.

And for Dylan's sake, she had to trust that he would.

"Was there anything else?"

She shook her head. "I'll see you next Wednesday."

"That reminds me—I'll probably be a little late bringing him home next week."

"You know I like him to keep to a schedule on school nights."

"I know, but Jillian has a recital in Southern Pines, and the program doesn't finish until eight and then it's an hour-and-a-half drive home again."

"You're going to make Dylan spend his time with you watching a bunch of five-year-olds dance?"

"One of those five-year-olds is his sister."

"Half-sister," she shot back, and immediately felt petty for making the distinction.

"If he doesn't want to come, he doesn't have to come," Jeff told her. "But I'm not missing my daughter's performance."

She noticed that he didn't offer to switch his scheduled visit with his son so that he could attend Jillian's recital but also spend some quality time with Dylan. No, he'd rather sacrifice his time with Dylan than reschedule it, and she couldn't help but feel frustrated on her son's behalf.

"I'll ask Dylan what he wants to do and let you know."

Over the next couple of weeks, Nate proved that he knew how to keep business separate from pleasure. During office hours, he never said or did anything that crossed the lines of their employer-employee relationship. But occasionally, in the evenings, he would send her quick text messages, not usually about anything specific but that would inevitably result in the exchange of a dozen more messages before they signed off.

She didn't think he was seeing anyone—she didn't know

when he would have the time. Since moving into the CFO's office, he'd taken his increased responsibilities seriously and was usually the first to arrive and the last to leave each day. On the last Friday in February, she planned to work late since Dylan was being picked up from school by his father and spending the weekend with him. But shortly after lunch, she started to feel unwell and skipped out early.

By the time she arrived home, she was so cold her teeth were practically chattering. She changed into a pair of yoga pants and a heavy sweater, pulled wool socks onto her feet, and climbed into bed with a cup of herbal tea. She only made it halfway through the drink before fatigue won out and she fell asleep.

She awoke, several hours later, when her cell phone chimed to indicate a text message.

Surprise! Night off, Chelsea texted. Do you want to catch a movie?

Sorry—already in bed, Allison typed back, her cold fingers fumbling over the keypad.

With…?

She couldn't even summon the energy to smile in response to her friend's question. It's actually a threesome: chills, headache, nausea.

You are sick—3 + U is a 4some.

YOU are sick, I'm ill.

Poor you! Can I bring you anything?

Just want to sleep.

Feel better soon! XO

Allison put the phone down on her bedside table, pulled the covers up to her chin and slept.

She was up several times in the night to race to the bathroom, but even when the meager contents of her stomach had been expelled, the nausea didn't subside. Since she hated dry-heaving more than she hated throwing up, she forced herself to sip on a can of ginger ale and nibble on a few saltine crackers.

She slept late and didn't awaken until she heard footsteps in the hall. Vaguely she remembered texting Chelsea and asking if she could pick up some chicken soup for her, because during one of her late-night forays into the kitchen, she'd discovered that there was none in the pantry.

But it wasn't Chelsea who came through the doorway into her bedroom—it was Nate.

Chapter Nine

She sat up, clutching the covers to her chest. "What are you doing here?"

"You texted me."

"I did not."

"You said that you wanted chicken soup." He held up the plastic container in his hand. "Chicken soup."

She closed her eyes on a moan. "I thought I was texting Chelsea."

"I figured." He put the soup on her bedside table, beside the thermometer and empty ginger ale can. "When was the last time you took your temperature?"

She pushed her hair away from her face. "Sometime last night."

"What was it?"

"One-oh-two."

He touched the back of his hand to her forehead. "You still feel warm."

She pulled away from his touch. "And sweaty. I think I should have a shower before I have that soup."

"Can you manage on your own?"

"You're not really offering to help me?"

He chuckled softly. "I could ask Mrs. Hanson to come over and give you a hand."

"Did she let you into the building again?"

"Yeah, I buzzed her because I didn't want to disturb you

if you were sleeping. She said she suspected you might be sick when you came home from work early yesterday."

Allison sighed. "Who needs a security system when there's Mrs. Hanson across the hall?"

"So do you want some help with that shower?"

"I think I can manage."

"Leave the door unlocked," he suggested. "I don't want to have to break it down if you fall over in the tub."

"I'm not going to fall over," she said, but she appreciated his consideration. If he truly was being considerate and didn't think he could use an unlocked door as an opportunity to peek at her while she was in the shower.

An idea that didn't seem completely out of the realm of possibility until she got a look at herself in the mirror and actually let out a shriek. The startled sound was still hanging in the air when Nate pushed through the door.

"What is it? What happened?"

She shook her head, and reached for the counter when the ground tilted beneath her feet. "Nothing."

He took a step closer, obviously concerned. "Then why did you scream?"

She felt ridiculous admitting the truth to him—and ridiculously vain. But she took it as a positive sign that she actually cared about her appearance today. Twenty-four hours earlier, she'd just wanted to curl up in a ball and pull the blankets over her head.

"Alli?" he prompted.

"I looked in the mirror," she finally confessed.

Somehow, he managed a smile. "It's not one of your best days," he acknowledged, "but you really don't look that bad."

"Am I dying?"

"What?"

"It's the only reason I can think of to explain why you're being so nice to me."

"Maybe I'm a nice guy."

"Maybe you are," she allowed.

"Are you still planning to take a shower?"

"I think we'll both feel better if I do."

"Just give a shout if you want me to wash your back."

She shoved him toward the door.

Upon receipt of Alli's text message asking for chicken soup, Nate had immediately realized that she'd sent it to him in error.

He could have called Chelsea and told her about the message. Probably that's what he should have done. He wasn't the nurturing type. Generally if someone he knew was sick, he kept his distance. He certainly didn't volunteer to play nursemaid. Playing doctor, on the other hand, might be something he could get into, but he knew Allison wasn't in any condition for those kinds of games right now.

But for some reason, her message had compelled him to stop by his parents' house and finagle a container of the homemade chicken soup that his mother always had in the freezer. Of course, asking his mother for the soup gave her an opening to ask questions of her own but, to his surprise, she didn't.

She'd done the same thing countless times when he'd been growing up. If he came home after curfew or she smelled beer on his breath, she never asked any questions—she just gave him that steady, patient stare that always led to him spilling his guts. Which was how he found himself telling her that he was taking the soup to Alli. If she was surprised that he'd make such an overture to a woman who was supposedly nothing more than his executive assistant, she didn't show it. All she said was that she hoped Alli was feeling better soon.

He poured the soup into a pot, then set it on the stove on low, to keep it warm until Allison was ready to eat it. He figured that was his good deed done and should score him some points for when she was feeling better. For now, he'd just wait until she was out of the shower and had eaten some soup, then he could tuck her back into her bed and be on his way. But he knew from experience being sick that it always felt better to stretch out on clean sheets.

No—he wasn't going to do it. Changing the sheets on her bed was too much of a domestic chore. He wasn't her boyfriend. They weren't even sleeping together anymore. Yeah, he hoped that might change, but if not, that was okay. There were plenty of other women around—even if he hadn't wanted any other women since he'd first kissed Allison. Because the realization made him uneasy, he shoved it aside.

Then he heard her coughing. Even though the closed bathroom door and over the sound of the running water, the harsh hacking sound made him cringe in sympathy. Sighing with resignation, he opened the door to what he guessed was the linen closet.

The shower shut off as he was plumping the pillows on her freshly made bed. He heard her moving around in the bathroom and tried not to think about her toweling off her wet and naked body, her silky skin glistening with moisture. When the hair dryer started up, he headed back to the kitchen to check on her soup.

She tracked him down a few minutes later. She'd dressed in a long-sleeved thermal-style shirt and a pair of plaid flannel pajama pants. Her hair, now dry, was tied back in a loose ponytail; her face was bare of makeup and pale except for the dark shadows beneath her eyes. She wouldn't win any beauty contests today, so why did he feel a tug in the vicinity of his heart? What was it about this woman that appealed to him on a level he'd never before experienced? And why did his fascination intrigue him as much as it terrified him?

Allison was wary about the soup.

It looked and smelled delicious, but the experience of the

past twenty-four hours warned her that whatever she put in her stomach might come back up again.

She sipped carefully from the spoon. The first tentative taste went down easily, so she followed it with a second. Before she knew it, the small bowl was empty.

"Feeling better now?" Nate asked.

She nodded.

"You look better."

She managed a wry smile. "I don't think it was possible to look any worse."

"The shower helped," he agreed. "But you've also got a little bit of color back in your cheeks since you ate."

"The soup was delicious."

"My mom's secret recipe."

"I'll do my best to keep it down," she promised.

And while it had felt good to sit at the table to eat, that effort had zapped the last of her energy. She pushed back her chair to carry her bowl and spoon to the sink, but he took them from her and set them down again.

"I'll take care of that when you're in bed," he told her.

Too tired to protest, she let him guide her back to the bedroom. He pulled back the covers and she lowered herself onto the mattress covered in a crisp pale blue sheet.

"You changed the sheets," she realized.

"I thought you'd sleep better in a fresh bed."

He'd brought her soup; he'd changed her sheets. He'd done more to take care of her in the space of two hours than her ex-husband had done in more than two years of marriage. The realization that this man—her boss and former lover—could show such compassion and consideration brought tears to her eyes.

When the first one slid down her cheek, Nate took an instinctive step back. "I can change them back," he offered.

She managed to choke out a laugh as she shook her head.

"I don't want them changed back. I just don't understand… why are you doing this?"

"Has no one ever taken care of you?"

"Not in a very long time," she admitted.

He pulled the covers up to her chin, as she still did for Dylan every night that he slept at home.

"Thank you," she said. "For everything."

"My pleasure."

She might have smiled at that, but she was too busy fighting against a yawn.

"Sleep now," he said, and touched his lips to her forehead. "I'll be here if you need anything."

"You don't have to stay."

"Maybe I want to."

"It's a Saturday night."

"Yes, it is," he confirmed.

"You must have something better to do on a Saturday night."

"Actually, I don't."

Her eyelids felt heavy, and she didn't have the strength to hold them open anymore. "I'm not going to have sex with you."

"Not tonight," he agreed.

But she didn't hear his response—she was already asleep.

Something changed between them that weekend.

Even more than after the weekend they'd spent together in her bed, their relationship shifted. There was another element now—a closeness and trust that hadn't been there before.

Allison stayed home from work on Monday, but Nathan texted her periodically throughout the day to make sure she was eating/drinking/resting. She went back to the office on Tuesday, and Nate left for Miami a few hours later.

She was thinking about him as she opened the mail that

afternoon. It was methodical work—slitting through the tops of the envelopes, sorting the contents into piles, tossing the junk into the trash. She didn't pay any attention to how they were addressed—not until she came across an envelope for John Garrett that was marked "Personal and Confidential."

A few similar envelopes had come across her desk before, but she hadn't seen one in more than a year, at least. Possibly two.

"Personal and Confidential" meant none of her business, and she set it aside to deliver to John at the earliest opportunity.

But she couldn't help wondering who was sending the letters. The handwriting on the envelope was undeniably feminine. She'd worked for the man for six years. She'd spent a lot of time with him and his family—his wife and their three sons—and she'd always noted how completely and utterly devoted he was to Ellen. It wasn't possible that he'd cheated on her. Allison didn't—couldn't—believe it.

She jolted when the phone rang, and her heart started to pound when she saw that it was her direct line. Probably Nate—which was just one more dilemma to add to her day. Should she tell him about the letter?

Her instinctive response was "no." It wasn't her place to tell him anything—especially when she didn't know for sure that there was anything to tell. But she'd never been very good at keeping secrets, so she tried to convince herself that she was reading too much into the feminine handwriting on an envelope addressed to his uncle.

She stuffed the letter into her purse to deliver to John at the earliest opportunity. Then she reached for the phone, but the call had already gone to voice mail.

Dylan's actual birthday was on Friday, but since it wasn't his weekend with his dad, Jeff promised that they would celebrate on the Wednesday before.

But at 2:33 p.m. on that day, Allison got a text message from her ex-husband saying that he was tied up at work and asking if she could get their son.

Dylan was surprised and—she could tell—a little disappointed by the change of plans, but he dutifully did his homework while he waited for his dad to show up. He was on his last page when Jeff finally buzzed up from the lobby.

"He's just finishing up his math, but he's ready to go," Allison told her ex-husband when he showed up at the door.

"Actually, we're not going anywhere."

"What are you talking about?"

He blew out a breath. "I have to cancel our plans for tonight."

She mentally counted to ten—in Spanish, because it required more thought and gave her a few extra seconds to try to control her reaction to his announcement. "You're canceling your plans to celebrate Dylan's birthday?"

"I have to."

"But you promised to take him to Buster Bear's." Not that the popular children's party location had been Dylan's choice, but she knew he'd been looking forward to celebrating with his dad.

"Because Jodie and I were going to take the whole family," Jeff explained, "but the girls both have the flu."

"So why can't you and Dylan go?"

"Because Jodie's pulling her hair out trying to deal with two sick kids and a baby."

"Dylan's going to be nine," she pointed out. "There aren't going to be many more years that he even wants to spend his birthday with either of us."

"I feel awful about this, but I don't have a choice. I did bring his gift, though," he said, and handed her a flat wrapped package.

A package that looked distressingly similar to another

one that she'd wrapped in different paper and hidden in her closet until Friday.

"It's the video game," she realized.

"Yeah, I didn't have a chance to get the jacket."

"And you're telling me now—two days before his birthday?" She kept her voice down so that Dylan wouldn't hear, but the low volume didn't disguise her anger or frustration.

"I don't need this crap from you, Allison. Not today."

The urge to slap him was so strong that her palm actually tingled in anticipation of making contact with his cheek. Instead, she shoved her hand into her pocket. "I think the problem is that I haven't given you nearly enough crap over the past six years. Dammit, Jeff, your son shouldn't be an afterthought."

"Hey, Dad." The subject of their discussion came running into the living room, his jacket already on. "I'm ready to go."

Jeff ruffled his hair. "I'm sorry, buddy, but I'm going to have to cancel tonight."

"Oh." Dylan's face fell.

"But I brought your birthday present."

The boy perked up a little at the sight of the gift. "Can I open it now?"

"Of course," his dad said.

He dutifully opened the card first, read the message, then tore off the bow and ripped open the paper. "Oh, wow. Cool."

"Is that the one you wanted?"

Dylan's head bobbed up and down. "This is the one where you can race all the big-name tracks or make your own. Do you wanna play it with me?"

"I wish I could," Jeff said. "But I can't stay tonight. Another time, though, I promise."

The boy nodded again, but with much less enthusiasm this time.

Jeff gave him a hug. "I'll see you soon, buddy."

"Okay."

As their son retreated back to his room, Allison walked her ex-husband to the door.

"Thanks for being so understanding, Allison."

"Don't thank me," she told him. "Because I *don't* understand—and neither does that little boy in there."

"He didn't seem too disappointed," Jeff said, obviously because it eased his conscience to believe it was true.

She just shook her head and opened the door to expedite his departure.

But with her own bout of the flu a recent and vivid memory, she couldn't help but feel sorry for what Jocelyn and Jillian were going through. "I hope the girls are feeling better soon."

Her ex-husband nodded. "I'll give Dylan a call on Friday.

"I'm sure he'd appreciate that."

And she knew Dylan would be happy to talk to his dad if Jeff did call, but she also knew he wouldn't sit around waiting for the phone to ring.

She closed the door and went to find Dylan. The video game had been tossed on his desk, on top of his homework, and he was lying on his bed, music blasting from his iPod.

She reached down to pluck the earbuds from his ears. "Come on—we're going out for dinner."

"Where?" he asked cautiously.

"How about Eli's Burgers & Fries?"

He pumped his fist in the air. "Yesss!"

"Then go get your shoes on."

She didn't have to tell him twice. He raced to the mat by the door to get his sneakers. She had her own coat and shoes on when she remembered the shepherd's pie that she'd taken out of the freezer when she'd thought she'd be eating alone tonight.

She detoured to the kitchen to put the container in the fridge. Of course, Dylan followed.

"Why are we going out to eat if you had shepherd's pie?"

"I decided I wasn't in the mood for shepherd's pie."

"It's because I was supposed to go out with Dad, isn't it?"

Her son, so wise beyond his years, and still a little boy at heart. "Are you going to question my motives or open the door so we can go get burgers?"

He reached for the door.

A bacon cheeseburger with curly fries and a chocolate shake were special treats for the middle of the week, but as she tucked Dylan into bed later that night, she worried that his birthday would end up being a disappointment to him.

She didn't believe in spoiling him, and he didn't always get what he wanted, but she knew the jacket was a big deal. He hadn't been too disappointed that it wasn't under the tree at Christmas, because his birthday hadn't been too far away.

Now his birthday was in two days and she knew he wasn't going to be happy with two copies of the same video game. Which meant that she had less than forty-eight hours to get her hands on a Ren D'Alesio jacket.

Chapter Ten

In the five weeks that he'd been in the CFO's office, Nathan had never heard Allison raise her voice to anyone. In fact, in all the years that she'd worked as his uncle's executive assistant, he'd never heard her sound anything but poised and professional. But Thursday afternoon, when he came back into the office after lunch with his brother, she sounded desperate.

"I'm calling from Charisma, North Carolina," she informed whoever was on the other end of the phone she had tucked between her ear and her shoulder. "The fact that your warehouse in California *might* have stock doesn't do me any good."

She clicked through search results on her computer screen as she listened to the reply on the other end of the line.

"Yes, Kentucky is closer," she acknowledged. "But still not a viable option when I need it tomorrow."

She nodded grimly. "You're absolutely right. I shouldn't have waited until the last minute. Thank you for your help," she said, then slammed the receiver into the cradle.

"Problem?" Nate asked.

She looked up at him. "I didn't hear you come in."

"Apparently." He leaned over her desk to look at her computer screen. "What are you doing?"

"Not shopping," she grumbled. "That would require actually finding what I need in order to buy it."

"What do you need?"

"A Ren D'Alesio jacket in youth L."

He unclipped his iPhone from his belt and started to text a message. "What's the occasion?"

She rubbed her eyes with the heels of her hands and sighed. "Dylan's birthday."

"When?"

"Tomorrow."

His brows rose. "The way you run things around here, I would have guessed you were the kind of mom who would have her son's presents all wrapped and ready two weeks before his birthday."

"*I* was giving him the video game he wanted—which *is* wrapped and ready," she said in her defense. "His dad said he would get the jacket, and then he showed up last night and gave Dylan the game."

His gaze shifted to the screen to read his brother's reply. "Miscommunication?"

Tears of frustration shone in her eyes. "Something like that."

But he could tell by the tension in her voice that it was a lot more than that.

"If your son's a Ren D'Alesio fan, I assume you know that he drives the number seven-twenty-two car for Garrett/Slater Racing and that my brother Daniel is part owner of that team?"

"I do," she agreed.

"So why didn't you ask me if I might be able to help with your birthday present dilemma?"

"I want to say that it was because I wouldn't feel right exploiting our working relationship for personal reasons, but the truth is, I was going to exhaust all other options first."

"Have you exhausted all those other options?"

She sighed. "Pretty much."

"And if I told you that Daniel is going to ensure that a youth L jacket is delivered here by noon tomorrow?" He held up his phone, showing her the confirmation he'd just received from his brother.

Her jaw actually dropped open. "For real?"

He nodded.

"I wouldn't know how I could possibly repay you," she said sincerely.

"You could say 'thank you' and invite me to come over for a piece of birthday cake," he suggested.

"Birthday cake?"

"It's a cake, usually decorated in honor of the occasion, sometimes with an appropriate number of candles to indicate the year being celebrated."

"I know what it is—I'm just not sure I understand why you want a piece of my son's birthday cake."

"I like cake," he said simply.

She closed the tabs linking her to several different online retailers. "Do you like spaghetti, too?"

"As a matter of fact, I do."

"Then you can come for dinner before the cake," she offered. "If you want."

"I'd like that."

"We usually eat at six."

"I'll be there," he told her.

"I should warn you—we don't often have guests for dinner, and Dylan can be extremely shy around people he doesn't know."

"I promise that I won't ask him to entertain me with a stand-up comedy routine—at least, not before cake."

Her lips curved, just a little. "Good call."

As Nate made his way to his own desk, he realized he was already looking forward to the following night.

Her son wasn't a fan of parties.

Allison had learned that when Dylan was in kindergarten and she'd invited five kids from his class to celebrate his fifth birthday. She'd invited Jeff and Jodie and the girls, too, but Jillian was just an infant and Jodie had been terrified of exposing her to the germs of so many other children, so they'd declined.

Notwithstanding their absence, Allison thought the party was a big hit—with everyone except the birthday boy. His guests had happily run around the apartment and played party games, eaten pizza and ice cream cake. But Dylan—a typical only child and atypical child—didn't like chaos and he didn't like anyone else touching his stuff.

Since then, she'd kept their celebrations simple and the guest list small. In fact, Allison and Dylan usually celebrated the occasion alone, unless "Aunt Chelsea" was available to join them. But Chelsea was working tonight, and Dylan was pouting despite the fact that she'd dropped off a gift on her way to the bar. The revelation that Mr. Garrett would be coming for dinner did not appease him.

He did seem pleased with the decorations, though. The Happy Birthday banner Allison had pinned to the dining room wall was flanked by bouquets of balloons, and the cake—chocolate with cherry filling and chocolate whipped icing from The Sweet Spot—was on the sideboard with nine candles strategically placed around his name. The jacket, delivered to the office earlier that day as promised, was wrapped in festive paper topped with a big red bow.

"When are we gonna eat?" Dylan wanted to know.

"About fifteen minutes after Mr. Garrett gets here," she explained for the tenth time. She didn't want to overcook the pasta, so she was waiting for Nate to arrive before she dumped it into the boiling water.

"Why is your boss coming to my birthday party?"

It didn't matter to Dylan that there would be only three of them at the table—the fact that it was his birthday and there were balloons and cake was enough to make it a party.

Because he's the only reason that you're getting what

you most want for your birthday. Of course, aloud she said only, "Because I thought it would be nice to invite him to have dinner with us."

Dylan plucked at a loose thread on the hem of his sweater. "Is he…your boyfriend?"

"What? *No.*"

"Oh." Her son sounded almost disappointed. "Why don't you have a boyfriend?"

Allison stirred the sauce that was simmering on the stove and wondered if she would ever understand the way her son's mind worked. "I don't have time for a boyfriend."

"Why not?"

"Because I'm too busy doing my job and being a mom and answering all of your questions."

He smiled at that. "But what about when I'm not here? Why don't you have a boyfriend then?"

"Because that's when I clean the house and do the laundry."

"Miss Aberdeen has a job *and* a boyfriend," he told her, naming his third grade teacher. "And they're gonna get married in the summer."

"That's great for her." And it explained the origin of his questions.

"Are you ever gonna to get married again?"

"I don't know, Dylan. But it's not a priority right now."

"I think you should get married again."

"Why is that?"

"Because I'm prob'ly not gonna live at home forever. One of these days, when I get a wife, I'm gonna have to find a place of my own."

"That's true," she agreed, holding back her smile.

"And when I move out, I don't want you to be lonely."

She slung an arm across his shoulders and pulled him close so that she could kiss the top of his head. "I appreciate your concern," she told him sincerely. "But I think we've got a few years before we need to worry about that."

He shrugged. "I dunno. Kayleigh Tippett said that she's gonna marry me."

Kayleigh Tippett lived in the apartment building across the street and was in Dylan's class at school. "And how do you feel about that?"

"I dunno," he said again. "She always shares her cookies with me, but she's kinda bossy."

"Then it's probably best if you keep your options open," she suggested, and breathed a sigh of relief when the intercom buzzed.

Of course, Nate's arrival meant the abrupt departure of her curious chatterbox son and the appearance of his extremely shy and introverted alter ego. But considering Dylan's chosen topic of conversation, she decided that wasn't a bad thing.

Dylan Caldwell was the shyest, quietest and most polite child Nate had ever met.

Not that he'd met a lot of kids, but it was inevitable that they crossed his path on occasion. And usually when they did, they were moving at full speed and full volume.

Andrew's daughter, Maura, was almost the same age as Allison's son, but that was about the only thing the two children had in common. His adorable niece didn't seem to understand the meaning of the words *quiet* or *still*. Dylan, by contrast, sat unobtrusively at the table, only answering questions that were directed to him, and even then, he did so with as few words as possible.

When Allison invited him to dinner, he thought it would be a good chance to spend some time with her son. Knowing how she doted on the boy, he figured that establishing a good rapport with him would be a step closer to Allison. Unfortunately, the kid didn't say more than a dozen words to him throughout the meal. He didn't say much more than that to his mother, but they seemed to have their own form of shorthand communication, no doubt a result of the fact that it had been just the two of them for so long. He felt as though he was on the outside looking in—and it surprised him to realize that he wished he was on the inside with them.

On a more positive note, the food was delicious. In addition to the spaghetti that Allison had promised, there was a green salad and crispy garlic bread.

When dinner was finished and the dishes cleared away, Allison lit the candles on the cake and set it in front of her son. Dylan raised himself up on his knees on the seat of the chair and closed his eyes tight as he made his wish and blew hard to extinguish each one of the nine candles.

Dylan opened his gift from Aunt Chelsea first—a Ren D'Alesio baseball cap and a book about the history of stock car racing. Allison handed him Nate's gift next—a limited edition die-cast scale replica model of the number 722 car. Dylan looked at him, his dark eyes—so much like his mother's—wide with awe.

"Your mom mentioned that you were a fan," Nate said.

The boy nodded. "I've never seen one like this," he admitted. "It's awesome. Thanks."

When Allison set her own gift on the table in front of him, Dylan bit down on his lower lip. He'd probably guessed, based on the size of the box, what was inside, and his excitement was palpable. At the same time, he almost seemed afraid to open it—just in case it wasn't what he wanted. No wonder Allison had been so eager to get the jacket for her son, and it made Nate grateful that he'd been able to help.

When Dylan was finally given the cue to open his last gift, he tore away the paper and ripped apart the box—and the look on his face when he lifted the jacket out of the box was one of stunned amazement.

"This is…" He seemed to be at a loss for words as he ran

his hands over the various crests, reverently traced the outline of the driver's number, then the replicated signature. In the end, he simply finished with, "Wow."

Then he slid off of his chair to wrap his arms around his mother and hug her tight. "Thank you! Thank you! Thank you!"

Allison smiled as she returned the embrace. As her eyes met Nate's over her son's head, she mouthed, *Thank you.*

He just nodded and hoped she'd still be grateful when Dylan found what was tucked inside the pocket of the jacket.

"Are you just going to look at it or are you going to try it on?" she asked.

Dylan grinned and slipped his arms into the sleeves. It was a little big, but she no doubt wanted to make sure he'd be able to wear it for more than one season.

He snapped the buttons to close the front, then tucked his hands in his pockets. His brow furrowed. "There's something in here."

"Probably tags," Allison guessed.

He pulled his hand out. "It's an envelope," he realized, and opened the flap. "And there's tickets inside."

"Tickets?" Allison looked from her son to Nate.

Of course, his deliberately neutral expression gave nothing away. But as Dylan's smile spread, she started to feel uneasy.

"For the race in Bristol."

Race? As in stock car race? Judging by the pure, unadulterated joy on her son's face, she'd guess her assumption was correct. And she hated that she would have to crush his enthusiasm.

"I don't know how those tickets got in there," she said, though her narrowed gaze shifted to Nate, suggesting otherwise. "But—"

"Don't say we can't go," Dylan interrupted. "Please, Mom. It's *Bristol*."

"Is that supposed to mean something to me?"

"It's the world's fastest half mile," her son explained.

"And Bristol is in Tennessee." She might not know stock car racing, but she knew geography. "And Tennessee is about a four-hour drive from here."

"Or an hour flight," Nate interjected.

"Not helping," she said.

Dylan looked at Nate, his excitement over the possibility overcoming his innate shyness—at least for the moment. "We could fly?"

"No, we cannot fly," Allison told him—both of them.

Her son looked at her pleadingly. "But I've never been on a plane."

"Because we can't afford—"

"Flights and accommodations are included with the tickets," Nate spoke up again.

Allison drew in a slow, deep breath and reminded herself that she had to handle this carefully or her son would never forgive her. But she was furious with Nate, that he'd gone ahead and made arrangements without even talking to her. And she was frustrated that he could give her son an opportunity that she never could. "Which is incredibly generous, but not something I could ever repay."

"It's a gift," Nate reminded her. "No repayment required."

"The model car was a gift. This is—"

"The best gift ever!" Dylan announced.

And in his eyes, it undoubtedly was, but even her son's enthusiasm couldn't override her reservations. Or silence the questions that echoed in her mind: Why was Nate doing this? What did he hope to gain?

"Why don't you go into the living room to play your new video game while Mr. Garrett helps me clear the table?" she suggested to Dylan.

Her son—thrilled to be released from his usual after-dinner chores in addition to his gifts—didn't need to be told twice.

"You're mad," Nathan guessed.

"You're perceptive." She stacked the cake plates and carried them to the kitchen to load into the dishwasher.

"Do you want me to apologize?"

She glanced up at him. "Are you sorry?"

"No," he admitted, setting the glasses on the counter.

"But you'd apologize anyway?"

"If it would stop you being mad at me."

She wiped her hands on a towel. "I'm not just mad, I'm infuriated. And I know I should be grateful—you've given him an opportunity that I never could. But I don't feel comfortable with the whole setup and I'm not sure why you'd go to so much trouble when—"

"I meant what I said," he interrupted to reassure her. "It's a gift. No payment required and no strings attached."

His generosity wasn't just overwhelming, it was baffling. "Why?"

"Because the way you described the whole family situation, it seemed to me like the kid's got a pretty rotten deal in the past and I figured it was time he got to do something that was all about him. I also thought that you might enjoy doing it with him so that, years from now, when he thinks back to his first stock car race, you'll be part of that memory."

She sighed, because he was absolutely right—she just hadn't expected him to be able to read the situation so accurately. "And, as you can see, he's thrilled by the prospect of going to Bristol."

"But you're wondering if this is all some kind of elaborate ploy to get you back into my bed," he guessed.

"It crossed my mind," she admitted. "But I can't imagine you'd go to that much effort for any woman."

"I would—for you," he said.

The admission unnerved her as much as the sincerity in his tone.

"Make no mistake, Alli—I do want you back in my bed. But when we make love again, it's going to be because you want me, too, not because you're feeling obligated or grateful."

Her traitorous heart hammered against her ribs. "Don't you mean *if*?"

"No, I mean *when*," he confirmed. "But the timetable is entirely in your hands."

"I thought…I mean…you never gave any indication… that you still wanted me."

"I haven't stopped wanting you," he assured her. "But I also wanted to make sure you knew that anything that happens between us outside of the office has nothing to do with work."

She nodded. "Are *you* going to Bristol?"

"Of course—the kid needs someone with him who knows what's going on."

She smiled at that. "But we wouldn't be sharing a room in Tennessee?"

"I don't have a lot of experience with kids, but even I'm smart enough to know that probably wouldn't be an arrangement that would work for you." He waited a beat. "Would it?"

She couldn't help but smile at the hopeful tone in his voice. "No, it wouldn't."

He sighed. "Then it's a good thing I've already booked separate rooms."

She was making coffee for Nate when Dylan ventured into the kitchen. He hovered in the background for a minute, as if trying to summon up the courage to say something. Conversation with new people had never come easily to him, and he'd already interacted with Nathan more than she'd anticipated.

"Do you want to play my new race game, Mr…Nate?" he

finally asked, remembering that Nate had insisted he call him by his given name.

Initiating conversation was a huge step for Dylan, and she could tell by the tone of his voice that he didn't hold out much hope of his invitation being accepted. She held her breath to see how Nate would respond, not just to the question but to her son.

"Can I be the number seven-twenty-two car?" he asked.

Dylan shook his head without even considering the request. "Nuh-uh—only I get to drive that one."

Nate sighed. "Four-fourteen?"

"Sure," her son agreed. "But we're racing Pocono so be careful on turn three—you don't want your back end to step out."

"I'll be careful on turn three," Nate promised.

He started to follow Dylan out of the room, then realized that he was abandoning Allison to finish the cleanup on her own. "Do you mind?" he asked her.

She shook her head. "No, I don't mind."

But as they went off to play video games together, she found herself questioning the truthfulness of her response. She couldn't object to her boss paying attention to her son, but in light of Dylan's recent interest in finding her a boyfriend, she was a little wary.

Because it was Friday night, and because it was his birthday, she let Dylan stay up past his usual bedtime. But at nine o'clock, she insisted that the current race was the last one. As they zoomed toward the finish line, each one trying to nudge the other out of the way, Allison was sure they were both going to crash and let the orange car running in third win the checkered flag. But Dylan assured her they were only "trading paint" and then, when he edged out Nate's car at the finish, he had to spin in circles, tearing up the infield before making his way to victory lane.

When the celebrations were finally done and Winner finished flashing on the screen, she directed her son to the shower. He didn't grumble too much, and he high-fived Nate on the way out and thanked him again for the "awesome" birthday present before going to do his mother's bidding.

"You want to see if you can beat me, too?" Nate asked, gesturing with his controller.

She shook her head. "I can't even watch Dylan play for too long without feeling dizzy."

Nate put both controllers back in the basket beneath the table, then reached for Allison's hand. He linked their fingers together and tugged her down onto the cushion beside him.

Sitting close to Nate made her feel dizzy, too, but in a completely different way. She wondered if she should shift to the other end of the sofa, to put some distance between them. But sitting close beside him, the warm strength of his thigh against hers, felt good. Maybe too good.

Over the past several weeks, she'd ignored her feelings for Nate, convinced that he was no longer interested and, even if he was, that he couldn't ever fit into her life. It was a well-known fact that he didn't do relationships, that he had no interest in a family of his own. But it had taken only five minutes of watching him with her son to have her questioning what she thought she knew about him.

And Dylan had basked in the undivided attention. She knew that her son loved his father and enjoyed his time with Jeff, but recently, there had been little time or attention that was his exclusively. She didn't blame Jeff for that—or she tried not to. She understood that he had a new wife and other children who needed him, too. But they were a cohesive family unit, and she wanted more for Dylan than stolen moments of time shared with siblings who had the benefit of living with both of their parents.

Nathan had given more time and attention to Dylan in three hours tonight than Jeff had done in the past three weeks. She knew it wasn't a fair comparison. Her boss had no personal obligations, no demands on his time. And seeing how quickly her son had overcome his usual reticence with him—no doubt helped along by the excited anticipation of seeing a live stock car race—only added to her concerns about the weekend they were going to spend together in Bristol.

Yes, she was worried about Dylan's expectations, but she was even more worried about her own.

Chapter Eleven

"What are you thinking about that put that furrow back between your brows?" Nate asked.

Allison shook her head. "Nothing, really."

"I don't think you have any reason to worry about Dylan—he's a great kid, Alli."

She smiled at that. "I think so."

"It's obvious that you have a good relationship with him."

"I try," she said. "Unfortunately, every day isn't cake and ice cream."

She heard the water shut off in the bathroom and shifted to the end of the sofa, away from Nate.

His brows lifted.

"I don't want Dylan getting the wrong idea about us."

"We were having a conversation—not making out."

"He already asked if you were my boyfriend."

"Why would he ask that?"

"Because I'm not in the habit of inviting men over for dinner."

"So what did you tell him?"

"The truth."

"You told him that we're not dating but we sometimes have earth-shattering sex together?"

Her cheeks flushed. "Just the first part because the 'have' is now a 'had' and therefore irrelevant."

"So you don't think about me anymore?"

"I think—no, I *know*—that a personal relationship with my boss is a recipe for disaster."

"You're the only one who gives a damn about my title."

"You don't think people in the office would have something to say if we started dating? You don't think your family would have something to say?"

"I don't care what other people think—even the people related to me. And you're more naive than I would have guessed if you honestly believe no one at the office suspects we've been seeing each other."

"Well, I do care," she said. "And *suspecting* isn't the same thing as *knowing*." But she couldn't deny that even the possibility of speculation bothered her.

"Why is this such a big issue for you?" he asked.

"There were two reasons I was thrilled to be hired at Garrett Furniture," she told him.

"The former CFO's handsome nephew being one of those reasons?"

She chuckled. "The former CFO has a lot of handsome nephews—and you were still in New York when I started working for your uncle."

"So what were the reasons?" he prompted.

"On-site day care and medical benefits. And while Dylan has obviously outgrown the need for day care, he has asthma, so the medical benefits are still essential."

"How bad is his asthma?"

"Not bad at all, on a day-to-day basis. But every once in a while, it's terrifying."

"I can't imagine," he admitted.

"He had a rough go of it when he was younger. He was in and out of the hospital a lot before he was properly diagnosed and we were able to get it under control."

"Well, you don't need to worry about medical benefits. Your job is not in jeopardy," he assured her. "No matter what happens between us, I promise you that."

"How can you make that promise?"

"I'm the boss," he reminded her. "And your employment is specifically protected by paragraph 114.6 of the Employee Handbook."

"I'll check that out," she said. "But right now, I should check on Dylan—make sure he's brushed his teeth and is tucked into bed."

"Is that my cue to leave?"

She shrugged. "It's getting late."

It wasn't really, but now that Dylan had left the room, they were both aware of the attraction sizzling in the air. An attraction that she hadn't decided what to do about and that he wasn't willing to act on with her son so close by.

He stood up and she followed him to the door, then offered her hand.

He took it, choosing to be amused rather than insulted by the gesture, and held it for a long moment, letting his thumb brush lightly over her knuckles, watching the awareness darken her eyes.

"Thanks for dinner."

"Thank *you*," she said. "Not just for the jacket but everything. You made Dylan's birthday celebration something truly special."

"Does that mean you're over being mad about the tickets?"

"It means that I'm getting there. Slowly."

"So I probably shouldn't do anything else to set you off."

"You shouldn't do anything else to set me off," she agreed.

"Would a good-night kiss be considered 'anything else'?"

"It might fit into that category."

"Then I guess—" his lips feathered lightly over hers "—I shouldn't—" and again "—kiss you good-night."

She closed her eyes, for just a second, as if savoring the

fleeting contact, then pressed her lips together. "You definitely...shouldn't...kiss me."

"Then I'll just say good night, Alli."

"Good night, Nate."

Chelsea stopped by to have coffee with Allison Saturday morning, which was clearly just an excuse to pry for details about dinner the night before.

"So how was your birthday, Dilly Bug?" she asked, when the sleepy-eyed boy finally wandered into the kitchen.

"Awesome!"

"Did you get cool stuff?"

"Really cool," he confirmed. And although Allison knew he was most excited about the upcoming trip to Bristol, he remembered to thank his "aunt" for her gift. "I'm gonna wear it for sure when we go to the race."

Chelsea sent Allison a questioning look before she focused her attention back on Dylan. "What race?"

"We're going to the fastest half-mile in the world."

"Bristol?" Chelsea immediately guessed, because working part-time in a sports bar for a dozen years had taught her almost everything anyone needed to know about sports—and more.

The little boy nodded enthusiastically. "Mom got me a D'Alesio jacket and there were tickets in the pocket."

"That's a lucky bonus."

"And Nate said we're gonna go on an airplane so we can be there to watch qualifying and everything." He opened the pantry and pulled out a box of his favorite cereal.

"Nate?" she said, looking at Allison, who busied herself pulling the milk out of the fridge for Dylan.

"Nate Garrett—Mom's boss." He dumped the cereal into a bowl, poured some milk over it, then took a spoon from the drawer.

"Sounds like a fun trip."

He nodded again, then looked at his mom. "Can I take this in the living room? I wanna watch qualifying."

"Go ahead," Allison agreed, albeit reluctantly. Because she knew that as soon as her son left the room, she would be inundated with questions.

Sure enough, Chelsea waited only until she heard the television come on in the other room before she asked, "Is it true? Are you really going to Tennessee with Nate Garrett?"

She nodded. "Tell me I'm not crazy."

"You're crazy," Chelsea said.

"Not quite the reassurance I was hoping for."

"You're the one who said that you couldn't risk any kind of personal involvement with your boss. And you don't even like stock car racing."

"I know. But Dylan does—and Nate set up this whole weekend for him, so how could I say no?"

"How you've managed to say no to anything the man asks is beyond me," Chelsea admitted. "And now, he did this—without any prompting—for your son?"

"I only asked if he could get the jacket. Actually, I didn't even get around to asking him that much—he knew I was having trouble finding it, so he asked his brother to help."

"Gotta love a man who takes charge," Chelsea said approvingly.

"My ex-husband liked to take charge," Allison reminded her.

"No, he liked to tell you what to do," her friend countered. "And he still does."

Allison couldn't deny it.

"In all the years that I've known Nate, I've never heard of him taking chicken soup to a sick friend or making plans to spend a weekend with a woman and her kid. And now he's taking you and your nine-year-old son to Bristol, making Dylan's biggest wish come true… Are you sharing a room?"

"No! Of course not."

"So he's done all of that and not even getting sex in return? That man is seriously smitten."

"Maybe he's hoping to get lucky despite insisting he has no expectations."

"He's a guy—of course he's hoping," Chelsea said. "But the fact that he's letting the choice be yours speaks volumes. He doesn't just want sex—he wants *you*." She got up to pour more coffee into her mug. "So—are you going to sleep with him?"

"No."

Her friend rolled her eyes. "He's one of the hottest single guys in Charisma—you could at least take a minute to think it over."

"I've spent a lot of minutes thinking about it," Allison confided, because Chelsea was her best friend and the only person she could admit it to. "But I can't do it—sleeping with the boss would make me a horrible cliché."

"Not if the sex was good," Chelsea countered. "Then it would make you a smart woman—and a satisfied employee."

She sighed, a little wistfully. "The sex would be great."

"So maybe you need to rethink your plans," her friend suggested.

"I can't," Allison insisted. "Because I know that one night would only make me want more."

"Why can't you have more?" Chelsea asked.

"Because Nate doesn't do more."

"It's March—almost two months since the night you spent together in St. Louis, which means that this is probably the longest relationship he's ever had with a woman."

"Except for the fact that we don't have a relationship."

"I think you do," Chelsea insisted. "You just don't want to admit it because you're as wary about relationships as he is."

"I'm not wary," she denied. "I'm just focusing on my son—that's the most important relationship in my life."

"So what does my Dilly Bug think of your new boy-friend?"

"He's not my boyfriend."

Chelsea just laughed.

She was starting to pack for the trip when Dylan was out with his dad Wednesday night. After saying goodbye to his son, Jeff asked to speak with her for a minute.

"Is something wrong?"

"No, I just wanted you to know that Jodie cleared our schedule for Saturday afternoon so we can take Dylan to Buster's to make up for missing his birthday."

She wondered if he would ever ask rather than tell her his plans. Of course, she knew it was at least partially her own fault that she'd always let him dictate the schedule of his visitation with Dylan because she wanted her son to spend as much time as possible with his father. But this time, she shook her head. "Sorry, that won't work."

"Why not?"

"Because we already have plans for the weekend."

"Change them," Jeff suggested.

"I can't."

He frowned. "Come on, Allison. I know I was short with you that night and I'm sorry, but it's not like you to hold a grudge."

"I'm not holding a grudge," she assured him. "And if we weren't going away, Dylan would be happy to go with you."

His scowl deepened. "Where are you going?"

"Tennessee."

"Why on earth would you go to Tennessee?"

"For the race at Bristol this weekend."

"You don't know the first thing about stock car racing."

She shrugged. "Apparently I'm going to learn."

"How did you manage to get tickets?"

"Garrett Furniture is one of the sponsors of the number seven-twenty-two car," she reminded him.

"And so they're giving out tickets to the employee of the month?"

"I mentioned to my boss that Dylan was a huge race fan, so Nate got the tickets for him for his birthday."

She'd never been a good liar, and though it wasn't really a lie, it wasn't the whole truth, and her ex-husband picked up on that. "Jesus, Allison—tell me you're not screwing him."

She was shocked by the crude choice of words as much as the question, and though it was none of his business if she was "screwing" Nate Garrett or anyone else, she had to ask, "Where did that come from?"

"Dylan told me that your boyfriend was here for dinner on his birthday."

"Well, Dylan was mistaken."

"Nathan Garrett wasn't here?"

"He was here, but he's not my boyfriend."

"You invited your boss for dinner?"

"Not that it's any of your business who I invite over for dinner, but Nate used his connections to get the Ren D'Alesio jacket that *you* were supposed to get for Dylan for his birthday—and to thank him, I invited him to come over so that he could see Dylan open it. And Nate gave us the tickets."

"Is he going to Tennessee with you?"

"He's going to Bristol for the race," she confirmed.

"I don't approve of this, Allison."

"Well, then, it's a good thing I don't need or want your approval."

"You need that job," he reminded her. "I don't have the kind of medical benefits that you do and all those inhalers Dylan needs cost a fortune."

"I'm well aware of our son's medical needs," she said coolly.

"Then don't jeopardize your job because you've got a crush on your boss."

She opened the door to hasten his exit. "Thanks for the advice—I'll see you next week."

The kid was practically vibrating with nervous energy.

Dylan was buckled into his seat beside his mother, his gaze glued to the sky outside the window, but he kept wrapping the loose end of the belt around his hand, then unwrapping it again.

Nate was a little apprehensive, too, because there was a lot riding on this weekend. He'd never had any concerns about hanging out with Andrew's daughter, Maura, but he'd never worried about making a good impression on her, either. Maybe the fact that she was his niece took some of the pressure off, because even if he said or did something stupid, their relationship was solid. But he barely knew Dylan, and he knew that if he screwed up, it would be over with Allison before it had even begun.

When Daniel had offered the tickets, he'd leaped at the chance to take Allison and her son to the race. It had seemed the perfect opportunity to win the kid over—or at least make a favorable first impression. But now he was wondering if he'd gone too big too soon. Maybe he should have started with a ninety-minute weekend matinee instead of a three-day weekend out of town.

He'd never fallen in love with stock car racing the way his younger brother had, but since Daniel had gone into partnership with Josh Slater and founded GSR, he'd come to appreciate the energy and excitement that surrounded every aspect of the sport. He thought it would be fun to share that with Allison's son. The boy was, in Nate's opinion, far too serious and quiet—except when Dylan talked about racing. Then his eyes lit up and enthusiasm filled his voice so that he looked and sounded like almost any other nine-year-old kid Nate had ever met.

Now that they were in the air and on their way to Bristol, Nate was thinking he should have opted for a race closer to home. Somewhere like Charlotte or Martinsville, where they could have gone to the race and returned home the same day. That way, if the experience was a complete bust, it would be over relatively quickly. Instead, he'd decided that a whole weekend was a good idea. He'd rarely ever spent a whole weekend with a woman, never mind a woman and her kid.

And Dylan looked as wary as Nate felt. Maybe it was the flight—Allison had told him that her son had never been on an airplane before.

"So what do you think of flying?" Nate asked him.

"I didn't think the plane would be so small," Dylan said.

"None of the major airlines fly direct from Raleigh to Bristol," he said, explaining why he'd decided to charter a plane for the trip. "And this is a six-seat Piper, owned by my friend Anthony—who also happens to be the pilot. If you have any questions about how the plane stays in the air, I'm sure he'd be happy to answer them."

The kid shook his head. "I looked it up. I know all about lift, gravity, thrust and drag."

"Then maybe you could answer his questions," he said.

Dylan frowned at that, as if he didn't get that Nate was joking. Allison covered her son's hand with her own, squeezed it.

Nate tried again. "Are you interested in aerodynamics?"

The kid shrugged. "I just like to know about a lot of things."

"There's nothing wrong with that," he assured him. "We wouldn't be able to fly to Bristol today if the Wright brothers hadn't displayed the same kind of curiosity."

"But sometimes I ask too many questions."

"I've noticed that you're quite the gabber."

It took the boy a minute, but this time he realized that Nate was only teasing, and he offered a shy smile in response.

"Mom's gonna have lots of questions this weekend," Dylan warned. "She doesn't know anything about racing."

"I know about restrictor plates now," she said.

"They don't use restrictor plates at Bristol," her son told her.

"Why not?"

"Because it's a short track."

"Oh."

But it was clear from her tone that she still didn't make the connection. Nate winked at Dylan, and the kid offered another shy smile in return.

"So if the race is on Sunday, why are we going to the track today?" Allison asked.

"Because before the drivers can race for the checkered flag, they have to qualify."

She frowned at that. "You mean, we might have come all this way and not even get to see Ren D'Alesio race?"

"He'll qualify," Dylan said with unwavering confidence.

"How does he qualify?"

As Anthony brought the plane smoothly down, Dylan patiently explained the procedure to his mother—the first-round qualifying that would take place on Friday, and the advantages of making that first cut, then the second round Saturday morning, and why some drivers would choose to stand on their time from the first round rather than participate in the second round.

The boy had obviously watched a lot of races and paid attention to the commentators. But if he'd never actually been to a race, he couldn't know how it really felt to be part of the action. The vibration of the ground beneath his feet as forty-plus cars rushed past so fast their distinctive paint schemes were nothing more than a blur of color.

The speedway was about a twenty-minute drive from the airport, and on the way, Dylan filled his mom in on Ren D'Alesio's stats—number of races, poles, wins and top-ten finishes. But he fell silent again when they arrived at the track and merged with the crowd of people.

The kid gaped at the lineup of haulers, their exteriors showcasing the colors, numbers and sponsors of the respective teams. He looked eagerly for the 722 hauler and seemed to be as much in awe of it as Nate suspected he would be when he got to see the actual vehicle Ren would be driving.

When they finally spotted the distinctive gold-and-green car, it was being checked over by the race inspectors, easily identified by OFFICIAL spelled out in block letters on their backs.

"What do the officials do?" Allison asked.

Nate waited to see if Dylan would answer, but the boy was too busy watching the inspection to pay any attention to his mother's question.

"They inspect the cars before every race to ensure that they're in compliance with the regulations of the specific track."

"What happens if a vehicle isn't in compliance?"

"It has to be fixed before the car can be put on the track for qualifying."

Dylan moved away from the fence as the 722 car was waved through.

"I didn't realize it was so technical," she admitted.

"She thought it was just a bunch of guys in fast cars who didn't know how to turn right," Dylan told him.

He looked at Allison, his brows raised.

Her cheeks colored. "That's what it looks like on TV," she said, just a little defensively.

"You've got a lot to learn," Nate said, as Dylan nodded his agreement.

They tracked down Daniel when they followed the 722

car back to the garage. He shook his brother's hand, said hello to Allison and put a lanyard around Dylan's neck.

The kid looked down at the hot pass inside the plastic cover, then back at Daniel with wordless awe, as if he'd just been handed the keys to the kingdom. And to a nine-year-old race fan, a hot pass was exactly that.

"What is it?" Allison asked, as Daniel gave matching lanyards to both her and Nate.

Dylan, who could probably give her an official definition and recite all the perks, was silent, stunned.

"It gives you access the garage and pit road, even when the track goes hot."

"Goes hot?" she echoed uncertainly.

"Usually an hour before the start of the race, everyone without a hot pass has to clear out of the area," Daniel clarified for her. "But today, with that pass, you can watch qualifying from up on top of the pit box if you want."

Dylan found his voice. "For real?"

Daniel chuckled. "For real. But you'll have to hang around awhile, because Ren is in the second half for qualifying."

Nate bought them pizza slices and soft drinks before they went to the watch the qualifying.

The crew chief was already on top of the pit box when they arrived, and he had headphones for all of them—to combat the noise, he explained, and so they could listen in to the communications between the driver and the garage.

Dylan followed the instructions he was given without question. He sat where he was told to sit, he put the headphones on and he settled back to watch. Only about a dozen cars had done their laps when Nate noticed that Allison was watching her son rather than the track. He shifted closer, so that he could talk to her without everyone on top of the pit box hearing their conversation. "Is something wrong?"

"I didn't realize the smells would be so strong."

"Race fuel and hot rubber," Nate told her.

"I'm fine, Mom," Dylan interjected, obviously more aware of the reason for her concern.

"His asthma," she said to Nate.

"Oh. Right." She'd mentioned it to him once before, but he wasn't entirely sure he understood what it meant. "We can move to the grandstand, if it's a problem."

"It's not a problem," Dylan said. Then, to his mom, "I've got my inhaler."

She hesitated a moment, then nodded.

But while Dylan watched the cars circle the track, she spent more time watching him.

When the first round of qualifying was complete—with Ren making the cut that exempted him from having to re-qualify the next day—they headed back to the hauler. Ren and Mike, his crew chief, were hanging out there, already looking forward to the race and discussing minor adjustments that should be made to the car before then. Ren felt the car had more to give and believed that if he'd pushed a little harder, he might have gotten the pole. His fastest lap had been less than half a second slower than the leader, but still only good enough for thirteenth spot.

Allison didn't seem to be paying much attention to the content of the conversation—she seemed more caught up in the fact that her son was right in the middle of it. Nate was surprised to find that the boy's shyness had disappeared in the face of his excitement and enthusiasm, and he was glad that the weekend was proving to be everything the kid hoped and imagined.

But he still wanted more: he wanted Allison back in his bed.

Chapter Twelve

Allison couldn't remember the last time she'd seen her son so animated, and she knew that she'd never be able to repay Nate for the gift of this weekend. But she hoped that buying dinner might be a start. He agreed on the condition that Dylan got to choose where they would eat.

That was how they ended up at the '50s-style diner across the street from their hotel. The floor was tiled in black and white, with chrome stools lined up at the soda fountain and red vinyl chairs around Formica tables for other diners. The walls were decorated with framed prints of vintage cars and posters advertising classic movies. And, of course, there was a Wurlitzer jukebox in the back corner where you could choose three golden oldies for a quarter.

The menu was updated with offerings that included not just hamburgers and hot dogs but also chicken and veggie burgers, with countless variations of each, and hand-dipped milkshakes. Dylan gorged himself like any nine-year-old boy, tackling a bacon cheeseburger, curly fries and a chocolate shake. But even before he was halfway through his meal, Allison could tell that the excitement of the day was beginning to catch up with him.

After dinner, they went back to the hotel—a Sweet Dream Inn, chosen because the hotel chain was a GSR sponsor. Allison and Dylan were in suite 810, and Nate was in 812, an adjoining suite.

Dylan had a quick shower, then she tucked him into bed,

not the least bit surprised that he was asleep almost before his head hit the pillow. She puttered around the room for a little while, partly because she wanted to make sure he was completely and deeply asleep and partly because she was debating her next move.

When we make love again, it's going to be because you want me, too.

There had never been any question that she wanted Nate—the question had been more about what would come after. If she got involved with him, would he end up breaking her heart? Because she knew it would end—with Nate, there was no chance of anything else. But even knowing that, she couldn't resist what he was offering, what she wanted.

She knocked on the adjoining door.

Nate responded immediately, almost as if he'd been waiting. "Is something wrong?"

"No, everything's fine," she hastened to assure him. "Great even. I just, um, wanted to thank you. For today. For everything."

"I'm glad Dylan had a good time."

"The best," she said. "And those were his words, not mine. You've done so much for him. Not just the race, but the whole weekend."

"I was a baseball fan when I was his age," Nate confided. "And I'll never forget the thrill of meeting Cal Ripken Junior."

"He'll never forget this weekend—or the part you played in making it happen. In his eyes, you're as much a hero as Ren D'Alesio now."

"I'm not anyone's hero," he warned her.

"You were my son's today," she said. "So thank you."

"I don't want you to be grateful."

"Well, I am. You did something amazing for my son and I can't help but feel appreciative." She drew a deep breath and shored up her courage. "But that's not why I knocked on this door."

"Why did you?"

She held his gaze. "Because I thought you might be able to make one of my wishes come true, too."

"Am I correct in assuming you don't want Ren D'Alesio's autograph?"

"I don't want Ren D'Alesio's autograph," she confirmed.

Nate didn't move. "So what do you want?"

"You."

He finally stepped away from the door, and she crossed the threshold.

Nate started to push the door shut, then reconsidered. "Should we keep this open?"

Allison shook her head.

"What if Dylan wakes up—or has an asthma attack?"

"He doesn't usually wake up in the night," she told him. "But we can keep the door slightly ajar, so I'll hear him if he does."

So he closed the door, but only partially, and pulled her into his arms.

He wanted to take his time, but they'd both wanted this—and fought against it—for too long to go slow now. He had her undressed before they made it across the room to his bed. He laid her down on top of the mattress and lowered himself over her.

He sucked her breasts, pulling first one nipple into his mouth, then the other. She gasped and sighed and rocked her hips. The way she was rubbing against him, there was no denying that she was wet and ready for him.

This time he had planned ahead—just in case—and he wasted no time in tearing open a condom package and sheathing himself. Then he drove into the moist heat between her thighs.

She gasped again, and her muscles clamped around him, pulsing her pleasure. She arched beneath him, pulling him deeper, and he felt the already tenuous thread of control start to slip from his fingers.

He caught her hands, held them over her head, and pressed his body against hers, pinning her to the mattress. "This isn't a race," he admonished softly.

"But I want—"

He nibbled on her lip, halting the flow of her words. "I know what you want, and I'll get you there. I promise."

And then he started to move, loving her slowly, deeply, endlessly. He kissed her lips, caressed her breasts, stroked her center. She gasped, she sighed and, finally, she came apart in his arms, shattering in unison with him.

Allison hadn't planned to fall asleep.

She didn't know that she had until she awakened in his arms. The glowing numbers of the clock on the bedside table revealed that it was 3:24. She breathed a sigh of relief, confident that Dylan, exhausted from all of the excitement of the previous day, would sleep for hours yet. But she should get back, so that he didn't wake up and find her bed empty.

She started to shift out of Nate's embrace, but his arms tightened around her.

"I have to go to my own room," she whispered in the darkness.

"Not yet." He rolled over on top of her. "I'm not done with you yet."

She felt the press of his erection against her belly, and the pulse of answering heat through her own veins. "So you're a morning person, are you?"

"Is it morning?"

She chuckled softly. "Or maybe you're just one of those guys who doesn't pay any attention to the clock when he's got a woman in his bed."

"Not a woman," he denied, brushing his lips to hers. "You."

They were simple words. Words that he'd probably spoken to countless women before her. But right now, with his body rising over and into her, she didn't care. Right now, she was the one in his bed, in his arms.

But even as her body responded to his touch, even as he drove her up and sent her flying over the edge, she held herself back from taking a bigger fall. Because she knew that if she gave him her whole heart, she would never get it back.

"Are you done with me now?" she asked, when she was finally able to gather enough breath to speak.

"Not even close," he said. "But I know you need to get back to your room before Dylan wakes up."

"I do." She brushed a soft kiss to his lips. "Thanks."

He didn't fall back to sleep right away.

After Allison left his bed, Nate couldn't stop thinking about the instinctive response he'd given when she'd asked if he was done with her.

Not even close.

It was true.

She was under his skin. She filled his thoughts when he was awake and haunted his dreams when he was asleep. He'd never been so preoccupied by a woman—any woman.

He wondered that an unexpected snowstorm could have had such an impact on his life, but everything had changed for him when he spent that night in St. Louis with Allison. Or maybe everything had changed at the Christmas party. He only wished he could be sure that she felt the same way.

He knew the fact that she'd spent the past few hours in his bed didn't magically alleviate all of her concerns about a relationship with him. And he couldn't blame her for that. She was wary of his reputation—a reputation he'd enjoyed building.

Unfortunately, he was now paying the price for it—having to convince the sexy single mom that he wasn't the careless and indiscriminate playboy he used to be. It wasn't going to be an easy task, but he wanted her not just to know that she could depend on him—but to actually do so.

When Allison finally returned to her room, she checked on Dylan, slipped into her pajamas, then fell face-first into her own bed.

She woke up several hours later to discover his was empty.

She wasn't surprised that he was up—a quick glance at the clock showed that it was almost 10:00 a.m. She couldn't remember the last time she'd slept so late—not that she'd gotten a lot of sleep. It had been almost five before she'd left Nate's room and returned to her own, at which time her son had been sleeping soundly.

But she was surprised that the room was quiet, making her wonder where Dylan might be and what he was doing. She wasn't really concerned. He wasn't the type of kid to wander too far on his own, especially in unfamiliar surroundings.

And then she noticed that the adjoining door was open.

Moving closer, she peeked through to see that Dylan was in Nate's sitting area, snuggled up in the middle of the sofa eating dry cereal out of a single-serve box from the mini-pantry. Nate was seated beside him and, judging from the sound emanating from the television, they were watching highlights of the qualifying that they'd both seen live the day before.

Looking at the two of them together, she felt a pang inside her chest to realize how much she wanted what Nathan was giving her son this weekend: a man who paid attention to him, who actually wanted to hang out with him.

Jeff had been a great dad in the beginning—attentive to

and doting on their baby. But his life was with Jodie now, his attention focused on their family. He still went through the motions with Dylan, because he was his son and his responsibility, and Jeff had always been big on responsibility. It was, after all, the reason he'd married her. He wasn't so big on warmth and affection.

She wouldn't have said Nate was, either, but he'd surprised her in so many little ways. Not just the trip, but the consideration he'd shown for her son's introverted personality. He'd given Dylan opportunities—so many wonderful and glorious opportunities—but he'd never pushed him beyond his comfort zone. He'd listened to what the boy wanted and had let him set the pace. He'd gone above and beyond for both of them this weekend, and seeing him with Dylan now, she was afraid her son was going to start to want more, expect more. And she knew that Nate wasn't a man who could give it.

Because a weekend away with a kid was one thing—being part of his life on a daily basis was another.

He'd been generous to a fault. Anything that Dylan expressed an interest in—T-shirts, pennants, posters—he bought for the boy. But far more than the merchandise, her son needed the time and attention that Nate gave him. She knew it didn't matter how much she made herself available to her little boy—he needed a man in his life on a more consistent basis. And if she wasn't careful, she might find herself dreaming about things that couldn't be.

"Are you guys going to lounge around here all day or are we going to go to the track?"

"The track!" Dylan voted.

"After a real breakfast," Nate suggested. "Man cannot live on dry cereal alone."

Dylan giggled, and Allison's heart swelled.

She couldn't remember the last time she'd heard such a

childish and carefree sound emanate from her son, and she knew that she would never forget this trip.

"Breakfast sounds good," she agreed.

"You going in your pajamas?" Nate asked.

Dylan giggled again.

She smiled. "Give me half an hour to shower and get dressed."

The rest of the weekend passed in a blur. Afterward, Allison was hard-pressed to recount a lot of specific details. She knew that Ren didn't take the checkered flag, but he came across the finish line in sixth place, which her son assured her was "an awesome run." She was pleased for the driver and the whole Garrett/Slater Racing team, but what made the strongest impression was the feeling of happiness that filled her heart to overflowing. And that happiness was the result of so many factors: the carefree sound of her son's laughter, the pure joy on his face, the slow emergence from his shell, the feeling of contentment when Nate linked his hand with hers and the giddy excitement of being naked in his arms.

And as they merged with the crowd exiting the stadium, Dylan's hands firmly clasped in each of hers and Nate's so that they didn't get separated, it occurred to her that they looked like a family—like so many other families around them. And the yearning sliced through her like a dagger.

She wanted to be part of a family again—not just for Dylan but for herself. But she knew that what they'd shared with Nate this weekend was only the illusion of family. It wasn't real and it wouldn't ever be real, and the longer she let herself cling to the fantasy, the more it was going to hurt when reality wrenched it out of her grasp.

It would be easier, although not painless, to let go before that happened. Which meant that when they got back to Charisma, she would take a step back, away from Nate. It was the only way to protect her son's heart—and her own.

She was so preoccupied with her own thoughts as they made their way to the car that it took her a while to notice that Dylan's breath was coming in short, shallow gasps. She'd been on high alert all weekend, worried that the excitement and the dust and fumes would trigger a flare-up of his asthma, but he'd been fine—until now. She pulled him out of the crowd and crouched down in front of him. She was conscious of Nate's presence behind her, but she kept her focus on her son. His face was pale and clammy and he coughed weakly.

"Relax," she said, tamping down the anxiety in her own belly to ensure that both her gaze and her voice were steady.

Dylan nodded, but she could read the familiar panic in his eyes.

Her hands were shaking as she opened her purse, locating both the bottle of water that she habitually carried and her son's emergency inhaler. She opened the water first and helped him take a few sips.

"Okay?"

He nodded again. She shook the medication, then removed the cover and passed the inhaler to him. Dylan closed his lips around the mouthpiece and pressed down on the pump.

"Breathe in," she reminded him. "Now hold."

She kept her attention focused on him, waited for his nod.

"Okay—one more," she suggested.

He did as she instructed, taking in a second dose of the medication.

"Is there anything I can do?" Nate asked.

She shook her head. "He's okay now."

Dylan still looked pale, but he was definitely breathing better and he wasn't making that wheezing sound that always made her blood run cold. She'd learned to cope with his asthma—both the daily regimen and the occasional flare-ups—but she still hated to see him suffer, hated even more knowing there was nothing she could really do to help.

He was clinging to her now, almost as if he might not be able to stand up on his own. She picked him up, thankful that he was on the small side for his age—barely four feet tall and not quite fifty pounds. But it wasn't going to be easy for her to carry him the rest of the way to the parking lot.

"Let me take him," Nate offered, obviously having come to the same conclusion.

She felt compelled to protest, because as great as he'd been with Dylan all weekend, her son seemed to prefer the comfort of his mom even over his dad when he was recovering from a flare-up. "Thanks, but—"

Nate didn't let her finish. He just lifted her son out of her arms and into his own. To her surprise, Dylan didn't protest. In fact, he curled an arm around Nate's neck, dropped his head onto his shoulder and closed his eyes.

The unhesitating display of trust and confidence worried her almost as much as her son's labored breathing.

It took them ten more minutes to make the trek to their rental car, another forty to get out of the parking lot, and thirty after that to the airport. The whole while that he was driving, Nate kept checking the rearview mirror to make sure Dylan was okay. His skin was still pale, and he suddenly looked not just younger than his nine years but fragile.

"Are you sure we shouldn't take him to the hospital?" he asked, as he took the turnoff to the airport.

"I'm sure."

"What if he has another attack while we're in the air?"

"He won't," she said. "But if he does, I have his inhaler, and if he did need to go to a hospital, I'd rather it was in Charisma where they have all of his medical records."

He nodded.

Anthony was waiting when they arrived. Having already

completed his preflight check, he announced that they were cleared for takeoff. Dylan was asleep, his head snuggled against his mother's side, almost before the wheels were off the ground.

The asthma attack—or flare-up, as Allison insisted on calling it—had freaked Nate out a little. He'd never seen anything like it before and he didn't think he wanted to again. Listening to the kid struggle for breath, he'd felt useless and helpless…and responsible.

"I'm sorry," he said to Allison now.

She seemed startled by the statement. "Why?"

"Because I didn't think about his asthma. When I made the arrangements for the weekend, I never considered that it would have a negative impact on his health."

"Don't be sorry," she said. "Because I'm not. And I guarantee you that Dylan isn't. In fact, I'm sure he would say that this was 'the *best* weekend *ever*.'"

He managed to smile at that.

"The truth is he might have had a flare-up even if we'd stayed at home this weekend."

"Now you're just trying to make me feel better."

"A little," she admitted. "But it's true. There are some common triggers—cigarette smoke and dust are big ones for Dylan, and he's more susceptible when he gets overexcited. And there are other times when his airways start to close up for no apparent reason."

"How do you stay so calm and unruffled?"

"It's an act," she admitted. "Because I know that I have to stay calm to keep him calm, but seeing him struggle for breath terrifies me—every single time."

Nate shook his head, a wry smile on his face. "You're an amazing mom, Alli."

"I try," she said. "And he makes it easy most of the time."

He hesitated for a moment. "Do you ever think about having more kids?"

She sighed and leaned back in her seat, her hand softly ruffling her son's hair as he slept. "When Dylan was younger, I used to think that it would be nice for him to have a brother or a sister. Now he has two sisters and a brother on his dad's side—" she shrugged "—and that doesn't quite seem to be the big happy family that I always wanted for him."

"What about what *you* want?" he pressed.

She looked away. "I'm old enough to know that I can't always have what I want."

Which didn't really answer his question at all.

Dylan woke up when they landed in Raleigh, then fell asleep again in the car when Nate drove them home. But he was relieved to see that the kid's color was better and he was breathing more normally. And when he lifted Dylan out of the car to carry him up to his apartment, he snuggled against him, and somehow the weight of the little boy in his arms lifted his heart.

Allison pulled back the covers on Dylan's bed so that Nate could put him down. Then she stripped off his shoes and socks, eased him back onto his pillow and pulled the sheet up over him again.

"I guess I should let you crash, too," Nate said, as they tiptoed out of Dylan's room.

She nodded as she walked him to the door. "It was a fabulous weekend but a busy one, and I am exhausted."

So he kissed her goodbye—and wished that she would ask him to stay.

Chapter Thirteen

Monday night, just before dinner, Nate showed up at Allison's apartment with a bag of souvenirs that Dylan had forgotten in the backseat of his car.

"Thank you," Allison said. "Dylan was asking for it as soon as he woke up this morning."

"I should have given it to you at the office," he admitted. "But then I wouldn't have had an excuse to stop by and see him."

"You came to see Dylan?"

"Dylan *and* you," he clarified.

She stepped away from the door so that he could enter. "He's in his bedroom—doing his homework."

"Then he won't catch me stealing a kiss from his mom," Nate said, pulling her close.

She kissed him back, because any pretense of indifference would be nothing more than that. The truth was, she wanted him too much. She wanted him to come in the door at dinnertime every night, to share every meal with her and Dylan, to hang out with her son and sleep with her in her bed. But wanting a real relationship with Nathan was like wanting to hold running water in her hands.

"I think I deserve a lot of credit," he said, when he finally eased his mouth from hers.

"You are very good at that," she told him.

"I wasn't referring to the kiss but my restraint—I've been

wanting to do that all day, but I managed to hold back until now."

"I appreciate your restraint." Though she'd recently begun to accept that many of her coworkers knew she'd been spending a lot of time with her boss outside the office. In the staff room that morning, no fewer than half a dozen people had asked about her trip and, since her weekend plans weren't usually noteworthy, she could only assume that the curiosity was actually about her involvement with Nathan.

He rubbed his lips lightly against hers again. "It was worth the wait."

She stepped out of his arms when the timer sounded on the oven. "I suppose you want to stay for dinner."

"I wouldn't turn down an invitation."

At the racetrack, he'd been a generous and kind friend to Dylan. In the bedroom, he'd been a thoughtful and considerate lover. At the office, he was a demanding but fair employer. She recognized and accepted him in each of those roles. What worried her was that those roles were starting to overlap, and it was getting harder for her to keep their relationship compartmentalized.

Nathan Garrett doesn't do relationships.

It was more than water cooler talk—it was the truth. He was thirty-three years old, and while he was rarely without female companionship, he'd never been married or engaged or even—at least in the four years since he'd moved back to Charisma from New York—had a serious relationship. There had been speculation, when he was dating Mallory, that she might be the one to get him to make a commitment, but it hadn't happened. And when they went their separate ways, no one was really surprised.

He was, everyone said, a love 'em and leave 'em kind of guy. So why was he still hanging around? Why was he being so nice and kind and reliable? Why was he making her think that she could actually depend on him?

These questions plagued her all through dinner. Thankfully, he didn't seem to notice her preoccupation as he and Dylan kept up a steady stream of chatter, recounting their favorite moments from the weekend, speculating on Ren's chances in the next race. She didn't pay much attention to their conversation—not until Dylan mentioned wanting to see a race at Daytona and Nate casually responded that he'd see what he could do. She stood up abruptly and began clearing the table.

Nate offered to help, but she waved him off. She couldn't talk to him right now, because she knew that if she did, she wouldn't be able to hold back her feelings. She was furious with Nate for letting her son hope for something that wouldn't ever happen—and even more furious with herself for hoping it would.

Nate retreated to the living room to play video games with Dylan. Though her son tried to bargain for another half hour, she refused to be swayed. It was a school night and almost his bedtime already. With a disappointed sigh, he said goodnight to Nate—then impulsively wrapped his arms around him in a quick hug before he went to get ready for bed.

Nate, reading her mood, didn't stay. He thanked her for dinner and kissed her goodbye, then he was gone.

She should have been relieved. Instead, she felt confused and ungrateful and—dammit all—sorry that he'd gone. But she pushed those emotions aside and went to tuck Dylan into bed.

He was already snuggled under the covers, thumbing through the pages of the race program he'd brought home from the weekend at Bristol.

Dylan had been passionate about stock car racing long before he ever met Nathan. But before his birthday, it hadn't seemed so real—at least not to Allison. Now that he'd been to an actual race, he was completely obsessed with every aspect of the sport.

"Do you think I could be a crew chief someday?"

"I think you can be whatever you want to be," she told him, because she didn't ever want him to feel as if any dream was out of his reach. And because she was grateful he didn't want to drive the cars around a track at two hundred miles per hour.

He closed the cover of the program and set it aside. "Is Nate your boyfriend now?"

"We're friends," she acknowledged.

"Does he kiss you and stuff?"

Oh Lord—where were these questions coming from? How was she supposed to respond? And what was the "stuff" to which he—at nine years of age—was referring?

"We're friends," she said again. "And Mr. Garrett— Nate—is also my boss, so it wouldn't be a good idea for him to be my boyfriend."

"Why not?"

"Because it would be awkward for us to work together when he stopped being my boyfriend."

Dylan frowned at that. "Why would he stop being your boyfriend?"

"Because sometimes relationships don't work out the way we want them to."

"Like you and Dad," he guessed.

"Yes, like me and your dad," she confirmed.

"But now dad's got Jodie, so you should have someone, too."

"And maybe someday I will."

"Why can't Nate be that someone?" he persisted. "Don't you like him?"

"Yes, I like him," she admitted. *Probably too much.*

"I like him, too."

"I know you do." She pushed his hair away from his face and bent down to touch her lips to his forehead.

"I should have wished for Nate."

"What do you mean?"

"For my birthday—when I made a wish before blowing out the candles. I wished for a Ren D'Alesio jacket, because I didn't really know Nate then. But now I wish that I'd wished for him to be my new dad."

The wistful tone proved to her how much he wanted—needed—a steady and supportive male presence. She knew that Dylan loved his father and that Jefferson returned his affection, but her son needed more than a few hours on Wednesday and every other weekend. And it worried her to realize that he was looking to Nate for that more.

He'd been beyond great the whole time that they were in Tennessee, but that fantasy weekend bore little resemblance to the reality of her life and the daily responsibilities of caring for and raising a child. Nate couldn't have any idea about that because he didn't do commitment, he didn't do long-term, he didn't do relationships. Because she knew all of that, she trusted that she was smart enough not to fall for him.

But her son, basking in the attention of a man who listened to what he had to say and enjoyed spending time with him, didn't know that Nate wouldn't stick around. And she didn't know if she could protect him from the heartache that would follow.

She'd been carrying the letter marked "Personal and Confidential" in her purse for weeks, hoping that John would stop by the office so that she'd have an opportunity to give it to him. Two days after she got back from Tennessee, he finally did.

When he smiled, it was the same warm, familiar smile she'd seen on his face every day for six years. It was a kind face, an honest face and—since the heart attack he'd suffered over the holidays—a weary face.

After a brief meeting with the new CFO, he offered to take Allison for coffee.

"I'm glad you came in today," she said, when she took a seat across from him. "There's something I need to give you."

"What's that?"

She pulled the envelope marked 'Personal and Confidential' out of her purse and handed it to him.

"Oh." He stared at the handwriting on the front for a long minute but made no effort to open it.

"Several envelopes like this have crossed your desk over the years," John noted, "but you've never asked me about them."

"I assumed *Personal and Confidential* meant just that."

He smiled. "But you must have questions."

"Of course," she admitted. "I also know the answers are none of my business."

Truthfully, she didn't want to know the secrets he was alluding to. Though the distinctly feminine handwriting triggered certain suspicions, she wasn't anxious to have those suspicions confirmed.

John lifted his cup to his lips again. "Let's talk about something else," he suggested. "How are things with Nate?"

"He's settled in without any problem," she said.

Her former boss's smile was indulgent. "That's great but not what I was asking."

"Oh?"

"I might be old but I'm not blind, and I can see that there's something between the two of you."

She felt her cheeks flush and dropped her gaze to her cup. "It's not…really…anything."

"He's a good man, Alli. I used to worry about his reputation," John admitted to her now. "One of the reasons I kept putting off my retirement is that I wasn't sure Nate was ready for the responsibility of the corner office.

"I had no doubts about his ability to do the job, but I wondered whether he would be able to balance the professional responsibilities with his personal life. In the past two months, he's grown and matured more than I anticipated, and I suspect that has as much to do with you as the promotion.

"So when you say that whatever is between you and Nate isn't really anything, I hope you're wrong. For both of your sakes."

If his insight had unnerved her, this statement outright baffled her. "I can't imagine that the board would approve of a relationship between the CFO and his executive assistant," she protested.

"No one should have the right to approve or disapprove of a personal relationship between consenting adults," John insisted. "And I promise that no one is going to have any issue with a relationship that is obviously so right for both of you."

Allison appreciated the sentiment, but she wasn't sure she believed it. Especially when she was finishing up her lunch in the staff room later that day and Melanie Hedley took the empty seat beside her.

"I heard that you spent the weekend in Tennessee with Nathan."

Allison hadn't expected that their mutual absence from the office on Friday would go unnoticed, but she was unnerved to realize that news of their getaway had spread so quickly and widely. "My son is a racing fan," she explained. "We went to see the race, and Nate was there, as well."

Melanie unwrapped a prepackaged sandwich from the cafeteria. "Did you have a good time?"

"Yes." She kept her response concise, aware that any information she gave would only serve as grist for the rumor mill.

"I owe you an explanation."

"About what?"

"My trip to Vail over the holidays."

She shook her head. "You don't—"

"I didn't go *with* Nathan," Melanie forged ahead, ignoring Allison's protest. "Not in that sense, anyway. We went to a couple of the same parties and had lunch that one day, but that was it."

"Why are you telling me this?"

"Because I've seen the way he looks at you."

"How does he look at me?" The question slipped out before her brain could still her lips.

Melanie's sigh was wistful. "The way most women only hope a man will look at her."

Allison wanted to believe it was true. More, she wanted to believe it could last. But as much as she enjoyed being with Nathan—and she knew that Dylan did, too—she couldn't help but worry. Because she knew that the more deeply he got involved in their lives, the bigger the void would be when he wasn't there anymore. She had to be prepared for that time—and try to prepare her son for the same eventuality.

The weekend in Tennessee had been a success on a lot of levels. Nate had had the pleasure of rekindling his relationship with Allison, and he'd also gotten to know her son. So he didn't understand why she'd taken not just one but a dozen steps back since they'd returned to Charisma.

He knew that she still believed there were people at the office who were unaware of their personal relationship and, because it seemed important to her, he was playing along. But he was growing increasingly frustrated by her determination to keep him at a distance.

Since Monday, when he'd stopped by her apartment, he hadn't seen her outside the office. They'd talked, via text messages and telephone, but every time he suggested they get together, she turned him down. On Tuesday, she had to help Dylan study for a science test; on Wednesday, Dylan's usual night with his dad, she already had plans to go to a movie with Chelsea; on Thursday, she had to take Mrs. Hanson to the airport, because her elderly neighbor was going to Boston to visit her sister.

On Friday, after they'd finished finalizing his itinerary for an upcoming trip to San Diego, he told her that he was going to his cousin's house that night to help with some minor home repairs.

"But I shouldn't be too late," he said. "And I'd like to come by to see you and Dylan afterward."

"Actually, I was thinking that it might be good for Dylan and I to have some one-on-one time tonight."

Which might have made sense to him if he'd spent every other night of the week with them. But since he hadn't been to her apartment since Monday, the implication of her statement was obvious. "You don't want to see me?"

"I don't want him—or me," she admitted, "to start thinking that hanging out with you on a Friday night is the norm."

"You don't think I'm going to stick," he realized.

"Because you don't," she said gently.

And he couldn't blame her for believing that. Because it was true—or it had been in the past. But with Alli, everything was different. Or maybe it was only different for him.

"Neither of us made any promises—and I'm not asking for any," she continued in the same reasonable tone. "We both know what is and what isn't, but I don't know how to explain it to Dylan, and I don't want him to start thinking it's something that it isn't."

"Do we?" he challenged.

She frowned. "Do we what?"

"Do we both know what is and what isn't?"

"I thought so," she said, just a little warily.

He wanted to push for a more complete answer—to make her define their relationship. But he wasn't sure what he hoped she would say, and he was afraid that he didn't want to hear her answer.

He'd always been careful to ensure that the women he dated didn't have any expectations, so that he was free to walk away without remorse when the relationship was done.

Whether that was a few weeks or a few months, the one constant was that he walked away.

But he didn't want to walk away from Allison and Dylan—not today, not tomorrow and not any time in the foreseeable future. It was the only thing he knew for certain. As for the rest, he honestly didn't have a clue.

Lauryn looked more wary than happy to see Nate and Andrew when they showed up at her door Friday night. On their previous visit, she'd let them hang the shelves in the baby's room but had balked at their offer to help with other tasks. Because he anticipated continued resistance, and because Rachel was working late finishing up the flowers for a wedding the next day, Andrew brought his daughter along.

"This is a surprise," Lauryn said when she opened the door. And though she eyed her adult cousins warily, the little girl got a warm smile and a hug.

"Mommy and I made cookies," Maura told her "aunt," offering the tin she carried.

"What kind of cookies?"

"There's chocolate chip and peanut butter."

"Peanut butter are my favorite," Lauryn admitted.

"We could have some with a glass of milk—cookies are always better with milk," Maura told her.

"That sounds like a great idea," she said, opening the door wider so that they could enter. "But why do I think your dad and Uncle Nate aren't here for milk and cookies?"

"They came to fix your railing," Maura said.

"Did they?"

"Maura—why don't you take those cookies into the kitchen while Uncle Nate and I talk to Aunt Lauryn?" Andrew suggested.

"Okay," the little girl agreed readily.

"You didn't know we were coming?" Nate said to Lauryn.

"Since you didn't call to tell me—and I know I didn't call to ask—how would I know?"

"I saw Rob at the store yesterday," Andrew said, referring to Play On—the local sporting goods store owned by Lauryn's husband. "He said he didn't have the right tools to fix the railing and asked if I could give him a hand because he's worried about you going up and down to the laundry room without something to hold on to."

"Why were you at the store?" Lauryn asked suspiciously.

"Maura wants to play Little League this year so I took her in to get a baseball glove."

"Oh." She still looked skeptical, but Nate could tell that she wanted to believe her husband cared enough to at least express concern, even if he wasn't prepared to do anything about it.

"Go have your cookies with Maura," Nate suggested. "We know where the basement is."

"It smells a little musty down there," she warned. "We had a bit of a leak after all that rain last week."

"There's a sealer you can get for foundation cracks," Andrew told her.

She looked away as she nodded. "Rob said he was going to look into it."

Nate bit his tongue. Her husband had said a lot of things since he'd married her—unfortunately, he had proven time and again that he was all talk and no action.

When she'd gone, he followed his brother down the stairs. "It baffles me that she ever saw anything in him."

"But she obviously did, or she wouldn't have married him."

"And now they're going to have a baby." He knew he should be happy for his cousin, because he knew how much she wanted a family of her own. But he also suspected that she was hoping a child might somehow miraculously fix all of the problems in her marriage, and he didn't see that happening.

"And Lauryn's going to be a great mom." Andrew assessed the wall—shaking his head at the holes where the previous railing had been nailed into the drywall but not secured.

"I have no doubt about that," Nate agreed. "I'm just afraid she'll end up being a single mom."

His brother set his toolbox down on the step. "If she does, she'll handle it."

"I can't imagine it's easy to take care of a baby without any help."

"As if she'd ever be alone in this family."

Nate smiled wryly at that. "Good point."

"Which makes me think that there's someone other than Lauryn on your mind," Andrew noted.

"Alli," he admitted.

His brother's brows lifted. "I heard something about the two of you, but I assumed—based on the conversation we had a few months back—that it was unfounded gossip. Because I know you wouldn't be so foolish and shortsighted as to sleep with your secretary."

"It's not as if we're going at it on her desk," he said. But then, because he knew his older brother had always been a stickler for the rules, he couldn't resist adding, "At least not during business hours."

Andrew shook his head as he released the end of the measuring tape. "And what's going to happen when you decide you've had enough—how are you going to feel about working with her then?"

Because he didn't know—couldn't imagine—he only shrugged. "We'll figure it out."

"Isn't it past time for you to be doing that?"

"What do you mean?"

"You've been seeing her for—how long now?"

Nate shrugged again. "A few months, I guess. On and off."

"That must be a record for you."

"I dated Mallory for almost six months."

"She's a flight attendant who was out of the country more than she was in it during those six months," Andrew reminded him. "That wasn't a relationship—it was a series of one-night stands with the same woman."

He scowled, uncomfortable to realize that his brother's assessment of the relationship was entirely correct.

"But at least she didn't work for you," Andrew pointed out.

"That was one of the reasons Allison didn't want to get involved," Nate admitted. "Actually, she had a lot of reasons she didn't want to get involved."

"Including her son?" his brother guessed.

He nodded.

"I heard you took both of them to Bristol last weekend."

"I did," he confirmed.

"How did that go?"

"Better even than I hoped. Dylan had a great time. Of course, Daniel set us up with complete access, so he got to go inside the garage and tour the hauler and meet Ren and his pit crew."

Andrew sat back on his heels and studied his brother.

"What?" Nate asked warily.

"You've really fallen for her—for both of them."

He scowled. "Just because we had a good time together doesn't mean I'm looking for anything more than that."

"You're right," Andrew agreed. "It was probably a relief to get home at the end of the weekend and dump them off at their place."

"I didn't 'dump them off.'"

"But you must have been happy to get back to the peace and quiet of your own condo. Spending a whole weekend with a woman and her kid must have worn on your nerves."

"Dylan's a good kid."

"So why are you hanging out with me instead of them tonight?"

He shrugged. "Alli said that she wanted to spend some time alone with her son tonight."

"Hmm."

"What does that mean?"

"I guess I was just thinking that maybe her take on the weekend wasn't the same as yours."

"She had a great time."

"I'm sure she did," Andrew placated. "But sometimes spending that much time with one person changes the way you see them."

"What are you suggesting—that she's bored with me?"

"I know that's never happened to you before, but it is a possibility."

"Like hell it is."

Andrew actually laughed.

"I'm glad that you're amused."

"It is kind of funny," his brother insisted. "You've spent the better part of thirty-three years avoiding any kind of committed relationship and now you've finally fallen for a woman who might not want to commit to you."

"I haven't fallen for her," he said, though the denial sounded false even to his own ears.

"You don't think so?"

He wasn't sure what to think. He couldn't deny that he had strong feelings for Allison, but he wasn't ready to put a label on those feelings. "It's a long way from enjoying being with a woman to falling for her."

"It might be a long way, but it's a fast drop," Andrew warned.

"Are you actually going to use that drill or just hold on to it?"

"What's your hurry? It's not like you've got a hot date to rush off to."

The sound of the drill drowned out his pithy reply.

Chapter Fourteen

Allison snatched up the receiver before the first buzz of the intercom had finished sounding.

Even though she'd told Nate not to come, as soon as she'd settled Dylan into bed, she realized how foolish that request had been. He was right—she didn't want to count on him always being there. But while she was trying to protect her heart—and Dylan's—against the disappointment they would inevitably feel when Nate walked away, they were missing out on precious time that they could spend with him.

"Hey, Allison. It's me."

Anticipating Nate's voice, she was disappointed to hear her ex-husband's instead. "What are you doing here, Jeff?"

"I wanted to see you."

"Do you know what time it is?"

"Is it too late?"

"Yes, it's too late," she said, baffled that he even needed to ask the question. "I tucked Dylan into bed more than an hour ago."

"I didn't come to see Dylan."

She couldn't imagine any other reason that he would be there. "Then what are you doing here?"

"I needed someone to talk to."

"Did hell freeze over? Because I can't imagine any other condition under which I would be your first choice for conversation."

"Please, Allison. Let me come up. Just for a minute."

She glanced down at her flannel pajamas and fuzzy slippers, then decided she didn't care. "All right."

She waited at the door, so that he didn't have to knock, and immediately saw that he wasn't entirely steady on his feet.

"You've been drinking," she realized.

"I had a few."

She could smell the yeasty scent of beer on his breath from three feet away. "A few dozen?"

"I don't need you to nag me right now."

"And I don't need a drunk ex-husband at my door, so why don't I call you a cab and send you home to your current wife?" she suggested.

"Don't. Please."

It was the "please" that got to her. Jeff wasn't in the habit of asking for anything, and she wasn't good at saying no. She stepped away from the door so that he could come in. "Did you and Jodie have a fight?"

"Not exactly." He followed her into the kitchen and dropped into a chair while she measured out the grounds to make a pot of coffee.

"Then what—exactly?" she prompted.

"Jodie told me she was pregnant, and I walked out."

Aside from the fact that Jefferson the Fifth wasn't even a year old, she remembered Jeff telling her—after the birth of his second son—that Jodie would finally be satisfied that she now had the boy she always wanted. Apparently, three kids hadn't been enough, and Allison didn't know whether to offer her ex-husband congratulations or condolences.

"We weren't planning on having any more kids," he said. "In fact, I had a vasectomy six weeks ago."

"I'm guessing she's more than six weeks pregnant."

"According to the doctor's calculations, nine weeks and four days."

She handed him a mug of coffee—black—then poured another for herself, adding a splash of cream.

He lifted his cup to his lips when she sat down across from him. "I don't want another kid," he admitted. "And she knew I didn't want another kid."

"She didn't get pregnant on her own," she pointed out.

"She told me she couldn't get pregnant while she was nursing."

"That's a common misconception," she told him.

He seemed to consider that as he continued to sip his coffee. "Do you think she actually believed it?" he finally asked.

"I wouldn't want to speculate as to what she believed, but I know that you'll love this baby as much as you love all of your other kids."

"I'm not feeling so warm and fuzzy toward my wife right now."

"Every marriage has bumps in the road."

He stared into his cup. "Do you ever wonder if we gave up on ours too easily?"

She shook her head. "Our marriage was doomed from the start, because you were still in love with Jodie when you married me."

"I thought I was," he admitted. "But maybe I was wrong."

She got up to put her cup in the sink. He followed, stepping up behind her, trapping her between the counter and his body.

He was Dylan's father, and because of that, she felt a certain amount of affection toward him, a bond through the child they shared. That was why she put her hand on his chest, holding him at a distance instead of knocking him flat on his ass like he deserved.

"Don't do something you'll regret even more than the hangover you're going to have in the morning."

He covered her hand with his own. "We were always good together."

She moved away from him, into the living room, leaving him to stumble after her. "We had a few sparks that fizzled long before our marriage did."

He frowned at her dismissive summary of their shared past. "Are you still dating your boss? Is that why you're acting like this?"

"You can sleep on the sofa," she said, and retrieved a blanket from the chest-style coffee table.

"You didn't answer my question," he told her.

"Because my relationship with Nathan is none of your business."

"Either you're screwing the guy who signs your paychecks or you're not."

"Good night, Jefferson." She threw the blanket at him, then hit the light switch on her way out, plunging the room and him into darkness.

Nate thought about his conversation with Andrew for a long time after they left Lauryn's house that night. His brother seemed to have a knack for asking the hard questions—the ones that Nate had been avoiding for too long.

He cared for Allison—there was no denying that. And while he'd been unwilling to put a label on his feelings or quantify his affection for her, he knew it was safe to say that his feelings for her went deeper than anything he'd ever felt for another woman. But was that love?

She'd become an integral part of his life—and not just because he saw her every day at the office. She was the first person he thought of when he had good news to share, the last person he wanted to talk to before he went to sleep at night and the only person he could imagine sharing every part of his life for the rest of his life. And that was a scary realization for a man who had spent the better part of his thirty-three years carefully avoiding any discussion of the future or long-term with respect to his personal relationships.

He wasn't prone to melodrama, so he would never say that he couldn't live without her. But he didn't want to live without her. When he imagined his life without Allison and Dylan in it, it was empty and lonely.

The challenge now was going to be convincing Allison that his feelings for her were real.

It was almost too easy to picture a future for the three of them together. And it wasn't outside the realm of possibility to think that they might want to expand their family with another child or two someday. Not that he was in any hurry to have a baby with Allison—he wanted to spend time with her and Dylan first—but the prospect didn't completely terrify him. In fact, he kind of liked the idea.

No one had ever accused him of being particularly sensitive or insightful, but over the past few months he'd noticed something about Allison. Whenever they were out anywhere together and she saw a family—a man and a woman with a child or children—her attention would shift and her expression would grow wistful. He knew that she'd lost both of her parents when she was young, and he suspected that what she really wanted was a family—for her son and for herself.

He'd been fortunate to be raised by two parents who loved their children and each other. And while he was happy that both of his brothers had fallen in love and chosen to follow the path of holy matrimony, he hadn't been eager to do the same. His mother insisted he would change his mind when he met the right woman. His sister-in-law, Kenna, liked to tease that he was so accustomed to women falling all over him, he wouldn't recognize the right one if she hit him over the head with a two-by-four.

Nate had suspected that might be true—until he kissed Allison at the Christmas party. From that moment, he hadn't been able to get her out of his mind, and while it had taken him a while, he now knew that she was the woman he wanted for the rest of his life. Now he had to convince her of the same thing.

With only the first inkling of a plan sketched out in his mind, he stopped at the Morning Glory Café and picked up an assortment of muffins before heading to Alli's apartment.

She buzzed him up, but it was Dylan who met him at the door.

"Nate!" Dylan's shyness seemed to be a thing of the past, at least so far as Nate was concerned. And it tickled him to no end the way the kid's whole face lit up when he saw him. Or maybe it was the bakery box in his hand that was responsible for his obvious pleasure. "Doughnuts?"

Nate offered him the box. "I don't know how your mom feels about dessert for breakfast, but I don't know anyone who doesn't like doughnuts."

"I love doughnuts—'specially chocolate ones."

"I'm sure there're one or two chocolate ones in there."

"You didn't say anything about stopping by this morning," Allison said.

He watched as Dylan disappeared into the kitchen with his breakfast, then drew her into his arms. "I wanted to surprise you."

"Well, you succeeded."

He lowered his mouth to hers, kissed her long and slow and deep. "Good morning."

She smiled at him, that soft half smile that never failed to tug at his heart. "It is now."

And then a man walked into the room.

A man who, judging by his unshaven jaw and heavy-lidded eyes, had just woken up. He scrubbed a hand over his face. "What time is it?" he asked in a gravelly voice.

"Almost ten," Allison told him.

"Jodie's going to kill me."

"Probably," she acknowledged. "But I did call her last night, to let her know that you were here."

He nodded. "Thanks for that. And for letting me crash."

"Maybe you could say hello to your son before you head home," she suggested.

The "son" confirmed Nate's suspicions that the man was Jefferson Caldwell the Fourth.

"Is he up?" Dylan's father asked.

"In the kitchen."

He moved in that direction.

Nate watched him go, then turned to Allison, a little less confused now but more than a little livid. "What the hell is your ex-husband doing here?" he demanded.

"He slept on the sofa last night," she admitted.

"Why?"

"Because, only a few months after agreeing that they weren't going to have any more kids, he found out that his wife is pregnant with their fourth child."

"What does that have to do with you?"

"Nothing," she admitted. "But he was angry and upset and he went on a bit of a bender and ended up at my door— what was I supposed to do?"

"Pour him into a cab and send him home," Nate suggested.

"He's Dylan's father," she reminded him.

"And who am I?" he demanded. "What is my role in your life?"

She eyed him warily. "Why are you doing this? Why now?"

"Because I deserve to know where I stand with you. Because every time I think we've taken one step forward, you take two steps back. I wanted to see you last night," he reminded her. "But you wanted some space. And I gave it to you—only to find out that you spent the night with your ex-husband."

"You're completely misinterpreting the situation."

"Maybe I am," he admitted. "But sofa or not—I don't want you letting him sleep here again."

"I don't care what you want," she shot back. "I might have to take orders from you in the office, but that's where it begins and ends."

"I'm not giving you orders—I'm trying to set some parameters for our relationship."

"We don't have a relationship. We just sleep together on occasion."

He stared at her for a long minute. "Is that what you really think?"

"You've never given any indication of anything more than that."

"Then you haven't been paying attention, honey, because while you were sleeping with me, I was falling in love with you."

She took a step back, stunned.

"Yeah—it caught me off guard, too," he admitted. "I certainly never planned for this to happen, and I definitely never planned to tell you like that, but there it is. And now that you know how I feel, we can finally move forward."

"But…you don't do relationships."

"I didn't think so, either, but we've started to build a pretty good one—you, me and Dylan."

The inclusion of her son—without any hesitation—filled her heart to overflowing. But that was a purely emotional response, and she couldn't afford to let her heart rule her head. She needed to be logical—and she needed Nate to be logical, too.

"Or maybe you just want what both of your brothers have," she suggested. "And with me and Dylan, you get the whole package."

"If you really believe that, you're not giving either you or your son enough credit," he admonished. "I love you, Alli. What's between us is more than I expected—more than I ever thought I wanted. But now that I've found it, found you, you should know that I have no intention of letting you go."

She hadn't expected this, didn't know how to respond. Her head was spinning even as her heart was leaping for joy. She wanted to believe him, to let herself hope, but she didn't understand what had changed, why he apparently wanted something he'd never wanted before. And how could she know what she wanted when she'd never considered that a future with Nate was a possibility? "What about what I want?"

He smiled. "We both want the same thing—you just haven't realized it yet."

"You think you know my mind better than I do?"

"No, but I know your heart."

"I don't even know my heart," she protested.

"Yes, you do—you're just afraid to acknowledge what you're feeling."

Her chin lifted. "I'm not afraid."

"Good. Go get dressed and I'll give you a chance to prove it."

She should have asked where they were going. Ordinarily, she would have pressed for details, but the whole declaration-of-love thing had made her head spin so that she could barely form coherent thoughts. When he'd told her to get dressed, she went to get dressed because she needed some time to process what he'd said.

I was falling in love with you.

Could she believe it? Did she dare even let herself hope it might be true?

Jeff hadn't broken her heart, but he'd broken her trust. When they'd exchanged vows, she'd intended to honor them. She hadn't expected to fall madly in love and live happily ever after, but she'd thought that they both wanted the same thing: a family for their son. And she'd believed they were both invested enough in that dream to do everything in their power to make it happen. When her husband told her that he was still in love with Jodie, she hadn't been angry or even hurt so much as disappointed.

"Haven't you ever loved somebody so much you just couldn't imagine your life without him?"

"I guess I haven't," she admitted.

"Well, someday you will, and when you do, you'll understand why I can't be with you when I'm in love with someone else."

"But...what about Dylan?"

"He'll always be my son."

"But we were supposed to be his family. Forever."

And she'd wanted that for her son. And for herself. Losing both of her parents had left an enormous void in her life—a void she'd been desperate to fill. Marrying Jeff and having his baby had finally begun to do that, had given her the illusion that they were a family—at least for a while.

She hadn't been looking for the head-over-heels kind of love that he claimed to share with Jodie. She wasn't even sure she believed it existed. But now, with Nate, she thought she was finally beginning to understand.

She was so preoccupied with her own thoughts she didn't worry about where they were going. In fact, it wasn't until he pulled into the long driveway leading to an old farmhouse that had obviously been added on to and renovated numerous times that uneasiness settled in her belly like a ball of lead.

"Where are we?"

"My parents' house."

"Why are we here?" Dylan piped up from the backseat.

"Because I wanted you and your mom to meet my family," Nate told him.

The explanation seemed to satisfy Dylan, but it only raised more questions in Allison's mind. Because she, of course, had met his parents before. In fact, she'd met most of his extended family. But those introductions had occurred when she was behind a desk at Garrett Furniture or at a company event.

Which was one of the reasons she felt so awkward now. She hadn't wanted her relationship with Nate to become office gossip, though she'd been powerless to prevent it. And even so, she'd suffered no negative repercussions. In fact, most of her coworkers seemed not just to accept but approve of the relationship. But his parents were a whole other story—and she had no idea how they would react to the news that their son was involved with his executive assistant.

Jane Garrett was watering the planters on her front porch when Nate pulled into the driveway, but she set the can down on the step and came to greet them.

"This is a pleasant surprise," she said, sounding more pleased than surprised.

"You remember Allison Caldwell, Mom?"

"Of course," she said, smiling at Allison. "It's wonderful to see you again."

"And this is her son, Dylan," Nate said.

"It's a pleasure to meet you, Dylan."

He looked hesitantly at his mom. "Thank you?"

"Your dad's around back with Maura," Jane said. "Why don't we go join them?"

They found David Garrett playing catch with his granddaughter.

"Spring training," he explained, waving to them from a distance. "Maura has decided she wants to play the hot corner this season, so she's got to work on making the throw from third to first."

Dylan watched them, undisguised yearning on his face.

"Do you want to play?" Jane asked him.

"I don't have a glove."

"We have a whole box of gloves in the garage," she told him. "Why don't you let Nate show you where they are so you can find one that fits?"

Allison expected him to refuse, to want to stay with his mom more than he wanted to play catch.

But when Nate said, "Come on," her son willingly fell into step behind him.

She watched them walk away, worried that Dylan was already so attached to Nate, he was willing to follow wherever he led.

"Can I get you something to drink?" Jane asked. "We've got lemonade and sweet tea, and I'll put a pot of coffee on, because I'm sure that's what Nate'll want."

"Coffee sounds good," Allison agreed.

She followed Nate's mom into the house.

"What did my son do to put that worried look on your face?" Jane asked, as she set the coffeemaker to brew.

"I really shouldn't play poker, should I?"

The older woman chuckled. "No, you definitely should not."

"I think I'm more confused than worried," Allison admitted.

"Men do have a way of muddling up the simplest things," Jane said. "Maybe I can help you figure it out?"

She had to smile at the woman's not-so-subtle prying. "I'm not sure I'd even know where to begin," she hedged.

Jane got out a sugar bowl and matching pitcher, which she filled with cream, then set both on a serving tray.

"I don't know what Nate has told you," Allison said hesitantly.

"He hasn't told me anything," Jane admitted, adding mugs to the tray. "But the fact that he brought you and your son here says it all for him."

"You might be making a bigger deal out of this than it is," Allison said, a warning to Nate's mother as much as herself.

"Falling in love is scary," Jane said. "Opening up your heart to someone else is always a risk. I'd say that falling in love with a Garrett goes beyond scary to downright terrifying, because none of them do anything by half measures.

"They demand one hundred percent—but they give one hundred percent, too. I'd almost abandoned hope that Nathan would find a woman he could love completely and forever, but I'm glad to see that he didn't." The coffee had finished brewing, and she added the carafe to the tray. "The only question unanswered is whether you can love him the same way."

Chapter Fifteen

They stayed for lunch, because Jane insisted. And Jane and David were both so natural and easygoing, it wasn't nearly as awkward as Allison had feared it might be. But she was still relieved when the meal was over and it was time to go, because she needed to think about Jane's question—and she needed to be sure that her answer wouldn't be unduly influenced by the presence of Nathan's wonderful family. Dylan, on the other hand, was obviously reluctant to leave and he held tight to Nathan's mom when he said goodbye.

Dylan had grandparents—Jeff's mom and dad—but he didn't see them very often and they'd never been overly affectionate with their eldest grandson. By contrast, David Garrett had talked to him like an equal, and he'd listened to what Dylan had to say. Not that he said much—after all, he'd only met the man a few hours earlier—but he did talk a little bit about baseball and stock car racing and what kind of condiments made the best burgers. And Jane Garrett had made no secret of the fact that she adored him from the get-go. She offered him food and drink and, after the burgers were gone, homemade chocolate chip cookies.

Then, as they were leaving, Jane had hugged Allison, too. It had been a long time since Allison had known the comfort of a maternal embrace, and although she didn't cling, as her son had done, she wanted to. She wanted to be part of Nate's warm and wonderful family, and it was exactly that wanting that she knew could be dangerous.

* * *

When they got back to the apartment, Allison gave her son permission to play video games because she didn't want him overhearing the conversation that she needed to have with Nathan.

When the sound from the living room confirmed that Dylan's attention was otherwise engaged, Nate said, "Are you going to tell me what I did wrong?"

"I can't believe you even have to ask."

"Was spending a few hours with my parents so horrible?"

"It wasn't horrible at all," she admitted. "Your parents are wonderful people."

"I'm glad you think so," he said. "Because they said the same thing about you and Dylan."

"I just feel like I was…ambushed."

"How do you figure?"

"Because you had to know that taking me—and my son—to meet your parents would make them speculate about our relationship."

"What I know," he told her, "is that it's traditional for a man to take the woman he wants to marry home to meet his parents."

"Ohmygod." She sat down, hard, because her legs were about to go out from under her.

"Was that a good or a bad 'ohmygod'?"

"I don't know."

"It's true," he said. "I want to be your husband and Dylan's stepfather. I want a life with both of you."

She swallowed. "And when did you come to this realization?"

"Last night. About two minutes after I figured out that I loved you. And I do—I love you, Alli."

Those simple words, sincerely spoken, made her heart stutter. She couldn't battle against him and her own desires, but she was still afraid to admit how much she wanted everything he was offering.

"I've never said those words to another woman," he admitted.

"And that's another point."

"What's another point?"

"You've dated half the female population in this town—"

"I'm not going to apologize for the fact that there were other women before you."

"I'm not asking for an apology," she told him.

He looked frustrated. "You just want to keep throwing them up in my face."

"I just don't understand why you think you want a future with me when you've never even had a long-term relationship before."

"I'd say the obvious and simplest explanation is that none of those other women was you."

She blew out a breath as her heart stuttered again. "It scares me," she admitted, "that you always seem to know just what to say to make me want to believe you."

"I love you, Alli. I've never said those words to another woman because I've never felt this way before, and if you believe nothing else, please believe that."

"I don't know what I'm feeling," she admitted. "I've tried so hard not to fall for you, because I was sure that if I did, you'd break my heart."

He took her hands. "I promise, if you give me your heart, I will only cherish and protect it—for now and forever."

She wanted to believe him. She wasn't sure she'd ever wanted anything more than she wanted to believe him. But he was Nathan Garrett—perennial playboy. How could she trust what he was saying? How could she trust that what he wanted today would still be what he wanted tomorrow?

But wasn't not knowing the very definition of trust? Could she give him the benefit of the doubt? Take a leap of faith? She wanted to—but there was more than her own heart at risk. She had to think of her son, whose heart was so much more vulnerable and fragile than her own.

He'd been so young when his parents separated that he had no memories—good or bad—of their time together. But he was already attached to Nate, and she worried that if things didn't work out for them, her son would be devastated.

But what if things did *work out?*

Then Dylan would finally have the full-time family she'd always wanted for him—and for herself.

Nate could tell that her resistance was weakening. Her eyes, always so expressive, swirled with emotion.

"It doesn't make any sense to me," she admitted. "How can you go from casual to committed in the blink of an eye?"

"It wasn't in the blink of an eye," he denied. "And my feelings were never as casual as you apparently believed."

She nibbled on her lower lip.

"I don't know why it's you—I only know that it is. You're *it* for me. You and Dylan. I want to share my life with you, build a family together. I want to be with you—both of you—today, tomorrow and always.

"I…"

Whatever she'd intended to say was cut off by Dylan's entrance into the kitchen. Apparently he'd grown bored with video games, as he now carried the glove and ball that David Garrett had let him bring home.

"Can we go to the park?" he asked hopefully.

"Can you give us a few more minutes, buddy?" Nate asked. "Your mom and I are in the middle of something."

Allison shook her head. "No—go to the park. Please. I need some time alone to think about this."

"*We* need to talk about it," he insisted, reluctant to leave her alone with her thoughts when he knew she would think of all kinds of reasons to back away from him again.

"I can't talk about it right now," she told him.

So he walked over to the park with Dylan, confident that the boy, at least, was in his corner.

He knew he'd caught Allison off guard when he told her he loved her, and he hadn't expected a reciprocal declaration—although he'd hoped. After all, it was the first time he'd ever said the words to a woman, and it would have been nice to hear her confirm that she felt the same way.

And he was pretty sure that she did. When he touched her, when he kissed her, she couldn't hide her feelings for him. But apparently she wasn't yet ready to admit them, either.

So he decided that he could give her time, but he wasn't going to give up.

"Are you and my mom fighting?" Dylan's tentative question pulled him out of his reverie.

"Did it sound like we were fighting?"

The boy shrugged. "She sounded like she sounds when she's trying not to yell at me."

"Your mom's a little annoyed with me," he admitted.

There weren't many people in the park today—a couple of kids flying kites, a teenager walking a dog, a mom with a baby in a stroller, an older couple down by the pond, feeding pieces of bread to the ducks.

"Are you gonna marry her?"

"Where did you hear that?" he asked cautiously.

"Maura told me she's never met anyone you dated before, so it probably means you're gonna marry my mom."

"That's the plan," he admitted. "If I can get her to go along with it."

Dylan sighed. "Good luck with that."

"You don't think I can persuade her?"

"Did she say 'we'll see'? 'Cause if she said 'we'll see,' she meant 'no.'"

Nate smiled at that. "She said she needed some time to think about it."

"That doesn't sound very promising," the boy warned.

"Well, I'm not going to give up."

"How come?"

"Because when you love someone, you don't walk away."

"You love my mom?"

"Yeah," he said. "And I happen to think her son's pretty terrific, too."

"Her…oh, me," Dylan realized, and offered a shy smile.

Nate tapped the brim of the boy's baseball cap. "I know it's been just you and your mom for a long time. Are you okay with the idea of a stepdad?"

The boy hesitated, and Nate's breath backed up in his lungs as he waited for a reply. It occurred to him then that he might have assumed too much—not just about Allison's feelings but Dylan's. After all, the boy already had a father—it was possible that he had no interest in what Nate was offering. It was possible that neither Allison nor her son needed him as much as he'd realized he needed them.

Dylan looked up at him. "I think so," he finally responded in a solemn tone. "If it was you."

And Nate's breath whooshed out of his lungs. "Okay, then," he said, striving to keep his tone light. "Let's play ball."

When the intercom buzzed only a few minutes after Nate and Dylan had gone, Allison assumed they'd forgotten something. When she realized it was Chelsea in the lobby, she was only too happy for her friend's company.

"Look what I found at the flea market." She held up a *Racing World* magazine with Ren D'Alesio on the cover. "It's near mint condition, from his rookie season, when he was still with Team D'Alesio."

"That's…great."

Chelsea rolled her eyes at the lackluster response. "Dylan will love it."

"I'm sure he will," she agreed. "But he's at the park with Nate right now."

At home in Allison's apartment, Chelsea went to the fridge and found a pitcher of sweet tea, poured herself a glass. "I thought you weren't going to see him this weekend."

"Apparently he had a different idea."

"Do you want a glass of this—" Chelsea held up the pitcher "—or do you need something stronger?"

Allison shook her head. "I'm fine." Then she sighed. "No, I'm not fine. But I'm not thirsty."

"What happened?"

"He took me and Dylan to his parents' house today."

"Oh. Wow. That's a pretty big step."

"A leap," Allison agreed. "But that's not even the biggest one."

"So tell me."

"Apparently he had some time to think last night, and he realized that he loves me and Dylan and wants to marry me so that the three of us can be a family."

Her friend's eyes got misty. "That is so…perfect."

"I didn't say yes."

Chelsea narrowed her gaze. "You better not have said no."

"I didn't know what to say. I've been so busy telling myself that this wasn't—couldn't be—a real relationship, that I didn't see it coming. How could I?"

"Honey, even I could see that he was heading in this direction."

"Another man—maybe," Allison allowed. "But this is Nathan Garrett—the guy who's never committed to a future any farther away than breakfast the morning after."

"Because he was waiting for the right woman," Chelsea told her.

"And what if I'm not the right woman?"

"He seems to think you are."

"How can he know when he has no experience with relationships?"

"Would you feel better if he had a failed marriage—or at least a broken engagement—in his past?"

"Maybe," she admitted.

"Do you know how crazy that sounds?"

She nodded.

"Which is usually a sure sign that you're head over heels crazy in love," Chelsea warned.

"I've never been all the way in love before," she confided.

"I know."

"He could break my heart."

"That's always a risk," her friend agreed. "But I don't think he will. I think he's the man who can finally give you the family you've always wanted, be the dad that Dylan deserves and the man who makes you happy for the rest of your life."

"When did you join the Nate Garrett fan club?"

"When I saw the sparkle come back into your eyes."

Allison pouted. "I thought you'd be on my side."

"I am. Always. But I'm sorry if I can't sympathize with the fact that there's a gorgeous, sexy, charming and very rich man who wants to be part of your life and had the audacity to take you to meet his parents and mention the possibility of marriage."

"Are you trying to make me feel ridiculous?"

"Is it working?"

"Yes," she admitted.

Chelsea grinned. "Good."

The ball diamond was empty, so they took up positions on the infield and began to toss the ball back and forth.

Dylan had a great arm, but he needed to work on his catching. He often closed his hand before the ball was in the pocket, which meant that the ball bounced off the glove and rolled away. But the kid had potential, and Nate thought it would be fun to work with him—maybe even coach him in Little League someday.

After about fifteen minutes, Nate noticed that Dylan was slowing down—hesitating before he threw the ball back and not rushing to retrieve it when he missed.

"You getting bored?" Nate asked him.

Dylan shook his head. But when he bent down to pick up the ball, he started to cough. And instead of throwing it back, he clutched it against his chest.

Something about his posture set off warning bells in Nate's mind. He jogged toward the boy, heard the wheezing as he expelled air from his lungs, his breathing obviously labored. He immediately recalled the flare-up he'd witnessed when they were leaving Bristol. But Allison had been there then, not just to recognize the signs but to help administer the medication.

Nate dropped to his knees beside the boy and tried to remember what she'd done. He picked him up and carried him to the player's bench, sitting him down and urging him to keep his back straight and take slow, deep breaths in through his nose.

"Do you have your inhaler?"

The boy nodded again and reached into his pocket, and Nate exhaled a shuddery sigh of relief. He took the device from Dylan and shook it vigorously, as he remembered seeing Allison do.

"It's okay, buddy. Just relax and get some of this medication into your lungs."

He knew that the panic that went hand in hand with an attack inevitably made the situation worse, so he tried to keep his voice level so the boy wouldn't realize how close Nate was to panicking himself.

Dylan put the inhaler in his mouth, pushed down on the

pump and drew in a slow, deep breath. Then he coughed again and shook his head.

"What's wrong?"

He tried the pump again, then tossed the inhaler aside.

"Emp-ty," he said, as a single tear slid down his cheek.

Empty?

It was the perfect word to describe the hollow feeling in Nate's chest. He already had his phone in his hand, intending to call Allison.

He dialed 9-1-1 instead.

Allison was grateful that Chelsea was still with her when Nate called.

Since he'd only gone across the street to the park with Dylan, she immediately knew that something was wrong.

"What happened?"

"Dylan had an asthma attack."

"Bad?"

"I don't know," he admitted. "We're at Mercy—"

"I'm on my way."

She didn't protest when her friend took the keys out of her shaking fingers. They'd made this trip several times before, although the last time had been more than a year earlier.

"Don't let him see how worried you are," Chelsea reminded Allison as they walked through the ER doors together.

"I know."

"And try not to jump all over Nate before he has a chance to tell you what happened."

"What happened is that I let them go to the park without me. No—I didn't just let them, I practically shoved them out the door. I was so preoccupied, I didn't think—"

"You can't be with Dylan every minute of every day," Chelsea interjected gently.

"I should have been there," she insisted.

"Nate was there."

"Nate's not his father."

"You're right." It was Nathan himself who responded to her statement. "I have no legal connection to Dylan or you—but I love him anyway, and I'm going crazy because none of the doctors or nurses will tell me anything because I'm not family. So maybe you can get some information from them."

She refused to feel guilty for speaking the truth, for putting that wounded look on his face. And while she did intend to talk to the doctor, she wanted some information from Nate first.

"Why didn't he use his rescue inhaler?" she asked him.

"He tried. I think it was empty."

"Empty?" Her eyes filled with tears. "Dammit, Nate."

"I didn't know," he said. "I'm so sorry, Alli."

She just shook her head. "Where is he?"

"They took him into an exam room—"

She pushed past him and rushed toward the nurses' desk, with Chelsea on her heels.

Allison's best friend had always seemed a little guarded around him, so Nate was surprised when Chelsea came out to the waiting room and sat down beside him.

"Alli's in mama bear mode right now," Chelsea said. "Don't take anything she says personally."

He nodded, but he knew that everything her friend had said was true. He'd been irresponsible. Allison had trusted him with her son, and now Dylan was in the hospital.

"It was an asthma attack—and hardly his first one."

"I thought—" He looked away but he didn't dare close his eyes, because every time he did, he saw the fear and panic on the little boy's face as he fought to draw air into his lungs. "I was terrified—I didn't know what I was going to do if the ambulance didn't get there on time."

"It is terrifying, especially the first time, because there's nothing really you can do. If the inhaler doesn't work or if he doesn't have it—and yes, I was with him once when that happened—the next step is to seek medical attention."

"Have you been through this more than once with him?"

"So many times I lost count," she admitted.

"I can't imagine."

"You aren't responsible for what happened."

"While I appreciate the sentiment, I'm not sure I agree. And it's obvious that Alli doesn't."

"It's hard for a parent to be rational when their child is hurting."

He just nodded.

"He's going to be fine," Chelsea said. "He's been given a reliever medication as well as an oral steroid and is already responding to treatment. Dr. Roberts said his heart rate and blood pressure are good, and his breathing is improving."

He nodded again.

She stretched her legs out in front of her and crossed her feet at the ankles, obviously settling in for a long wait. "Do you have a ring?"

The abrupt change of topic caught him off guard. "What?"

"If you expect Allison to take your proposal seriously, you need a ring. Otherwise it seems like an impulse—and one she might think you'll later regret."

"I don't have a ring yet," he admitted. "I was planning to take Dylan with me to pick one out, so that he knows he's a part of it, too."

"Oh." Chelsea's eyes filled with tears. "That's good. She'll love that."

Nate could only hope that she was right.

While Nate was talking to Chelsea, Allison was on the phone with her ex-husband.

She knew their son was going to be fine, but she also knew that if the incident had happened when Dylan was in his father's care, she'd want to know about it. Of course, Jeff was a veteran of ER visits, so he asked all the usual questions and she reassured him that Dylan was okay—and now that she'd seen her son, she was willing to believe it. Jeff opted not to make the trip to the hospital but promised that he would stop by to see Dylan the next day.

After she hung up with Jeff, she went to find Chelsea, surprised to find Nathan was still in the waiting room, too.

Nate's not his father.

The words she'd practically snapped out at her friend echoed in the back of her mind. Maybe she'd spoken the truth, but her tone had been angry and accusatory, and though she hadn't intended to hurt Nathan, she couldn't deny that had been the result. Another truth was that Nathan had given her son more time and attention over the past month than the man who'd contributed to his DNA. Even now, even after the way she'd treated him, even while Jeff was at home with his new family, Nate was still there, pacing the waiting room and worrying about her son.

He can be the dad that Dylan deserves.

As Chelsea's words echoed in the back of her mind, Allison realized that he already was. In so many ways, he'd proven not only that he was capable of making a commitment, but he'd done so. She'd just refused to see it.

She'd been on her own for so long with Dylan, so accustomed to doing things on her own, that she wasn't sure she knew how to share her life. But she wanted to share it with Nate, if that was what he still wanted, too.

Chelsea spotted her first. "Any update?"

"Everything's good. Dr. Roberts just wants to keep an eye on him for another hour or so to make sure, but he figures we can go home after that."

"That's great," Chelsea said. "I'm just going to go in to say goodbye to him before I head home to get ready for work."

"You don't have your car," Allison said.

"I'll catch a cab."

Her friend kissed her cheek and walked out, leaving Allison alone with Nate. Well, alone with Nate and the half dozen other people who were waiting for medical attention.

"Do you want to see him?" she finally asked.

He nodded.

She turned and led the way, pulling back the curtain of an exam cubicle where Dylan was asleep on the bed. Nate hovered just inside the curtain, looking worried.

"He's fine," Allison assured him. "These episodes just wear him out."

She sat on a hard plastic chair beside the bed and reached for Dylan's hand. His eyelids flickered but didn't open. Nate took the chair on the other side of her.

"I owe you an apology," she said quietly.

"No, you don't," he denied.

But she nodded. "I blamed you because it was easier than accepting my own responsibility for what happened. I *never* let Dylan go anywhere without making sure that he has his inhaler with him. But I was distracted and confused—"

"That was my fault, too."

She shook her head. "None of this is your fault. You called 9-1-1. You kept him calm until the ambulance got there. You stayed with him, so that he wasn't alone."

"He wouldn't have needed the ambulance if I'd made sure he had a working inhaler before we left the apartment."

"Next time you will."

He looked at her hopefully. "You're going to let there be a next time?"

She managed a wry smile. "If all of the drama hasn't completely scared you off."

"I was terrified," he admitted. "But I'm not going anywhere. Like I told Dylan earlier—when you love someone, you don't walk away." He took her free hand, linked their fingers together. "And I'm not walking away from either of you."

She looked at their joined hands for a long minute, grateful not just for his support and his strength but for everything he'd added to her life just by being part of it. "I'm glad, because I love you, too," she finally admitted.

"Enough to marry me?"

Her eyes filled with tears. "Are you really proposing to me in a hospital cubicle?"

"I know you deserve candlelight and flowers. And a ring—Chelsea told me that I should have a ring. But I don't want to wait any longer." He released her hand and dropped to one knee beside her chair. "Allison Caldwell, will you marry me?"

"The where and the how don't matter," she assured him. "Only the who—and since you're the man I love, I want to say yes, but I need to talk to Dylan about this first."

"Say yes," Dylan said.

She turned to see that her son was now wide awake and grinning. "Don't you think we should talk about this?"

"Nah. Nate and I already talked—it's good."

He said it so simply, and with so much confidence, she knew it *was* good. And that it was going to get even better.

"Still on my knee here," Nathan reminded her. "Waiting for an answer."

"The answer is yes," she told him. "Definitely yes."

He stood up and lifted her into his arms, holding her tight, as if he wasn't ever going to let her go.

"I guess our relationship won't be a secret at work now," she noted.

He chuckled. "You're the only one who ever thought it was."

"Since it's not, do I get a ring?"

"As long as I get you and Dylan, you can have whatever you want."

"You." She touched her lips to his. "I want you."

"You've got me," he promised. "For now and forever."

* * * * *

Resolutely Polly held the glass up over the man's face and tipped it. A perfect stream of cold water fell like rain onto the peacefully slumbering face below.

Polly didn't quite know what to expect: anger, shock, contrition, or even no reaction at all. He was so very deeply asleep after all. But what she *didn't* expect was for one eye to open lazily, for a smile to play around the disturbingly well-cut mouth, or for a hand to shoot out and grab her wrist.

Caught by surprise, she stumbled forward, falling against the chaise as that hand sneaked around her waist, pulling her down, pulling her close.

"Bonjour, chérie."

His voice was low, gravelly with sleep, and deeply, unmistakably French.

"If you wanted me to wake up you only had to ask."

"What do you think you're doing?"

"Saying *au revoir,* of course."

He had shifted position and was leaning against the back of the chaise, his eyes skimming every inch of her until she wanted to wrap her arms around her torso, shielding herself from his insolent gaze.

"Au revoir?"

"Of course." He raised an eyebrow. "As you are dressed to leave I thought you were saying goodbye. But if it was more of a good morning…" the smile widened "…even better."

"I am not saying *au revoir,* or good morning, or anything but *What on earth are you doing in my office and where are your clothes?"*

THE HEIRESS'S
SECRET BABY

BY
JESSICA GILMORE

Published in Great Britain 2015
by Mills & Boon, an imprint of Harlequin (UK) Limited,
Eton House, 18-24 Paradise Road, Richmond, Surrey, TW9 1SR

© 2015 Jessica Gilmore

ISBN: 978-0-263-25110-4

23-0215

Harlequin (UK) Limited's policy is to use papers that are natural, renewable and recyclable products and made from wood grown in sustainable forests. The logging and manufacturing processes conform to the legal environmental regulations of the country of origin.

Printed and bound in Spain
by CPI, Barcelona

An ex au-pair, bookseller, marketing manager and sea-front trader, **Jessica Gilmore** now works for an environmental charity in York. Married with one daughter, one fluffy dog and two dog-loathing cats, she spends her time avoiding housework and can usually be found with her nose in a book. Jessica writes emotional romance with a hint of humour, a splash of sunshine and a great deal of delicious food—and equally delicious heroes.

For Jo M

It seems pretty fitting that a book with a Parisian setting is dedicated to you just as we plan our girls' trip to Paris! I'm not sure how you have managed to be so positive and supportive and brilliant during the past five years; I am completely in awe of your strength. Thank you so much for being such a fantastic friend to me and an inspiration (and ever-patient hairstylist) to Abs.

Here's to Paris and most of all to medical advances and to a happy, healthy future xxx

CHAPTER ONE

My Secret Bucket List

~~Swim in the sea, naked~~
~~NB: in azure warm seas, not in the North Sea~~
~~Sleep out under the stars~~
~~Have sex on the beach~~
~~NB: the real deal, not the cocktail~~
~~Drink an authentic margarita~~
Fall in love in Paris

POLLY READ THE list through for the last time, feeling the carefree *joie de vivre* fall away and the old, familiar cloaks of respectability and responsibility settling back onto her shoulders. They were a little heavy, but maybe that was to be expected after three months away.

Three months, five wishes. And she'd achieved four out of the five, which wasn't bad going. The heaviness lifted for a second as the highlights of the last three months flashed through her mind and then it descended again.

What had she been thinking? She might as well have written the list in a silver pen and decorated it with pink love hearts and butterflies, pinning it on her wall next to a lipstick-kiss-covered poster of a pre-pubescent boy band.

Polly pulled the page out of her diary and, without allowing herself a second's pause to reconsider, tore it into pieces. It was time to reposition her three-month sabbatical into something more appropriate for the new CEO of a company with a multimillion-pound turnover.

She chewed on the end of her pen for a moment and then started a new list.

My Bucket List

~~Travel to the Galapagos Islands~~
See the Northern Lights
~~Walk the Inca Trail~~
Write a book
See tigers in the wild

There, two achieved, three to aspire to and all perfectly respectable. Not a grain of sand in any place it definitely shouldn't be…

The large luxurious town car drew to a smooth halt and jolted her back into the present day, away from dangerous memories. 'We're here, Miss Rafferty. Are you sure you don't want me to take you home first?'

Polly looked up from her diary and drew in a breath at the sight of the massive golden stone building stretching all the way down the block. She *was* home. Back at the famous department store founded by her great-grandfather. She hadn't expected to ever see it again, let alone to walk in as mistress of all that she surveyed.

She stared at the huge picture windows flanking the iconic marble steps, her heart swelling with a potent mixture of love and pride. Each window told a tale and sold a dream. Rafferty's could give you anything, make you anyone—if you had the money to pay for it.

'This will be fine, Petyr, thank you. But please arrange for my bags to be taken back to Hopeford and for the concierge service to collect and launder them.'

She didn't want to set foot in Rafferty's carrying her rucksack stuffed as it was with sarongs, bikinis and walking boots, no matter how prestigious the brand names on them. Polly had spent a productive night at a hotel in Miami turning herself back into Miss Polly Rafferty from Miss Carefree Backpacker—all it had taken was a little shopping, a manicure and a wash and blow-dry.

She was back and she was ready.

Petyr opened the car door for her and Polly slid out onto the pavement, breathing in deeply as she did so. Car fumes, perfume, hot concrete, fried food—London in the height of summer. How she'd missed it. She pulled down her skirt hem and wriggled her toes experimentally. The heels felt a little constrictive after three months of bare feet, flip-flops and walking boots but her feet would adjust back. She would adjust back. After all, this was her real dream; her time out had been nothing but a diversion along the way.

Polly lifted her new workbag onto her shoulder and headed straight for the main entrance. She was going in.

'Hello, Rachel.'

Oh, it had felt good walking through the hallowed halls, greeting the staff she knew by name and seeing the new ones jump as they realised just who was casting a quick, appraising eye over them. Good to see gossiping staff spring apart and how everyone suddenly seemed to find work to do.

Good that nobody dared to catch her eye. There must have been talk after her abrupt disappearance but it didn't seem to have affected her standing. She allowed herself a small sigh of relief.

But it was also good to go in through the Staff Only door, to be buzzed in by old Alf and see the welcome on

his face. Alf had worked for Rafferty's since before Polly's
father was born and had always had a bar of chocolate and
a kind word for the small girl desperately trailing after her
grandfather, wanting, *needing*, to be included.

And it was good to be here, back in the light-filled foyer
where her assistant had her desk. Not that Rachel seemed
to share her enthusiasm judging by her open-mouthed expression and panicked eyes, and the way her fingers shook
as she gathered together a sheaf of papers.

'Miss Rafferty? We weren't expecting you back just
yet.'

'I did let you know my flight details,' Polly said coolly.
It wasn't like Rachel to be so disorganised. And at the very
least a friendly 'welcome back' would have been polite.

Rachel threw an anxious glance towards the door to
Polly's office. 'Well yes.' She got up out of her chair and
walked around her desk to stand in front of the door, block-
ing Polly's path. 'But I thought you would go home first.
I didn't expect to see you today.'

'I hope my early appearance isn't too much of an inconvenience.' What was the girl hiding? Perhaps Raff had
decorated her office in high gloss and black leather during his brief sojourn as CEO. 'As you can see I decided to
come straight here.' Polly gave her assistant a cool glance,
waiting for her to move aside.

'You've come straight from the airport?' Rachel
wouldn't—or couldn't—meet her eye but stood her ground.
'You must be tired and thirsty. Why don't you go to the
staff canteen and I'll arrange for them to bring you coffee
and something to eat?'

'Coffee does sound lovely,' Polly agreed. 'But I'd rather
have it *in* my office if you don't mind. Please call and arrange it. Thank you, Rachel.'

Rachel stood there for a long second, indecision clear

on her face before she moved slowly to one side. 'Yes, Miss Rafferty.'

Polly nodded curtly at her still-hovering assistant. Things had obviously got slack under Raff's reign. She hoped it wouldn't take too long to get things back on track—or to get herself back on track; no more lie-ins, long walks on beaches where the sand was so fine it felt like silk underfoot, no more swimming in balmy seas or drinking rum cocktails under the light of so many stars it was like being in an alternate universe.

No. She was back to work, routine and normality, which was great. A girl couldn't relax for ever, right?

Slowly Polly turned the chrome handle and opened her office door, relishing the cool polished feel of the metal under her hand. Like much of the interior throughout the store the door handle was one of the original art deco fittings chosen by her great-grandfather back in the nineteen twenties. His legacy lived on in every fitting and fixture. She loved the weight of history that fell onto her shoulders as soon as she walked into the building. Her name, her blood, her legacy.

She stood on the threshold for a second and breathed in. It was finally hers. Everything she had worked for, everything she had dreamed of—this was her office, her store, her way.

And yet it had all felt so unachievable just three months ago. Despite four years as vice CEO and the last of those years as acting CEO while her grandfather stood back from the company he loved as fiercely as Polly herself did, she had walked away. After her grandfather had told her he was finally stepping down and installing Polly's twin brother Raff in his place she had dropped her swipe card on the desk, collected her bag and walked out.

The next day she had been on a plane to South America. She had left her home, her cat and her company—and replaced them with a frivolous bucket list.

Three months later that memory still had the power to wind her.

But here she was, back at the helm and nothing and no one was going to stand in her way.

The relief at seeing her office unchanged swept over her; the sunshine streaming in through the stained-glass floor-to-ceiling windows highlighting the wood panelling, tiled floors and her beautiful walnut desk—the very same one commissioned by her great-grandfather for this room in nineteen twenty-five—the bookshelves and photos, her chaise longue, her...

Hang on. Her eyes skittered back; that hadn't been there before.

Or rather *he* hadn't.

Nope, Polly was pretty sure she would have remembered if she'd left a half-naked sleeping beauty on her antique chaise longue when she'd stormed out.

Frankly, the mood she'd been in, she probably would have taken him with her.

She moved a little closer, uncomfortably aware of her heels tapping on the tiled floor, and contemplated the newest addition to her office.

He was lying on his front, his arm pillowing his head, just the curve of a sharply defined cheekbone and a shock of dark hair falling over his forehead visible. His jeans were snug, low, riding deep on his back exposing every vertebrae on his naked torso.

It was a tanned torso, a deep olive, and although slim, almost to the point of leanness, every muscle was clearly defined. On his lower back a tree blossomed, a silhouette whose branches reached up to his middle vertebrae. Polly fought an urge to reach out and trace one of the narrow lines with her fingers. She didn't normally like tattoos but this one was oddly beautiful, almost mesmerising in its intricacy.

What was she doing? She shouldn't be standing here admiring the interloper. He needed to wake up and get out. No matter how peaceful he looked.

Polly coughed, a short, polite noise. It was as effectual as an umbrella in a hurricane. She coughed again, louder, more irritated.

He didn't even stir.

'Excuse me.' Her voice was soft, polite. Polly shook her head in disgust; this was her office. Why was *she* the one pussyfooting around? 'Excuse me!'

This time there was some effect, just a little; a faint murmur and a shift in his position as he rolled onto his side. She couldn't help flickering a quick glance along the lean length. Yep, the front matched the back, a smattering of fine dark hair tangled on his upper chest, another silky patch emphasising the muscles on his abdomen before tapering into a line that ran down inside the low-slung jeans.

Polly swallowed, her mouth suddenly in need of some kind of moisture. No, she scolded herself, tearing her eyes away, heat flushing through her. Just because he was in her office she didn't have the right to stand here and objectify him. She gave the room a quick once-over relieved that no one was there to witness her behaviour; she was the CEO for goodness' sake, she had to set an example.

This had gone on long enough. This was a place of business, not a doss house for disreputable if attractive young men to slumber in, or a hidey-hole for her PA's latest boyfriend. Whoever he was she was going to have to shake him awake. Right *now*.

If only he were wearing a shirt. Or anything. Touching that bronzed skin felt intrusive, intimate.

'For goodness' sake, are you woman or wombat?' she muttered, balling her fingers into a fist.

'Hello.' She reached over and took a tentative hold of one firm shoulder, his skin warm and smooth against her hand. 'Wake up.' She gave a little shake but it was like shaking a statue.

All she wanted was to sit at her desk and start working. Alone. Was that too much to ask? Anger and adrenaline flooded through her system; it had been a long journey, she was jet-lagged and irritated and in need of a sit-down and a coffee. She'd had enough. Officially.

Polly turned and walked crisply towards her small en-suite cloakroom and bathroom, this time uncaring of the loud tap of her heels. The door swung open to reveal a wide, airy space with room for coats and shoes plus a walk-in wardrobe where Polly stored a selection of outfits for the frequent occasions where she went straight from work to a social function. She gave the room a quick glance, relieved to see no trace of Raff's presence. It was as if he had been wiped out of the store's memory.

That was fine by her. He had made it quite clear he wanted nothing to do with Rafferty's—and although they were twins they had never been good at sharing.

Another door led into the well-equipped bathroom. Polly allowed herself one longing glance at the walk-in shower before grabbing a glass from the shelf and filling it with water, making sure the cold tap ran for a few seconds first for maximum chill. Then, quickly so that she didn't lose her nerve, she swivelled on her heel and marched back over to the chaise longue, standing over the interloper.

He had moved again, lying supine, half on his back, half on his side revealing more of his features. Long, thick lashes lay peacefully on cheekbones so finely sculpted it looked as if a master stonemason had been at work, eyebrows arching arrogantly above.

His wide mouth was slightly parted. Sensual, a little voice whispered to Polly. A mouth made for sin.

She ignored the voice. And she ignored the slight jibe of her conscience; she needed him awake and leaving; if he wouldn't respond to gentler methods then what choice did she have?

Resolutely Polly held the glass up over the man's face and tipped it. For one long moment she held it still so that the water was perfectly balanced right at the rim, clear drops so very close to spilling over the thin edge.

And then she allowed her hand to move the glass over the tipping point, a perfect stream of cold water falling like rain onto the peacefully slumbering face below.

Polly didn't quite know what to expect; anger, shock, contrition or even no reaction at all. He was so very deeply asleep after all. But what she didn't expect was for one red-rimmed eye to lazily open, for a smile to play around the disturbingly well-cut mouth or for a hand to shoot out and grab her wrist.

Caught by surprise, she stumbled forward, falling against the chaise as the hand snuck around her waist, pulling her down, pulling her close.

'Bonjour, chérie.' His voice was low, gravelly with sleep and deeply, unmistakeably French. 'If you wanted me to wake up you only had to ask.'

It was the shock, that was all. Otherwise she would have moved, called for help, disentangled herself from the strong arm anchoring her firmly against the bare chest. And she would never, ever have allowed his other hand to slip around her neck in an oddly sweet caress while he angled his mouth towards hers—would have moved away

long before the hard mouth claimed hers in a distinctly
unsleepy way.

It was definitely the shock keeping her paralysed under
his touch—and she was definitely *not* leaning into the kiss,
opening herself up to the pressure of his mouth on hers,
the touch of his hand moving up her back, slipping round
her ribcage, brushing against the swell of her breast.

Hang on, his hand was where?

Polly pulled away, jumping up off the chaise, resisting
the urge to scrub the kiss off her tingling mouth.

Or to lean back down and let him claim her again.

'What do you think you're doing?'

'Saying *au revoir* of course.' He had shifted position
and was leaning against the back of the chaise, his eyes
skimming every inch of her until she wanted to wrap her
arms around her torso, shielding herself from his insolent gaze.

'Au revoir?' Was she going mad? Where were the panicked apologies and the scuttling out of her office?

'Of course.' He raised an eyebrow. 'As you are dressed
to leave I thought you were saying goodbye. But if it was
more of a good morning...' the smile widened '...even
better.'

'I am not saying *au revoir* or good morning or anything
but *what on earth are you doing in my office and where
are your clothes*?'

She hadn't meant to tag on the last line but with the
imprint of his hand still burning her back and the taste of
him taunting her mouth she really needed to be looking
at something other than what seemed like acres of taut,
tanned bare flesh.

Surely now, now he would show some contrition, some
shame. But no, he was what? Laughing? He was mad or
drunk or both and she was going to call Security right now.

'Of course, your office! Polly, *bonjour*. I am charmed to meet you.'

What? He knew her name? She took an instinctive step backwards as he slid off the chaise, as graceful as a panther, and took a step towards her, hand held out.

'Who are you and what are you doing here?' She stepped back a little further, one hand groping for the phone ready to call for help.

'I am so very sorry.' He was smiling as if the whole situation were nothing but a huge joke. 'I fell asleep here, last night, and was confused when you woke me.' His eyes laughed at her, shamelessly. 'It's not the first time I've been awakened by a glass of water. I am Gabriel Beaufils, your new vice CEO. My friends call me Gabe. I hope you will too.'

No, that was no better, she was still looking at him as if he were an escaped convict. Not surprisingly, Gabe thought ruefully. What had he been thinking?

He hadn't. He'd been dreaming, stuck in that hazy world between sleep and wakefulness when he'd felt a warm hand on his shoulder followed by the chill shock of the water and, confused, had thought it some kind of game. After three weeks of eighteen-hour days, making sure he was fully and firmly ensconced at Rafferty's before the formidable Polly Rafferty returned, he wasn't as switched on as he should be.

Well, his wake-up call had been brutal. It was bad enough from Polly's point of view that he had been catapulted in without her say-so or knowledge—and a wake-up kiss probably wasn't the wisest way to make a good impression. He needed to make up the lost ground, and fast.

He smiled at her, pouring as much winning charm into the smile as he could.

There was no answering smile, not even in her darkly

shadowed eyes. The bruised circles were the only hint of tiredness even though she must have come straight here from the airport. Her dark gold hair was twisted up into a neat knot and her suit looked freshly laundered. Yet for all the business-style armour there was something oddly vulnerable in the blue eyes, the determined set of her almost too-slender frame.

'Gabriel Beaufils?' There was a hint of recognition in her voice. 'You were working for Desmoulins?'

'*Oui*, as Digital Director.' He debated mentioning the tripling of profits in the proud old Parisian store's web business but decided against it. Yet. That little but pertinent detail might come in handy and he didn't want to play his hand too soon.

'I don't recall hiring a new vice CEO.' There was nothing fragile in her voice. It was cold enough to freeze the water still dripping over his torso. 'Even if I had, that doesn't explain why you were sleeping in my office and appear to have mislaid your top.'

Nor why you kissed me. She might not have said the words but they were implied, hung accusingly in the air.

No, better to forget about the kiss, delightful as it had been. Strange to think that the huge-eyed, fragile-looking woman opposite had responded so openly, so ardently, that she would taste of sweetness and spice.

Damn it, he was supposed to be forgetting about the kiss.

'Polly, *je suis désolé*.' This situation was not irredeemable no matter how it seemed right now. It wasn't often that Gabe thought himself lucky to have three older sisters but right now they were a blessing; he was used to disapproving glares and turning the stickiest of situations right around.

'I have been using this office until you returned—we

didn't know if you would want to take over your grandfather's office or stay in here. But once again I was working too late and missed the last train back to Hopeford. It was easier to crash out on the couch rather than find a hotel so late. If I had known you were coming in this morning…'

He threw his hands out in a placatory gesture.

It didn't work. If anything she looked even more suspicious. 'Hopeford? Why would you be staying there?'

A sinking feeling hit Gabe. On a scale of one to ten this whole situation was hitting one hundred on the awkward chart. If she wasn't happy about having a vice CEO she hadn't handpicked then she was going to love having a strange houseguest!

'Cat-feeding. Raff was worried Mr Simpkins would get lonely.' He smiled as winningly as he could but there was no response from her.

Okay, charm wasn't working, businesslike might. 'I do have an apartment arranged,' he explained. 'But unfortunately, just before I was going to move in, the neighbour's basement extension caused a massive subsidence in the whole street. I can quite easily go to a hotel if it's a problem but as your house was empty and I was homeless…' He shrugged. It had made perfect sense at the time.

Apparently not to Polly. 'You're staying in my *house*? Where is Raff? Why isn't he there?'

'He was in Jordan, now I think he's in Australia but he should be back soon.' It had been hard to keep up with the other Rafferty twin's travels.

'Australia? What on earth is he doing there?' She sank down into the large chair behind her desk with an audible sigh of relief, probably worn out by the weight of all the questions she had fired at him. Gabe's head was spinning from them all.

'I thought Raff would wait until I got back before taking off again,' Polly murmured, her voice so low that Gabe hardly caught her words.

If Gabriel had to narrow all his criticisms of his own family down to just one thing it would be the complete lack of respect for personal space—physically *and* mentally. Every thought, every feeling, every pain, every movement was up for general discussion, dissection and in the worst-case scenario culminating in a family conference.

His middle sister, Celine, would even video call in from New Zealand, unwilling to let a small matter like time zones and distance prevent her from getting her two cen-times' worth in.

The possibility of anybody in the Beaufils household not knowing the exact whereabouts of any member of their family at any given time was completely inconceivable. Sometimes Gabe suspected they had all been microchipped at birth. How could Polly Rafferty have no idea where her own twin brother was or what he was doing?

She looked up at him, the navy-blue eyes dark. 'I think I might be more jet-lagged than I realised,' she said slowly. 'Let me get this straight. You are working, here, at Raffer-ty's, as the vice CEO and living at Hopeford. In my house.'

'Temporarily,' Gabe clarified. 'Your house, that is.'

She closed her eyes.

A knock at the door jolted her back to wakefulness, the eyes snapping open.

'Yes?'

The door opened, followed a moment later by Rachel, who was carrying a large tray. She flickered a sympathetic glance over at Gabe and he couldn't resist winking back.

'Your coffee, Miss Rafferty.' Rachel set the tray onto the desk and smiled at Gabe. 'I brought your usual smoothie, Mr Beaufils,' she said in a much lighter tone. 'The chef has your muesli ready. I said you might prefer to eat it in the staff canteen this morning. Oh, and dry-cleaning has sent your clean shirt up. I'll just take it through for you.'

'*Merci*, Rachel.'

Polly had begun to pour her coffee but stopped mid flow, her eyes narrowed and fixed on her assistant.

'You were aware that Mr Beaufils was here? In my office?'

'Well, he often works late…' Rachel said.

'And you didn't think to warn me?'

'I…'

'Tell Building Services I need to see them this morning. Mr Beaufils obviously needs his own sleeping and breakfasting area. Oh, and his own assistant. Get on to HR. We'll discuss the rest later.'

'Yes, Miss Rafferty.' Rachel bobbed out with a sigh of relief, returning a second later with a crisply wrapped shirt, which she handed to Gabe before exiting the office and closing the door.

'Nice girl, very competent.' Gabe sauntered over to the tray and picked up his usual smoothie. It had taken a few days for the chef to get the mixture just right but it was pretty close to perfection now. He took it over to the chaise and sipped but could feel Polly's eyes on him and looked over at her with a faintly enquiring smile.

'Are you quite comfortable?' she asked. 'Are you sure you don't want to ask for your muesli in here? Take a shower before getting dressed? How about a massage?'

He bit back a smile at the sarcastic tone in her voice. 'A shower would be lovely, thank you.' He downed the shake, feeling the cool liquid hit the back of his throat, the vitamins working their way into his system. 'Don't worry about showing me the way. I know my way around.'

'Hold on.' But she was too late, Gabriel Beaufils had disappeared into the cloakroom.

Polly jumped to her feet but came to a stop. She was hardly going to follow him into the shower, was she?

Not that he would mind—he'd probably just ask her to pass him the towel! After all he had no compunction about parading around her office half naked. No wonder Rachel was smitten. Smoothies and muesli indeed.

The phone on her desk blared. It was probably the kitchen wondering if Gabe wanted a lightly poached egg with his breakfast. Polly glared at it before pressing the speakerphone button.

'Polly Rafferty.'

'You're home, then.' Familiar grizzled, curt tones.

'Hello, Grandfather. I hope you're feeling better.' He at least hadn't expected her to go back to Hopeford before returning to work. But then Charles Rafferty had never actually taken a holiday—*his* bucket list probably read 'spend more time in the office'.

Her grandfather merely grunted. 'Hope you're ready to get down to some serious work after your little holiday.' Polly bit back the obvious retorts; it hadn't been a holiday, she had left the company after barely taking a long week-end off in the last five years.

But what was the point? Words wouldn't change him.

'Have you met Beaufils yet?'

Polly couldn't stop her eyes flicking towards the cloak-room door. 'I've seen him,' she said drily. 'Confident young man.'

'He's Vincent's boy, Gabriel. You know Chateau Beaufils of course, we've been their exclusive UK stockist for decades. He's the only son.'

'That doesn't explain why he's here.' Her voice was sharper than she had intended.

She didn't want her grandfather to know how much Gabe's presence had shaken her.

'Oh, he's not here because of the vineyard although that's a good connection of course. Man did some great things at Desmoulins, which is why I snapped him up. Thought he'd be good balance for you.'

'Good balance for me?' Polly wasn't sure whether she wanted to laugh or cry. Balance or replacement? If he couldn't have Raff did her grandfather want this young man instead? Just how much did she have to do before he finally accepted her? 'I really think I should have been consulted.'

'No.' Her grandfather's answer was as sharp as it was unequivocal. 'Vice CEO is a board decision. We need someone with different strengths from you, not someone you can ride roughshod over.'

Talk about the pot and the kettle. Polly glared at the phone.

'He knows the European markets and is very, very strong digitally, so I want him in charge of all e-commerce. Oh, and Polly? It's going to take a few weeks before his apartment is sound again. It won't bother you to have him at yours until then? You barely spend any time there as it is.'

Despite her best intentions Polly found her attention wandering back to the moment she had first seen Gabe sprawled on her chaise. The line of his back, the strong leanness of him, the delicacy of that intricate tattoo spiralling up his spine.

Thank goodness her grandfather wasn't here to see the flush on her cheeks.

Her first instinct was to demand they find Gabriel Beaufils alternative accommodation a long, long way from her house and home. And yet…it might be useful to keep him close. What was that they said about friends and enemies?

'I can't imagine there's much to excite him in Hopeford,' she said sweetly. 'But of course he can stay.'

The more she could find out about Gabriel Beaufils, the easier it would be to outmanoeuvre him. She was in charge of Rafferty's at last and no smoothie-drinking, bare-chested, charming Frenchman was going to change that.

CHAPTER TWO

GABE FINISHED TOWEL-DRYING his hair and grabbed the clean shirt Rachel had brought him. Pulling it on, he began to button it up slowly, once again running the morning's unexpected events through his mind. What had he been thinking?

He hadn't been thinking, that was the problem, he'd been reacting. A sure sign he'd allowed himself to mix business and pleasure that bit too often. Not enough sleep and too many office flirtations.

What a first impression! Although he wasn't sure what had thrown her more—the kiss or the news of his appointment.

He couldn't blame her for being less than pleased with either but he was here and he was staying put. Unlike Polly Rafferty he didn't have the advantage of bearing the founder's name, but he was just twenty-eight, already the vice CEO of Rafferty's and his goal of running his own company by thirty was looking eminently doable.

Things were nicely on track to get the results he needed, to learn everything he could and in two years look for the opportunity he needed to achieve his goal. Because life was short. Nobody knew that better than Gabe.

He pushed the thought away as he strode out of the bathroom and along the passage that led to the office. It was time to eat some humble pie.

'Nice shower?'

Gabe came to a halt and stared at Polly Rafferty. Was that a smile on her face?

'Rachel tells me you've been working all hours,' she continued. 'I just want to thank you. Obviously it was less than ideal that I wasn't back before Raff left but it's such a relief that you were here to help out.'

'I was more than happy to step in.' Gabe leant against the door frame and watched her through narrow eyes.

Polly seemed oblivious to his gaze. She was leaning back in his chair—correction, her chair—completely at her ease. She had taken off her jacket and it hung on the hat stand in the corner, her bag tossed carelessly on the floor beneath it. Her laptop was plugged into the keyboard and monitor, his own laptop folded and put aside. Several sheets of paper were stacked on the gleaming mahogany desk, a red pen lying on top of one, the crossed-out lines and scribbled notes implying great industry. It was as if she had never been away.

As if he had never been there.

Polly looked up, pen in hand. 'You haven't had breakfast so I suggest you take an hour or so while I get to grips with a few things here, then we can discuss how it's going to work moving forward. Starting with a permanent office and an assistant for you.' She couldn't be more gracious.

In fact she was the perfect hostess. Gabe suppressed a smile; he couldn't help approving of her tactics. Polly was throwing down the gauntlet. Oh, politely and with some degree of charm but, still, she was making it clear that absence or no absence this was her company and he was the incomer.

'You don't want your grandfather's office?' he asked. 'I assumed that you would want to move in there.'

A flicker of sadness ran over her face disturbing the blandly pleasant mask. 'This room belonged to my great-grandfather. The furniture and décor is just as it was, just as he chose. I'm staying here.'

But she wasn't going to offer him the bigger room either; he'd stake his reputation on it.

'I don't need an hour.' He pushed off the door frame. 'I am quite happy to start in fifteen minutes.'

'That's very sweet of you, Gabe.' The smile was back. 'But please, take an hour. I'll see you then.'

The dismissal was clear. Round one to Polly Rafferty.

That was okay. Gabe didn't care about individual rounds. He cared about the final prize. He inclined his head as he moved towards the door. 'Of course, take as long as you need to settle back in. Oh and, Polly? Welcome back.'

Polly held onto the smile as long as it took for the door to close behind the tall Frenchman then slumped forward with a sigh. It had taken her just a few minutes to reclaim the office but it still didn't feel like hers. It smelt different, of soap and a fresh citrusy cologne, of leather and whatever was in that disgusting green drink Gabe had tossed down so easily. She'd sniffed the glass when he was in the shower and recoiled in horror—until then she didn't think anything could be as vile as the look of the smoothie, but she'd been wrong.

Her coffee smelt off too. It must be the jet lag and all the travelling she'd done in the last week—nothing smelt right at the moment. Her stomach had twisted with nausea at the mere thought of caffeine or alcohol and even the eggs she had tried to eat at the airport.

Polly pushed the thought away. Whining that she was tired and that she felt ill wouldn't get her anywhere. She needed to hit the ground running and not stop.

Walking over to the massive art deco windows that dominated the office, she peered through their tinted panes at the street below. Coloured in red and green it looked like a film maker's whimsical view of the vibrant West End. Polly had always loved the strange slant the glass gave on the world. It helped her think clearly, think differently—helped her see problems in a new way.

And right now she needed all her wits about her.

'Gabriel Beaufils,' she said aloud, her mind conjuring up unbidden the tall man lounging at his ease, jeans riding low, bare chested, the water still dripping from his wet hair. What did that tell her?

That he was shameless. That he was beautiful.

Polly shook her head impatiently, replacing the image in her mind with the man that had just left. Leaning insouciantly against the door, wet hair slicked back. Still in jeans but now they were more sedately paired with a crisp white linen shirt. No tie. Laughter in his eyes.

That was better. Now what could she deduce from that? He didn't care what people thought about him, what she thought about him. That he was confident and utterly secure in his charm. That he was underestimating her.

She could work with that.

What else? Polly pulled herself away from the view and returned to her desk, running her fingers possessively over the polished wood. *Okay, let's do this.* She pulled up a search engine and typed in his name. 'Who are you, Monsieur Beaufils?' she murmured as she hit enter.

The page instantly filled with several engines. He had left quite the digital trail.

Polly sat back and began to read. Some of it she knew. He was from an affluent background, his family the proud makers of a venerable brand of wine. However, Gabe had left home in his late teens, gone to college in the States and stayed on to do his MBA while working at one of the biggest retail chains there.

'Good,' she muttered, returning to the results page and scanning the next paragraph, an article written about him just a few months ago. 'What else?'

Two years ago he had returned home to France, to Paris, to take charge of digital sales at Desmoulins. The young up-and-coming whizz-kid introducing innovation into one of Paris's most venerable *grande dames* had made quite a stir. Was that what he was planning to do here?

So much for his business history. Personal life? She moved through several lines of results. Nothing. Either he was very discreet or he didn't have a private life.

Polly's mouth tingled as if his lips were still hovering above hers. Despite herself she flicked her tongue over them as if she could still taste him. Discreet it was. That was a very practised kiss.

She took the cursor back to the top of the page and hit the images button. Instantly the page filled with photos of Gabe, smiling, serious, in a suit…in head-to-toe Lycra.

Hang on? He was wearing *what*?

She hovered over the image of Gabe walking out of a lake, wetsuit half undone, and Polly resisted the urge to zoom in on his chest. She checked the caption. He was a triathlete.

Gabriel Beaufils. Confident, charming, discreet and competitive.

She could handle that.

A smile curved her mouth. This was going to be almost too easy.

'I hope I didn't keep you waiting. I got caught up in something.'

As a matter of fact he was precisely on time—Polly would bet money that Gabe Beaufils had been standing outside the office watching a stopwatch to make sure he walked back in exactly one hour after she had dismissed him.

She would have done the same thing herself. Interesting.

Not that she was going to let him know that. She kept her eyes locked on her computer screen, giving every impression that she too was busy. 'I hope you had a nice breakfast.'

'Yes, thank you, most important meal of the day.' There was a dark hint of laughter in his voice.

'So they say.' She looked up and smiled. 'I'm usually too busy to remember to eat it.'

She had meant the glance and the smile to be brief, dismissive, but there was an intensity in his answering look that ensnared her. How could eyes be so dark, so knowing? Heat burned her cheeks, a shiver of awareness deep inside.

Reluctantly she pulled her gaze away, staring mindlessly at her computer screen, reading the same nonsensical sentence over and over again.

'You should take care of yourself, Polly.' His voice was low, caressing. 'Neglecting your body is not wise.'

'I don't neglect my body.' She wanted to pull the defensive words back as soon as she had uttered them.

'I exercise and eat well,' she clarified not entirely truthfully but she didn't want to admit to her snacking habits to him. Not when he was evidently so healthy. And fit. It took every ounce of willpower she had not to look up again, to sweep her eyes over him from head to toe, lingering on the muscles she knew were lurking under that crisp white shirt. 'I just don't make a big deal of it.'

She pushed her chair back and stood. 'I am going to do a walkabout,' she said. 'Would you care to accompany me?'

He stayed still for a moment, that curiously intent look still in his eyes, and then nodded courteously as he pulled the door open and held it for her.

Polly sensed his every movement as he followed her back out into the light, glass-walled foyer, awareness prickling her spine.

Rachel looked up as they walked by, curiosity clear on her face. Polly had no doubt that she was emailing all of her friends with a highly scurrilous account of her boss's encounter with a half-naked Frenchman. Let her; Polly would fill her PA's forthcoming days so completely that she wouldn't even be able to dream about gossiping.

It wasn't far from her office to one of the discreet doors that led out onto the shop floor. This was what Rafferty's was all about. No matter how essential the office functions were they existed for one purpose—to keep the iconic store in business. Polly ensured that every finance assistant, every marketing executive spent at least one week a year on the shop floor. Just as her great-grandfather had done. She herself spent most of December on the shop floor serving, restocking and assisting. The buzz and adrenaline rush were addictive.

'I've spoken to Building Services,' she said as she slid her pass through the door lock, turning with one hand on the handle to face Gabe. 'I am going to turn Grandfather's old office into the boardroom. It's bigger than any of the meeting rooms, far too big for one person—and I think he'll be pleased with the gesture. He is still President of the Board.'

Polly knew everyone expected her to move into the vast corner suite but couldn't face the thought of occupying her grandfather's chair, feeling him second-guessing her all the time, disapproving of every change she made.

'And me?' It was said with a self-deprecating and very Gallic shrug but Polly wasn't fooled. There was a sharpness in his eyes.

'The old boardroom.' It was a neat solution. Polly got to

keep her office, her grandfather would hopefully feel honoured and Gabe would get a brand-new office in keeping with his position. But not a Rafferty office, not one with history steeped in its walls.

'Building Services are confident they can create a room for your assistant with no major infrastructure changes and there's already a perfectly good cloakroom. You can start picking wallpaper and furniture this week and it should be ready end of next week.'

'And where do I work in the meantime?' His voice was still mild but Polly was aware of a stillness about him, a quiet confidence in his gaze. She didn't want to push too far, not yet. Reluctantly she discarded her plan that he sit in her foyer, with Rachel, or that she find him a spare desk in one of the bigger, open-plan offices where the rest of the backroom staff worked.

'We can fit a second desk in my room,' she said. 'Just until you're settled. But, Gabe? No more sleeping in the office, no more using my assistant to sort out your laundry and…' she swallowed but kept her gaze and voice firm '…you remain fully dressed and act appropriately at all times. Understood?'

Gabe's mouth quirked. 'Of course,' he murmured.

'Good.' She pushed the door open.

This was it, this was where the magic happened.

Polly blinked as she stepped out. They had entered the home furnishings department on the top floor and the lights were switched to full, purposely dazzling to best showcase the silks, cushions, throws, ceramics, silverware and all the other luxury items Rafferty's told their customers were essential for a comfortable home. Beneath them were floors and galleries devoted to technology, books, toys, food and, of course, fashion.

Polly's heart swelled and she clenched her fists. She was home.

And yet everything had changed. She had changed.

She had hoped that being back would ground her again but it was odd walking through the galleries with Gabe. If her staff greeted her with their usual respect, they greeted him with something warmer.

And how on earth did he know every name after what? Three or four weeks?

'*Bonjour*, Emily.' Polly narrowed her eyes at him as they entered the world-famous haberdashery room. Had his accent thickened as he greeted the attractive redhead who had turned the department into the must-go destination for a new generation of craft lovers?

'How is your cat? Did the operation go well?' He had moved nearer to Emily, smiling down at her intimately.

Polly's head snapped round. No way. He knew the names of every staff member and all about the health of their pets too?

'Yes, thank you, Mr Beaufils, she's desperate to go outside but she's doing really well.' Emily was smiling back, her voice a little breathy.

'They can be such a responsibility, *non*? I 'ave…'

Had he just dropped an aitch? *Really?* Polly had known him for what, an hour? And she already knew perfectly well that Gabe spoke perfect, almost accentless English. Unless, it seemed, he was talking to petite redheads. She coughed and could have sworn she saw a glimmer of laughter in the depths of his almost-black eyes as he continued.

'I 'ave been looking after Mademoiselle Rafferty's cat for the last few weeks. He is a rascal, that one. Such a huge responsibility.'

'They are,' Emily said earnestly, her huge eyes fixed on his. 'But worth it.'

'*Oui*, the way they purr. So trusting.'

That was it. Polly felt ill just listening. 'So greedy,' she said briskly. 'And so prone to eviscerating small mammals under the bed. If you're ready, Gabe, shall we continue? Nice work,' she said to Emily, unable to keep a sarcastic tone from her voice. 'Keep it up.' And without a backwards glance she swept from the department.

It had been an interesting morning. Gabe was well aware that he had been well and truly sized up, tested and judged. What the verdict was he had no idea.

Nor, truth be told, was he that interested. He had his own weighing up to do.

Tough, but not as tough as she thought. Surprisingly stylish for someone who lived and breathed work; the sharp little suit she was wearing would pass muster in the most exclusive streets in Paris—unusual for an Englishwoman. He liked how she wasn't afraid of her height, accentuating it with heels, the blonde hair swept up into a knot adding an extra couple of centimetres.

And she wasn't going to give him an inch. The solution to the offices was masterful. It was going to be fun working with her.

He loved a good game.

Gabe strode through the foyer, smiling at Rachel as she looked up with a blush. Maybe he should have gone a little easier on the flirting. He wouldn't make that mistake with his own assistant—he would request a guy or, even better, a motherly woman who would keep all unwanted callers away and feed him home-made cake. He made a note to keep an eye on the 'interests' section of any applicants' CVs.

He opened the door to Polly's office without knocking; after all they were sharing it.

'This is going to be fun,' he said as Polly looked up from her computer screen, trying unsuccessfully to hide her irritation at the interruption. 'Roomies, housemates. We should take a road trip too, complete the set.'

Bed mates would really make it a full hand but he wasn't going to suggest that. Totally inappropriate. But, despite himself, his eyes wandered over her face, skimming over the smattering of freckles high on her cheeks, the wide mouth, the pointed little chin. She kissed like she spoke— with passion and purpose—but there was none of the coolness and poise. No, there was heat simmering away behind that cool façade.

Heat he was better off pretending he knew nothing about.

'I'll let you have a lift in the company car. Will that do?' She looked unamused. 'Did you decide on office furniture? There's a temporary desk for you there.' She nodded over towards the wall where a second desk had already been set up, a monitor and phone installed on its gleaming surface.

'I'll be here a week or two at the most according to Building Services and then you're free of me.'

'Hardly,' she muttered so low he could barely make out her words then spoke out in her usual crisp tones. 'Are you available to talk now?'

'*Certainement*, if you need me to be.' He didn't mean to let his voice drop or to drawl the words out quite so suggestively but the colour rising swiftly in her cheeks showed their effect all too clearly. 'It would be good to start again, properly,' he clarified.

'Good.' Polly waited until he had taken his seat at his new desk. It wasn't quite as good a position as hers, which faced the incredible windows. When Gabe had sat there absorbed in his work he would look absently up every so often, only to be struck anew by the light, the simple art-istry of the stylised floral design.

Now his view was the bookshelves that lined the op-posite wall—and Polly, her desk directly in his eyeline. She swivelled her chair towards him, a notepad and pen poised in her hand, her legs crossed.

The only way this was going to work was if he behaved himself in thought and deed. But he was a mere man after all and better souls than him would find it hard to stop their gaze skimming over the long willowy figure and the neatly crossed legs. Incredibly long, ridiculously shapely legs. Of course they were.

'You've got a pretty impressive CV,' she said finally. 'Why Rafferty's?'

'That means a lot coming from you,' he said honestly. 'Oh, come on,' as her brows rose in surprise. 'Polly Raf-ferty, you set the standard, you must know that. I came here to work with you.'

'With me?'

'Don't misunderstand me, there's a lot you can learn from me as well. In some ways Rafferty's is stuck in the Dark Ages, especially digitally. But, you have done some great things here over the last few years. I have no prob-lem admitting there are still things I need to learn if I am going to be a CEO by the time I'm thirty...'

'Here?'

He raised an eyebrow. 'Would you let me?'

'You'd have to kill me first.' She shook her head, her colour high.

'That's what I thought. No, maybe a start-up, or even my own business. I'll see nearer the time.'

'You're ambitious. It took me until I was thirty-one to make it.' Her eyes met his coolly, the blue of her eyes dark.

'I know.' He grinned. 'A little competition keeps me

focused.' He shrugged. 'Rafferty's is possibly the most famous store in Europe if not the world. It's the missing piece in my experience—and I have a lot to offer you as well. It's a win-win situation.'

She leant back. 'Prove it. What would you change?'

He grinned. 'Are you ready for it? You only just got back.'

The corners of her mouth turned up, the smallest of smiles. 'Don't pull your punches. I can take it.'

'Okay then.' He jumped out of the chair and began to pace up and down the room. It was always easier to think on his feet; those months of being confined to bed had left him with a horror of inaction.

'Your social media lacks identity and your online advertising is practically non-existent—it's untargeted and unplanned, effectively just a redesign of your print advertising. I suggest you employ a digital marketing consultant to train your existing staff. Emily is very capable. She just needs guidance and some confidence.'

He looked across for a reaction but she was busy scribbling notes. Gabe rolled his eyes. 'This is part of the problem. You're what? Writing longhand?'

'I think better with paper and pen. I'll type them up later.' Her voice was defensive.

'*Non*, the whole company needs to think digitally. The sales force need tablets so they can check sizes and styles at the touch of a button, mix and match styles.'

'We have a personal touch here. We don't need to rely on tablets…'

'You need both,' he said flatly. 'But what you really need is a new website.'

There was a long moment of incredulous silence. 'But it's only three years old. Do you *know* how much we spent on it?'

Polly was no longer leaning back. She was ramrod-straight, her eyes sparkling, more in anger than excitement, Gabe thought. 'Too much and it's obsolete. Come on, Polly.' His words tumbled over each other, his accent thickened in his effort to convince her.

'Do you want a website that's fine and gets the job done or do you want one that's a window into the very soul of Rafferty's? You have no other stores anywhere—this is it. Your Internet business *is* your worldwide business and that's where the expansion lies.'

'What do you have in mind?'

This was what made him tick, made his blood pump, the adrenaline flow—planning, innovating, creating. It was better than finishing a marathon, hell, sometimes it was better than sex. 'A site that is visually stunning, one that creates the feel and the look of the store as much as possible. Each department would be organised by gallery, exactly as you are laid out here so that customers get to experience the look, the feel of Rafferty's—but virtually. Online assistants would be available twenty-four hours to chat and advise and, most importantly, the chance to personalise the experience. Why should people buy from Rafferty's online when there are hundreds, thousands of alternatives?'

She didn't answer, probably couldn't.

'If we make it better than all the rest then Rafferty's is the store that customers will choose. They can upload their measurements, their photos and have virtual fittings—that way, they can order with certainty, knowing that the clothes will fit and suit them. Cut down on returns and make the whole shopping experience fun and interactive.'

'How much?'

'It won't be cheap,' he admitted. 'Not to build, maintain or staff. But it will be spectacular.'

She didn't speak for a minute or so, staring straight ahead at the window before nodding decisively. 'There's a board meeting next week. Can you have a researched and costed paper ready for then?'

Researched *and* costed? *'Oui.'* If he had to work all day and night. 'So, what about you?'

'What about me?'

'There must be something you want to do, something to stamp your identity firmly on the store.'

'I have been running the company for the last year,' she reminded him, her voice a little frosty.

'But now it's official…' If she wasn't itching to make some changes he had severely underestimated her.

She didn't answer for a moment, her eyes fixed unseeingly on the windows. 'We have never expanded,' she said after a while. 'We always wanted to keep Rafferty's as a destination store, somewhere people could aspire to visit. And it works, we're on so many tourist tick lists; they buy teddies or tea in branded jars, eat in the tea room and take their Rafferty's bag home. And with the Internet there isn't any real need for bricks-and-mortar shops elsewhere.'

'But?'

'But we've become a little staid,' Polly said. She rolled her shoulders as she spoke, stretching out her neck. Gabe tried not to stare, not to notice how graceful her movements were, as she turned her attention to her hair, unpinning it and letting the dark blonde tendrils fall free.

Polly sighed, running her fingers through her hair before beginning to twist it back into a looser, lower knot. It felt almost voyeuristic standing there watching her fingers busy themselves in the tangle of tresses.

'We were one of the first stores in London to stock bikinis. Can you imagine—amidst the post-war austerity, the rationing and a London still two decades and a generation from swinging…my great-grandfather brought several bikinis over from Paris. There were letters of outrage to *The Times*.

'We were the first to unveil the latest trends, to sell miniskirts. We were *always* cutting edge and now we're part of a tour that includes Buckingham Palace and Madame Tussauds.' The contempt was clear in her voice. 'We're doing well financially, really well, but we're no longer cutting edge. We're safe, steady, middle-aged.' Polly wrinkled her nose as she spoke.

It was true; Rafferty's was a byword for elegance, taste and design but not for innovation, not any more. Even Gabe's own digital vision could only sell the existing ranges. But it was fabulously profitable with a brand recognition that was through the roof; wasn't that enough? 'Can a store this size actually be cutting edge any more? Surely that's the Internet's role…'

'I disagree.' She shook her head vehemently. 'We have the space, the knowledge, the passion and the history. The problem is, it takes a lot for us to take on a new designer or a new range, to hand over valuable floor space to somebody little known and unproven—and if they have already established themselves then we're just following, not innovating.'

'So, what do you plan to do about it?' This was more like it. Her eyes were focused again, sharp.

'Pop-ups.'

'Pardon?'

'Pop-ups. Bright, fun and relatively low cost. We can create a pop-up area in store for new designers whether it's clothes, jewellery, shoes—we'll champion new talent right here at Rafferty's. Sponsor a graduate show during London fashion week in the main gallery.'

That made a lot of sense.

'But I don't just want to draw people here. I want to go out and find them—it could be a great opportunity to take Rafferty's out of the city as well. Where do we have the biggest footfall?'

It was a good thing he'd pulled those eighteen-hour days; he could answer with utter confidence. 'The food hall.'

'Exactly! The British are finally understanding food—no, don't pull a superior gourmet French face at me. They are and you know it. There are hundreds of food festivals throughout the country and I want us to start having a presence at the very best of them. And not just food festivals. I want us at Glyndebourne, Henley, the Edinburgh Festival Fringe. Anywhere there's a buzz I want Rafferty's. Exclusive invitation-only previews to create excitement, with takeaway afternoon teas and Rafferty's hampers—filled with a selection of our bestselling products as souvenirs.'

Gabe rubbed his chin. 'Will it make a profit?'

'Yes, but not a massive one,' she conceded. 'But it *will* revitalise us, introduce us to the younger market who may think we're too staid for them. Make us more current and more exciting. And that market will be your domestic digital users.'

Gabe could feel it, the roar of adrenaline, the tightening in his gut that meant something new, something exhilarating was in the air. 'It would create a great buzz on social media.'

She nodded, her whole face lit up. 'It all works together, doesn't it? I am presenting at the board meeting too. It's less investment up front than you will need—but this is something untried and untested and the current board are a little conservative. You support me and, once I've checked your finances and conclusions, I'll support your digital

paper. We'll have a lot more impact if we're united. Deal?'
She held out her hand.

Gabe worked alone. He preferred it that way. Sure, he
had good relationships with his colleagues, liked to make
sure they were all onside but he didn't want or brook in-
terference.

Freedom at home and at work. That way he never had
to worry about letting anyone down.

But this was a great opportunity—to be part of the team
dragging Rafferty's into a new age. How could he refuse?
He took her hand, cool and elegant just like its owner.

'Deal.'

CHAPTER THREE

POLLY KICKED OFF her shoes with a sigh of relief. She was home, the sun was shining and it was Friday evening. This was exactly what she needed to get over this pesky jet lag. Surely the tiredness, the constant nausea and the lack of appetite should have gone by now?

It wasn't exactly a weekend break, she still had a lot of work to do if she was to wow the board in a week's time, but she could do it at home either in the little sunshine-drenched study at the back of the cottage or in the timber-beamed, book-lined sitting room. Away from the office.

Usually her office was a sanctuary but right now it felt alien. Gabe seemed to fill every corner of it. His gym gear in her cloakroom, a variety of equally disgusting smoothies on the table and, worst of all, Gabe himself.

He was so *active*, always on the phone, pacing round, chatting to every member of staff as if they were his long-lost best friend.

Even his typing was a loud, banging, flamboyant display. She couldn't think, couldn't concentrate when he was in the room.

But, although he had been living in Hopeford, in her house, for several weeks there was no trace of Gabe in the living areas of the cottage; his few possessions were kept neatly put away in the guest bedroom. Not that she'd snooped, obviously, but she had felt a need to reacquaint herself with her home, visiting every room, reminding herself of its quirks and corners.

It was odd being back after such a long absence. The cottage was clean, aired and well stocked, the rambling garden weeded and watered all thanks to the concierge service she employed to take care of her home. Mr Simpkins, the handsome ginger cat she'd inherited when she'd bought the house, was plump and sleek and bearing no discernible grudge after their time apart. But everything felt smaller, more claustrophobic.

For three months she had been someone else. Someone with no purpose, no expectations. It had been disconcerting and yet so freeing.

But that was over. She was home now and she had a lot to do. Friday night usually meant her laptop, a glass of wine and a takeaway. Polly put her hand to her stomach and swallowed hard; maybe she'd forego the latter two this week.

And think about a doctor's appointment if the tiredness and nausea didn't go away soon.

Hang on a second, what was that? Polly had visitors so rarely that it took another sharp decisive peal of the doorbell before she moved. Probably Gabe.

'If he can't keep hold of his keys how can I trust him with Rafferty's online strategy?' she asked Mr Simpkins. He merely yawned and turned over, stretching out in a patch of early evening sunshine.

Walking down the wide stairs towards the hallway, she took a moment to look around; at the polished, oiled beams, the old flagstoned floor, the gilt mirror by the hat stand, the fresh flowers on the antique table. It had all been chosen, placed and cared for by someone else. She lived here but was it really hers?

The doorbell rang again, impatiently. 'I'm coming,' she called, trying to keep the irritation out of her voice. It was hardly her fault that he had forgotten his keys. Unlocking the door, she pulled it open.

It wasn't Gabe.

Tall, broad, hair the same colour as hers and eyes the exact same shade of dark blue. A face she knew as well as she knew her own. A face she hadn't seen in four years. Polly clung onto the door frame, disbelief flooding through her. 'Raff?'

'I still have a key.' He held it up. 'But I didn't think you'd want me just walking in.'

'But, what are you doing here? I thought you were in Jordan. Or Australia?'

'Sorry to disappoint you. Can I come in?'

'Sorry?' Polly gaped at him as his words sank in. 'Yes, of course.'

She stepped back, her mind still grasping for a reason her twin brother was here in her sleepy home town, not trying to save the world, one war zone at a time.

Raff faced her, the love and warmth in his eyes bringing a lump to her throat. How on earth had four years gone by since she had last seen him? 'Come here.' He took her in his arms. It had been so long since he had held her, since she had allowed herself to lean on him.

'It's so good to see you,' he said into her hair. Polly tightened her grip.

It wasn't Raff's fault their grandfather had favoured him, wanted him to take over the store. Yet somehow it had been easier to hold him culpable.

'Hi, heavenly twin,' she murmured and took comfort in his low rumble of laughter. They had been named for the Heavenly Twins, Castor and Pollux, but Polly had escaped with a feminine version of her name. Her brother had been less lucky; nobody, apart from their grandparents, used it—Raff preferred a shorter version of their surname.

'Thanks for looking after everything.' She disentangled herself slowly, although the temptation to lean in and not let go was overwhelming. She led him down the wide hallway towards the kitchen. 'Looking after the house, Mr Simpkins.' She swallowed, hard and painful. 'Taking over at Rafferty's.'

'You needed my help, of course I stepped in.' He paused. 'I wish you'd called, Pol. Told me what was going on. I didn't mind but it would have been good if we had worked together, sorted it out together.'

'After four years? I couldn't,' she admitted, heading over to the fridge so that she didn't have to face him. 'You stayed away, Raff. You went away, left me behind and you didn't come back. Ever.' She swallowed painfully. 'I didn't even know whose side you were on—if you had spoken to Grandfather, knew what he was planning, if you wanted Rafferty's.' That had been her worst fear, that her twin had colluded with her grandfather.

Raff sounded incredulous. 'Surely you didn't think I would agree? That I would take Rafferty's away from you?'

'Grandfather made it very clear that nothing I had done, nothing I could do was enough to compete with your Y chromosome.' She turned, forced herself to meet the understanding in his eyes. 'It destroyed me.'

Raff winced. 'Polly, I spent three months running Rafferty's while you were gone and I hated every minute of it. How you manage I don't know. But even if I had come back and experienced an epiphany about the joys of retail I *still* wouldn't have agreed. I don't deserve it and you do. You've worked for it, you live it, love it. Even Grandfather had to admit in the end that his desire to see me in Father's place was wrong, that his fierce determination for a male heir was utterly crazy. I've agreed to join the board as a family member but that's it. You're CEO, you're in charge.'

Polly grabbed a cold beer and threw it to her twin, who caught it deftly with one hand, and pulled out a bottle of white wine for herself. She checked the label: Chateau Beaufils Chardonnay Semillon. One of Gabe's, then.

'So where have you been?' Raff was leaning against the kitchen counter. He raised the beer. 'Cheers.'

'Oh, here and there.' Polly's cheeks heated up and she busied herself with looking for a corkscrew. *Remember the new bucket list,* she told herself, ruthlessly pushing the more reprehensible details of her time away out of her mind. 'I went backpacking. In South America.' She flashed him a smile. 'Just like you always said I should.'

He smirked. 'When you say backpacking, you mean five-star hotels and air-conditioned tours?'

'Sometimes,' Polly admitted, breathing a sigh of relief as the stubborn cork finally began to give way. She eased it out carefully, wrinkling her nose as the aroma hit her. She held the bottle out to Raff. 'Is this corked?'

He took it and inhaled. 'I don't think so.'

She shrugged, and poured a small amount into a glass. She didn't sip it though; just the sight of the straw-coloured liquid caused her stomach to roll ominously. She put the glass down. 'But I did my fair share of rucksacks and walking boots too, along the Inca trail and other places.' She grinned across at him. 'You wouldn't have recognised me, braids in my hair, a sarong, all my worldly goods in one bag.'

'I had no idea where you were.' He didn't sound accusatory; he didn't need to. She had read his emails, listened to his voicemails. She knew how much worry she'd caused him.

'I didn't want you to. I didn't want pity or advice or

anything but time to figure out who I was, who I wanted to be if I wasn't going to run Rafferty's.'

'And?'

'I was still figuring it out when Clara emailed me telling me to come home. So, don't think I'm not glad to see you but why are you here? Did you miss Mr Simpkins?'

'My shirts don't look the same without a covering of ginger fur,' he agreed. 'Polly, there's something I need to tell you.' He turned his beer bottle round and round, his gaze fixed on it. 'I'm not going to be working in the field any more. I've accepted a job at the headquarters of Doctors Everywhere instead and I'm moving here, to Hopeford.'

Polly stared. 'But you love your job. Why on earth would you change it? And you're moving here? Hang on!' She looked at him suspiciously. 'Do you want to move back in? I'm not running a doss centre for young executive males who are quite capable of finding their own places, you know.'

'For who?' His face cleared. 'Oh, Gabe? He's still here? How are you getting on with him?'

'No.' She shook her head, unwilling to discuss her absent houseguest. 'No changing the subject. What's going on?'

Raff took a deep breath. 'You're not the only one who's been working things out recently. I have to admit I was pissed when you left with no word—I hotfooted it straight here, convinced that Clara knew where you were. I was determined to get it out of her, drag you back and get on with my life.'

'She didn't. I didn't even really know what my plans were.'

His mouth twisted into a smile. 'I know that now but things were a bit hostile for a while.' He shook his head. 'I can't believe it's only been a few months since I met her, that there was a time I didn't know her. Thing is, Pol, meeting Clara changed everything. I'm engaged. That's why I'm staying in the UK, that's why I'm moving to Hopeford. I'm marrying Clara.'

'Bonsoir?'

Polly should get off the sofa, should open her laptop, look as if she were working.

But she couldn't. Her appetite for the game, the competition had gone.

'Hi.' She looked up wearily as Gabe walked into the room. He was so tall his head nearly brushed the beams on the low ceiling.

'Nice run?' she continued. Small talk was good; it was easy. It stopped her having to think.

'Oui.' He stretched, seemingly unaware that his T-shirt was riding up and exposing an inch of flat, toned abdomen. 'A quick ten kilometres. It ruins the buzz though, getting the train after. I might try biking back to Hopeford one evening. What is it? Just fifty kilometres?'

'Just,' she echoed.

Gabe looked at her curiously. 'Are you okay?'

'Yes, no.' She gave a wry laugh. 'I don't really know. Raff's engaged.'

'Your brother? That's amazing. We should celebrate.'

'We should,' she agreed.

The dark eyes turned to her, their expression keen. 'You're not happy?'

'Of course I am,' Polly defended herself and then sighed. 'I am,' she repeated. 'It's just he's moving here, to Hopeford. He's marrying my closest friend and joining the board at Rafferty's.'

She shook her head. 'I feel like I am being a total cow,' she admitted. 'It's just, I have spent my whole life competing against him—and he wins without even taking part.

'And now…' she looked down at her hands '…now he's moving to my town, will be on the board of my company and is marrying the one person I can confide in. It feels like there's nowhere I am just me, not Raff's twin sister.'

The silence stretched out between them.

'I have three sisters,' he said after a while. 'I'm the youngest. It can be hard to find your place.'

Polly looked over at him. 'Is that why you're here? Not working at the vineyard?'

'Partly. And because I needed to prove some things to myself.' He walked over to Mr Simpkins, who was lying on the cushion-covered window seat set into the wall on the far side of the chimney breast.

Gabe should have been an incongruous presence in the white-walled, book-lined sitting room, the soft furnishings and details were so feminine, so English country cottage. He was too young, too indisputably French, too tall, too *male* for the low-beamed, cosy room. And yet he looked utterly at home reaching over to run one hand down Mr Simpkins' spine.

He was wearing jeans, his dark hair falling over his forehead, his pallor emphasised by the deep shadows under his dark eyes and the black stubble covering his jaw. He worked so late each night, rising at dawn to fit in yet another session in the gym—and the lack of sleep showed.

Polly watched the long, lean fingers' firm caress as her cat flattened himself in suppliant pleasure and felt a jolt in the pit of her stomach, a sudden insistent ache of desire as her nerve endings remembered the way his hand had settled in the curve of her waist, those same fingers moving up along her body, making her purr almost as loudly as Mr Simpkins.

'Is that why you went away?' he asked, all his attention seemingly on the writhing cat. 'Because of your brother?'

Polly flushed, partly in shame at having to admit her own second-class status to a relative stranger—and half in embarrassment at her reaction to the slow, sure strokes from Gabe's capable-looking hands.

'Partly,' she admitted. 'I had to get away, learn who I was without Rafferty's.'

'And did you?' He looked directly at her then, his eyes almost black and impossibly dark. 'Learn who you are?'

Polly thought back. To blisters and high altitudes. To the simple joy of a shower after a five-day trek. To long twilight walks on the beach. To lying back and watching the stars, the balmy breeze warm on her bare skin. To the lack of responsibility. To taking risks.

It had been fun but ultimately meaningless.

'No,' she said. 'I saw some amazing things, did amazing things and I had fun. But there was nothing to find out. Without Rafferty's I don't have anything…I'm no one.'

'That's not true.' His voice was low, intimate.

'It is,' she argued. 'But Raff? He is utterly and completely himself. I think I've always envied that. And now he has Clara—which is great, she's lovely and I'm sure they'll be very happy. But my brother and best friend getting married? It leaves me with no one.'

She heard her words echo as she said them and flushed. 'I am the most selfish beast, ignore me, Gabe. I'm tired and fluey and having a pathetic moment. It'll pass!'

He regarded her quietly. 'And you don't eat,' he said after a while. 'Come on, I'll cook.'

Polly was still protesting as Gabe rummaged through the fridge, trying to find something he could make into a meal a Frenchman could be proud of. It might have to be a simple omelette, he decided, pulling the eggs out of the fridge along with a courgette, some cheese and the end of some chorizo.

'You really don't have to cook for me,' she said. 'I'm quite happy with some bread and cheese.'

'Do you ever cook?' He looked at the gleaming range cooker, the beautiful copper saucepans hanging from their hooks looking as blemish free as the day they were bought.

'I butter bread and slice cheese. Occasionally I shred a lettuce.'

'That is some variety.'

'I know.'

He continued to chop onions as she watched.

'So you're a business whizz-kid, a gourmet chef, a tri-athlete. Is there anything you can't do?'

'I've never backpacked.'

'Didn't fancy the dirt and blisters?'

'I didn't have the time.' Gabe scraped the onions into the pan and tipped it expertly so they were evenly covered in oil. 'I went to university late and had a lot of time to make up. No chance to slack off.'

Polly was sitting at the counter, her chin propped in her hands. 'Is that why you set yourself such a punishing schedule now?'

Was it? All Gabe knew was that once you'd spent a year confined to bed, without the strength to get a glass of water, watching your classmates grow up without you, that once you knew just what losing someone meant then you had to make the most of every single second.

'You can sleep when you're dead,' he said. It was all too true; he'd thought about that long enough.

Now he just wanted to live every moment.

Polly continued to watch as he whisked the eggs. 'What do your parents think? Of you working away? Did they expect you to work with them?'

Ouch, that was direct. 'They found it hard to adjust.' He poured the eggs into the pan with a flourish. 'They wanted me to go to university nearby, stay in Provence. When I said I was going to Boston they were hurt. But they got over it.'

On the surface at least. The very worst part of being ill had been the despair in his parents' faces whenever they thought he wasn't watching. Or the forced positivity when they knew he was. It made it hard to say no to them.

'You're the son and heir.' There was no hiding the bitterness in her words. 'Of course they expect a lot.'

His mouth curved into a wry smile. 'Son? *Oui.* Heir? That remains to be seen. Celine is studying vineyard management in New Zealand and Claire is doing a very good job of opening the chateau up to guests and tourists while presenting them with a perfect trio of grandchildren.'

'Three!' She straightened up, pulling her hair back into a knot as she did so. He watched, fascinated, as she gathered up the silky golden strands and twisted them ruthlessly, tucking the end under. It wouldn't take much to make it spill free. Just one touch.

'Three in three years,' he confirmed. 'And Natalie is expecting her second. She takes care of all the advertising and marketing. So you see I have some formidable rivals for the vineyard. If I wanted it that is.'

'Isn't it funny? You and Raff could have it all on a plate. And you don't even want it.'

'We still have to work,' he argued. 'No one I work with cares what my parents do. Raff had to work his way up at Doctors Everywhere. It's exactly the same. Pass me a plate, will you?'

Polly got up and took two plates off the dresser, handing them over. Gabe shredded some lettuce and added a couple of tomatoes before cutting the omelette in half and sliding it onto a plate.

'*Voilà,*' he said, sliding it towards her.

'Thanks, Gabe, this looks great.' Her hair was coming loose and she gathered it up again, beginning the familiar twisting motion as she re-knotted it, before picking up her fork.

'I have worked at Rafferty's since I was legally allowed to get a job. Before that I spent every moment there.' Her voice was wistful, filled with love.

Gabe pictured the iconic store, its large dome and art deco façade dominating the expensive London street on which it was situated. It was always busy, exuding wealth and glamour and style. Exciting and as restless as its patrons, prowling in search of the bag, the outfit, the décor that would make them unique, special. It was easy to see why she loved it.

But then his mind turned to the chateau, to the acres and acres of vines, the scent of lavender and the scarlet flash of poppies. The old grey building, covered in ivy. He loved the buzz of retail but had to admit that no shop, no matter how magical, could match his home. The look in her eyes, the note in her voice spoke of the same deep connection.

'It's your home,' he said.

'Yes!' Polly pointed her fork at him. 'That's it. But only temporarily. It was made very clear to me that I could work there but it was never going to be mine. Grandfather even wanted me to study History of Art instead of business, not that I took any notice of him.'

So much dwelling on the past; if Gabe had done that he would still be in Provence, weeping in the graveyard. 'But now look at you. In charge of the whole store.'

Polly took a bite of the omelette, her face thoughtful. 'I told you I went away to find myself. The truth is I had no choice. Grandfather came to see me three months ago and told me he was signing Rafferty's over to Raff.' She laughed but there was no humour in the sound.

'My ex had just got engaged and Grandfather was concerned for me, or so he said. He thought I was leaving it too late, "letting the good ones get away".' She swallowed. 'He said it was for my own good—I should concentrate on marriage, have children before it's too late.'

'That was unkind.'

'It hurt me.' It obviously still did, her voice and her face full of pain. 'So I left my job, my home and I went away to try and work out who I was without Rafferty's. But then Raff walked away, for good this time, and I came back.'

She looked at Gabe, a gleam of speculation in her eyes. 'I have to admit I was thrown when I got back to find you already in place. At first I thought Grandfather was trying to replace Raff, but now?' She shook her head, once more dislodging the precarious knot of hair. 'I wonder what kind of game he's playing.'

'Maybe, he just knows I'm good at my job.'

'Oh, that will be part of it,' she agreed. 'But with Raff engaged I'll bet there's something else. It wouldn't be the first time he's played matchmaker. You've got to admit it's convenient, working together, living together.' Her voice trailed off.

'And I thought it was an over-ambitious developer tunnelling under my building. Your grandfather must have some extraordinary powers.'

'You have no idea,' Polly said darkly. 'He's pretty unscrupulous.' She shook her head. 'He just can't stop interfering.'

'You are just speculating. Besides, what does it matter? He can play all he wants.' Gabe made an effort to speak calmly but his heart was thudding so loudly he was surprised the kitchen wasn't shaking. Marriage? Children? If

Charles Rafferty was looking at Gabe to fulfil his dynastic dreams he had a long, long wait ahead. 'We don't have to join in. Not on his terms.'

Light, fun and short-lived. That was all he wanted, all he could cope with. Polly Rafferty was many impressive things but were light and fun part of her enticing package? She hid it well if so.

But getting under her skin *was* fun. He was pretty sure, by the way her gaze lingered on his mouth, by the sudden flush that highlighted her cheeks occasionally, that she hadn't forgotten about that kiss.

And he certainly hadn't—not for want of trying.

'Of course we don't.' She sounded more like her usual self. 'I've never allowed myself to follow the path Grandfather thinks suitable. I'm not going to start now he has finally retired. I'm still so tired, I'm probably imagining things. You're not my type at all. Even Grandfather must see that.'

This was where a wise man would stay silent. 'I'm not?'

The soft words caught her, echoing round and around her head.

'Of course not, you're an exercise-mad smoothie drinker who flirts inappropriately with half my staff.' Polly tried to keep her voice light but she could feel inappropriate heat rushing to her cheeks, a sweet insistent ache pulsing in her chest, reverberating all the way down to the pit of her stomach. She didn't want to look at him yet somehow she had turned, caught in his dark gaze. 'Not to mention that we work together.'

Had he leaned in closer? The dark eyes were even more intent than usual, black pools she was drawn to, the kind of bottomless depths girls could drown in. 'I won't tell if you don't.'

'Tell what?' But her tone lacked conviction even to herself. 'Gabe, I…' Polly wasn't entirely sure what she had been planning to say, whether she was going to lean in, close the distance between them and pull him in close—or turn away and tell him to grow up and stop with the innuendoes. She knew the sensible choice, the logical choice and yet she hesitated.

But the kitchen seemed to have shrunk, the space suddenly, suffocatingly small, the air so stuffy she could hardly breathe, the tumult in her stomach churning. She gasped for a breath, realising her mistake too late, pushing her stool back and running for the downstairs cloakroom horrifyingly aware that she wasn't going to make it.

'I am so humiliated.' Polly leant forward until her forehead touched the kitchen counter, grateful for the coolness of the granite. 'Thank you for taking care of me.'

That wasn't quite enough but she didn't want to articulate all the reasons for her gratitude. The gentle way he had rubbed her back, held her hair back from her face, waited with her until the last spasm had passed. 'You're good with sick people.' She looked up and smiled but he didn't return her admittedly pathetic attempt, his eyes filled with an unexpected pain.

'I have some experience.' His face was unreadable but his voice was gentle.

'I wasn't drunk.' Bad enough that it had happened; it would be far worse if he thought she was some kind of lush.

'You hadn't eaten. Even one glass could have that effect.' He looked at the glass she had poured earlier.

'I didn't even have one sip,' she protested. 'Just the smell made me feel ill. I must have picked up some kind of bug.'

He put a hand on her shoulder, just that one light touch sending shivers down her spine. 'You should eat something now, some crackers maybe.'

'No.' Not crackers. Her body was very insistent. 'I need…' She paused, thought. She *was* a little hungry, now the churning had stopped. 'Hang on.' She pushed herself to her feet and walked over to the stone pantry.

Polly opened the door that led to the old-fashioned, walk-in cold room and looked at the shelves that lined the walls, at the marble meat shelf at the far end.

'I know they're here somewhere. I saw them just the other day. I would never buy them. They must be Raff's, vile things. Aha!' Her hand closed triumphantly on a cardboard box. 'Got you.'

She hauled her prize triumphantly out, grabbing a bowl off the oak dresser and setting them both onto the counter. 'Cornflakes! Now I need sugar, lots of sugar. And milk, cold, rich milk. I never usually crave milk.' She pushed the thought away. 'Must be the bug. Maybe I need calcium?'

Raff hadn't said a word, just watched, eyes narrowed, as Polly poured a gigantic bowl of cornflakes, sprinkled them liberally with sugar and added almost a pint of milk to the already brimming bowl. 'This looks amazing,' she told him, almost purring with contentment.

'That looks disgusting. Like something my sister would eat when she's pregnant.'

The word hung there, echoing around the room. Polly put her spoon down and stared at him.

'It's just a bug.' But her voice was wobbling.

'Of course.' He sounded unsure, almost embarrassed, the accent thickening.

'Mixed with jet lag.'

'I know.'

'I'm not…'

'I didn't mean to infer that you were. I'm sorry.'

'But…what if I *am*?'

CHAPTER FOUR

WAS SHE? COULD she be? It should be impossible. It was impossible! Only technically...

Only technically it wasn't.

'Oh no,' she whispered. She looked up at Gabe. He was leaning against the kitchen counter, his face inscrutable. 'It was only once.'

His mouth twisted. 'That's all it takes, *ma chérie*.'

'How could I have been so stupid? What was I thinking?' She pushed the bowl of cornflakes back across the counter. They were rapidly going soggy and her nausea rose again at their mushy state. 'Obviously I wasn't thinking. I was trying not to, that was the point.'

But she had to think now; there was no point in giving into the rising panic swelling inside her. Her throat might be closing up in fear, her palms damp but she could override her body's signals. If only she'd done that ten weeks ago...

Ten weeks! And she hadn't even suspected, putting the nausea and the tiredness down to stress, jet lag, a bug.

It could still be! Two and two didn't always make four did it? Not in some obscure pure mathematical plane. Probably.

'I need a test.'

'Oui.' He was still expressionless. 'In the morning I'll...'

'Not in the morning!' Was he crazy? Did he think she was going to sit around and wait all night when liberation could be just around the corner? 'There's a twenty-four-hour supermarket in Dartingdon, I'll get one from there.'

She was on her feet as she said it. Thank goodness for modern twenty-four-seven life.

'You can't drive.'

She stopped still, swivelled and stared. 'I already said I didn't drink anything.'

'No.' He shook his head. 'But you're in shock. It isn't safe.'

So her hands were shaking a little, her legs slightly weak. She'd be fine. She'd driven the route a thousand times.

'And what if you throw up again?'

'Then I'll pull over. You don't have to take care of me, Gabe. I was big enough to get myself into this mess, I am certainly capable of sorting it out. I don't need anyone.'

His eyes bored into hers. 'If that's true then how did this happen?'

Ouch! That was well and truly below the belt. 'Want me to draw you a diagram?' She could hear the tremor of anger running through her voice and tried to rein it back.

'You fell out with your family here, went to find your-self, felt lost and lonely and so you what? Fell for the first smile and compliment?'

Polly stood stock-still, ice-cold anger running through her veins, her bones, every nerve and sinew. How dared he?

How dared he be so right?

'That wasn't what happened. Not that it has anything to do with you.' Shaking with a toxic mixture of righteous anger, adrenaline and nausea, she marched over to the counter to grab her car keys but before her hand could close on the fob it was whisked away in a decisive mas-culine hand.

'I'll go.'

'We drive on the left here. And do you even know where Dartingdon is?' she added slightly lamely. Polly wanted to prove a point but part of her knew he was right. Annoyingly. She was barely fit to run a bath let alone drive twisty country roads.

'I'm a big boy. I'll figure it out.'

'No.' All the anger had drained. Now she was just weary, utterly, achingly tired. 'You can drive but I'll navigate. And I'll scream if you take my beloved car even one centimetre over onto the wrong side.'

He regarded her levelly then nodded. 'Okay. I still think you would be better staying here.'

But she was adamant. Polly had never waited for things to be brought to her—she'd never have made it this far if she had. 'I can't wait that long,' she admitted. 'I need to know straight away.'

'And then what?'

That was the million-dollar question. 'Then I can plan. Everything's better with a plan.'

She was quiet. So quiet Gabe would almost swear that she was asleep except when he glanced over he could see the glare of her phone illuminating the whites of her eyes.

'Concentrate on the road,' she snapped but he could sense the worry under the anger. He had got used to that, with Marie. In the end when the pain had got too much, as the fear and anger and sheer bloody unfairness had overtaken her she had been cross all the time, barely able to be civil, even to those she loved.

Especially to those she loved.

'I am,' he said. He couldn't resist one little provocative grenade. 'If you drove a proper car…'

'This is a proper car!'

'It's a grown-up's toy,' he teased. It actually handled

pretty well, the small body taking the many twists and turns of the Oxfordshire country roads surprisingly well. 'Shame you'll have to get rid of it.'

He could feel her stiffen beside him. 'What do you mean?'

'It's a two-seater…' He didn't have to say any more. From the intake of breath he knew his point had hit home.

'Possibly not. We'll know soon enough.' But there wasn't any hope in her voice.

She didn't say anything for the next few miles. Despite his confidence earlier, this was the first time Gabe had actually driven a left-hand drive and it required most of his concentration to stay on the correct side of the road as he navigated the narrow curves. He wasn't helped by the car; low slung and powerful, she was absurdly responsive to his slightest touch, almost as if she were desperate to speed on.

Although there were no street lights in this country corner it wasn't too hard to see his way as he drove through hedge-lined lanes, fields almost at their ripest stretching out on both sides towards gently rolling hills. The summer solstice was nearly upon them and it was barely dark out, more of a gloomy dull grey. Like his mood.

There was no reason for him to feel so…so what? Slighted? Gabe sighed; he really needed to get over himself. One kiss did not equal any kind of relationship.

And if it did he would be headed the other way, right back to France.

It was just, if Polly Rafferty had really indulged in a night of meaningless, no-holds-barred, anonymous sex he wished she'd indulged with him.

He could be wrong, she might often go out prowling bars and clubs for one-night stands but he would bet the oldest bottle of wine in the vineyard's formidably stocked cellars that this had been a one-off occasion. And pregnant or not she was unlikely to indulge again.

'This doesn't have to change anything. It *doesn't* change anything.' Her voice penetrated his thoughts. Gabe risked a glance across at his reluctant passenger. Polly had pulled herself upright and was looking straight ahead, her jaw firmly set. 'The timing is awful but I could make it work.'

'Didn't you want children?'

There was another long pause. 'I don't *know* children,' she said after a while. 'I don't know how families work, normal ones. Raff and I were raised by our grandparents and they sent us away to school when we were small. It's not something I've ever thought about.' She huffed out a small laugh. 'Not every woman hits thirty and starts counting down her biological clock, you know.'

'But your house, it's begging for a family.' Five bedrooms, the large garden full of hidden corners and climbable trees. Despite the low ceilings and homely furnishings it felt too big, too echoey for just two people. And she had been living there alone for three years.

'It's just a building.' Her voice was dismissive.

Gabe shrugged. He was no psychologist but he had been through enough counselling—support groups, family therapy, grief counselling, chronic illness groups—to know a little bit about the subconscious. The cottage was a family-home wish come true.

'If you say so.'

She shifted, turned to look at him. 'How about you? Dreams of *petits enfants* clustering around your knee one day?'

'I'm a good uncle,' he said shortly.

'Guys can say that, can't they? No pressure to settle down, get married, churn out kids. You have all the time in the world.'

'None of us know how much time we have.' He meant to say it lightly but the words came out too quick, too bitter. He shot her a quick glance. 'I had cancer in my teens, a lymphoma. It teaches you to take nothing for granted.'

Polly gasped, a loud audible intake of breath as she put her hand to her mouth. 'Oh, Gabe. I am so sorry. I didn't mean…'

'It's fine.' This was why he hated people knowing. A brush with mortality and they never treated you the same way again. It was as if you were tainted with the mark of Death's scythe, a constant reminder that no one was safe.

'Besides, I can't.' The words were out before he knew it, the darkness beginning to shadow the car giving it the seal of a confessional, somewhere safe.

'Can't what?'

'Have children. Probably. Chemotherapy, stem-cell treatment…' His voice trailed off; he didn't need to add the rest.

'Oh.' Understanding dawned in the long drawn-out syllable. 'Didn't they freeze any?' Her hand was back over her mouth. 'I'm sorry. I didn't mean to intrude.'

'They didn't think it would have any long-term effects.' He smiled wryly. 'I was seventeen. To be honest it was the last thing I was thinking about—or my parents thought about. But it took longer, needed stronger drugs than they expected. It's okay. I'd rather be healthy.'

Her hand had crept to her stomach. 'Of course.'

'They did say it can change in time but I have never been tested. There's no point. I don't want them anyway,' he surprised himself by offering. 'The worst part of being ill was seeing my parents suffer. I'm not sure I'm strong enough to put myself through that.'

'I watched my father die.' Her voice was flat. 'That wasn't much fun either.'

They didn't speak the rest of the way there. Gabe was too absorbed in his thoughts and Polly had returned to jabbing furiously at her phone as if it could give her all the answers she needed.

Following the signs, he navigated his way around the roundabouts that ringed the old town, pulling off into an ugly development of warehouses and cavernous shops.

'We're here,' he said.

Polly didn't move, just looked out of the window at the neon orange streetlamps and the parking signs. 'Okay.'

'Why don't I go for you?' he suggested but she was already shaking her head.

'Thank you but I really need to do this by myself.'

'Are you sure you have enough?'

Polly bit her lip. Maybe two each of five different brands was slightly excessive but she had to make sure. If Gabe was potentially harbouring an alien life form inside him he would want to know one hundred per cent too.

'No.' She twisted the bag nervously. 'Do you think I should have got three of each?'

'I think you should leave at least one test on the shelves, just in case someone else is tearing through the night in need of answers.'

'Let's just get home.' She tugged impatiently at the car door, glaring at Gabe as he made no move to unlock it.

'Are you sure?'

She stared at him. 'What? You want to pop out for a nice meal first? Maybe go for a moonlight stroll? Of course I'm sure.'

He didn't react. 'I meant maybe you wanted to take the test now. Find out one way or another.'

'Oh.' How had he guessed?

Polly looked around the car park. There were several

chain restaurants but they were all showing signs of closing for the night. Or the supermarket toilets; they would still be open.

She bit back a hysterical giggle. She had never actually imagined taking a pregnancy test, let alone taking it in the strip-lit anonymity of a supermarket loo. It wasn't the cosy scene depicted in the adverts.

But then she wasn't the hopeful woman on the advert either.

'There's nowhere here.'

'Not here exactly.' Finally he clicked the button and the doors unlocked. 'We can find somewhere a little more salubrious than this.'

It took him less than five minutes to exit the car park and start back round the ring road, retracing their earlier route.

'Don't worry,' he said as Polly looked worriedly at the sign pointing the way back to Hopeford. 'I've got an idea.'

'I trust you.' And she did. Maybe because she had nobody else—not even herself.

At the Hopeford roundabout Gabe took a different exit, driving into the car park of a large redbrick building. Polly must have driven past it dozens of times but had never registered it before. Why would she? Anonymous roadside hotels offering business deals and cheap weddings weren't her usual style.

'Wait here.' He was gone before she could formulate a reply. Resentment rose up inside her. Who was he to tell her what to do? She half rose out of her seat, determined to follow him, to regain control.

But no, she reminded herself, she had relinquished control, tonight at least. Polly sank back into her seat and tried to control the panicked race of her heart.

The bag was on her lap, the sharp edges of the boxes an

uncomfortable fit against her thighs. Pulling out a handful, Polly turned them this way and that, reading the fine print on them curiously. Fancy being thirty-one and never having even properly seen a pregnancy test before!

But why would she have? She had been good to study with but she had never been the kind of friend others turned to. Not for panicked confidences and surreptitious tests in the school bathrooms or university toilets.

And she had never been the type to slip up herself. Not careful Polly Rafferty.

Not until now.

How could she have not known? Suspected that the bug she just couldn't shift might be something more? But she had continued with the pills her doctor had prescribed her for her trip, relieved to be spared the inconvenience of her monthly cycle, and missed nature's most glaring warning.

'Okay,' she muttered. How hard could taking one of these be? A blue line, two pink lines, a cross for yes. A positive sign? That was a little presumptuous. Another simply said 'pregnant'. She swallowed, hard, the lump in her throat making the simple act difficult. Painful.

She jumped as a knock sounded on her window, muttering as the packets fell to the floor. She hastily gathered them up. They felt wrong, like contraband. It was as if just being seen with them branded her in some unwanted way.

Looking up, she saw Gabe. He must have seen her reading the packets. Heat flooded through her and she took a deep breath, trying her best to summon her usual poise.

She opened the door. 'Hi.'

'They have a room we can use.' He stood aside as she got out of the car and waited while she gathered the dropped boxes, stuffing them into the carrier bag.

'Won't they wonder why we are checking in so late with no luggage?'

Gabe huffed out a short laugh. 'Polly. They will think we are illicit lovers looking for a bed for an hour, or travellers realising we need a bed for the night. Or, more likely, they won't think at all. Come on.'

He took the bag from her as if it were nothing, as if it didn't carry the key to her hopes and dreams. To the freedom she had never even appreciated until this moment.

'Come on.' He strode off towards the hotel.

Polly hesitated. Maybe she could wait until she got home after all. In fact maybe she could just wait, wait for this nightmare to be over.

Her hand crept to her abdomen and stayed there. What if? There was only one way to find out.

The hotel lobby was as anonymous as the outside, the floor tiled in a nondescript beige, the walls a coffee colour accented by meaningless abstract prints, the whole set off by fake oak fittings. Gabe led the way confidently past the desk and Polly noted how the receptionists' eyes followed him.

And how their eyes rested on her in jealous appraisal, making her all too aware of her old tracksuit, her lack of make-up. She lifted her head; let them speculate, let them judge.

They walked along a long corridor, doors at regular intervals on either side. 'Aha, *voici*,' Gabe muttered and stopped in front of one of the white wooden doors.

Number twenty-six. Such a random number, bland and meaningless. It didn't feel prophetic.

He opened the door with the key card and stood aside to let Polly enter. Her eyes swept around the room. The main part of the room was taken up by a large double bed made up in white linen with a crimson throw and matching pillows. The same tired abstracts were on the walls of the room; a TV and a sizeable desk completed the simple layout.

The door to her right stood open to reveal a white tiled bathroom.

The bathroom.

Panic whooshed through her and Polly put out a hand to steady herself against the wall. It was time.

What if she was pregnant?

What if she wasn't?

The thought froze her. That was what she wanted. Wasn't it?

'I'm going to order some food. I didn't manage more than a couple of forkfuls of that omelette. You should eat. What do you want?' Gabe's voice broke through her paralysis like a spoon stirring slowly through thick treacle.

Polly blinked at him, trying to make sense of the words. How could he even think of food at a time like this? 'I'm not hungry.'

'I'm ordering for you anyway. I'm going to have a beer. What do you want to drink?' He flashed a look at the bag on the bed. 'You're going to need a lot of liquid to get through that lot.'

As if the whole episode weren't mortifying enough. Why hadn't they invented tests you breathed on?

Gabe sat down on the bed and kicked off his shoes, one hand reaching for the menu, the other for the TV control. He looked like a man completely happy with his surroundings as he swung his legs onto the bed and reclined.

The bed.

The one and only.

'This is a double room.'

He grinned at her. 'I can see why they made you CEO.'

'You booked us a double?'

'I took the room they had available so that you—' he

cast a speaking glance at the bag next to him '—could get on and do what you have to do. I might as well be comfortable, fed and watered while I wait. Panic not, princess. Your virtue is safe with me.'

Or what was left of it, she silently filled in the rest of the sentence. What was she thinking anyway? She was potentially pregnant, definitely sick, had bags under her eyes big enough for a whole week's worth of groceries and was wearing an old tracksuit, her freshly washed hair pulled back into a knot. Clothes she had put on after puking over her outfit, floor and cloakroom. She wasn't exactly a catch.

To be honest she was surprised Gabe hadn't got them separate rooms, not a double. Anything less sexy than Polly Rafferty right now was hard to imagine.

'Right then.' She took a tremulous step forward, then another, leaning forward and grabbing the bag. 'Let's do this thing.'

He looked up from the menu, his eyes dark with concern. 'Do you want…I mean is there anything I can do?'

'You can hardly pee on a stick for me,' Polly snapped. She took a breath, her cheeks heating up. Great, she could add scarlet and sweaty to her long list of desirable attributes. 'No, really. I don't think either of us will ever recover if you come in there with me.'

The tiles were cold on her cheek and hands and beginning to chill the rest of her body. She should move, get up.

But getting up was a pretty tall order right now. In fact, Polly wasn't sure she was ever going to move again; she could spend the rest of her life curled up here, right?

Curled up in a foetal position. Now that was pretty damn ironic.

A bang on the hotel room door made her start. But of course, Gabe was there. He would take care of it.

She heard the mumbling of voices and the clink of crockery. If only they would shut up. Quiet was good. The bedroom door swung shut with a resounding *thunk*.

Good, peace again.

'Polly.'

Drat the man. If she didn't answer maybe he would go away.

'Polly, your food is here.'

The tiles had gone from cold to numbing. Polly liked numb. It was peaceful.

'Polly, if you don't answer me right now I am going to break down the door.'

He wouldn't, would he?

'Final warning, three, two...'

'Go away.' Was that her voice so clear and strong? She thought it would be croaky with years of misuse. But after all it had only been fifteen minutes since she had shut the door.

It just felt like centuries.

'Polly Rafferty, open the door this instant and come and eat some food.'

She pulled a face in the direction of the door.

'Now!'

Her peace had evaporated. He was evidently not going to give up.

'I'm coming.'

She rolled round and clambered painfully to her feet, hugging herself as the cold from the floor permeated every pore, and walked slowly to the door, twisted the lock and inched the door open. 'Satisfied?'

'I ordered you chips. And bread. Carbs are good for sore stomachs.'

'I thought you only ordered things full of vitamins.'

He didn't answer, just walked away to lift the silver covers off the plates on the desk.

'You're having chips as well?' Wonders would never cease. She'd bet half her trust fund that he would go on an extra run tomorrow and not stop until he had burnt off every calorie and gram of fat.

'I wasn't sure that you would cope with the smell of anything else.'

He hadn't asked about the test, not even with his eyes.

'They're positive.'

A flash of something then; sorrow, a hint of anger but both overshadowed with concern. 'They all agree?'

'I only managed to take six, even after drinking a gallon of water.'

She sank onto the bed. 'Oh, God, positive. What do I do?'

He handed her a plate. 'Tomorrow you plan. But now… now you eat.'

Polly was showing no sign of wanting to leave the hotel room. She had managed to eat a few chips and drink the tea he'd ordered. Now she was lying on the bed seemingly absorbed in the music videos playing on the TV.

But Gabe could tell she wasn't hearing a note.

He put the empty plates out into the corridor and walked back into the room. Polly hadn't moved, not even a centimetre. With one eye on her, as cautious as if she were a feral cat, Gabe sat back onto the bed and stretched out alongside her. Close but not touching.

He put his hands behind his head and stared at the ceiling. The plaster was perfectly smooth, as featureless as the rest of the hotel.

'I can't bake.'

He turned his head to look at her. She was still propped up on the pillows and staring at the TV.

'That's okay.'

'Of course it's not okay. You have to be able to bake. No one cares if a mother has an MBA or an amazing job. It's the cupcakes that count. I can't sew either.'

'No, but you work somewhere full of people who can do both those things so why care?'

She moved slowly until she was propped on her side looking at him. Her eyes were almost navy blue, matching the shadows deepening under them. Her skin pale under the rapidly fading tan. 'I bet your mother can bake and sew.'

'*Oui*, but she doesn't have an MBA.'

She didn't answer, just continued to look at him, her eyes searching his face as if he had all the answers.

'I don't know his surname.'

Cold rage swirled. How could anyone seduce this woman and just walk away? There were women who knew the game, who enjoyed playing, who wanted little more than a night or two. They were the ones you played with. 'We can find him.'

'You think?' The hope in her voice was killing. But then she shook her head. 'I don't see how. All I know is that he's Danish. What a mess. He probably wouldn't want to be involved, but he should know.'

'Who is he?'

'Markus. I met him in Mancora after I finished the Inca trail—he was about my age, recently divorced. A little lost.' She tried for a smile. 'Like me.'

'And I thought this was it, my life here, at Rafferty's, was over, that I needed to start again. I needed to be a new Polly.'

'That's a shame,' he said, keeping his voice level despite every trembling instinct. 'I kind of like the old Polly.'

'Me too,' she whispered as if it were a confession. 'But

old Polly had failed. No job, nobody who cared about me. Oh, I dated, had serious relationships but I always walked away. Relationships need compromise, you see. Only what they wanted was for *me* to compromise. For *me* to work less hours, to attend *their* work dos. To make the relationship work I had to be less. They could just keep on doing what they were doing.'

'Fools.'

Her mouth curved upwards. 'I thought so. I would leave and move on. But old Polly never learnt. She always went out with successful men, businessmen, suits and chauffeured cars and busy schedules and she always, always failed. So why not try someone new? Someone different?'

That had always been Gabe's philosophy. New, different, meaningless. It didn't sound so pretty on her lips.

'It makes sense.' In a warped way it did. He understood exactly why she had thrown caution to the wind.

'I had a list, of things I had never done, things most people did in their teens and early twenties. Swim naked, sleep under the stars.' She flushed. 'Have sex on a beach.' She shook her head. 'It sounds so childish.'

'No, it doesn't.' Gabe knew what it was like to miss out on things. He hadn't gone to teen parties, hadn't experimented with girls or beer or flirted with danger. Instead he'd hovered on the brink of death, he'd fallen in love, he'd lost everything.

'I've never done any of those things either,' he confided, trying to push away the image of Polly, tall and willowy, tanned bare skin glowing in the moonlight.

'It was supposed to mean nothing. Only now…' Her voice trailed off. 'I've messed up so badly. I finally have everything I always wanted but I don't know what to do.'

'You don't have to figure it out tonight.' Gabe was supposed to be keeping his distance, supposed to be the chauffeur, nothing more, but watching her tears spill out, hot and heavy, he couldn't not act. Without thought he edged closer, pulled her in, wrapped his arms around her and allowed her body to settle along his.

She fitted like a glove, her head on his shoulder, her chest against his, hip against hip.

'How could I mess up like this? I have never ever put a foot wrong. The one time I allow myself to just act, to not think and it explodes all over my dreams. I need to be a CEO, not a mother.'

'Who says you can't be both? When I was diagnosed I had so many plans. Plans to pull the hottest girl at school, to captain the rugby team. Plans to ace my exams. I had to rethink everything. In the end my plan was to live. And I did.'

'And the other things?' she asked softly.

'I didn't pull the hottest girl in school, but I fell in love with someone much better.' Gabe tightened his grip and tried not to remember Marie crying in his arms. 'I gave up rugby but took up marathons and triathlons—and I still aced my exams. Plans change, they adapt, you'll be fine.'

'How?'

Gabe sighed. It took time, adjustment, pain—but she wasn't ready to hear that. Not yet. 'We can figure it out tomorrow. It's all going to be okay. I promise, it's going to be okay.'

CHAPTER FIVE

IT WAS WARM, the mattress firm and comfortable but not quite as firm and comfortable as the bare chest she was nestled against. Polly sighed and rolled in a little closer, allowing her hand to slip round the firm midriff to trail along the smooth back.

Hang on. Skin? Muscle?

She snatched her hand back and rolled away, swallowing back the all too familiar nausea that hit her the moment she moved. And with it reality came crashing through the sleep fog, harsh, bitter. Terrifying.

She lay there trying to summon up enough strength to move, and doing her best to ignore the almost overwhelming temptation to move closer to Gabe, to put her arm back around him, snuggle in close and go back to sleep.

Getting into bed with strange men had got her into this situation. It looked as if she hadn't learned anything!

Not that the two cases were at all the same. She was still fully dressed in the tracksuit she had thrown on last night.

She was still pregnant.

An ache began to throb, squeezing the side of her temples, the sticky soreness of her eyes an unwelcome reminder of the tears she had shed the night before. The weakness she had displayed.

Polly put her hand over her mouth, stifling the groan that threatened to escape. What had she done? She had *cried*. Cried in front of Gabriel Beaufils of all people. She had just handed him the keys to utter humiliation. How could she spin this situation as a positive thing when he could expose her any second? Tell everyone that she had messed up.

That she was fallible.

But would he? Heat burned her cheeks as she remembered his gentleness, his words, his confidences.

No, somehow Polly knew deep down that he wouldn't expose her. But he would still *know*. Know that she wasn't strong, that she had allowed herself to lean on him.

It couldn't happen again.

'Morning.'

Polly turned her head slowly. Gabe was propped up on one elbow facing her. His expression was warm, radiating concern. Concern that she didn't need or want.

Polly slowly pulled herself up to a seating position, glad that the nausea seemed to have abated after that first rush.

'I thought we had a deal,' she said.

'A deal?' He looked surprised.

'That you were going to keep your shirt on.'

A slow appreciative smile spread over his face. It wasn't fair, Polly thought as the breath hitched in her throat. He already had soulful eyes and a well-cut jawline. Adding a smile that made you want to respond in kind, that sent a jolt of appreciation into the pit of your stomach, gave you a sudden urge to reach out and trace the firm mouth was too much.

'That agreement was only for the office,' he said. 'We are no longer in the office.'

'No.' Polly looked around at the generic bland furnishings. 'We certainly aren't. I'm sorry.'

'No need.'

'There's every need,' she corrected him. 'I dragged you out here. I'm pretty sure this isn't your usual style.'

Gabe's eyes swept over the room, coming to rest on Polly. She fought the urge to fidget, to straighten her mussed hair, pull at her baggy top.

'I don't know,' he said. 'I've had worse evenings.'

Polly stared at him, an unexpected bubble of laughter rising. 'Of course you have,' she said. 'What's more fun than a little vomit, a crazy late-night car ride and a night with a weeping woman in a downmarket hotel?'

'It was more than a little vomit. How are you feeling?'

Polly put a hand to her stomach, allowing it to linger there for a moment. Somewhere in there was the beginning of new life. A life she had created.

'Better,' she said, surprised that it was true. She thought for a moment, savouring the hollow feeling that had miraculously appeared. 'Hungry. Really hungry.'

'Room service?'

Polly shook her head. 'I need to get out,' she said. 'Although…' she looked at herself '…I'm not really fit to be seen.' But she didn't want to go home yet.

'How hungry are you?'

She was grateful that he didn't insult her intelligence by telling her that she looked fine. She had eyes and she still had the tattered remnants of her pride.

'Why?'

'If you can wait half an hour,' he suggested, 'I'll pop back to that supermarket and pick up a toothbrush and hairbrush and anything else you need. Then I think we should go out for the day.'

'Go out?' Polly leant back and eyed him suspiciously. 'To do what? We have papers to write, remember?'

'We've both put in a ridiculous amount of hours this week.' Gabe rolled off the bed unperturbed and picked up his T-shirt from the floor, shaking it out fastidiously before putting it back on. 'And it was an emotional evening.'

He smiled across at her as he said it, taking any possible sting out of the words. 'I need a walk, some fresh air and a change of scenery. Are you in?'

A vision of her laptop floated into Polly's mind. The half-written report. The statistics and recommendations and examples. The spreadsheet full of costings and projections and risk analysis. 'I should work,' she said, pulling her hair out of its ponytail and running her fingers through the tangled lengths.

Gabe didn't say anything, just regarded her levelly. Polly glared back.

'Last chance.'

She should work. She'd just had three months off, for goodness' sake. So what if she felt as if a steamroller had run her over physically and emotionally before reversing and finishing the job? She wasn't paid to have feelings or problems or illnesses.

She should work.

Polly glanced over at the window. The sun was peeping in around the blinds. Was that birds she could hear singing, their tuneful chirps not quite masked by the roar of passing traffic? She'd spent all of the previous summer indoors, working. The strangest part about travelling had been adjusting to being outdoors, the blissful heat as the sun soaked into her weary bones. She had missed out on so many summery weekends.

And next summer everything would be completely changed. There would be another person to take care of.

She glared at Gabe, who was still waiting, arms folded and an enquiring eyebrow raised.

'Oh, okay then. Let me write you a shopping list.'

Polly spent the entire half-hour of Gabe's absence in the hotel's surprisingly powerful shower, letting the hot jets blast away the kinks in her shoulders and back, beat the tangles out of her hair and massage the worry out of her mind. By the time Gabe rapped softly on the door she felt vaguely human again.

Wrapping the towel tightly around her, she took the proffered carrier bag Gabe handed through the bathroom door. Polly was conscious of an unprecedented intimacy. Gabe had selected her clothes, underwear, her shoes.

It was disconcerting, made her feel vulnerable. Which was ridiculous; she often ordered outfits or lingerie when she needed a quick change for an unexpected meeting or lunch. They were picked out and delivered by any one of the many anonymous salesmen or women she employed and she never felt a moment's hesitation about wearing things they had handled.

She didn't even pick her own toothpaste; her concierge service took care of all her household purchases.

But Polly couldn't help staring at the pretty lilac bra and pants, the sleeveless, fifties-style summer dress in a vibrant blue, the flared skirt ending just before her knees. Had he just grabbed the first things he had seen—or were they chosen especially for her?

Either way it was a choice between the dress or the tracksuit she'd slept in.

Slowly Polly slipped on the underwear and buttoned up the dress, her hands uncharacteristically clumsy. They fitted perfectly. Her figure was unchanged—for now.

Luckily she always carried a selection of miniatures from her favourite make-up brands with her and in just a few minutes she was ready, tinted moisturiser hiding the last of the damage from the evening's tears, mascara and some lip gloss an armour to help her through the day. Slipping her feet into the flowered flip-flops Gabe had provided, she stepped out of the bathroom strangely shy.

'Better?' she asked.

'That colour suits you. I thought it would.' There was a huskiness in his voice that reached deep inside her and tugged, a sweet sensual pull that made her sway towards him.

'Matches my eyes,' she said, aware what a lame comment it was but needing to say something, to try and break the hypnotic spell his words had cast.

'Non.' Gabe was still staring at her as if she were something deliciously edible. 'Your eyes are darker.'

Polly felt exposed before the hunger in his eyes. The dip of the dress suddenly seemed horribly low-cut, the hemline indecently short, her arms too bare. 'I've never worn a supermarket dress before,' she said.

'No.' He gave a quick bark of laughter and just like that the air of sensuality that had been swelling, filling the room, disappeared. 'Polly Rafferty in prêt-à-porter. There's a first for everything.'

'I wear ready-to-wear all the time,' she protested.

'Designer diffusion ranges?' He laughed again as she nodded. 'What about while you were away?'

'It pays to buy quality. It lasts longer,' she told him, unwilling to admit that even her travelling sarong had cost more than the entire outfit she was currently wearing. 'Now, I believe you promised me breakfast and then we need to decide what we're going to do.'

'We could just drive and see where we end up,' Gabe suggested.

'Oh, no, if I am taking a day off it needs to be well planned so I make the most of it,' Polly told him. 'And if you think I'm letting you drive my car one more time you're crazy. My nerves won't take the strain.'

Gabe grinned. 'We'll see,' was all he said. 'Come on, Polly. Let's go and organise a day of spontaneous fun.'

* * *

Of course it had begun to rain. Why had he given up the golden beaches of California or the flower-strewn meadows of his home for this grey, drizzly island?

Although Paris could be rainy too, Gabe conceded. But somehow in Paris even the rain had a certain style. In the English countryside it was just wet.

'Thoughts, Mr Spontaneity?'

Gabe sat back in his seat and considered. The prospects weren't appealing: a walk, a tour round a stately home, a visit to yet another of the exquisite market towns where the old houses were built from the golden stone with which the region abounded. If they were going to do that they might as well return to Hopeford—the most exquisite and golden and historic of the lot.

The sea? But they were in the middle of the country and the nearest coast was over one hundred miles away.

He could, if he hadn't been overcome with a ridiculous chivalry, have been on a train into the city right now. A visit to the gym, a couple of hours in the office and then a few beers in Kensington with some other émigrés. But there had been something vulnerable about the elegant Polly Rafferty slumped on a cheap hotel bed, that golden hair piled up into an untidy ponytail, red-eyed, white-faced. The circumstances couldn't have been more different, the women more different, but for one heart-stopping moment she had reminded him of Marie.

Of Marie as she began to give up.

The irony was that he had spent the last ten years turning away from women who provoked even the smallest reminder of his ex. One hint of vulnerability, of neediness and he was gone—so why was he sitting here watching the rain lash the windscreen on a magical mystery tour to nowhere?

Was it because he respected Polly? Knew that once she adjusted she would pick herself up and walk tall, head high, daring anyone to criticise her choices?

Or because he instinctively knew that she hid her weaknesses from the world. He might have been in the right place at the right time—or the wrong place at the wrong time—for her to collapse on him the way she had.

No matter why his usual 'turn tail and run' instincts weren't functioning normally. Not yet.

But they would. He didn't have to worry.

'What do you want to do?' He turned the question onto her.

'Not get wet?' Polly glared at the windscreen as if she could stop the rain with pure force of will. 'I took the day off to enjoy the sunshine. Besides, my new outfit doesn't include a cardigan or an umbrella.'

'It was warm just an hour ago. I forgot to factor in the crazy British weather.'

'Between May and September it's wise to carry an umbrella, a wrap and sunscreen at all times. Let that be your first lesson in British life. That and always have an indoor alternative.'

'I would suggest lunch but after that breakfast you just ate…' he said slyly.

'I'm eating for two!' The colour rose high in her cheeks. 'And I've barely eaten anything for the last week or two. I was in a major calorie deficit. Hang on, what does that sign say?'

Gabe peered through the slanting rain at the colourful poster, gamely flapping in the wet and cold. 'Probably some kind of fete,' he said. 'The British summer, always wet and cold and yet full of outdoor events. You're an optimistic isle, I'll give you that. Or crazy,' he added thoughtfully.

'No, it's not that. Oh!' With that squeal she put the indicator on and turned down the winding lane indicated by the poster. 'It's a Vintage Festival. Do you mind?'

'As long as it's dry and indoors.'

'What? Mr Triathlete scared of a little rain?'

'*Non*, just a man from the South of France who likes summer to be just that, summery.'

'Oh, boy, are you in the wrong country.'

The small country lane was long and winding and it took Polly a few moments to navigate its twists and turns before she followed another sign that took them through wrought-iron gates and up a sweeping, tree-lined driveway. Gabe caught a glimpse of large, graceful house before the road took them round to a busy car park.

'Wow.' Polly's voice was full of envy as she pulled to a stop, her eyes eagerly looking around. 'People have come in style.'

Hers was by no means the only modern car there but even her sporty two-seater was put firmly in the shade by the array of well-loved vintage cars from all eras. 'If I'd known we were coming I'd have brought Raff's Porsche,' Polly said sadly. 'It's a seventies car so not really vintage but older than this.'

The look she gave her own car was scathing, which, Gabe thought, was a little rich considering the fuss she had made over him driving it the night before.

'Aren't they gorgeous?' She had jumped out of the car, heedless of the rain, which had lightened to a drizzle, and was trailing her hand over a cream Austin Healey. 'And look at that Morris Minor, it's pristine. Wow, what great condition. Somebody loves you, don't they, baby?' she crooned.

Crooned. To a car. To an *old* car.

'They are very nice,' Gabe said politely as he joined her. 'For old cars.'

'Shh!' Polly threw him a scathing glance. 'They'll hear you. Don't listen to the nasty man,' she told the Austin consolingly. 'He's French.'

'We have old cars in France too,' Gabe said indignantly, stung by the slur to his country. 'I just prefer mine new.'

She patted his arm consolingly. 'This might not be the right place for you. Come on.'

It was a new side to Polly. Excited, eager, playful. It was a side he bet her staff never saw, that barely anybody saw.

'So, where are we?' Gabe asked as they walked along the chipping-strewn path that took them through a small wooded area and towards the house. Bunting was strung along the path, dripping wet yet defiantly cheerful.

'Geographically I'm not entirely sure, socially we're at a vintage festival.'

Clear as mud. 'Which is?'

Polly stopped and turned. 'Surely people go to them in France?'

'Possibly,' he said imperturbably. 'I, however, have not.'

'You are in for such a treat,' she said, grabbing his arm and pulling him along. 'There's usually stalls where you can buy anything old: clothes, furniture, jewellery. And tea and cakes, and makeovers and dancing. Loads of people come all dressed up in their favourite decade, mostly forties and fifties but you do get twenties and sixties as well.'

Gabe looked at her curiously. 'Do you go to these a lot?'

Her face fell. 'Not any more,' she said. 'Which is a shame because there are loads now, big affairs like this one looks to be. But I did go to a few vintage clubs and smaller affairs when I was at university. I've always loved the twenties; you know, flappers and jazz and the art deco style. Everything that was around when Rafferty's was founded.'

'Why don't you go any more?'

She sighed. 'The usual,' she said. 'Time—or lack of. I used to collect nineteen twenties accessories; costume jewellery, compacts, that kind of thing, but I haven't even wandered into an antique shop for a couple of years. Ooh.' Her face lit up. 'This is great timing. We could have a vintage pop-up at Rafferty's? Our centenary is in just a few years. We could have a whole series of twenties-inspired events leading up to that?'

Gabe had no intention of still being there in a few years but he could picture it perfectly. 'Is this just so you can dress up as a flapper?'

'Of course.' She looked down at her outfit. 'Although today I am loosely channelling the fifties. You must have known we were coming here when you picked out the dress.'

Gabe could see the house clearly now; they had ended up at a stately home after all. But this was a place gone back in time, to the middle of the last century if not back to its seventeenth-century roots.

The path had brought them out onto a large terrace at the back of the house overlooking lawns and ornamental gardens that seamlessly seemed to merge into the fields beyond. The furthest lawn was covered with an array of carnival rides, none of which was younger than Gabe, horses going round and round in a never-ending circle, helter-skelters and coconut shies.

Tables and chairs were dotted all around the terrace and lawns, served by a selection of vintage ice-cream vans parked in a row by the entrance gate, some selling the eponymous food, others cream teas, cakes or drinks.

'It's beautiful,' Polly breathed, still hanging onto his arm, her gaze transfixed on the scene before them. 'Doesn't everyone look fabulous? We're completely underdressed, especially you!'

Swing music was coming from the house, clearly audible through the parade of open doors. Parading in and out were people from another era: brightly lipsticked women with elaborate hair accompanied by men in old-fashioned military uniforms. Behind them girls with big skirts and ponytails were chatting to men with Brylcreemed hair and attitude to match. It was all pretty cool—if you were into fancy dress.

It had never been Gabe's kind of thing. Life was a mystery as it was; why complicate it by pretending to be someone you weren't? By emulating the lives of those long gone?

'It's a good thing the rain's stopped.'

Polly huffed. 'And people say the English are obsessed with the weather. Come on, Gabe. Let's go in.'

'What do you think?' Polly twirled around in front of Gabe, She hadn't been able to resist the opportunity to have her hair pin-curled and it hadn't taken much to persuade her into the accompanying makeover.

Or a new outfit. 'You look like you're from a film,' he said. Polly wasn't sure whether he meant it as a compliment or not but decided to go with it.

'That's the idea.' She looked down at the pink-flowered silk tea dress. 'It's not twenties but it will do. You need something too. A coat. Or a hat! We should get you a hat. This is so much fun. Why haven't I done this for so long?'

She led the protesting Gabe over to a stall specialising in military overcoats. 'I hope they have a French coat,' she said. 'Army, air force or navy?'

She knew she was chattering a bit too much, was being a little too impulsive, happily trying—and buying—anything that took her fancy.

It was better than thinking or worrying. She was almost fooling herself that everything was okay, that nothing had changed.

She wasn't fooling Gabe though. She could see it in his eyes.

'Lighten up.' She held a coat up against him. 'You're the one who wanted a day out, a change of scenery, remember?'

'Oui.' But his smile seemed forced, concern still radiating from him. Concern for her.

Unwanted, unneeded.

Suddenly the dress seemed shabby rather than chic, the lipstick heavy on her mouth. She had just wanted a day to forget about everything, a day with no responsibilities or decisions.

'I need some air.' She pushed past him, ignoring his surprised exclamation.

The swing band was still going strong in the ballroom and couples were engaging in gymnastics on the dance floor, a series of complicated lifts and kicks. At any other time Polly would have stopped to watch, to join in with the onlookers enthusiastically applauding each daring move, but she felt stifled, too hot, too enclosed. She wandered over to the terrace, stopping at one of the ice-cream vans to buy a sparkling water and took it over to a table where she examined her impulse purchases.

They were a mixed bag. A few old crime novels, a rather lovely, shell-shaped compact still with the wrist chain attached, two rose-covered side plates and a matching cake stand and some bunting made out of old dress material. It might look nice in the baby's room, she thought idly.

The baby's room.

Her breath whooshed out of her body and she held onto the iron table, glad of the cold metal beneath her palm, anchoring her to the world. She was pregnant. That was her reality and no amount of impromptu days out could change that.

But the expected panic, the gnawing pain in her stomach didn't materialise. Instead she felt light; it was okay. She didn't have a plan or any idea what to do next but it was okay.

For what must be the hundredth time that week Polly put her hand on her stomach but not in illness, or shock, or horror.

'Hello,' she whispered.

Nobody answered, there was no resulting flutter or any acknowledgement of her words, yet everything had changed.

She wasn't going to be alone any more.

'Would you like an ice cream?'

Polly pulled her hand away as if she had been caught doing something wrong.

'I'm okay,' she began, but the words died on her lips. 'What are you wearing?'

'They didn't have any French coats,' he said. 'So I got a hat instead.'

The trilby should have looked incongruous with the jeans and T-shirt, but somehow he made it look edgy.

Disturbingly sexy.

'It suits you.'

'What have you got there?' Gabe nodded at the bags spread over the table.

'Bits and bobs, bunting.' She looked up, met his eyes. 'For the baby's room.'

He tipped the trilby back; the gesture made him look almost heartbreakingly young, like a World War Two pilot heading back to base for a final mission.

'I hope he likes flowers, then,' he said doubtfully.

Polly gathered the bunting back up, stuffing it into the

bag. 'He might be a she, and either way no child of mine will be constrained by gender constructs.' She was aware that she sounded stuffy and that laughter was lurking in his watchful dark eyes.

For a moment she had a view of another path. One where the man teasing her wasn't a momentary diversion in her journey. One where the baby wasn't a shock to deal with but a welcome and much anticipated event.

A world where she might bicker playfully over the suitability of floral bunting, the colour of the paint, where to put the cot and the name of the first teddy bear. Where she wouldn't be doing this alone.

'So do you?' Gabe broke in on her thoughts.

She blinked, confused. Did she what? Want to take a different path? It was a little late for that.

'Polly? Ice cream?'

'Oh. No, no thank you. Actually, I think I want a walk. The grounds look spectacular.' Walk away from her thoughts and the sudden, unwanted regrets.

Gabe cast a doubtful look at the sky. 'Those clouds are pretty dark.'

Rolling her eyes, Polly got up and picked up her bags. 'You have a hat to keep you dry. Honestly, Gabe, you're not going to last five minutes in England if you can't cope with a bit of rain.'

'A bit? Not a problem. This nasty drizzle…' his accent elongated the word contemptuously '…it's not natural. I can't understand why the Normans didn't just turn straight around and go home as soon as they landed and saw the sky.'

'Exactly.' Polly began to walk away from the house, across the wet lawns and towards a small path covered in wood chippings that led through the cluster of trees. 'Romans, Vikings, Normans—rainy or not we're still quite the prize.'

Apart from a disbelieving snort Gabe didn't reply and they walked towards the woods in a companionable silence. After a moment Gabe reached across and took the carrier bags from her. Polly froze for a moment and then loosened her fingers and allowed him to relieve her of her load.

They wandered along for a few more moments, the air heavy with the promise of summer rain. Polly inhaled, enjoying the freshness of the countryside; the heady scent of wet leaves mixed with the damp earth and sawdust from the path.

They rounded a corner and the trees came to an abrupt end; in front of them a pretty ornamental lake stretched ahead, the path skirting the edge.

'Okay, Mr Spontaneity, right or left?'

'What is that?' Gabe sounded startled. 'Have we stumbled onto the set of a horror film?'

Polly followed his disbelieving gaze and saw a dark grey stone tower perched on the edge of the lake, the jagged edge of the spire reaching up into the sky.

'It's a folly. You know...' as he looked at her in query '...a couple of centuries ago it was the craze to build some kind of gothic ruin in a picturesque place. Around the time you were chopping aristocrats' heads off.'

'This is exactly why we were chopping off heads, if they squandered money on such crazy projects.'

'Hence the name. Want to take a look? There might be a princess for you to rescue at the top, or a prince in need of my knightly skills.'

It only took a few minutes to reach the base of the tower and Polly stood on tiptoe trying to get a look inside but the

narrow slits that passed for ground-floor windows were
set too high. 'Where's the door?'

Gabe had wandered off around to the other side. 'Here.
Are you sure you want to risk it? You might disappear,
never to be seen again, kidnapped to be the bride of a
headless horseman.'

Polly joined him by the heavy oak door, the hinges exaggerated iron studs. 'Is it locked?'

'Only one way to find out.' Gabe grasped the heavy iron
ring and turned it and, with a creak so loud Polly jumped,
the door swung open.

'Ready? It looks dark in there.'

'So *you* are scared of ghosts?' she teased.

'*Non*, not ghosts. Spiders and rats on the other hand I
am not so keen on.'

Rats? Polly shuddered, an involuntary movement of
complete horror. She edged back. 'You think there are
rats?'

'Hundreds. And cockroaches too,' he added helpfully.

Polly glared at him. 'Move aside, I'm going in.'

With an exaggerated bow Gabe stood aside, allowing
her to precede him into the room.

'There are no stairs, how disappointing. Definitely no
stranded royalty for us to rescue.' Polly swivelled slowly,
taking in the large circular room paved in grey flagstones,
the steep sides rising all the way up to the pointed tip of
the tower. There were no other floors but it was mercifully
dry. And free of any evidence of rat infestations.

'I still don't understand. What is it for?' Gabe had followed her in.

Polly flung her arms open as she turned. 'Probably
somewhere for illicit trysts.'

'Ah, for the nobleman to meet the maid.' He leant back
against the wall of the tower, arms crossed, face full of

amusement, the hat still tilted back on his head giving him a rakish air.

Polly tilted her chin and stared up at the windows and considered. 'Or for the lady of the house to meet the game-keeper. Or maybe the stable boy.'

She looked across at Gabe to share the joke but he had gone still, his gaze focused intently on Polly. 'Is that what you would have done? Snuck out to meet the gamekeeper?'

Polly felt a jolt of heat hit the pit of her stomach as their eyes snagged and held, a flash of that first, unacknowledged attraction zipping between them.

'Or the stable boy.' Was that her voice? So husky.

'Of course. What would you have done with the stable boy in this room far away from everyone and everything?' His eyes were so dark, so intense it was hard to look into them, not to be swallowed up in their depths. Polly dropped her gaze to his mouth. Remembered how sure it had been. How demanding.

The heat spread.

'I don't know,' she lied, her mind filled with irresistible images of Gabe, those long legs clad in breeches, a shirt open at the neck. Her mouth dried. She could feel the heat of his gaze, scorching her where she stood, her whole body burning where it fell upon her.

But she couldn't move, desire humming deep in her veins, thrilling to the caress of his eyes.

'Non?' He pushed off the wall, walking towards her with sure, graceful strides. 'You came here to talk? To touch?' He raised one hand to her face, sliding a finger down her cheek, the lightest of embraces.

'Maybe,' she whispered.

The memory of their earlier kiss was throbbing through her. She could taste him, feel his arms around hers, the lean strength in his hold, the deftness of his touch. He was so close. She only had to step forward, lean against him, raise her face to his.

The desire pounded harder, her heart beating an insistent drum, every pulse point throbbing with her need to close in. To take the kiss further, explore him.

Just one step.

'What's this?'

'Cool, it's a castle!'

Excitable voices outside as sudden, as shocking as the cold water she had poured on Gabe just a few days ago. As shocking, as sobering. Polly took a step back.

'I think…' She took a breath, tried to get her ragged breathing under control. 'I'm tired. Maybe it's time to go home.'

Home. Sanity. Sense. There might be an undeniable attraction between them but now was not the time to act on it. Not while everything was changing, not while she was so vulnerable.

Polly walked across the room and picked up the bags Gabe had left by the wall. Without looking back she left the tower, and left the moment behind.

CHAPTER SIX

'DO YOU WANT to go over these papers before the meeting?'

Polly sat back in her chair and frowned as Gabe folded his long, lean frame into the chair opposite her desk. 'Now you have your own office it would be polite if you knocked.'

'Of course.' Not that he looked in the slightest bit put out, more amused. 'Do you?'

'Do I what?'

His eyebrows shot up. 'Want to go over the papers, of course. The board meeting *is* this afternoon.'

Oh, yes. That. In just a couple of hours her grandfather, Raff and the rest of the board would be sitting in Rafferty's renowned tearooms being suitably feasted before the meeting began.

She was expected to attend. Polly repressed a sigh. Normally she looked forward to these occasions, the buttering-up of contacts, starting to get her case across to the more swayable board members before the official business began, working out whose vote she could count on.

But today the usual thrill was missing; there was so much at stake; her return, Raff on the Board. Consolidating her position before she announced her news.

'We could have gone over the papers last night,' she pointed out, trying to prevent a waspish note from creeping into her voice.

Of course Gabe was free to do whatever he liked; she wasn't his landlady or wife. But surely it was plain good manners to let her know that he wasn't going to be back that night—or even that week.

Not that it was any of her business where he slept. As long as he looked refreshed, smart and in control for the meeting and was well prepared that was all that mattered. Whatever else he got up to—and who he got up to it with— was of no interest to Polly.

It wasn't jealousy that twisted her stomach as she watched him lean in that inch too close to Cordelia from Lingerie or to Amy from Accounts, those liquid brown eyes fixed soulfully on his unwitting victim, the way he murmured low and sweet. No, it was worry about an HR nightmare begging to happen. It was morning sickness.

'I was working late last night,' he said mildly. 'Some of my best contacts are in the U.S. West Coast so it was long past closing by the time I finished getting the information I needed. It was easier to stay here—sleeping in my own office, you'll be glad to hear.' His smile was fleeting but intimate and Polly's breath hitched in her throat.

Unbidden, a memory of her first sight of him flashed through her mind, the strength in that lean body, the tattoo whose lines and curves haunted her dreams.

'I don't think our insurance covers overnight stays. You should stay in a hotel or get the town car home.' She knew she sounded prim. That was fine; prim was good.

'Yes, ma'am.' Another amused look, as if they were sharing a joke only known to the two of them.

Polly inhaled, long and painful. Her heart *wasn't* picking up speed. For goodness' sake, one night of being held, of having her back rubbed and her hair stroked and she was a mushy wreck. It must be the hormones; the same ones that had her tearing up at life insurance adverts.

'So, are you ready now?' Gabe pulled out his smartphone and a USB stick.

'Ready?'

'To go over the papers,' he said patiently.

'Oh, yes. The papers.'

Yep. Hormones. Mush. And apparently turning her into Echo, which, she thought, looking over at the nonchalant man lounging opposite, made him Narcissus. Her eyes flickered over long legs outstretched, shirt collar unbuttoned, sleeves rolled up and day-old stubble; he looked more like an aftershave model than a Vice CEO.

Well, if the Greek allegory fitted…

Regardless, she was no sappy nymph, wafting around in hope of a smile.

'Are you okay?'

'Fine.' She summoned up as much poise as she could. 'Let's get on with this. We don't have much time.'

He looked at her critically, concern etched onto his face. 'Is it the baby? Do you need to lie down?'

'I'm pregnant, Gabe.' No, the ground didn't open up as she said the words out loud, nor did her grandfather appear in an accusatory puff of smoke. 'I'm not ill.'

If he heard the stiffness in her voice he didn't react, firing more questions at her like tiny, yet intensely irritating arrows pricking away at her conscience. 'Are you eating properly? Have you made a doctor's appointment yet?'

Oh, my goodness. It was like being stuck at a baby shower with no easy way of escape—only this time she hadn't primed Rachel to call her with a prefabricated crisis after twenty minutes as she did every time she couldn't get out of the sickly sweet events. If he even mentioned stretch marks or yoga or stitches then one of them would be headed straight out of the window. And she didn't much care which one it was.

'Look, I really appreciate what you did for me last weekend.' There, she said it quite normally despite her urge to grind the words out through gritted teeth. 'But this really isn't any of your business and I would appreciate it if you just…' She searched for a polite way to tell him to butt out. 'Just don't discuss it any more,' she said a little lamely.

He quirked an eyebrow. 'You seem very stressed, Polly. Have you considered yoga?'

Breathe, breathe again and again. It was no good. 'Butt out, Gabe!'

He put his hands up in surrender but his eyes were laughing. 'I'm sorry. Business first. Of course.'

'Good.' But she was unsettled. What if he was right? Should she see a doctor? It was probably the first thing most women did.

What if her independence hurt the baby? Polly clenched her fists; she wanted to reach down again, to cradle her stomach and make a silent vow to the baby that, unorthodox as its beginnings were, as much of a shock the whole thing was, she would do her best to keep it safe. Do her best to love it. But with those mocking eyes fixed on her she wouldn't allow herself to show any signs of softening.

'Hang on.' She couldn't look at Gabe. It felt like giving in. 'I'm just going to call my GP. I'll be with you as soon as I can'

She looked tired. Pale, drawn and thin. And vulnerable. It was a good thing he was hardened against vulnerable women.

'Thanks, yes. I will.' Her conversation at an end, Polly put down the phone and leant forward until her head touched the desk, her hands clasped in front of her. He could see the breaths shuddering through her. Slowly she straightened, pulling at the pins that held her hair in place, running her hands through the freed strands.

'I'm sorry, Gabe, but I need to go in right now.' She

smiled, a brief perfunctory smile that didn't go anywhere near her eyes. 'Perils of being a Rafferty. They like to see us early.'

'Sounds like a benefit to me.' It never ceased to amaze Gabe how those with good health took it for granted. He'd been like that once, heedless of his body and strength, unknowing what a miracle every breath, every step, every sensation was.

'Daddy was so young when he had his stroke, they worry about blood pressure.' She was gathering her papers and phone together to put into her bag. 'I tried to put them off until tomorrow but it was easier just to agree to go in. I know we need to talk about the papers. We'll just have to skip the board lunch.'

'I could come with you. We can talk on the way, better use of both our time.' His suggestion had nothing to do with seeing her reluctance to go, knowing how tough it must be to face so many changes alone.

She stopped dead and stared at him. 'You want to come to the doctor's with me? Why ever would you want to do that? I would have thought you of all people would have had enough of anything medical.'

'I'm not planning to come in with you and hold your hand, just to discuss business on the way.'

'I'm walking,' she said, almost defiantly. 'It's only a mile away and the sun's out. I could do with some fresh air.'

'Air sounds good,' he agreed. 'I missed out on a run yesterday. If you're good I might even buy you a frozen yogurt on the way back.'

Rafferty's was situated in the heart of London, not far from the bustle of Oxford Street, close to the rarefied boutiques of Bond Street. Tourists, commuters, shoppers and workers pounded the pavements in an endless throng of busy chatter and purposeful movement. There were times when Gabe would catch the scent of car exhausts, cigarettes, fried food and perfume and feel such a longing for the flower-filled air of Provence it almost choked him.

And there were times when these crowded streets felt like home. When knowing the shortcuts, the local shops, the alleyways, the cafés and bars off the tourist track, which tube stop was next, when it was quicker to walk was instinct. It gave him a certain satisfaction, a sense of belonging.

But Polly didn't need to belong. She might have moved to a quiet town miles from the capital but London ran through her veins, was in her blood. It was evident in her confidence, the way she moved through the crowd, never putting a foot out of place, seamlessly blending in.

And yet she'd chosen to leave. The city girl living in a sleepy rural town. The defiantly single woman living in a house made for an old-fashioned family with several children and a large golden dog. What was real? Did she even know?

'Do you miss London?'

'I'm here every day.'

'To work, not to play.' He grinned at her, but there was no responsive smile.

She didn't answer for a while. 'Everyone thought I was crazy when I moved to Hopeford—even though I bought my five-bedroom cottage for the same price as my two-bedroom flat,' she said eventually. 'People in their twenties *come* to London, they don't leave it—they only move out when they have children, or if they want to totally reinvent themselves.'

'People come to London for the same reason,' he said, but so quietly he wasn't sure whether or not she heard him.

'I went to Hopeford on a whim,' she said. She still wasn't

looking at him, almost talking to herself. 'It was Sunday. I was working as usual. I lived around here, in a beautiful flat, walking distance to Rafferty's. I worked all the time.'

'You still do.' Not that he could talk. But at least he had his training to break up the days, refresh his brain. Polly lived with her laptop switched on.

'That Sunday I was in by six a.m. I couldn't sleep. And by eleven I was done. No emails to send, no reports to read or write, no plans to check. And I didn't know what to do with myself. I had all this time and no way to fill it. It was terrifying.

'So I went for a walk. I was heading towards Regent's Park, I think, planning to go to the zoo. It's what we did as kids for a treat. Raff was already gone. Maybe I was missing him. Anyway I ended up at Marylebone. There was a train to Hopeford and I liked the name—*hope*. So I jumped on.' She shook her head. 'It felt so daring, just travelling to a strange place on a whim. And then I got there and it was like another world.'

'It's very pretty.'

'And very quiet. I couldn't believe it. No shops were open, nobody was working, people were just walking, or gardening or cooking. When you live and work in London you forget that people live like that. We sell the tools, you know, the sheets and the candles and the saucepans and the garden furniture but it feels a little like make-believe. I didn't want it to be make-believe any more. I wanted it to be real.

'So you moved?'

She laughed. 'No one could believe it; *I* didn't really believe it. It was the most impulsive thing I ever did. Well, until a few weeks ago anyway.'

'Are you happy there?'

There was a long pause. Nimbly she skirted a large

group of tourists taking photos of a mime artist and the window shoppers milling outside the many boutiques.

'Yes,' she said finally. 'I am.'

'Not everything needs to be planned out,' he said softly. 'Sometimes just going with your instinct is the right path.'

She stopped and stared at him. 'Are we still talking about Hopeford?' she asked.

He shrugged. 'Just making conversation.'

'Well, don't.' She gestured at a glass door, sober and discreet in a Georgian building. 'We're here. Meet me afterwards? We still have to talk about work, remember?'

'I'll come in with you.' The words were out before he had a chance to think them through. 'There's always a lot of hanging around at these places. We can talk inside.'

Polly knew she should be attending to everything that Dr Vishal was saying but it was so alien she couldn't get a grip on it.

Was this really her body? Her future? Now the nausea was dying down she looked and felt the same as always. Maybe she had made a really embarrassing mistake and it had been a bug after all?

'You're fine, but I want you to make sure you do everything I am recommending.' The doctor broke into Polly's thoughts. 'Vitamins and rest and midwife appointments. Careful blood-pressure monitoring, some light exercise and proper food,' she said, frowning at Polly. 'You're too thin, Polly. If you can't or won't cook then there are some good meal-delivery services. Lots of protein and vegetables.'

'I'll arrange it,' Polly promised. It was almost a shame Gabe was moving out; he took food seriously enough.

'Are you ready?'

'For what?'

'To see your baby of course. If you go with Sasha she'll

get you ready for your scan. We do them in house now although once your hospital referral goes through they'll want to scan again and sort out any extra blood tests.'

Polly followed Sasha, her brain whirling. A scan. Her hand fluttered to her stomach again. This was going to make the whole thing horribly real—unless it was a phantom-bug-baby after all.

Gabe was sitting on a chair in the corridor, his long legs sprawled out before him, frowning at the phone in his hand as he briskly typed out a message, but as Polly came close he shoved the phone into his pocket and got to his feet.

'Everything okay?'

'I think so. I have a long list of instructions. You'd like them; they use words like exercise and vitamins.'

'That's my language,' he agreed. 'Are you ready? We've still got an hour and a half until the meeting.'

'I've just…' Polly waved towards the nurse. 'A scan. To check everything is, you know, okay. I won't be long.'

'You're very welcome to come with us,' Sasha said with a bright smile. 'Ready to meet baby?'

Confused words of refusal rose to Polly's lips but when she started to speak nothing came out. Of course she didn't *need* company but it might be nice to have some backup, someone to reassure her that she wasn't imagining the whole thing.

Indecision was writ clearly on his face as he ran a hand over the dark stubble. 'Why not?' he said after a moment.

'No, don't worry,' she began but he was already on his feet.

'Come on,' he said. 'Let's go and see who's been causing you so much trouble.'

Gabe had seen more than his fair share of scan pictures. From the moment of his eldest niece's conception it felt as if he had been asked to admire thousands of fuzzy pictures of alien blobs. It wasn't just his family; more and more friends and colleagues were replacing their social media ID photos with what, he was fairly sure, was an identikit picture.

Secretly Gabe wondered if the whole thing was a scam, if there was just one photo that had been mocked up several years ago and was palmed off on every expectant couple. They probably made a fortune out of it.

The nurse led them into a small room. A chill shivered down Gabe's spine and his stomach clenched. The dull green walls, the blind at the window, the metal bed surrounded by machinery. It was a different country, a different patient and yet utterly, achingly familiar.

Old pains began to pulse in his limbs, scars to throb. He swallowed hard, trying to control his breathing. A cool hand touched his arm. Gabe braced himself for pity.

But all there was in the clear blue eyes was understanding. 'You can wait outside,' Polly said softly. 'It's fine.'

How did she know? How could she know?

He took a deep breath. 'I'm okay. Makes a nice change to not be the one on the bed.'

The hand lingered, squeezed. 'Thanks.' She didn't say anything else, just sat on the bed, her hands clasped, and waited for instructions.

Gabe folded himself into a chair while Polly was fussed over, the moment before frozen in his mind. He didn't often speak of his time in hospital, those days were over, but when it did come up there were usually two reactions: cloying pity or brisk heartiness.

It wasn't often anyone showed tact and understanding. He hadn't expected it from Polly; she was such a cat that walked alone. Why did she hide it? The sense of humour, the love of vintage accessories, her compassion? Did she feel that the human made her weak?

'Okay now, can you just lift your top?' The nurse's voice broke into his thoughts. The language was different but the tone exactly the same as the many, many nurses he had interacted with over the years: brisk, matter-of-fact.

Polly obediently rolled up the silk T-shirt, wincing as she did so, and Gabe tried not to laugh as he caught her expression—the carefully chosen top was going to get horribly creased. She was dressed for a board meeting not a doctor's appointment. Resolutely Gabe dragged his eyes away from the long legs lying supine on the bed, only to find himself staring at a flat stomach, the colour of warm honey.

It was a completely inappropriate time to stare but he couldn't help himself. She was on the thin side of slender, her ribs clearly visible. The cream fitted top set off the remains of her holiday tan; Gabe could hear her words echoing in his head: '*swimming naked in the sea*'. Just how much of her was honey brown?

He looked away quickly, trying to cleanse his mind of images of long limbs in clear waters, the hair floating languorously on the sea's surface. A lithe mermaid, dangerously desirable.

'This may be a little chilly,' the nurse warned her—'*it'll be utterly freezing*', Gabe translated mentally and by Polly's quick shudder as the gel touched her belly knew he was right. 'Okay.' The nurse was smiling at him. 'Ready to say hello?'

The language was cloying, the situation somewhat surreal and the nurse evidently under the assumption that he was responsible for Polly's situation but any embarrassment dissolved the second the nurse ran the scanner over

Polly's stomach. The screen wavered for a second and then there, in sharp focus, there it was.

Gabe stared at the screen. People used the word 'miracle' all the time until it lost any meaning but surely, *surely* this alien person floating around in Polly's body was a miracle?

He was so used to associating hospitals with pain and death he had completely forgotten what else they represented: life.

'It's still tiny,' the nurse told them. 'But perfect.'

Gabe looked over at Polly. Her head was turned to the screen; she was utterly transfixed. He didn't know if she had even heard the nurse.

'Is everything okay, as it should be?' he asked.

'It's still early days, you're what? Eleven weeks? But everything looks like it's right on track. The hospital will want to scan you again in about two to three weeks. All the details are in your pack. Do you want a photo?'

The ubiquitous photo. Suddenly Gabe could see the point of them after all. Why wouldn't you want to monitor every second?

He looked over at Polly but she didn't respond. But of course she would. Wouldn't she? '*Si*, I mean, please.'

Polly still hadn't spoken.

'Polly? Is everything okay?'

She blinked, once, twice as if released from a dream and then turned to him, her face transformed, lit up with an inner joy. It almost hurt to look at her.

'Oh yes,' she said. 'Everything is perfect.'

The contrast was completely surreal. One moment she was lying down, almost helpless as she deferred to the judgement and expertise of others, less than two hours later she had been on her feet, standing in front of a group of suited, booted, note-scribbling board members. Here she was the expert, the one in control, setting the pace and the agenda.

If she couldn't still feel the chill of the gel, sticky on her stomach, if she hadn't glanced down to see, with a shock of surprise, that she was no longer wearing the cream, fitted silk top but a sharply tailored pink shirt, she would think she had imagined her morning.

This was her future. A world of contrasts.

'That went well.' Her grandfather was sat at the head of the table. If his gaze lingered a little longingly on the bookcases that used to be filled with his belongings, if he eyed the pictures on the wall with barely hidden nostalgia then Polly couldn't blame him. The store was his life, his legacy.

As it was hers.

'Really interesting presentation, Pol,' Raff said. Her twin had spent his first meeting as a member of the Rafferty's board watching and listening intently but not jumping in. Not yet, although he had asked a few penetrating questions.

Polly knew him too well to think that he didn't have decided opinions—or that he wouldn't voice them—but he had been a supportive presence for her first official meeting as CEO.

She smiled at him, a rush of love for him flooding her. Despite their past disagreements and the long absences he was still part of her. And he would be part of her baby's life too, unconditionally, that went without saying. 'Thank you, Raff. For everything.'

'I love the pop-up idea—both in store and out. Where do you think you'll start?'

'In store,' she said, dragging her mind back to the matter at hand.

'We can use the centre of the Great Hall. It's mostly

used for themed displays anyway. I've found this great
designer who uses vintage fabrics and jewellery and re-
works them into a more modern design but still with a
hint of history. They're something really special and tie
in brilliantly with the building and best of all she's completely unknown. We would be a great launch pad for her
and it's exactly the kind of thing I'm looking for. Unique
and creative.'

'And start branching out with the food when?' Her
grandfather might sound casual but his gaze was as sharp
as ever.

Much as she wanted to get started, Polly knew this
couldn't be rushed. 'Next year. We've left it too late in the
season to start properly—all the best festivals are booked
up and there's no point starting anywhere else. But we
are investigating doing a few surprise pop-ups locally so
that we can test some concepts—Hyde Park, South Bank,
Hampstead Heath. Picnics and Pimms, that kind of thing.
We're in the process of applying for licences.'

'Dip your toe in, eh? Not a bad plan.' Her grandfather
shifted his gaze over to Gabe, who was busy packing up
his laptop. 'That's all very well, but I still don't know about
this digital strategy of yours. It's risky.'

'Not mine, Gabe's,' Polly corrected. 'I agree, it is a lot
of money—but you were the one who told me to hand all
digital concerns over to him.'

'What's your gut instinct?'

She hesitated as Gabe snapped his briefcase shut and
turned his attention to the trio at the table, his eyes intent on her. 'Truth is I'm torn,' she admitted. 'I think it's
innovative and brilliant, but the technology is untried at
this scale and the outlay huge. My heart tells me to go for
it but my head is a lot more cautious. But, if we wait, and
someone else gets in first, then we lose both the competi-

tive edge and the PR advantage. Gabe, what do you think? Honestly.'

Gabe leant back against the wall, arms folded, and regarded them intently. Polly willed him to dig deep, to find something that convinced her, convinced her family.

'My parents use something a little similar,' he said after a long moment. 'It's not as all singing and dancing as the concept I presented but their web and digital presence is very different from their competitors'—much more interactive, presenting the vineyard, restaurant and B&B virtually just as it is in reality. Why don't you come over and see? See how the physical matches up with the online and Natalie can talk you through click-through rates, bookings and the uplift in spend.'

Polly shifted nervously. 'Go to Provence?' Go to Gabe's home. Meet his parents and sisters, see the place he had grown up in?

A further blurring of the lines she kept trying to draw— and ended up rubbing out.

'That's an excellent idea,' Raff said warmly. 'I think that's exactly what we need, to see something similar and grasp just how it works in practice. You should go, Polly.' He looked at Gabe. 'If Pol agrees it's a goer then you have my vote.'

'I agree.' Her grandfather was looking at her thoughtfully. 'Take your time, look at every angle and then report back. If Raff and I are a yes then the rest will fall into line. But it needs your unequivocal approval, Polly. It's too much of a gamble for half-hearted efforts.'

'If we go this weekend the wine festival is on.' Gabe was checking his phone as he spoke. 'They have all kinds of stalls—wine, obviously, food, entertainment. Could be good research for planning just what the Rafferty pop-up brand will be.'

Polly nodded, to all intents and purposes solely focused on the matter at hand—but her mind was churning. This was all a little cosy.

She had spent the last week trying to re-establish much-needed boundaries—and so evidently had he. Now they had separate offices, now he spent so little time in Hope-ford, she could convince herself that her evening of weakness was a one-off anomaly. A symptom of shock.

But if that *was* the case then what harm could a weekend do? It was just a working weekend like any other, she reminded herself. In fact it was probably a good thing, a chance to prove to herself that she was in control, in every way. 'It sounds perfect,' she said. 'Count me in.'

CHAPTER SEVEN

'WHAT A SHAME we didn't get to see some of Paris, but it was easier to fly in to Toulouse. I would have liked to have shown you around Desmoulins.' British retail royalty meeting the cream of Parisian style; it would have been an interesting introduction.

Now they were in his country, on his turf, Gabe was back behind the wheel, waving a protesting Polly into the passenger seat, refusing to listen to her attempts to direct him; no phone sat nav could possibly know the roads, the shortcuts better than the returning native.

'I've never been to Paris.' She was looking out of the window, seemingly absorbed in the scenery. It was worth looking at, the undulating hills and bright fields of lavender and sunflowers. At one point Provence had felt too rural, too stiflingly parochial to hold him. Now his blood thrilled to the scented air. He was home.

'You must have. A woman like you! Business, romance, shopping…'

She was shaking her head. 'Nope. Business I conduct in London. Romance?' She smiled wryly. 'I didn't really take time in my twenties for romantic breaks and the least said about this year, the better.' She rubbed her stomach. Gabe had noticed how often her hand crept there instinctively, unthinkingly, as if she had a primal need to connect with the life within.

'And I shop at Rafferty's of course. Or Milan or New York if I do want a busman's holiday.'

'But…' He was incredulous. Surely everyone came to Paris at some point in their lives. 'But what about fashion week?'

She shook her head. 'That's the buyers' job. I can't predict the next season's hits and I don't need to. I pay people with far more flair to do it.'

Oh, she had flair. It helped that she was almost model tall and model thin; it made it easy for her to wear clothes designed with willowy slenderness in mind. But she wore them with a panache that didn't come from the designer. It was innate. Even today, casual in a pair of skinny jeans and a yellow flowery top, she turned heads.

'But why? It takes what? Two and a half hours by train? It's a day trip.'

Polly smiled. A little self-consciously. 'It's silly.'

Gabe turned to look at her. Now he was intrigued; what on earth made Polly Rafferty blush in embarrassment?

'I can keep a secret.'

'I know.' She winced. 'You already know far too many of mine. I can't give you any more.'

She had a point. It was odd, knowing things not even her brother knew. Tied them together in a way that wasn't as unwelcome as it should be. He should even the score, make them equals.

Gabe turned his concentration back to the road ahead, navigating a tight bend before answering. 'That's fair. How about I tell you two of mine and then you answer?'

She leant back in her seat and considered. 'They have to be embarrassing secrets. Or deeply personal. Things you have never told anyone.'

'Okay.' He took a deep breath. Gabe was a businessman; he had always done what he needed to to get ahead. A little stretching of the truth here, taking a gamble on an assumption there. Nothing dishonest or illegal—more a prevarication.

But he couldn't prevaricate here; Polly was right. He did owe her a secret or two.

He just had so many to choose from. It might be nice to let one or two of them out, to lighten the load.

Gabe concentrated on the road ahead, his hands gripping the steering wheel so tightly his knuckles were white. 'When I was ill I hated my parents so much I couldn't even look at them when they came to visit.'

He heard her inhale, a long, shuddering breath. But she didn't protest or tell him he must be mistaken. 'Why?'

'Because they hurt so damn much. Every needle in my vein pierced them twice as hard, when I retched, they doubled over. My illness nearly killed them. They wanted me to live, to fight, so badly that when I slipped back I knew I was failing them. My illness failed them.'

He could feel it again: the shame of causing so much hurt, the anger that they needed him to be strong when it was almost too much. The responsibility of having to fight, to stay alive for them.

'They must love you a lot.' Her voice was a little wistful.

'They do. And I love them but it's a lot. You have to be strong for yourself in that situation, single-minded. Their need distracted me. Added too much pressure.'

'Is that why you don't want children?'

He thought back to her scan, to the life pulsing inside her, the unexpected protectiveness that had engulfed him and picked his words carefully.

'Our lives are so fragile, our happiness so dependent on others. I've been cancer free for nearly ten years, Polly. But it could come back. I don't want to put a wife or a child through the suffering I put my parents through. I don't want to suffer like that for someone else. Is it worth it?'

There was a pause and he knew without looking that her hand would be back at her midriff.

'I hope so,' she said after a while.

He continued driving while she busied herself with her phone. 'You still haven't told me your second secret.' She was looking away again. It was like being in the seal of the confessional: intimate and confidential.

Gabe didn't even consider before he answered. 'Ever since I kissed you in the office I've wanted to do it again.'

Another silence. This one more loaded. He was achingly aware of her proximity, of her bare arms, the blonde hair piled precariously in a loose knot, the hitch in her breath as he spoke.

His words had unlocked a desire he didn't even know he carried, one he had hidden, locked down. The kiss had been totally inappropriate. They were colleagues; she was his boss. He didn't want or need anything complicated— and nothing about Polly Rafferty was simple.

She was prickly and bossy. She didn't know the names of half her staff and was rude to and demanding of the ones she did know. She worked all the time. She was pregnant.

Sure, she was conventionally pretty with her mass of blonde silky hair, her dark blue eyes and legs that went on for ever but that was just the surface. It was the inappropriately intimate conversations with cars, that carefully hidden vulnerability and her way of looking into a man's soul and seeing just what it was that made him tick that made her dangerous.

It made her formidable. It made her utterly desirable.

'What does the tree mean?' Her words pierced the thickened atmosphere, the soft voice a little unsteady, her hands twisting on her lap.

'Pardon?'

'Your tattoo? What does it mean?'

His mouth twisted. 'My mother didn't cry once during any of my treatment but she wept when I showed her that tattoo. And not with pride.'

'I think it's beautiful.' Her voice was almost shy.

'It's life,' he told her. 'I wanted my body to reflect growth and hope, not death.'

'My mother told me you should visit Paris to fall in love.' Polly changed the subject abruptly. 'That's why I've never been.'

'You've never fallen in love?'

'I've been in "like",' she said. 'I've been in companionable comfort. I've desired.' Did her eyes flicker towards Gabe at the last word?

His chest tightened at the thought, the blood pulsing hot and thick around his body.

'But, no. I haven't been in love.' She bit her lip. 'That is rather shameful for a woman of thirty-one, isn't it?'

'Non.' The word was strong, vehement. 'Real love is rare, precious. Many of us will never experience it.' He'd thought he'd found it once. Had watched it slip away.

'My mother left home when I was eight. Our father died a couple of years later but he was in a home all that time.' Her voice faltered. 'We found him, Raff and I. He'd had a stroke. He needed full-time care and we were a mess. My mother just couldn't cope. People always took care of her, you see. She was one of those fragile women, all eyes and a way of looking at you as if you were all that mattered. She went away for a rest and just never returned, found someone else to take care of her.'

'I'm sorry.' The words were inadequate.

'Oh, it was a long time ago, and I think I always knew. Knew she couldn't be relied on. It was harder on Raff. He absolutely adored her. But for some reason I never forgot her words. She said she'd been to Paris before, with friends, boyfriends, but when she went with Daddy the city turned into a magical wonderland and she knew…'

'Knew what?'

'That she was in love,' she said simply. 'And she made me promise her, promise I would never go to Paris until I was sure I was ready to fall in love. It's funny, I have spent my whole life not being my mother, not relying on anyone else, always doing my duty. But I kept my promise.'

Her mouth curved into a reminiscent smile. 'She also told me to always wear lipstick, make sure my hair was brushed and to wear the best shoes I can afford. I never forgot that advice either.'

'Even on the Inca trail?'

She exhaled, an amused bubble of laughter. 'Especially then.'

'I hope you get to Paris one day.' She deserved it, deserved to have the trip of her dreams, to experience the world's most romantic city with somebody who loved her by her side.

But the thought of her strolling hand in hand through the city streets with some unknown other, cruising down the Seine, kissing on the Pont des Arts, made his whole body tense up, jealousy coursing through his veins.

It was ridiculous; he had no reason to be jealous.

Jealousy implied need. Implied caring. Sure he liked Polly, respected her, was attracted to her. But that was all.

If she worked somewhere else, if she weren't pregnant then she would be perfect—for a while. She was as busy as he was, as focused as he was, she wouldn't want him to take care of her, to text or call five times a day. She wouldn't care if he went away for a weekend's training or decided to pull an all-nighter at the office.

And when she talked about the likes, the companionable comforts and the desires of her past there was no hint of regret. She moved on without a second's thought. Just as he did.

But she *was* his boss and she *was* going to have a baby and there was no point dwelling on what-might-have-beens. Because the boss situation would change one day but the baby situation most definitely wouldn't. And that made her even more off-limits than ever. She deserved someone who would want a family, someone to take her to Paris.

'You may even fall in love there,' he added.

'Maybe.' She didn't sound convinced. 'It's a fairytale, though, isn't it? Not real life. Because, although Mummy had that perfect moment, it didn't mean enough in the end, didn't stop her bailing when things became rough.'

'No.' There was nothing else to say.

She took out a few pins and let her hair fall, before gathering it up and twisting it into a tighter knot, a few strands escaping in the breeze. 'It was a sharp lesson. If you rely on someone else you are vulnerable. You need to be self-sufficient, to protect yourself.' She sighed. 'It would be nice to meet someone who understood that, who didn't think being independent means not caring.'

She shook her head. 'One day I'll go to Paris, on my own. Or take the baby.'

'You could go to Disneyland.'

She grimaced. 'I am so not ready for this.'

Gabe glanced over. 'You will be,' he said. 'I think you are going to do just fine.'

There was something intimidating about meeting other people's families. Mingling, small talk, conferences, cocktail parties, those posed no fear at all for Polly. But the intimacy and warmth of family homes chilled her.

Even at school she'd hated the invites back to other girls'

houses for the holidays. It was all so alien: in-jokes and traditions, bickering, knowing your place was secure. So different from the formality of her grandparents' house, a place more like a museum than a home for two children.

Throw in a different language, a tangle of small children and in-laws and her arrival at the Beaufils chateau was a scene right out of her worst fears. She was seized upon, hugged, kissed and exclaimed over by what felt like an endless stream of people.

'It is lovely to meet you.' Madame Beaufils linked an arm through Polly's and whisked her through the imposing front door.

'Thank you so much for having me.' Polly did her best to relax. She wasn't really that comfortable with physicality, more of a handshake than a hug person, but she couldn't work out how to disentangle herself without causing offence. 'Your home is beautiful.'

No fakery needed here. Polly had grown up accustomed to a luxurious home; her grandfather still lived in the old Queen Anne manor house in the Berkshire countryside that she and Raff had been brought up in. But the weathered old chateau with its ivy-covered walls, surrounded by lovingly tended gardens that stretched into the vineyards beyond, had something her childhood home lacked.

It had heart.

There were pictures everywhere: photos, framed children's paintings, portraits and certificates. The furniture in the huge hall at the centre of the house was well chosen, chic but loved, the sofa a little frayed, the mirror spotted with age.

'It's a mess,' Gabe's mother said dismissively. 'We put our money into renovating the old barns for the B&B and wedding business, and for turning the wings of the house into apartments for Natalie and Claire and their families.

But I like it like this. It feels as if my children are still here with me.' She looked longingly at a large photo of a laughing, dark-eyed girl.'

'That's Celine,' she said with a sigh. 'My biggest fear is that she will meet someone in New Zealand and never return to us. It was worse when Gabe was in the States. Paris was better but at least he's just over the Channel. I can almost breathe again.'

It must be claustrophobic to be needed like that, Polly thought with a stab of sympathy for the absent Celine. But a small, irrepressible part of her couldn't help wondering what it would be like. Her grandmother was certainly miffed if Polly didn't meet her for tea and accompany her shopping when she was in town, and her grandfather liked updates on the store. But neither of them needed Polly for herself. Any granddaughter would have done.

'I've put you in the blue room.' Madame Beaufils led Polly up the grand circular staircase dominating the great hall. 'It has its own en-suite so you will be quite private. Why don't you take a moment to freshen up and then come back down for some lunch before we show you around?' She smiled. 'Natalie is very excited at the thought of showing off her website to you. She has been compiling numbers all week!'

The room she showed Polly to was lovely. It was very simple with high ceilings, dark polished floorboards and whitewashed walls with a huge wooden bedstead dominating one end of the room. The bed was made up with a blue throw and pillows; it looked so inviting Polly didn't dare sit down in case the fatigue pulsing away at her temples took over.

Instead she walked over to the large French windows and flung open the shutters to step out onto the narrow balcony. Her room was at the back of the house overlooking the peaceful-looking garden and the rows of vines beyond. She had never seen anything so vibrant, even on her travels—the green of the vines contrasting with the purple hues of the lavender in the distance, set off by an impossibly blue sky. Polly breathed in, feeling the rich air fill her lungs and, for the first time since that devastating conversation with her grandfather all those months ago, she felt at peace.

She reluctantly tore herself away from the view and took her toiletry bag into the pretty bathroom adjoining her room, emptying out her compact and lipgloss. It was time to apply her armour.

Or was it?

Polly stared at the deep berry red she favoured and then slowly set it back down.

She didn't need to hide. Not today. Instead she loosened her hair and brushed it out, allowing it to fall naturally down her back.

With one last longing glance at the inviting-looking bed, Polly took a deep breath and opened the door. She was ready.

She found the family in the garden, congregated around a large cast-iron table set under a large shady tree. It was already set for lunch and at the sight of the plates piled high with breads, salad, cheese and meat Polly's increasingly capricious appetite perked up.

Oh no, what if it was one of those days? It was all or nothing at the moment; mostly nothing, but when she did want to eat she had no stop mechanism. She hoped she didn't eat the Beaufils family out of house and home.

She could imagine them, gathered together in twenty years' time, telling tales of the Englishwoman who couldn't stop eating.

Polly leant on the corner of the house content just to

watch them for a moment. Everyone was talking, words tumbling out, interrupting each other with expansive hand gestures. Polly's French was pretty good but she was completely confused by the rapid crossfire of laughing conversation.

The laughter was loud and often. Each peal rang through her, making it harder and harder to take a step forward, to interrupt. Not wanting to break into the reunion, for the lively chatter to turn into the inevitable formal chitchat a stranger's presence would cause.

And the longer she stood there, the more impossible that step seemed.

She had never seen Gabe so utterly relaxed. Sitting at the head of the table, he had one plump toddler held firmly on his knee, another was crawling at his feet, attempting occasionally to climb up his denim-clad legs. His mother was pouring him wine, one sister showing him something on her iPad, his father grasping his arm as he made his point.

He was totally immersed, somehow paying attention to each member of his family. A smile of thanks, a nod of acknowledgement, a firm capturing of sticky fingers. Son, brother, uncle, the heart of his family. How could he want to escape this? If this was Polly's family she would never ever want to leave.

It was as if he could hear her thoughts. Gabe's head snapped up and he looked straight over at Polly, his dark gaze unwavering. She didn't want him to think her a coward, wanted to step out with her head held high but she was paralysed, held still by the understanding in his eyes.

She should have felt exposed, weak, but instead it was as if he was cloaking her in warmth, sending strength into suddenly aching limbs. It was almost painful when he dragged his eyes away, handing the toddler on his knee to his mother and scooping up the one by his feet as he rose gracefully out of his chair, walking over to Polly and expertly avoiding the small hands trying to grab his nose.

'*Bonjour*, Polly, this is Mathilde. She doesn't speak English yet but you must forgive her. Her French is terrible too.'

'Your French was terrible too when you were two, and it's not much better now,' interrupted a petite dark-haired woman with a vivacious grin as she came over to join them. She lifted the protesting small girl out of her uncle's arms, cuddling her close with a consoling kiss before turning to Polly.

'We must all be a bit much for you. It gets very loud when we are en masse. Especially when we have all the babies with us. I'm Natalie. I'm sure you didn't get a chance to work out who was who earlier.'

'It's lovely to meet you.' Polly couldn't help her gaze dropping to focus on the woman's large bump.

Natalie followed her gaze and grimaced. 'I know, I am enormous.' She shook her head ruefully. 'The doctor assures me it's not twins. I blame Maman's cooking. There's nothing like eating for two.'

'Not at all,' Polly said quickly. 'I was just thinking how well you look.'

Well. Happy and secure. Could that be her future?

'Come, sit and eat. Would you like some wine? *Non?* How about some grape juice made from our own vines? It's very refreshing.'

Polly allowed herself to be led to the table, to have her glass filled with the chilled juice, her plate filled with a tempting selection of breads, salads and meats, and did her best to join in with the conversation, which kept lapsing into French.

'*En anglais,*' Madame Beaufils said reprovingly. She

turned to Polly. 'I am so sorry, Polly. You must think us very rude.'

'Not at all. I think you are very happy to see Gabe. Please, don't speak English on my account. It will do me good to try and get along. My French is sadly rusty.'

'But so many of our hotel guests are English it does us good to speak it,' Claire said. Gabe's oldest sister was the quietest of the family, much of her time taken in attending to one of the two small children sitting by her side. A third slept quietly in a pram under the tree. 'I want these three to grow up with perfect English.'

Polly eyed the eldest child; he was no more than three, she thought, although children's ages were a mystery to her. One she would soon be solving. Despite many longing glances at a football in the middle of the lawn he was sitting upright on his chair eating daintily. 'He's very good,' she said. Maybe French children *did* have better manners.

Claire grinned. 'He's been bribed. Uncle Gabe will come and play trains with him if he eats all his lunch and behaves. Don't let him fool you. He's not usually this angelic.'

'How do you do it?' Polly looked from Claire to Natalie, both so laid-back, dressed simply but elegantly, not a hair out of place. 'Raise them and run this place?'

'With help!' Claire said emphatically and Natalie nodded in laughing agreement.

'I have an au pair, Maman is always on hand and my husband does a great deal.'

Polly smiled automatically but her mind was racing, calculating. She didn't have a mother or a husband—but she could buy in help. After all, she paid people to clean her house, buy her groceries, mow her lawn. Why not to raise her child?

Polly put the bread she was holding back on her plate

untasted. It sounded so cold. She looked over at the small boy trying so hard to be good and wished he were free to run free, to tear into his food with gusto. That her presence didn't constrain him.

She didn't want to recreate her childhood, to raise a perfectly behaved child painfully trying to live up to impossibly high expectations. She wanted...she wanted *this*. Loud, argumentative, affectionate and close. If she was going to have a child then she wanted a real family: wellies and mud and a big golden dog, the whole lot.

Well, maybe not a dog; Mr Simpkins would never cope.

Summoning up her best French, she leant over to the small boy. 'Bonjour, Jean. I love trains,' she said. 'When you've finished eating do you think you could show me?'

Jean put his bread down and regarded her with solemn dark eyes. 'I have cars too,' he said after a pause. 'Do you like cars too?'

'I adore cars,' Polly told him. 'Especially old ones.'

CHAPTER EIGHT

'YOUR FAMILY ARE lovely.'

It seemed odd to be alone with Gabe again after twenty-four hours of almost continuous company. After playing cars with Jean for a surprisingly enjoyable hour she had had a comprehensive tour of the vineyard and B&B accommodation followed by another long, laughter-filled family meal, this one enhanced by Claire and Natalie's charming husbands.

Visiting a vineyard and refusing to sample any of the products might seem eccentric but nobody had commented. Thank goodness she was past the sickness stage, otherwise she might have disgraced herself as soon as she entered the bottling room and storage cellars with their strong, distinct, alcoholic odour.

Gabe slid her a sidelong look. 'They like you.'

A glow spread through her at his words. She had been at the vineyard for such a short time, a stranger speaking a different language, but she felt a connection to the Beaufils family. It was nice to know it wasn't one-sided.

'Especially Jean,' he added. 'I think you've ousted me from number one. Luckily for me Mathilde still thinks I'm perfect.'

Polly rolled her eyes. 'They all seem very blinkered where you're concerned. Did I see your mother make your smoothie this morning?'

'She likes to,' he said with an annoying smirk, every inch the youngest child. 'I even managed to drag Papa out for a run. Well, more of a jog but it was a start. He eats too much—drinks too much. It's an occupational hazard.'

'How does your father feel about Claire and Natalie's innovations?' Polly asked. There were no traces of the power struggles she had experienced with her grandfather—but they could be good at putting on a public face. She knew all about that; public solidarity was part of the Rafferty code.

'He is overjoyed they are still at home, that they love the vineyard as much as he does.' Gabe pulled an expressive face. 'If he could keep us all there he would. I know he hopes Celine will come back and take over the wine production.'

'And you?'

'There's no place for me there, not now. My horizons are wider. I return home for holidays, weekends. I don't have the time to come back often.'

'I don't think there's any lack of ambition at the vineyard.' Polly had spent the morning with Natalie looking at all the digital innovations the Frenchwoman had introduced. It was impressive, a seamless interface between the physical world and the digital marketplace. 'Natalie is far ahead of much bigger businesses. There's an app for everything. And I think Claire plans to make it *the* premier events and hospitality venue in the country. She'll do it too, if she has the capital.'

'I can help out there.'

'I think they'd rather have your input than your money. Oh, I don't mean come back home to live. But they miss you.' She grinned at him. 'Talk about the prodigal son. If you get this kind of reaction after a few weeks in London I can't imagine what your mother feeds Celine when she comes home.'

'A full fatted calf.' He looked over at her. 'What did they say?'

A flush rose on her cheeks. She didn't want Gabe to think she'd been talking about him, probing for secrets and tales. But his family had been all too eager to share stories with her.

Almost as if she were his girlfriend, not his boss.

A wave of longing swept through her as unexpected as it was unwelcome. What would it be like to be welcomed into the bosom of a family such as this? To be part of a large, loving, chaotic throng? To have a place around the enormous scrubbed pine table that dominated the kitchen? To know your steps in the carefully choreographed dance of a family meal. Even Mathilde and Jean had gone straight to a drawer to collect and fold napkins. The sons-in-law were kept busy fetching and carrying.

Polly alone had had no role. The guest, set apart.

'They said you don't come home enough but they understand that you're busy.' Polly chose her words carefully. 'That as they look at expanding it would be good to have your input, only they know how it's hard for you to get away.'

Their eyes followed him everywhere, their need echoing out. They adored him, would absorb him back in if he gave them the chance. Polly could see how it smothered him, why he stayed away even as she wondered what it would be like, to be loved so comprehensively.

'Papa often talks about expanding.' Gabe was dismissive. 'Yet, he never does.'

'He might do if you were there to talk it through with him.' Polly could hear the tart note in her voice but didn't try to rein it in. 'Your sisters are specialists, great at what they do but very focused. You however are trained in managing the bigger picture. You should give him some time beyond a morning jog.'

There was a pained silence. 'One day here and you're the expert on my family.'

Words of apology rose to her lips but she swallowed them back. 'I don't need to be an expert. It's completely plain to anyone with eyes. I'm not saying move back home, but you could talk his plans through with him, advise him.'

'Maybe.'

'I know you needed to get away—and you did, you created a life away from them. Well…' she considered him '…you created a *career* away from them.'

Gabe's mouth was set tight, a muscle pulsing in his jaw. 'I don't see the distinction.'

'I know,' she said sadly. 'You and I are birds of a feather. We think success at work, achieving career goals is all that matters, all that defines us. But, Gabe, I *had* nothing else. The only approval I ever got was work-related—and I begrudged it. But you? You could announce you were giving it all up tomorrow to go back and, I don't know, create art out of vine leaves and they would still welcome you home and support you all the way.'

His mouth twitched. 'Art out of vine leaves?'

'It might be a thing.'

He didn't say anything for a few minutes, his eyes set on the road ahead. Polly sat back in her seat, losing herself in the vibrant scenery. What must it be like to grow up surrounded by so much colourful beauty?

'Why does it matter to you?' His words were so unexpected it took a moment for Polly to comprehend them.

'Why does what matter?' But she knew what he meant.

'My family, my place there.'

Her cheeks heated. 'It doesn't mean a thing to me personally,' she said. 'But I like your parents, your sisters. It seems a shame, that's all. I like you…' Her words hung there. Polly wanted to grab them, take them back.

But they *were* out there. So she might as well be completely honest. 'I like you,' she said again. *In for a penny,* she thought.

'I'm not keen on the workaholic who flirts with my assistant, the smell of those smoothies would turn my stomach even if I wasn't pregnant and I have very strong, negative views on people who turn up to work in Lycra cycling shorts.' Even if they did look as good as on Gabe. You had to have good legs to pull off the tightly fitting shorts. Gabe rocked them.

Some staff members had taken to standing near the staff entrance when he came back from his lunch time bike ride.

'Don't spare my feelings.' But there was a quirk at the side of his mouth as he tried to hide a reluctant smile.

'I really dislike the way you take one girl out for a drink and another the next day. I know you don't cross any lines or break promises, but it creates discord and I won't have that in my store. But…' she took a deep breath '…I do admire the way you remember everyone's name and what they do. I am a little envious of the rapport you have with my staff already. I don't doubt you'll be a CEO by thirty because you're focused and innovative and put the hours in.'

'Should I be blushing?'

'And I don't know what I would have done without you last week.' There, she had said it.

'Oh, Polly.' He shook his head, the smile gone. 'You would have been absolutely fine.'

'Maybe,' she agreed. 'I am used to doing things alone. I would have *coped*. I'd have had to. But it was nice not having to. Maybe it's the time I had away, maybe it's the hormones whooshing around turning everything upside down, but I am actually glad, glad that there is going to be something in my life apart from work. It may not be planned, the circumstances aren't ideal but I think the baby is a good thing for me.'

She smiled ruefully. 'Of course if you repeat that to anyone I will kill you.'

'I'd expect nothing less.'

'But you already have things outside work. Nieces and nephews and a family—and you keep yourself apart. I know why, I understand why. I just wonder...' She paused, trying to pick her words carefully. 'I just think maybe it's time you open yourself back up to them. Don't you think you've punished them enough?'

'I'm not punishing them.'

'Aren't you?' She pulled at her hair, twisting it round in her hand as she looked at him, at the set of his jaw, the line of his mouth. The dark chill in his eyes. 'Punishment? Atonement? Proving something? Whatever it is you're doing it's been ten years. I think it's time you gave them a break. I think you should give yourself a break. Before it's too late.'

Polly's words echoed round and round in Gabe's head despite his attempts to push them away, far away out of his subconscious.

Punishment.

She was right, damn her. But not as right as she thought she was. He wasn't punishing them.

He was punishing himself. For falling ill, for causing them such pain and anxiety.

For all the petty, nasty resentment he had allowed to build up during that long year of pain. Resentment towards his parents for their need and worry. Towards his sisters for their health.

He didn't speak for the rest of the journey. Polly didn't try to engage him in conversation, scribbling notes in her ever-present notebook instead but occasionally shooting him concerned glances.

Glances he pretended not to see. If he didn't engage

then he didn't need to speak and he could lock it all back up, deep inside.

Where it needed to be.

It took a while to find a parking space in the small riverside town of Vignonel. Sleepy for fifty weeks of the year, it was transformed into an international hub by the annual food and drink festival held there every summer. Over the years it had grown to include culture, local crafts and music, and every year thousands of people descended there from all over the world to dance, drink and eat.

They had all descended today, it seemed.

'This is where we've been going wrong,' Polly said after they were finally parked and had begun to thread their way through the main thoroughfare that led towards the main town square. 'We don't go out and find our suppliers any more. People come and pitch to us. Chris and the rest of his team should be here, searching out the best local producers and stocking them.'

'Yes.' But he barely heard her words, his attention snagged by the large church dominating the town square. His heart began to speed up and despite the heat of the day a cold sweat covered his hands.

He swallowed, a bitter taste coating his mouth. 'There's a lot to see,' he managed to say in as normal a tone as possible. 'We'll cover more ground if we split up.'

A fleeting expression flashed in Polly's blue eyes. For a moment Gabe wondered if he had hurt her feelings but dismissed the arrogant notion as her head snapped up and she became her usual focused self.

'Good idea.' She pulled out her notebook and pen. 'We'll compare notes when we meet up. Look out for suppliers but I am more interested in what makes a stall successful, what draws people in. The look, the branding, the offer.'

'The technology?' Gabe couldn't help giving the

leather-bound book a pointed look and Polly hugged it to her chest protectively.

'What? I don't have to worry about the battery running out or a system relapse wiping everything.'

'No, you just have to keep it dry and hope you don't lose it.' They had reached an information point and he picked up a map and guide, handing it to Polly. Her hand was cool, soft. Comforting. A sudden urge to take it in his, to stroll through the streets together, no notebooks, no reports, no memories, hit him but he pushed it aside. It took more effort than he cared for to refocus.

'I promised Claire I'd call in at her tourism and marketing pavilion.' Was she really so oblivious to his momentary inner struggle? Evidently so. She was frowning at the map in utter concentration. 'If I look at that part of the market why don't you go into the wine quarter to start? Your father's there on the regional wine stand this afternoon. And no...' her eyes met his clearly '...I'm not interfering, just being polite.'

She held his gaze, cool and self-possessed before inclining her head, a curiously old-fashioned gesture. 'I'll see you back here, then.'

Gabe watched as she swivelled and walked away, her head held high, the dark gold sweep of hair still loose, covering the slim line of her back. It was odd to see her hair down, not in the customary loose knot, for her to leave it unfettered. It made her seem younger, relaxed.

What would it be like to tangle his hand in that hair? Let the silken tresses fold around his fingers?

She was wearing the pink dress she'd bought at the vintage fair and as Gabe followed the proud, straight figure as she disappeared into the crowd he had a curious sense of being out of time.

Okay, time to push such fanciful thoughts out of his

head, time to get on. To find his father, say hello, compliment him on the stall and the vintage just as Polly suggested.

As for the rest? It was ridiculous. He wasn't punishing them. He was protecting them.

Protecting himself.

If you had no ties then you couldn't get hurt. It was that simple.

The food and drink quarter was situated on one of the several windy streets that led off the square, opposite the church. Just a few minutes' walk up there and he would be among old friends and neighbours, watching his father do what he did best—enthusing about wine.

A smile curved his lips as he pictured the scene: a laughing group of tourists pulled in by his father's practised patter, sipping and tasting before parting with what would no doubt be a considerable amount of money.

Just a few minutes' walk. He should go, say hi.

He could even offer to help.

Gabe stood for a moment and then slowly turned to face the church.

A deep breath shuddered through him as if an icy fist had clenched his heart.

He hadn't set foot in that church for ten years and yet he could clearly picture the aged, wooden beams, see the sunlight dancing through the coloured glass in the ancient windows, the expression on the faces of the cold marble statues. He could smell the incense as it burned hot and heavy.

He could see the coffin.

Without conscious thought, without decision, he walked across the tree-lined square, away from the festival, past the church, to the narrow street that led out of town. Towards the old walled cemetery.

To Marie's grave.

Was it really ten years since he had stood by the open grave, pale faced and dry eyed as the white coffin had been slowly and solemnly lowered in?

White! She would have been horrified! Demanded black and velvet with silver clasps—or nothing at all, a quiet spot in a wooded glade. No X to mark the spot.

But burials weren't for the dead, they were for those left behind and her parents had needed every last trimming to get them through the day.

His mouth tightened. He hadn't written or contacted the Declors for years, unable to face another visit down memory lane. Not wanting to sit in the claustrophobic *salon*, sipping wine while looking through photo albums preserving the memory of a dead girl, pink cheeked and full of health. He had never known that girl. The Marie he had known had been like him, clad with a hospital pallor.

They were supposed to live or die together. He hadn't kept his part of the deal. Had she known, when she slipped away, that he wouldn't be joining her? Not yet.

Which was the worst betrayal? That he hadn't died with her or that she hadn't lived with him?

Had she forgiven him? He wasn't sure he had forgiven her yet. Or himself.

'Gabe?'

He jumped, a shiver running down his spine at the softly breathed words.

'Gabe!' No, not a ghost. Not unless Marie had developed a clipped English accent in the last ten years, had swapped the Converse low tops for high-heeled sandals that tapped smartly on the old cobbles.

He stopped and turned. Waited. Relieved to have the present intrude on the past.

'Claire was so busy I didn't like to disturb her.' Polly

stopped as she reached the tall figure, her hand automatically going up to nervously knot her hair, only to fall away as she spoke. 'I wondered if maybe you wanted some lunch, if I could buy you some lunch. I…er…I crossed a line earlier. I need to apologise.'

She let a shuddering breath go and waited.

Lunch, work, an excuse not to face up to the past, to push it away for another decade.

'That would be nice,' he said after a long moment. 'But there's somewhere I need to go first. Polly, I'd really like it if you came with me.'

The river rushed along, white-topped as it bubbled over rocks and dropped over mini falls. The path along it was flat, easy walking. Left the mind free to wander.

Polly wasn't entirely sure that this was a good thing. She searched for something to say.

Nothing.

Now didn't seem appropriate to discuss work and she had already ventured into personal territory once that day. Look how well that had gone down, a clear indication to mind her own business.

Only… It was just…

He had asked her to come along.

She hadn't gone all the way into the rather macabre cemetery with its carved headstones, statues and family vaults, as different from a tidy Church Of England graveyard as a Brie from Cheddar, rather she had waited by the wall as Gabe had walked steadily to a white marble gravestone, topped with a carved cherub, and dropped to one knee in front of it. He had stayed there for five minutes, head bowed. Polly couldn't tell if he was weeping, praying or just frozen in silent contemplation. Either way discomforting shivers had rippled down her spine.

She had witnessed something deeply personal.

So she should say something, right? Wasn't that the normal thing to do when someone allowed you to see a part of their soul?

Only it had never happened before. She had no compass for this kind of thing. No guidance.

Even at her very proper boarding school there hadn't been a lesson on how to handle this kind of situation.

How to greet an ambassador? Yes. Royal garden party etiquette? Of course.

But this? She was clueless. She was going to have to go in blind.

'Are you okay?'

Not the most insightful or original icebreaker in the world, but it was a start.

'Oui.' Gabe turned, looked at her, the dark eyes unreadable. 'Thank you.'

Polly stopped, tilting her head up to meet his gaze. 'What for? I didn't do anything.'

He shrugged. 'For being there. I needed a friend.'

Her eyes dropped; she was suddenly, oddly shy. 'I owe you.' Unable to resume looking at him, she started walking again and he fell into step beside her. 'Who was it?'

He sighed, low and deep. 'Who was your first love, Polly?'

'My what?' Flustered, she pushed her hair away from her face. 'I don't know. I thought we'd already covered that I don't really do love.'

'But there must have been someone, a crush, a passion. Someone who made your world that bit more exciting, your pulse beat that bit faster. Someone who made your blood heat up with just the thought of them.' His voice was low, his accent more pronounced than usual; each word hit her deep inside, burning.

You.

But she didn't say the word; she couldn't. That wasn't who she was, what they were. They might have crossed a line from colleagues to friends but the next line, from friends to lovers, was too far, too high, too unattainable.

And Polly didn't have many friends. She didn't want to screw this new understanding up.

First love? She dragged her mind back, to her lonely teenage years.

'I had a huge crush on my school friend's brother,' she admitted. 'I was sixteen and staying there one Christmas holidays. He kissed me on New Year and I went back to school convinced we were an item. When I next saw him he was with his girlfriend and barely acknowledged me.' She grimaced. 'I wept for a week. What a silly idiot I was.'

'Non.' To her surprise he reached over and took her hand. His long fingers laced through hers. Every millimetre where his skin touched hers was immediately sensitised, tiny electric shocks darting up her arm, piercing the core of her.

She shivered, all her attention on her hand, on her fingers, on the way he was touching her, the light caress.

It wasn't enough.

Just friends, remember? she told herself sternly. But who was she fooling? As *if* it were enough.

'That's how we learn, that complete single-mindedness of the teenage heart.'

'Learn what?'

His fingers tightened on hers. 'That feelings are not always worth the price.'

'Gabe.' Her voice was husky with the unexpected need. 'Who was she?'

'Marie.' The sound of loss and regret pulsed through her. 'She was sixteen.'

'Like I was,' she breathed, absurdly glad to find some tenuous link between her teenaged self and his ghostly lover.

'Same age as you were,' he agreed. 'Only I didn't find someone else. She left me.'

'You met in hospital?' It was all beginning to fall into place.

He nodded, his fingers almost painfully tight but Polly didn't care, welcomed his grip, anchoring him to her. 'It's not like anywhere else,' he said. 'Everything is distilled down. You're defined by your illness but underneath? Underneath you're still a person, a teenager desperate to act out and find yourself, and the steroid bloating and the hair loss and the bruising and burns? None of it changes that. Marie and I met and we knew each other. Instantly.'

A shocking, unwanted jolt of jealousy hit her and Polly swallowed it back. It was unworthy. Of her and of the story he was confiding in her.

'Tell me about her.' She wanted to know everything.

'She was understanding and acceptance. She was anger and rebellion and gallows humour. Just like me. It was…' he paused, searching for the right word '…intense. I don't know if we'd met in normal life if we'd have even liked each other. But then? Then she was all that I wanted, all that I needed. We were going to make it together or fail together.' He laughed softly, bitterly. 'The hubris of youth. But it didn't turn out the way we planned. I was so angry that she left me behind.'

'And now?'

'And now I am a decade older. That time is a memory, and Marie…' He swallowed. 'I don't even think of her day to day. I don't think of the boy I was. I took that time and I locked it away. I got well, I left Provence, left France, went away to college and I reinvented myself.'

'You're a survivor.'

She stopped and turned to face him. One hand was still held tightly in his; she allowed the other to drift up, to touch his cheek, to run along the defined line of his cheekbone and along the darkly stubbled jaw.

'You did what you had to do to survive. That makes you pretty darn amazing.'

He looked down at her, a pulse beating wildly in his cheek, the eyes almost black with pain. 'I forgot how to feel,' he said hoarsely. 'It hurt too much. Loss and pain and need. It was easier to smile and flirt and work and leave all that messy emotional stuff locked away. With Marie.'

'I know,' Polly whispered. She stared up at him. 'Emotions hurt.'

'Coming back, coming home, I can't forget. It's in every look, every word. My parents see me and they remember it all, all the hurt I caused them. And I see her, on every street corner, in every field. I see my broken promises.'

'You must have loved her very much.' Polly could hear the wistfulness in her voice and winced inwardly.

'Love?' He laughed softly. 'We were too young and fiery for love. I needed her, adored her, but love?' He looked right at her, gold flecks in his eyes mesmerising her. 'I don't know what love is either, Polly.'

She took a step towards him, eyes still fixed on his. The one small step had brought her into full contact, her chest pressed against his, hips against hips. She slid the hand cupping his face around his neck, allowing her fingers to run through the ends of his hair.

'Neither do I,' she said. 'I know want.' She stood on tiptoe and pressed a kiss on the pulse in his throat. He quivered. 'I know need.' Emboldened, she moved her mouth up and nipped his ear lobe. 'I know desire. Sometimes they're enough, they have to be enough.'

Her mouth moved to his, to drop a light butterfly kiss on

the firm lips. She had only meant to comfort him, to take his mind off the past but one small step, three small kisses, three dangerous words shifted the mood, charged the air.

'Are they?' he asked, his eyes burning a question.

Polly couldn't answer, couldn't speak, could only nod as he continued to look hard into her eyes, into her soul.

She had no idea what he saw reflected there, all she knew was that she was boneless with desire, burning up with the unexpected, unwanted, but very real need pulsing through her, his body branding her, claiming her at every point they touched.

She didn't want him to think, didn't want any regrets, she just wanted him to hold her tight, wanted to taste him. She pulled her hand out of his, the momentary loss of contact chilling her until she slid her arm around his waist, working her hand under his T-shirt to feel the firm skin underneath. There under her fingers was the tattoo. She traced it from memory feeling him shudder under her touch.

'Goddammit, Polly,' he groaned. 'I'm trying…'

'Don't.'

It was all he needed. With a smothered cry of frustration, of need, he gave in, his arms pulling her in tight, one hand on her back, the other tangling in her hair.

He looked one last time, searching her face and whatever he saw there was enough because he lowered his mouth to hers. Claimed her. And she allowed it. Allowed herself to lose herself in his mouth, his hands, his hard, strong body. Today at least, in this moment, it was all she could give him.

And she would give all that he could take.

CHAPTER NINE

'OH, NO!'

Polly had barely waited until the plane had landed and the seat-belt light was switched off before she had pulled her phone out and switched it on.

Keeping busy. Avoiding conversation. Just as she had done all last night, all morning. Chatting to his mother, going on yet another guided tour with Claire, bathing Mathilde.

Avoiding conversation. Avoiding physical contact. Avoiding Gabe.

Gabe closed his eyes. It wasn't as if he had been trying to get her alone either.

It was all too *real*. The taste of her, cinnamon spicy and sweet. The softness of her hair, the warmth and smoothness of her skin. The exquisite torture of her hands, roaming over him as if she could learn him by heart…

He took a long, deep breath, willing away the evocative memories. Willing away the urge to reach over, take her hands and draw her back to him. To lose himself in her again.

What had he been thinking? Necking like teenagers on a riverside path! Gabe couldn't remember the last time he had been content to hold and be held. To kiss, to touch with no expectation, no hurry to move on to the next stage. It wasn't just their admittedly exposed location. It was as if they were the teenage selves they had exhumed, armed with all that shy and explosive passion. No need to take it further. Content just to explore, to be.

No need to go further. Not then. And not since either.

It was probably all for the best. Every reason he had listed against getting involved with Polly still stood. Was valid. Even with the memory of the kiss thudding through him.

He opened his eyes and stared at the back of the airline seat. Yep, definitely all for the best.

'Honestly, does he never think?' Polly was still muttering as she glared at her phone as if it could answer her.

'Problems?' Gabe swung himself out of his seat and opened the overhead locker to collect their bags.

'Grandfather.' It was said expressively. 'He wants to meet us at the house when we get back. My house. He's asked Raff. It hasn't even occurred to him that we might be tired.'

'Why should it?' Gabe swung Polly's neat overnight bag down and set it onto his seat. 'It's not even three in the afternoon. It's the middle of your working day. Besides, have you ever put tiredness before business before? It's not like he knows that you're pregnant.'

'That's not the point...'

'Polly.' He put his own bag onto the floor and turned to face her, taking in the dark circles under her eyes. She looked as if she had slept as well as he had. Was it the heat or the baby keeping her awake—or was she, like him, taunted by the memory of soft lips and caressing hands? Had she got out of bed several times, determined to creep down the landing hall to tap at his door only to fall back onto the bed unsure what to say, what to do?

'You need to tell him.'

She turned the full force of her glare on him but Gabe simply shouldered her bag and collected his own. 'It's time, Polly. Everything's looking good. You've accepted it. You need your family.'

She blinked, the long dark lashes falling in confusion. 'My family isn't like yours. We don't do unconditional love.'

'Then it's time you changed that,' he said and walked off along the nearly empty aisle.

She didn't speak to him again as they exited the airport and found their way to her car and this time, when Gabe held out his hand for her keys, she didn't protest, handing them over almost absent-mindedly. He had expected her to spend the journey back to Hopeford as she had every other moment that day, tapping on her laptop or phone or scribbling in her notebook, but she simply laid her head back on the headrest and stared out of the window.

It didn't take them long; the small airport was conveniently close to Hopeford and it was less than an hour later when Gabe turned into the narrow lane and parked outside the cottage. An old red Porsche was already parked there along with a Mercedes saloon.

'Great, the cavalry are already here.'

Gabe shot her a concerned look. Where was the cool, collected Polly, in charge of everything and everyone? Where was the insistently questioning Polly, forcing him to face up to some unpalatable truths?

'Is that Raff's car? The vintage one?' Surely a mention of vintage cars would cheer her up.

'It was our father's. He got Daddy's car, I got Mummy's jewellery, the bits she left behind anyway. Never say that the Raffertys aren't conventional.'

She opened the door and slid out. 'Let's do this. Leave the bags, Gabe. We'll get them later.'

Gabe slowly exited the car and watched her. It was incredible seeing the way she breathed in, the mask slipping over her as she tilted her head up, straightened her back. She was every inch Polly Rafferty, CEO. On the outside at least.

He fell into step beside her but she didn't look at him as she marched up the small path that wound from the road through her flower-filled front garden to the wooden front door.

Twisting the handle, she made a face as the door opened with no need for a key. 'Hello,' she called as she pushed it open. 'If you're burglars then there isn't anything worth taking. If it's Raff how the hell did you get in?'

'Ah, that's my fault. I abused my position as your concierge service but I thought you would prefer to come home to a prepared dinner and a settled-in grandparent.' A woman with a heart-shaped face, wavy red-gold hair and the greenest eyes Gabe had ever seen came through from the kitchen, smiling a little shyly. 'Hi, Polly. I'm so sorry I haven't been round before today. Good trip?'

Polly stood stock-still for a moment and Gabe felt her take an audible deep breath as if steeling herself before she moved forward, her face wreathed in smiles. 'Clara! I should have known. It's so good to see you. Let me see...' She grabbed Clara's left hand and stared at the antique emerald ring on her third finger.

'I know it's customary to say congratulations but as Raff's twin I can't square it with my conscience if I don't first say *run*. I lived with him for eighteen years and you are far too good for him.'

Clara was glowing with happiness. 'It's too late. Summer would never forgive me. He's promised to take her to two theme parks in Florida this year.'

Polly shook her head. 'That's my brother. He always targets the weak spot! Congratulations, Clara. I hope you will be very happy. Have you met Gabe yet? Gabe, this is Clara, my brother's fiancée.'

'No, we haven't met but I know Raff, of course. Please accept my felicitations.' Gabe shook her hand warmly and smiled down into the green eyes.

'Polly, I am so sorry,' Clara whispered. 'I said you would probably be too tired for a meeting now, and the last thing you would want was your house invaded, but your grandfather was so insistent. I got Dad to make some food I can heat up, just a lasagne and salad, and Sue will clean it all up tomorrow so, really, all you have to do is eat.'

Polly didn't know how she would have managed without Clara's concierge service to manage her life over the last three years; she had never been more grateful for her friend's organisational powers.

'That's okay.' Polly gave Clara's hand a squeeze. 'But I hope you're sticking around. You're part of the family now. Where is everyone?'

Clara smiled back at her friend. 'Thanks, Polly. They're in the sitting room. Oh, and just to warn you before you go in, your grandmother is there as well.'

'What? With Grandfather? In the same room? Good God, thank goodness I don't have any priceless antiques.'

Polly led the way through the low-beamed door into the pretty sitting room. Gabe was so used to seeing the house empty it was a shock to find the room full of people. Charles Rafferty was ensconced on the straight-backed armchair by the unlit fire, his despised stick by his side. A white-haired, regal-looking woman with an unmistakeable look of the Rafferty twins in her straight nose and shrewd blue eyes was sitting on the sofa talking to Raff while a dark-haired girl of ten or so was lying on the floor whispering softly to Mr Simpkins as he purred around her hand.

'This is quite the welcoming committee.' Polly looked

calm and collected as she walked in. 'Hello, Grandmother.' She went over to the sofa and kissed the older lady's cheek. 'Raff.' A cool nod at her brother. 'Grandfather.' Another nod. 'Hi, Summer, how was Australia?'

'Polly!' The girl scrambled to her feet. 'Do you know you're going to be my aunt?'

'I do.' Polly stepped over and gave her a quick hug. 'My first niece. I'm looking forward to it.'

There was an ache at the back of Gabe's throat as he watched her dance so awkwardly around her family. She was right: he kept his at arm's length but it didn't matter. They would always be there, love him, have a space for him. Nothing he could do would provoke this kind of cold and formal reception.

He *should* go home more often. Talk to his papa about his future plans. Help out a little.

'Sorry for gatecrashing, Pol.' Raff was twinkling up at his sister. 'Grandfather insisted.'

'Clara explained. It's okay, of course you're all welcome but there's not much I can tell you today. Gabe and I haven't had an opportunity to pull our research together, although after seeing what Natalie is doing with the software on a smaller scale I have to say I'm very close to being completely convinced if we can make the numbers add up…'

'This isn't about Rafferty's,' her grandfather interrupted and Gabe could feel the shock reverberate through Polly as her cheeks whitened and she took a step closer to her grandfather's chair.

'Not about Rafferty's? Are you ill? I knew you should have stepped down earlier!'

'Charles isn't ill, at least, no worse than he was before the angina attack.' Polly's grandmother spoke calmly and Polly held her stare, looking for and apparently finding reassurance.

'Then what?'

'Polly dear, your grandfather and I are going to re-marry.'

Polly looked down the wooden table at her family and resisted the urge to rub her eyes. It was ironic, just last night she would have given anything to have her family congregated in her kitchen the way the Beaufils did, all eating together.

And here they were. Sure, it was a little more formal, a tad more awkward than in the Provence farmhouse. Summer was unusually tongue-tied and Gabe evidently embarrassed about being caught up in the family drama. Clara...

Clara only had eyes for Raff and he for her.

A hollow pit opened up in Polly's stomach. What would it be like for someone to look at her like that? As if she were the answer to every question? To every prayer.

Yesterday with Gabe she had come close. Close to letting him in. Colour flushed her cheeks as she remembered. She had almost begged him. No wonder he couldn't meet her eyes.

'Not hungry, Polly?' Clara looked pointedly at Polly's almost untouched plate.

'Sorry, Clara. Please don't tell your father. It was delicious as always. I'm just tired, I guess.' Without meaning to, Polly allowed her eyes to wander over to Gabe, somehow at the head of the table. Of *her* table. He looked completely at ease, mid-conversation with her grandfather, long fingers playing on the stem of his wine glass.

Fingers that just yesterday had been playing on her skin.

Polly shivered. How could a kiss be that sensual? More erotic than the most practised lovemaking?

What would it have been like if they had been somewhere more private? If they had gone further? If she had been able to explore that tattoo the way she had burned to, tracing it with the tip of her finger. With kisses. With her tongue, slick on salty skin.

She clenched her hands, allowing the nails to dig into her palms. She was at dinner, for goodness' sake. With her grandparents.

With her brother.

With Gabe…

He looked up, with that sixth sense he seemed to possess whenever she thought about him, eyes dark and intent.

'We should celebrate,' he said abruptly. 'Two engagements require champagne.'

'Yes, of course.' She should have thought of that. It was her house after all. And she was the only one without news to celebrate. Publicly at least. 'There's a couple of bottles out back.'

'I'll get them.' He pushed his chair back and disappeared into the pantry, reappearing with one of the bottles that had been chilling in the old stone cold room.

'Summer, *ma chérie*, could you go to the cupboard there and get me six of the long glasses? *Oui*, clever girl.' He flashed his warmest smile at the small girl as Summer proudly put the glasses on the table and Polly pushed her still-full wine glass to one side.

It had been easier to accept the glass and not touch it rather than face any questions. Gabe was right, she needed to say something. But how?

With an expert twist Gabe loosed the cork and began to pour the bubble-filled amber liquid into the first glass, handing the first to her grandmother and the second to Clara. When every glass had been filled and handed around every face turned expectantly to Polly.

Of course. This was her role. Head of the family firm.

She got to her feet, trying to drag her thoughts back to

the here and now, to the unexpected news that had greeted her return home.

'So there are two engagements to celebrate,' she said, keeping her voice as steady as she could. Raff and Clara were smiling up at her, her grandparents regarding her with more warmth than she had seen from them in a long time.

Her eyes flickered to Gabe. His eyes were fixed on her, expression inscrutable.

'I know my job involves looking for trends and seeing what lies ahead so all I can say is that thank goodness I don't run a dating agency because I didn't predict either of these. But that doesn't mean that I'm not truly happy for you all. Clara, you've been my closest friend in Hopeford.'

So close that I haven't seen you since I returned, a little voice whispered but Polly ignored it.

'I know how much Raff loves you and I know he will do everything he can to make you happy—and when Raff sets his mind to something he usually achieves it!

'And Grandfather, Grandmother. Thank you for raising Raff and me. I know it wasn't easy, that we weren't easy. I know it put a strain on you. I'm just glad you've found your way back together after thirteen years. You're the most formidable team I know. So.' She held her glass high. 'To the Raffertys. Congratulations.'

'The Raffertys,' they chorused, glasses held to hers before they sipped.

Polly put her glass down thankfully.

'Aunty Polly,' Summer's voice rang out clearly. 'Why aren't you drinking yours?'

Every eye turned to Polly and she sank back into her seat, instinctively looking over at Gabe for help.

But he just sat there.

'You didn't drink any wine either.' Raff sounded accusatory.

For goodness' sake, wasn't a girl allowed to not drink? It wasn't as if she were a lush!

But maybe Gabe was right. They had to know soon enough and although a big announcement hadn't been her plan maybe it would be better to tell them all in one fell swoop. Like ripping off a plaster.

Polly took a breath, feeling the air shudder through her.

'I have a little announcement of my own. This isn't quite how I wanted to do it…' she looked around the table, desperate for some reassurance '…but I suppose there isn't an easy way so I'm just going to say it. I'm pregnant.'

'That's great, Polly.' But Clara's voice was lost as both Raff and her grandfather sprang to their feet.

'Pregnant?'

'You'll marry her, of course!' Her grandfather was glaring at Gabe.

'What do you mean, pregnant?'

So much for extending the celebrations.

The noise levels rose. Polly couldn't think, didn't know which angry, accusatory face to answer first. 'Stop it!' She had risen to her feet as well, hands crashing down onto the table, rattling the crockery and silverware.

'Come on, Summer, let's go for a walk.' Clara threw her an apologetic glance as she shepherded her daughter from the table. 'We'll talk later, Polly. It's great news. Raff?' Her eyes bored into her fiancé, an implicit warning. 'I'll see you at home.'

Raff sank back into his seat. 'Sorry, Polly. It was just, it was a shock.'

Charles Rafferty wasn't so easily cowed. He was still on his feet and glaring over at Gabe. 'Well?' he demanded.

'Grandfather!' Polly said sharply. 'For goodness' sake. You are not some medieval knight, much as you might wish it, and I am *not* some dishonoured damsel to be married off to avoid a scandal. This is a good thing and it has *nothing* to do with Gabe.'

Maybe she had put too much emphasis on the 'nothing', she conceded as the Frenchman whitened, and added: 'I've only known him a few weeks.'

'Then whose is it?'

'Mine,' she said firmly. 'This is the twenty-first century, I am thirty-one and I am quite capable of doing this alone.'

'Yes, dear, we know how independent you are.' Her grandmother sounded like a dowager duchess from the turn of the last century. 'But what your grandfather means is who fathered it? Unless you went to one of those clinics,' she said a little doubtfully.

If only she had! That would be so much easier to admit.

'Someone I met travelling.' She held up her hand. 'I don't know his surname. Obviously if I had foreseen this I would have exchanged business cards but I didn't. So it's up to me. And you, if you want to be involved.'

'Of course we do, dear, don't be so melodramatic.'

But her grandmother's words were negated by her grandfather's expression. Shock, disapproval, horror, disgust passing over his face in rapid but sickening procession.

'A granddaughter of mine? Besmirching the family name with some dreadlocked backpacker? I told you to get married, Polly. I told you to settle down…'

'With respect, *monsieur*, that's enough.' Now Gabe was on his feet. 'Polly has done nothing wrong. It may not be your preferred path for her but she is going to be a great mother—and a great CEO.'

'A single mother in charge of Rafferty's?' Charles Rafferty huffed out a disparaging laugh. 'I thought you had more sense than that, Beaufils. As for you, Polly, I knew letting you take over was a mistake. I should have stuck with my gut instinct.'

The blood rushed from her cheeks and her knees weakened. He'd admitted it. He didn't want her. Her appointment, her career was nothing but a mistake in his eyes.

'Clara's a single mother,' Raff said. His voice was mild but there was a steely glint in his eyes. 'At least she was. Polly, I'm sorry, you…' He rubbed his jaw, the blue eyes rueful. 'You surprised me but you're not alone. I hope you know that. Clara and I are right here.' Polly nodded, numb inside, her eyes returning to her grandfather, still standing up, still glaring.

'You two always did stick together,' he said. 'It doesn't change anything. It's hard enough for any working mother to be at the top, impossible for a woman on her own. It's not old-fashioned, it's common sense.'

'There are plenty of single parents at Rafferty's, men and women.' Gabe's voice was soft but it cut through the tense air, drawing all the attention away from Polly, and she folded herself back into her chair, clasping her hands together to keep them from trembling.

'The only person, *monsieur*, who sees a problem here is you. Which is ironic because if you had seen her worth earlier, if you hadn't pushed her away, then maybe she wouldn't be in this position. You need to think very carefully about how you treat and value your granddaughter before you lose her for ever—and the great-grandchild she is carrying.'

Charles Rafferty paled and Polly and Raff exchanged a concerned glance as he sat down heavily in his chair. His tongue wasn't weakened though. 'I thought we had established that this has nothing to do with you.'

Gabe didn't quail under the withering tone. '*Non?* Who held her hair when she was sick? Who sat with her during the first scan? I didn't ask to be involved but she has no one else. You make it quite clear that she can't come to you.'

Charles Rafferty gasped, a shuddering intake of breath, and Polly was back on her feet. Before she could move round to him Raff had passed their grandfather a glass of water and her grandmother had moved round to him, her usually aloof expression one of concern.

This was all getting horribly out of hand. 'Gabe!' How dared he? How dared he try and explain away her actions? Interfere? 'A word? In private?'

Still trembling but now more with anger than with shock, she led him outside. Normally her garden was one of her favourite spots with shady, hidden spaces and a stream running across the bottom. Today it was just somewhere convenient.

'How dare you talk to my grandfather like that? What the hell do you think you're doing?'

His mouth hardened into a thin line. 'Standing up for you.'

The nerve of him! 'I didn't ask you to.'

His eyes narrowed contemptuously. '*Non?* I must have misunderstood the beseeching look you threw me when you sat there mute as your family shouted at you.'

'I didn't, at least I didn't mean for you to attack my grandfather! I don't need help. I am quite capable of standing up for myself.'

'*Oui*, keep telling yourself that.'

The words were thrown at her, sharp as arrows, and she quailed under them. 'What do you mean by that?'

'What I say. You tell me, you tell yourself that you don't need anything—anyone.' His eyes had darkened with an unbearable sympathy. 'But you're still just a little girl tugging at her grandfather's sleeve wanting attention. Without it, you allow yourself to be nothing.'

Polly hadn't known words could hurt before, not physically, but each of Gabe's words was like a sharp stab in her chest. 'How dare you…?'

'He rules the board, he rules you. He uses his health to keep you quiet and his disapproval to keep you tame. When he said you couldn't take over, did you stay to fight, to prove him wrong? No, you ran away.'

How had this happened? How had the passion and need of yesterday turned into these cruel words, ripping her apart?

'I couldn't stay. You know that.'

'You *chose* not to stay.' He laughed, not unkindly but the tone didn't matter. The unbearable sympathy on his face didn't matter. The words were all that mattered and they were harsh.

They were true. He had seen inside her and he was stripping her to the bone.

'You were quick enough to label me a coward, to judge me, but you know what, Polly? You were right when you said we were just the same. We define ourselves through work because without it? What is there? Who are we? Nothing.'

Polly stood there looking at him. She had thought that she knew him. Knew the feel of his mouth, the taste of him. The way the muscles on his shoulders moved, the play of them under her hands.

She'd thought that she understood him. That he might be coming to understand her. Maybe he did, all too well. She was defenceless.

'Get out,' she said, proud when her voice didn't waver. When the threatened tears didn't fall. 'Get out and leave me alone.'

He stood there for a long moment looking at her. She didn't move, didn't waver.

'You need people in your corner, Polly,' he said softly. 'People who will be there for you no matter what. Pick wisely.'

And he was gone.

Tears trembled behind her eyes but she blinked them back. *You don't cry, remember?*

She took a deep breath, almost doubling over at the unexpected ache in her chest, the raw, exposed pain and grief, like Prometheus torn open, awaiting the eagles. She had lost everything. Her grandfather. Gabe.

But no. She straightened, her hand splayed open on her still-flat stomach. Not everything.

She could do this. She could absolutely do this alone. Gabe was wrong. In every way.

Slowly she turned and walked back to the kitchen. Her family were at the table where she had left them and she was relieved to see colour in her grandfather's cheeks. Maybe she could fix this. She had to fix something.

'I'm sorry about what Gabe said.' She took her seat and picked up her water glass, relieved that her hands had stopped shaking enough for her to drink. 'He was out of line.'

She bowed her head and waited for more reproach and anger to be heaped on her.

'Charles.' Her grandmother spoke sharply and her grandfather leant forward, reaching for one of Polly's hands.

She couldn't remember the last time he had touched her first; she was usually the one bestowing a dutiful kiss on his cheek.

It felt comforting to have her hand in his. Unbidden, Gabe's words sprang into her mind. *'You're still just a little girl tugging at her grandfather's sleeve.'*

'I'm sorry, Polly.' Charles Rafferty's voice was a little wavery, his speech unusually slow and Polly's chest tightened with love and fear. 'I was shocked and I reacted badly. I said some terrible things and I hope you can forgive me, my dear.'

An apology? From the formidable Mr Rafferty? 'I'm sorry too,' she said, squeezing his fingers. When had they got so frail? 'I should have told you earlier. I needed time to process everything, to deal with it all, but I should have come to you.'

'You always were independent,' he said.

Was she? Polly wondered. Or did she just want to be thought that way? Was Gabe right?

'I didn't mean for this to happen.' She looked at her grandparents, pleading for them to understand. They might not be perfect but they were the only parental figures she had. She needed them. 'I was lost and met someone as lonely as me. He was nice, a teacher in Copenhagen and recently divorced. I *have* tried to track him down but with no picture or surname the private investigator wasn't hopeful. He gave it a week and then told me to save my money. You know how much I missed Daddy. I hate the fact that my baby will grow up not knowing his or her father.'

'Polly dearest.' Her grandmother was suspiciously bright eyed. 'Did Gabriel say something about a scan? I don't suppose there's a picture…'

A glimmer of something that felt a little like hope skimmed through Polly. 'There is a picture,' she said. 'Would you like to see it?'

CHAPTER TEN

'IT DIDN'T LOOK this dark on the tin.' Polly stood back from the wall and stared at the first splash of paint. 'I'm not intending to raise a baby Goth.'

'It'll be lighter when it dries.' Clara joined her and looked doubtfully at the wall. 'I hope. Are you sure you don't want me to find somebody to do it for you?'

'No, I am doing it all myself. My baby, my walls, my botch paint job in deepest purple.' Polly glanced at the tin. 'It's supposed to be lilac lace.'

'You *can* outsource some of the work, you know. To Raff or to me. I do special discounts for family…'

'I might consider outsourcing the actual birth part. That looks a little scary.' The books Clara had given her were piled high on the chest of drawers in the sunny room at the back of the house Polly had decided on for the nursery. After a quick flick through the graphic words and even more graphic pictures Polly had put them aside vowing not to go anywhere near them again.

There was some protection in ignorance.

'Sorry, Polly, there are some things even you can't delegate away.' Clara dipped her paintbrush in the deep colour and began to apply it to the walls in sweeping strokes. 'Talking of delegation, have you spoken to Gabe?' She sounded disinterested but the sly glance she slid Polly belied the light tone.

'I've sat in meetings with him.'

'Let me rephrase that. Have you had a conversation

with Gabe, just the two of you, that hasn't involved spread-sheets, budgets and forecasts?'

'That would be a negative.'

Clara added a bit more paint to her brush. 'Polly,' she said slowly. 'We've known each other for a while and I like to think that although we've never touched on anything really deep we're good friends.'

Polly bit her lip. Truth was Clara was her only friend. And yet she knew so little about the woman who was going to marry her twin. 'Of course we are, and I am delighted you're going to be my sister.'

'And the aunt of the lucky future possessor of these walls,' Clara agreed. 'So I hope you don't mind me pry-ing a little bit but what is going on with you and Gabe?'

That was easy enough to answer. 'We're colleagues.'

'That's all?' Clara persisted.

Polly sighed and put her paintbrush down on the news-paper she'd spread over the furniture, before sliding onto the floor and hugging her knees. 'We kissed. Twice. Well, once was an accident.'

Not the other. No, the other had been wonderfully in-tentional.

'Don't you hate those accidental kisses?' Clara mur-mured, laughter in her voice.

Now she had started confiding Polly couldn't bear to stop. It was almost a relief to let the words spill out. 'We talked. Spent some time together.' It didn't sound much. Not the bare, bald facts. 'He was there when I needed him. And he was brilliant; patient and helpful and understand-ing. He's good to work with too, sparky and innovative and pushes me…' Her voice trailed off.

'Sounds good.' Clara was still painting. It was easier talking to her back than to have to face her, see concern or sympathy in her eyes.

'It was. I've only known him a couple of weeks but I thought maybe we had a connection.' Polly pulled at her ponytail. 'It's stupid, hormones playing up. I should have known better. Neither of us are looking for anything, want anything. In a different time or place maybe we could have had a thing. But the timing was off.'

And she didn't want a 'thing'. Not any more. Not with anyone. Especially not with Gabe.

She'd spent her twenties valuing her independence, her ability to walk away. It didn't seem such an achievement any more.

Clara painted another streak of colour onto the wall and stood back to assess the effect. Her voice was still light, conversational. 'You don't need to be looking to find it. I wasn't, Raff wasn't. We tried hard not to fall in love but it was too strong.'

Love? Polly swallowed hard, her heartbeat speeding up. 'Who said anything about love?'

'No one. Yet. But you said yourself there's a connection; he pushes you, understands you—and the kisses were good enough to make your voice go hazy just thinking about them. Even if one *was* an accident.'

Clara put her paintbrush down beside Polly's and slid into place beside her. 'It might not be love, Polly, not yet. But it sounds pretty close to me. I don't know why you've pushed him away, nor why he has let you. But isn't it worth trying swallowing your pride?'

'I miss him,' Polly admitted.

But it was more than that. She'd lived alone in this big old house for so long, had never felt lonely in it before. But now his absence was in every room.

It was ridiculous; he'd hardly spent any time there as it was.

It was the same at work. Sometimes she would look up

from her desk and glance over at the empty space where his desk had so briefly sat. It was so quiet without him typing loudly, his continuous conversations. The room so still without his pacing up and down. She would listen jealously for some mention of his name, to find out who he was flirting with this week.

But the staff grapevine was quiet.

And she *was* lonely. Raff and Clara were doing their best, almost overwhelming her with dinners and visits, trying to include her in everything. And she appreciated it, she really did. Only they were so very together.

It made her feel her solitary state even more.

She had never cared about being alone before. Or allowed herself to admit it.

'He took you to the hospital, helped when you were sick, what makes you think he doesn't want more? Have you asked him?' Clara was pushing but Polly didn't mind. The last few weeks, his last words had been going round and round in her head like an overactive carousel until she was so giddy she couldn't think. This was her opportunity to get it all straight.

To get over it.

'I don't need to. He's…' Polly searched for the right word. 'He's complex, Clara. He has this amazing family.' She could hear the wistfulness in her own voice and cringed. 'They're really supportive and loving, like yours if you multiplied your family by three, the noise level by ten, added in a host of toddlers and moved to France.'

'Just like my family, then.'

'Yours was the happiest, most together family I knew until I met the Beaufils,' Polly admitted.

'So he has the family you always wanted,' Clara said shrewdly. 'I still don't see the problem.'

'He was ill, really ill in his teens and it nearly killed his parents.' Polly winced as she pictured the pain in his dark eyes. 'I don't know whether he really blames them for caring so much or himself for causing so much pain. I think it's a mixture of both. Throw in a first love who died in her teens and you have one emotionally mixed-up man.'

'We all have our scars, but most of us are redeemable. For the right person.'

'That's just it.' Clara had got it. 'I'm *not* the right person, Clara. Gabe needs someone who understands him, someone with the patience to wait for him, to help him. Me? I have a business to run, a baby on the way. I have no idea how a functioning family works. I can't help him! He deserves better.'

Clara didn't say anything for a long moment and then she got up and picked up the paintbrush. 'It's a lot, I agree,' she said. 'But you've never backed down from anything daunting before. If you think you and he have a chance, if you think it might, could be love, then you should go for it. But, Polly, if you're backing down out of fear, then you're letting yourself down and you're letting Gabe down. Be sure before you let him walk away.'

He still had a key in his pocket but using it just didn't feel right. Not with her car parked outside and the windows flung open.

A part of Gabe had hoped that Polly was out, working maybe or with her brother, that he could have nipped in, gathered his stuff and left again leaving no trace.

Taking a deep breath, he pressed the doorbell. How hard could this be? After all, they saw each other every day at work. They sent emails, held meetings. It was all fine.

Polite. Formal. Fine.

There was a pause and then the sound of light footsteps running down the stairs before the door was pulled open.

'I left it open for you…oh!' Polly stepped back, her eyes huge with surprise. 'You're not Clara.'

'Non,' he agreed.

'She was just here, helping me paint and popped out for sandwiches so I thought, I assumed…' Her voice trailed off.

'Paint?' That made sense, he thought as his gaze travelled up her despite his best intentions to stay cool and focused. Bare feet, long tanned legs in a pair of cut-off denim shorts. Who would have thought the elegant Polly Rafferty even owned such disreputable-looking garments, fraying and paint splattered?

Her vest top was falling off one shoulder, revealing a delicate lilac bra strap.

Lilac. The colour he had bought her. It might even be the same set. His breath hitched, his heartbeat speeding up, blood pounding around his body in a relentless march.

No. He dragged his mind back to the matter at hand. They weren't on those kinds of terms, not any more.

They had almost got in too deep; he'd allowed her in too deep. Thank goodness Polly had seen sense.

Her hands tightened on the door. 'I'm decorating the baby's room purple, to go with the bunting. Only it's a little darker than I thought, more bordello than nursery.'

'It might lighten when it dries.' He shifted his weight onto the other foot. Such a non-conversation. As if they were mere acquaintances.

'That's the hope,' Polly said.

She still hadn't asked him in.

'I just wanted to return your key and get the last of my things.'

'Oh.' Her eyelashes dropped, veiling her eyes. 'Of course, come in.'

She opened the door fully, stepping aside as she did so. 'Is your flat fixed?'

Gabe grimaced. 'Unfortunately not. The underground cinema and gym is proving most expensive for my oligarch neighbour. He's still paying hotel bills for at least twenty people.'

'Including you?'

He shrugged. 'There's a gym. It's convenient for work. No more trains.'

'That's good.'

Gabe stepped over the threshold and stopped, unwanted regret and nostalgia twisting his stomach. The scent of fresh flowers mixed with beeswax and that spicy scent Polly favoured, a dark cinnamon, hit him. It smelled like home.

Only it wasn't. Not any more. It never really had been.

She was right to have pushed him away. What did he have to offer? Financial security? She had her own. No, what Polly needed was emotional security.

The one thing he couldn't offer.

She deserved it. Deserved more than a coward who spent his life hiding from his own family so that he didn't have to face up to the possibility of losing them. Of letting them down.

'I don't have much.' He needed to pack, to get out and leave the memories behind. Start afresh.

She turned to him, one hand twisting her ponytail, the other playing with the frayed cotton on her shorts. 'Gabe, I'm sorry,' she said.

What? 'No, I should apologise to you.' He squeezed his eyes shut. 'I was harsh. Unfair.'

'You were right.' She exhaled. 'You just gave me some home truths. I didn't want to hear them, to admit them. That doesn't stop them being true.' She huffed out a laugh.

'There doesn't seem to be a warning sign with us, does there? We just say whatever is in our heads and damn the consequences. I've never been so honest with anyone before.'

'No, me neither.'

'I'm not sure I like it.' She moved away towards the kitchen. 'Would you like a coffee?'

Gabe had intended to make a quick exit but he recognised the offer for what it was: a peace offering. 'Do you have decaf?'

'A month ago I would have laughed in your face but pregnancy does strange things to a woman. I have decaf and a whole selection of herbal teas, each more vile than the rest.'

'I could make you a smoothie,' he suggested and laughed, the tension broken by the horror in her eyes.

'Spinach and beetroot and those horrid seeds? I'm pregnant, not crazy.' She busied herself at the expensive coffee machine and Gabe leant on the counter, idly looking at the papers there. One letter caught his eye and he read a few lines before realising it was personal. He pushed it away just as she looked over.

Awkward, as if he had been caught purposely snooping, he gestured at the letter. 'You have a hospital appointment?'

'Yes. Clara's agreed to accompany me.'

His duties were well and truly over. He was free, to concentrate on work, to train for the Alpine triathlon in the autumn. To live his life the way he wanted it with no interruptions.

It was all going back to normal.

Polly walked back over, a steaming cup of coffee in her hand. 'Gabe.' She put the coffee down next to him. 'I really need to thank you. For everything.'

He shrugged. 'I was here. Anyone would have done the same.'

'Maybe, but you stepped up, more than once. You didn't have to. Not just with the practical stuff.'

She pulled up a stool and sank onto it, pulling the letter from the hospital over towards her, folding it over and over. 'I've been thinking a lot lately. About what I want from my life. I guess the pregnancy would have forced me to make some changes anyway but it's not just that. You *made* me think. About the kind of person, the kind of parent I want to be. My work, Rafferty's, is incredibly important, that won't change. But it's not enough. It shouldn't be enough. I don't want to turn into a female version of Grandfather, putting the business before family, before happiness.

'I'm going to have a baby.' Her eyes were shining. Gabe had seen Polly experience a whole range of emotions about the pregnancy: shock, grief, acceptance. But not joy like this. Not before today. 'And I want that baby to have a family. I think, deep down, there's a bit of me that's always wanted your kind of family. Ironic, isn't it? When you find them too much?'

'Swap?' he offered.

'In a heartbeat.' She folded the paper again. 'I can't conjure up parents and a partner for the baby, but I want him or her to grow up with love and laughter and security. Clara and Raff will help, if I let them. And I will. I need to start letting people in. So thank you. For helping me realise that.'

'You're welcome.' The words almost stuck in his throat.

She smiled at him but there was sadness in her eyes. 'I just hope you find what you're looking for,' she said.

Gabe wanted to make some flippant comment but she was right. They *were* always honest with each other, no matter what the consequences. 'I'm not looking for much.

Another year healthy? Another goal achieved?' It didn't sound like much but it was all he had.

'I wish I could have helped you, the way you've helped me. It's not that I don't want to try, arrogant as that sounds, but I do. I like you, Gabe.' The colour flared on her cheeks.

Gabe wanted to speak out. To tell her that she had helped, that with her he had finally confronted memories locked away for too long.

To tell her how much he liked her too. That he lay awake at night replaying every single moment of that kiss, his skin heating where she had touched him.

But he didn't know how to.

Polly took a deep breath. 'I don't know what love is, not really. But I think we were close. At least, I was close. The closest I've ever been. But I have the baby to think of, the security I have promised it. Right now, it needs me to be putting it first, to be strong for it.'

She reached over and took his hand, her fingers soft in his. He curled his hand round hers, holding them tight and she raised his hand to her lips, dropping a kiss onto his knuckles. 'My mother didn't put us first. Or second or anywhere. Her need for love came before anything else. I guess I overcompensated, desperate to show the world that I didn't need anyone. That I wasn't like her. Now I wonder if maybe I took it too far. But now isn't the time to worry about that. I can't put myself first, not any more.'

'No.' What else was there to say?

'I do believe that there's someone out there who'll show you that life isn't a challenge or a goal, it's a blessing.' She closed her eyes, blinking back a tear. 'I have to admit I'm a little jealous of that someone.' Her voice was so low he hardly heard the words. 'Maybe you'll do it on your own. You're strong enough, goodness knows. The burdens you bear. The misplaced guilt.'

'I'm happy for you, really I am. But I'm fine.' He tried to smile. 'I don't need fixing.'

So much for honesty. He was utterly broken and they both knew it.

Breathe. Breathe. Breathe. It wasn't easy training for an Alpine triathlon in a busy, flat city like London. It was a particularly gruelling trial, a lake swim followed by a ninety-kilometre cycle-ride and a full marathon run. Although the trails didn't go too high up into the Tyrolean mountains it was a hilly course.

Just finishing wasn't an option. He wanted a winning time.

There was nothing better than pushing his body to its limits. Proving he was no longer at its mercy, that his mind was in control at all times.

Control. He'd lost it the past few weeks. It was time to regain it.

Gabe stopped, leaning against a tree, and took a swig of water. It didn't take long for fitness levels to drop. For an easy ten-kilometre jog to become a challenge.

He just needed to get his rhythm back, to regain that blissful state where all he knew was the thud of his feet, the beating of his heart.

Instead he ran to a soundtrack of Polly's voice, sad, resigned, defeated. *I like you.*

And he'd said? He'd said nothing. Because what could he say?

I wish I could have helped you, the way you've helped me.

Of course she did. She was an achiever. Polly Rafferty didn't like to leave tasks unfinished, a list unticked. She'd wanted to see him reconciled with his family, the past dealt with.

She was getting her happy ever after, she just wanted the same for him.

It was a shame life just wasn't that tidy.

Gabe set off again, wiping the perspiration off his forehead as he increased the tempo. He didn't need a happy ever after. He didn't deserve one.

But she did.

She deserved the whole damn fairy tale. Paris at her feet.

He just hoped that she would meet someone who recognised that.

The thought reverberated around his head, the echo getting louder and louder.

Someone else.

His stomach clenched and Gabe skidded to a stop, bending forward to alleviate the cramp, hand on his side.

No, he didn't want that for her at all.

Oh, how he wished he could be that altruistic, that selfless, that he could put her needs first. But he didn't think he could survive watching her laugh with another man, talking cars with another man, showing off vintage designs to another man, fired up as she planned business and strategy with another man.

Kissing another man.

Raising her child with another man.

And there would be someone else. For all her brave talk about going it alone, there would be. She might not have fallen in love in the past but she'd had partners whenever she needed them. How long before the new, softer Polly was snapped up? Opened up her heart to some lucky man?

They'd be queuing around the block.

And he was just going to let them?

Gabe straightened up, oblivious to the people walking around him, the sighs and tuts from commuters unwilling to step around a human being in their well-trodden path.

Of course he wasn't going to let them!

I like you, she had said. More than once. What must it have taken for the proud Polly Rafferty to say those words? And he hadn't reacted. Hadn't told her.

That he liked her too.

It was time he did.

If Polly wanted to have the whole white-picket-fence dream while running the world's most famous department store then she was going to need the best by her side.

And Gabe had always liked a challenge.

CHAPTER ELEVEN

'GOOD MORNING, RACHEL.'

Polly smiled at her assistant. Rachel had done her job beautifully. Unable to bear some big announcement of her pregnancy, Polly had, instead, confided in her PA. The news had spread around the store in less than a day, just as Polly had known it would.

At some point she would have to have a word with the gossip-loving woman about confidentiality and discretion. But not yet, not when she had just used Rachel to her advantage.

'Good morning, Miss Rafferty. There is a mint tea on your desk and Chef says that he has a summer fruit compote and a breakfast omelette for you this morning.'

It was surprising—and rather sweet—how many of her staff had taken the news of her pregnancy and turned it into a project. The kitchen sent up nutritious meals three times a day and were hopefully awaiting outlandish cravings so that they could rise to whatever challenge she set.

The make-up department manager had put together an entire basket of pre-natal oils, creams and bath salts and was sourcing and testing the very best in post-natal and baby unguents. As for the personal shoppers, not only were they putting aside more clothes than triplets could easily get through, they were also ensuring she would be the chicest mother-to-be in London.

Polly had always felt respected rather than liked—she had encouraged it. This new two-way process was a little disconcerting. But she was rather enjoying the interest and attention. It didn't feel as intrusive as she had feared, more warm and friendly.

Only Gabe was nowhere to be seen. He seemed to be constantly in meetings although he sent detailed emails and was obviously working as hard as ever. It wasn't hard to deduce that he was avoiding her.

She shouldn't have used words like love.

But somehow Polly couldn't bring herself to feel regret or embarrassment. She'd tried.

A little at least.

'Oh, Miss Rafferty, there's been a change to your afternoon appointment. The one with the web developer?'

'Has he postponed?'

Up to now Polly had left all the details about the possible new website with Gabe, but she wanted to check some final budgets and meet the developer herself before making the final recommendation.

Finding a mutually convenient date had been problematic—and now he couldn't make it? She hoped this wasn't a portent of his professional reliability.

'He's stuck in Paris and asked if you would mind going there instead?'

'To Paris?' Polly echoed. 'That's…'

'Less time to get to than Edinburgh,' Rachel said, putting a pile of papers onto the desk. 'I've booked you onto the noon Eurostar so a taxi will be here to take you to St Pancras for eleven. A car will collect you at the other end.'

Rachel looked a little anxious. 'I have done the right thing, haven't I? It's just you told me to use my initiative more and I know you want to talk to him yourself before making a final decision…'

'No, you did right. As you say it's quicker than Edinburgh.' Polly scooped up the pile of papers, including her passport, she kept it at work for just this reason, and retreated into her office.

Sorry, Mummy, looks like I won't be keeping my word after all, she thought. But maybe this is a good thing. Demystify Paris as part of her new start.

Baby steps.

It was so comfortable in Business Class that Polly realised with a jump that she had almost nodded off. *I think I preferred the nausea to the tiredness,* she thought as she jolted back to awareness when the train braked, the papers still unread on the table in front of her, her laptop reverted to sleep mode. There were times when she eyed the couch in her office longingly, desperate to stretch out and just close her eyes.

Until she remembered Gabe sprawled out. The firm toned lines of his body, the tree spiralling up his back.

The couch seemed a lot less safe then.

Polly pulled her mind back to the present. She had enough to do without daydreaming and dwelling on the past, including finding her way around a totally strange city. Paris might be quicker to get to than Edinburgh but it felt a lot more alien.

Luckily she didn't have to think or organise herself at all; a driver was waiting for her as she stepped out of the bustling, light-filled Gare du Nord station with its imposing Gothic façade and, before she had a chance to take in the fact she was actually in Paris at last, he had pulled away into the heavy traffic.

It was only then that Polly realised she had no idea where the meeting was being held. He could be taking her anywhere. She shuffled through the papers Rachel had handed her, looking for some kind of clue.

Nothing. Budgets, technical specs, nothing of any use.

She felt so helpless, the annoyance itched away at her. The tiredness was bad enough; the effort it was taking to function at her usual level was soul destroying. Clara's re-assurances that it wouldn't last, that she would be back to full capacity in just a couple of weeks, were little comfort. She couldn't afford to slack at any point.

Nobody had said it would be easy—and 'nobody' was right—but she couldn't let that derail her. Her grandfather might have apologised but she wasn't going to give him the slightest opportunity to think she couldn't cope.

The car drew up outside an imposing-looking hotel built of the golden stone Polly had already noticed in abundance as they drove down the wide boulevards. Each floor was populated with quaint balconies while colourful flower baskets softened the rather regal effect.

The driver had come around to open her door. *'Mademoiselle?'*

'I'm meeting him here?' she asked, puzzled. Polly knew a five-star hotel when she saw one and this looked top end. This kind of old-world luxury seemed a peculiar choice for a cutting-edge developer. Maybe it was a post-modern thing she wasn't cool enough to understand.

Either way she was here now—and the hotel certainly was Paris at its opulent best. The Eiffel Tower was clearly visible from the pavement and the foyer reminded her a little of Rafferty's with its art-deco-inspired floor and grand pillars. Polly looked around. How was she supposed to work out which particular bar, restaurant or café she was meeting her contact in—and what *was* his name again?

'Can I help you?' The intimidatingly chic receptionist spoke in perfect English. How did she know? Did they have a nationality detector at the door?

'Yes, I am Polly Rafferty and I am supposed…'

'Ah, Mademoiselle Rafferty. I have your key here. There is nothing to sign. It is all taken care of.'

'Key?' Polly took it in her hand. It was a key too, a heavy gold one, not an anonymous card. 'No, I'm not staying. I am meant to be meeting…' She thought hard. Nope. Nothing. Had Rachel ever told her the name? 'Someone,' she finished lamely.

'Yes, I know. Pierre will show you the way.'

It was a bit like being in a Hitchcock plot. Polly fully expected Cary Grant to walk past as the dapper porter showed her to the lift, not betraying by one eyebrow how odd it was for her to be checking in without as much as an overnight bag.

If checking in she was. Maybe he was merely showing her to a meeting room?

The lift went up. And up and up.

'Penthouse?' she queried. It was an odd place for a meeting room. Pierre merely motioned for her to follow and led her to a white door, the only one in a grand, formal-looking corridor richly papered in a gold and black oriental print.

I'm being kidnapped and I am far too English and polite to scream for help, Polly thought as she put the key into the lock and turned it. The door swung open and she found herself looking at quite the most perfect hotel suite she had ever seen.

The door opened into a large sitting room. Polly stepped in, her attention immediately captured by two floor-to-ceiling windows, both flung open and leading out onto one of the pretty balconies she had admired on the way in. Perfectly visible through both was a to-die-for view of the Eiffel Tower, majestically dominating the horizon.

Polly turned slowly, taking in her luxurious surroundings. The suite was decorated in shades of lavender and silver, the cool colours perfectly setting off the rich mahogany tones in the woodwork. Two sofas, lavishly heaped with cushions, surrounded the dark wooden coffee table and lavender silk curtains framed that perfect city view.

Polly stepped further in, looking back at Pierre for confirmation, but he had gone, closing the door behind him. She was alone.

If this was a kidnap then it was a luxuriously comfortable kidnapping. Her gaze stopped on a plate on the coffee table. A kidnapping complete with a plate of delicately coloured macaroons.

Polly had never stayed anywhere this beautiful. It wasn't that she couldn't afford to, but, her recent trip aside, she really only travelled for business and that was on Rafferty's budget. She stayed in good hotels, in comfortable, spacious rooms fully outfitted for the business traveller, but she would never charge a suite like this to her expense account.

And it had never occurred to her to book this kind of luxury for herself. What had she been thinking? From now on it was suites all the way.

She wandered around taking in each lavish detail. All the accessories from the light switches to the lamps, the vases to the mirrors, had a nineteen twenties art deco vibe to them. In fact, Polly narrowed her eyes, she was no expert but that fruit bowl looked pretty genuine to her.

If the bathroom had an enormous roll-top bath, vast, thick towels and an array of scented creams and bubbles then Polly had either died and entered her own personal heaven or was in some kind of weird reality show tailored to her every need.

She tiptoed through the large bedroom, noting with approval the terrace off it, complete with sun loungers, and entered the bathroom.

Oh! It was utterly perfect.

Would it be very wrong to have a bath when she was supposed to be prepping for the oddest business meeting she had experienced in ten years of work?

Reality asserted itself. A chill ran through her.

What kind of meeting was this? She should go back into the sitting room and take advantage of her solitude to complete the prep work she had neglected on the way here. More importantly she should phone Rachel and find out what on earth was going on.

Maybe, if this was all a mistake, she could book the suite anyway. After all, she was here now. She was finally in Paris. It would be a shame to just turn around and make her way tamely home now that her mother's spell was broken.

With a last longing glance at the bath Polly returned to the sitting room, resisting the urge to bounce on the bed as she passed it.

It was all just as gorgeous when she walked back into the main room but it just didn't have the same effect. The suite felt too big, too spacious. Too lonely.

This was why she had never stayed anywhere like this. This was a suite made for two. For lovers. From the massive bed to the double tub, the twin sun loungers to the sumptuous robes, it was a place heavy with romantic possibilities.

Polly walked over to the window and out onto the balcony, looking at the Eiffel Tower more like a set from a film than an actual view. What would it be like to be here with someone else? Sipping champagne—or, for her, right now, some kind of fruit cordial—and watching the city below?

What would it be like to stay here with Gabe?

Polly tried to push the thought away but it stuck there,

persistent. She had shared so much with him the last few weeks. If only she could share this too. Had she tried hard enough to get through to him? After all, she had pretty much told him that she was giving up and putting the baby first.

Had that been the right thing to do? It had certainly been the sensible thing, the logical thing.

But should she have fought harder?

Her hands clenched. In her desperation to prove that she wasn't her mother, had she thrown away her only chance at happiness?

A soft knock at the door pulled her out of her introspection and she gave the view one last, longing look. It was time to work.

She should have the meeting and then, maybe, she would think again. Make a final decision. Stick with it this time. She couldn't keep second-guessing her choices.

She didn't usually. Maybe this was a sign that she had got it wrong…

Another knock, a little louder this time.

'Yes, I'm coming…' If only she could remember his name!

She was going to have to wing it. Polly walked over to the darkly panelled door and opened it, words of apologetic welcome on her lips.

Only to falter back as she clocked the tall, dark-haired man on the threshold.

'Gabe? Are you in this meeting as well? Thank goodness. I am woefully ill prepared. I can't even remember the developer's name. Although I *will* deny it if you quote me on that.'

Gabe didn't say anything and she continued, the words tumbling out. 'Do you have any idea why he has arranged to meet us in such an odd place? Although it is completely beautiful. You should see it, it's like a slice of heaven. With macaroons *and* views.'

Okay, she was definitely gabbling.

But better gabbling than grabbing him by his lapels and dragging him in close. Better gabbling than flinging her arms around his neck and pressing her lips to his.

But, oh! How she wanted to. Especially now.

Her eyes took him in greedily. It was unfair. No man should look so good. It wasn't as if he were dressed any differently from his usual smart-casual style. Perfectly cut grey trousers, white linen shirt open at the neck, hair falling over his forehead, heavy stubble shadowing his sharply cut jaw. Standard Gabe.

Utterly irresistible.

How could she walk away?

She couldn't. She wouldn't.

She would try again, fight harder. Both she and the baby needed her to fight. Needed Gabe in their lives.

She stood aside as he strolled into the room. *'Bonjour,* Polly.'

She was going to make him see. If she could only figure out how.

She was biting her lip, looking thoroughly confused. It was kind of adorable seeing Polly off-kilter.

'I spent the last two years here in Paris,' he said, walking over to the window and looking out at the spectacular view.

It was like seeing the city for the first time, seeing it through her eyes. Golden, exciting, full of possibilities.

'I know, you were working at Desmoulins.'

'I had an apartment not far from here. I got up, jogged to work, worked, ate out, met friends, worked out. All in Paris.'

He took a step out onto the balcony and breathed in the city air. Car fumes, cooking smells, the river. It had always choked him before but today it was welcome. Felt fresher somehow.

Polly stood in the room for a moment and then came out to join him, looking around her in awe. 'It's even more beautiful than I thought it would be. It must have been hard to leave.'

Gabe shrugged. 'Not really. It was just a place. A place to climb up the ladder a little further. It didn't mean more to me than New York or San Francisco.'

'Oh.'

'I was hoping that if I came back to Paris with you, if I walked the streets with you, then that might change.

'I was hoping it would become magical.'

The words hung there. Anxiously Gabe scanned her face but he couldn't read her expression.

'I don't understand,' she said finally. 'Is this a test? If I don't feel the pea through twenty mattresses I'm not a princess and we're not worth fighting for? Is that what you mean?'

'*Non.*' She hadn't understood. His heart speeded up; he could feel it thumping through his chest. 'Polly, you told me to go and like a coward, like a fool, I went.'

He grimaced. 'I told myself it was for the best, that I was doing it for you. But I don't think it can be for the best. I don't think anyone can feel the way I feel about you, love you the way I love you, and not be with you.'

He'd said it. Surely the sun should burn a little brighter, the birds sing louder. Some acknowledgement somewhere that he had finally cracked open his shell.

'I don't understand.' She turned to him, eyes huge and clouded with an emotion he couldn't identify. 'What about the meeting?'

Damn the meeting. What about his words? He'd rushed in, confused her. 'It's not until Monday. I asked Rachel to get you here early so we could have the weekend. The weekend for you to try and see the magic, see if I'm worthy.' He swallowed. Had he misjudged so badly?

'If you want to, that is. Your ticket will let you return today if you would rather, or you can have the room on your own. It's paid for, it's yours…'

He paused, waiting, heart thudding as the seconds passed.

Her voice was small. 'You arranged all this?'

'*Oui.* For you. Although,' he added fairly, 'Rachel helped.'

Her mouth turned up. A smile. It was like a medal awarding him hope. 'I had no idea. I guess she can be discreet after all.'

'I tried to plan it all. I looked up all the romantic things to do in Paris but they all seem to involve champagne or cocktails, which is no fun for you. And I thought, if we need a list to find the magic then something is wrong. So I tried again.'

'You did?' She took a step closer, the tilt on her mouth more pronounced, a gleam of hope in her eyes.

'I thought, what would Polly like? And I knew.' At least, he hoped he knew. 'Old Paris. Shopping at all the best vintage and antique shops, strolling around Montmartre paying our respects to the artists of the past. The Catacombs.'

It wasn't too exhaustive an itinerary, not for three days. Organised enough for Polly to have a sense of purpose, fluid enough for some spontaneity.

Her mouth trembled. 'What if there isn't any?'

'Any what?'

Her eyes closed briefly, the long lashes sweeping down. 'Any magic?'

Gabe's heart thudded, audibly, painfully. 'Polly,' he said, taking her hands in his. 'For me there is magic wherever you are. I don't need a walk around old streets to prove that. I can't wait to show Paris to you, can't wait to see you buy out the vintage shops or discover a new café with you, but I don't need to do these things. I just want to do them for you. With you.'

Her hands folded around his. 'Really?' she whispered. 'What about next week, next month, next year?'

He tightened his hold, drawing a caressing finger along her hands. 'I can't tell you I'm not afraid,' he said honestly. 'Your life is changing so quickly and if we do this, mine will too. I didn't want to cause my parents more pain. The thought of putting you through that…' He inhaled, a deep painful breath.

'I got given my life back but somewhere along the way I forgot to live it. It was easier not to care. I thought I was in control. I set goals. I worked, I ran, I didn't stop. The more I worked, the harder I pushed my body, the less I had to think. I thought I had found a way to conquer my demons, a way to take charge, but I was hiding. And then you came along and ripped my hiding place to shreds.'

'I'm sorry.' Tears were trembling on her lashes and he released one of her hands to capture the sparkling drop.

'Don't be. I've been more alive the last few weeks than I was in the last ten years. I worked away this week,' he confessed. 'Stayed at the vineyard, spent time with my parents.' He smiled at her. 'Trying to get my number one spot back with Jean. You're right, of course, there's a lot I can help them with even in England. Advice, contracts, that kind of thing.'

'I'm glad. They're so lovely.'

'That's funny, they say the same about you. I have to

admit there's a bit of me that thinks you'll agree just to spend more time with my parents.'

'Agree to what?'

'To marry me.'

Polly blinked. Had she heard him right? 'To what?'

Gabe squeezed her hands tighter. It was almost painful but she was glad of the contact. It was proof that she was actually here, on a balcony in Paris, being proposed to.

'I should be on one knee…'

'No,' she said quickly. 'Just say it again.'

'I don't have a ring. I hoped we might include some jewellers on our antique trail, find something vintage. Sapphires, like your eyes. I was going to wait till then but I can't,' he confessed, the dark eyes so full of love it almost hurt to keep looking into them. 'Polly Rafferty, *je t'aime*. And if you would do me the honour of letting me in, of being my wife, then I promise I will always love you. And the baby. I'll be the best husband, the best father I can be. I want to start living again, Polly. I want to start living with you by my side.'

Polly struggled to find the right words. She couldn't. She had no idea what to say. 'And Mr Simpkins?'

'He has always had my heart,' he assured her, his face lightening with hope, with love. 'Mr Simpkins, Rafferty's, Hopeford. Everything you love, I love too. And I hope you feel the same way about my home, my family. My heart belongs to you.'

'And you have mine.' It wasn't so hard to say the words after all. 'I know the future is utterly terrifying. But with you by my side I can face it, whatever it holds.'

Gabe let go of her hands, reaching up to cup her face, pushing her hair back, his hands tangling themselves in its lengths. 'Are you sure?'

Polly slipped her hands around his waist, pulled him in closer. 'I've never been surer of anything. I love you too, Gabe. I think I loved you from that very first day. I had never met anyone so infuriating, so annoying, so challenging.' She smiled up at him. 'Anyone I fancied more.'

'I thought you were going to slap my face.'

'The accidental kiss? I think it was meant to be.' She stood on her tiptoes and found his mouth at last, cool and firm and sure. 'I think we were meant to be. I think it was magic.'

EPILOGUE

POLLY DIDN'T THINK Rafferty's had ever looked more beautiful. Her talented window dressers had moved some of the make-up counters and beauty areas back, draping the rest in purple and cream fabric, and suspended huge intricate paper sculptures in the same colours from the ceiling. Upstairs, she knew the tearooms were decorated in similar colours ready to welcome her wedding guests.

A stage dominated the middle of the floor, right under the point of the iconic dome. Cream vases, the size of a small child, were filled with silver branches creating an ethereal woodland effect.

The chairs were set in a wide semi-circle around the stage, each row flanked with a massive altar candle, the flames casting a dancing light over the room, discreetly backed up with the store's lowlights.

They were usually open until nine in the evening on a Saturday but today, for her wedding, Rafferty's had done something even the Blitz had never forced them to do.

They had closed early.

Most of the seats were already filled. Suited men and elegantly dressed women in a bright assortment of colours whispered and snapped pictures of the fairy-tale scene. There were several overexcited children fidgeting beside their parents, tugging at their best clothes, and Polly breathed a sigh of relief knowing she had a room put aside for them, complete with films, toys and paid babysitters to watch over the younger guests.

Peeking over the balcony, Polly spotted her grandparents, regal in the front row, entertaining Monsieur and Madame Beaufils. Her heart gave a little squeeze of joy, her family. All together.

'Are you ready?' Clara touched her shoulder softly.

Polly shivered. 'I think so. I didn't expect to be nervous but now that we're here I'm beginning to wish that we'd run away and got married in secret.'

Clara laughed. 'Summer would never have forgiven you. This is her moment of glory. I wouldn't have forgiven you either and nor would Hope. It's not every three-month-old who gets to be a bridesmaid.' She dropped a kiss on her niece's's fuzzy head.

'She looks gorgeous,' Polly agreed, beaming at her small baby who was trying her best to eat the silk sleeve of her cream dress.

'Best dressed girl in the room.'

'For now.' Polly eyed her daughter darkly. 'I have three changes with me. I'm not sure that will be enough.'

'It's a good thing there's a whole baby department just one level up.'

'Clara…' Polly pulled at her skirt, her fingers nervous. '…will I do?'

The other woman smiled. 'You're beautiful,' she said.

Polly inhaled, a long deep breath. Her dress was simple, an ankle-length cream sheath, her loose hair held off her face with a beaded band. It was an utterly simple yet perfectly elegant outfit; a Rafferty's original, copied from one of the old designs Polly had found in the archives.

Clara smoothed down her own purple dress, a loose design that skimmed over her stomach, flattering the bump. There would be less than six months between the cousins and Polly couldn't wait to meet Raff's child. The smaller bridesmaids, Summer and Hope, were looking uncommonly neat and tidy in cream. For now. The chances of them ending the evening in their current outfits were pretty slim. Especially Hope, who was currently averaging four changes a day.

'I don't know.' Polly watched as Hope fiddled with the delicate platinum bangle she had given Clara as a brides-maid gift. 'You were a pretty gorgeous bride.'

'I was marrying Raff,' Clara said simply, her green eyes glowing with love. 'I would have been happy with a sack and a takeaway.'

Polly grinned, she knew full well that Clara had adored every moment of her winter wedding to Raff. She would have preferred something smaller herself but Gabe wanted the world to see them become a family.

And she could deny him nothing.

They had started adoption proceedings as soon as they could but Gabe couldn't have adored Hope more if he had fathered her, and, Polly thought loyally, he had in every way that mattered—from holding Polly's hand through the long, arduous labour to night feeds and nappy changes.

The assembled guests had been talking quietly but when two tall men made their way to the front the murmuring ceased and heads craned to get a better look at the groom and his best man.

Dressed in identical morning suits, the two men couldn't have looked more different. Although they were of a simi-lar height Raff was built on broad lines, his hair as blond as Polly's own, his brand of good looks deceptively boy-ish. Gabe was leaner, darker with a more dangerously at-tractive demeanour.

'They're there,' she told her friend shivering with an-ticipation as her grandfather climbed the sweeping stairs to join them, pride beaming in his face as he readied him-self to escort his granddaughter down the makeshift aisle.

Polly gripped Clara's hand tightly and then took a deep breath, turning to greet her grandfather father with a kiss. She was ready.

Clara was poised, ready to go first, Hope in her arm, then Summer would follow on. Waiting out front, sprinkled throughout the congregation was her grandmother, her parents-in-law to be and all three of Gabe's sisters with assorted husbands and children. Waiting for her at the bottom of the aisle was her brother, tugging at his cravat.

And Gabe. Her fiancé, father of her child. His eyes were fixed on hers, a small, private smile just for her on those well-cut lips.

This time last year she had had no one. Now she was just ten minutes and a few words away from a huge, extended, noisy, chaotic, loving family. A challenging, questioning, adoring, supportive husband. She had a daughter, dependent on her for everything.

There was a time all this would have terrified her. But now?

Polly smiled back at Gabe. 'I love you,' she mouthed.

His sensual mouth curved. *'Je t'aime,'* he mouthed back.

Polly Rafferty was completely and utterly happy.

* * * * *

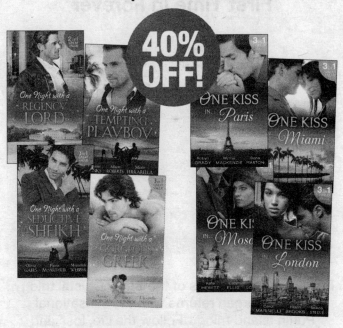

MILLS & BOON®

Why not subscribe?
Never miss a title and save money too!

Here's what's available to you if you join the
exclusive **Mills & Boon Book Club** today:

✦ *Titles up to a month ahead of the shops*
✦ *Amazing discounts*
✦ *Free P&P*
✦ *Earn Bonus Book points that can be redeemed
   against other titles and gifts*
✦ *Choose from monthly or pre-paid plans*

Still want more?
Well, if you join today we'll even give you
50% OFF your first parcel!

So visit **www.millsandboon.co.uk/subs**
or call Customer Relations on 020 8288 2888
to be a part of this exclusive Book Club!

SUBS_2014

MILLS & BOON®

Cherish™

EXPERIENCE THE ULTIMATE RUSH OF FALLING IN LOVE

A sneak peek at next month's titles...

In stores from 20th February 2015:

- **The Renegade Billionaire** – Rebecca Winters
  and **Her Perfect Proposal** – Lynne Marshall

- **Reunited with Her Italian Ex** – Lucy Gordon
  and **Mendoza's Secret Fortune** – Marie Ferrarella

In stores from 6th March 2015:

- **The Playboy of Rome** – Jennifer Faye
  and **The Baby Bonanza** – Jacqueline Diamond

- **Her Knight in the Outback** – Nikki Logan
  and **From City Girl to Rancher's Wife** – Ami Weaver

Available at WHSmith, Tesco, Asda, Eason, Amazon and Apple

Just can't wait?
Buy our books online a month before they hit the shops!
visit www.millsandboon.co.uk

These books are also available in eBook format!